Dear Rep. Ocasi

This book was written for kids
with climate grief who were coming
into my office after getting over
lyme disease. They were refusing
to get a job or go to school because
'the world was going to end'

Starseed contains humor, real-time
climate solutions + hope..,

Could we possibly connect
on ways to move the climate
needle in a positive direction?
Thank you for all you do
(and you are in part 4, Ecocide...)
                    In Appreciation,
Dr Richard Horowitz
    www. starseed-revolution. com
pri email: Kalachakra108@aol.com
    cell 845-797-1482.

ADVANCE PRAISE FOR
STARSEED R/EVOLUTION

"Physicians and allied health care practitioners across the globe have a sacred responsibility to protect the wellbeing of our patients from the many risks of climate change. In this highly entertaining romp through galaxies, Starseed civilizations, and magical universes, Dr. Richard Horowitz provides a mirror for humanity to witness the foibles and vulnerabilities of a civilization hell bent on its own destruction. He gives practical solutions to reverse our present course of environmental degradation. Spanning topics from personal empowerment, medicinal mushrooms, healthy aging, sustainable wellness, ecological medicine, consciousness expansion, and the power of the mind, *Starseed R/evolution* urges us to wake up and laugh our way to a more enlightened, saner, and healthier future."

—**Dr. Andrew Weil**, author of *8 Weeks to Optimum Health* and *Healthy Aging*

"After decades treating Lyme disease, Dr. Richard Horowitz has heard every conspiracy theory under the Sun. In *Starseed R/evolution: The Awakening*, he wraps them all into a rollicking commentary on our species' existential plight. In this outrageous science fiction adventure, a quirky human-alien prince describes a future overrun by the current era's most haunting fears and tropes: a climate crisis so severe extinction seems certain, alien (that's ET) sleeper cells, and the deliberate poisoning of a public under siege. In the course of creating a campy intergalactic metaverse, Horowitz manages to illuminate real world looming perils, propose some clear solutions, and make it loads of fun."

—**Pamela Weintraub**, senior editor, *Aeon*; co-founder, Science Literacy Foundation; and author, *Cure Unknown*

"*Starseed R/evolution: The Awakening* by Dr. Richard Horowitz is an amazing and skillfully written book by a talented author, with humor, wisdom, and vital information on how to save the planet during our unfolding climate emergency. The book entices the reader to explore the deepest questions of existence, ultimately illustrating how the paths of love and compassion can and will create miracles."

—**Bernie Siegel**, MD, author of *Love, Medicine and Miracles*, *No Endings, Only Beginnings*, and *Three Men Six Lives*

"Global warming is rapidly increasing acute and chronic health problems including nutritional deficiencies, lack of potable water and food, heat related illness, worsening environmental toxicity, and rising vector-borne diseases. *Starseed R/evolution* is an engaging, highly entertaining novel which outlines a clear path for humanity's salvation, providing hope for future generations."

—**Mark Hyman, MD**, *New York Times* bestselling author of
The Pegan Diet

"In the future, we will need to look back to assess what we did and didn't do to address climate change. This unique work, set in the future, lays out in a satirical but alarming way a scenario that should scare us all into acting on climate today. Highly recommended."

—**Mark Z. Jacobson**, Professor of Civil and Environmental
Engineering, Stanford University

"During our climate emergency, in order to sustain life on this planet, human beings have to take responsibility for our life and the life of all that lives on Mother Earth. Love is an inherent quality of all life on the planet and *Starseed R/evolution* explores that and helps to bring that reality into being."

—**Brant Secunda**, Huichol Shaman, Healer, and Ceremonial Leader

"This book is a rousing alert about the need for overcoming climate change and pollution problems on Earth, and the control that certain groups have over humanity. It is also a unique introduction to Arcturians and other extraterrestrial beings and Starseeds. It is a positive depiction of humans and ETs working together to overcome evil influences, to save all life on Earth, and to create goodness for all. Richard's spiritual practices and suggestions for ways to save the Earth are inspiring."

—**Barbara Lamb**, M.S., MFT, CHT, longtime regression
therapist, author

"Starseeds generally perceive themselves beyond their physical human body and intuitively sense themselves as multi-dimensional vast beings. They bring knowledge gained from other lifetimes and on other planetary bodies. They are often sensitive to vibrational frequencies that others cannot perceive. In the past they have been burned as witches; today they want to alter the perilous road humanity is traveling down. Climate change is the most serious disaster awaiting the human race; Starseeds are hoping to inspire those in power to change their ways and embrace the idea of healing the Earth, rather than harming her. A Revolution is indeed needed, one that joins all of us on Earth as One Family."

—**Margaret Doner**, author of *Merlin's Handbook for Seekers and Starseeds, The Path of the Human-Incarnated Angel and Starseed,* and *Merlin's War: The Battle between the Family of Light and Family of Dark*

"Many normal and healthy people around the world, from all walks of life, believe themselves to be in regular contact with beings from outer space, as ET encounters occur in numerous ways. As a trained therapist, I have worked with many individuals who have claimed to have had these remarkable experiences. The process of waking up to this multidimensional reality can be difficult, but the results are positively life changing, such as spiritual transformation and expanded awareness. *Starseed R/evolution: The Awakening*, is an extraordinary novel that goes way beyond the 'science fiction' genre. It provides a mirror for humanity to understand not only its strengths and weaknesses along with our Starseed origins and lineages, but provides a clear road map and practical instructions on how to actually awaken our enlightened potential, saving ourselves and the planet in the process. This highly entertaining novel is a must read to understand the new realities that are now emerging on planet Earth."

—**Mary Rodwell**, Principal of ACERN (Australian Close Encounter Resource Network), author of *Awakening: How Extraterrestrial Contact Can Transform Your Life* and *The New Human: Awakening to Our Cosmic Heritage*

"It is only from the genius of creative explorers that we will ever find a way out of our current climate predicament. Thus enters Dr. Richard Horowitz and his revolutionary *Starseed R/evolution*. Horowitz's timely and entertaining romp through the universe wakes people up to our present environmental dangers. But the adventurous and often hilarious spirit of the book is to break all boundaries of confined beliefs and make the reader available to the solutions that will help us think outside the box of conditioned cultural limitation. The writer takes on the persona of Prince Ian, a higher dimensional ET, whose teachings provide us with hope to ascend and reach our highest potential before it's too late. In this mixed genre classic, the truth to save future generations can be heard."

—**Alan Steinfeld,** author of *Making Contact: Preparing for the New Realities of Extraterrestrial Existence*

"Astrology is the mathematical science and art of how movements in the heavens affects all life on Earth. We are presently experiencing a radical and revolutionary shift from the Age of Pisces into the Age of Aquarius, which will establish innovative and revolutionary social systems based on equality, humanitarianism, cooperation, and community. These new paradigms will benefit humanity by accessing enlightened consciousness and shifting 'reality' in a positive direction. Prince Ian of Arcturus, the half-alien/half-human hybrid protagonist of *Starseed R/evolution*, as an Aquarius with an Aquarius rising, is the perfect harbinger to bring in this new age. Prince Ian explains, with wit and wisdom, how shifts in philosophy, ethics, and the science of consciousness can help lead us out of the darkness of our climate crisis. In our time of need, the world would do well to listen to this 'little Prince.'"

—**Anne Ortelee**, Certified Astrologer, ISAR CAP, PMAFA, OPA, NCGR-PAA

"*Starseed R/evolution* is a hilarious science fiction satire that offers a creative way to educate our young and older generations alike about our climate emergency. The humor, philosophical, scientific, and spiritual solutions should give hope to all of us, ensuring our children have a safer future."

—**Ally Hilfiger**, author of *Bite Me: How Lyme Disease Stole My Childhood, Made Me Crazy, and Almost Killed Me*

"Dr. Richard Horowitz has managed what seems unachievable. He has created a marvelously entertaining, but terribly troubled, fictional world that is, of course, all too close to the real one. Amid elements of magic, fantasy, science fiction, and characters both historic and futuristic, he tells the story of a civilization that teeters on the edge because of its own mistakes, greed, and intransigence. As an investigative reporter who has documented the role of climate change in spreading disease-toting ticks around the planet, I can relate all too well to the challenges of future earthlings to escape the threats besetting them. It's my hope that the world Horowitz paints—of princesses and Reptilians, a book of everlasting life, astrology, meditation, and families sprouted from Starseeds—will inspire the doubters to become believers. There is hope for a healthier planet, for growth and rebirth, if civilizations and generations see and embrace the flickering but determined light. This is a book I would want my grandsons to read."

—**Mary Beth Pfeiffer**, author of *Lyme: The First Epidemic of Climate Change*

STARSEED R/EVOLUTION

THE AWAKENING

STARSEED R/EVOLUTION

THE AWAKENING

DR. RICHARD HOROWITZ

PERMUTED
PRESS

A PERMUTED PRESS BOOK
ISBN: 978-1-63758-169-8
ISBN (eBook): 978-1-63758-170-4

Cover Image by Elizabeth Kelly
Cover Design by Cody Corcoran
Interior Design by Yoni Limor

Oprah Image: © 2021 Bat Boy LLC - Weekly World News and related marks
are trademarks of Bat Boy LLC. Weekly World News salutes Dr. Horowitz for supporting his narrative with our reliable and prescient reporting.

PERMUTED
PRESS

Permuted Press, LLC
New York • Nashville
permutedpress.com

Published in the United States of America
1 2 3 4 5 6 7 8 9 10

PREFACE

This work of science, science-fiction, reality, and fantasy, is loosely based on Starseed lore from Margaret Doner, author of several books, including *Merlin's War: The Battle Between the Family of Light and the Family of Dark, Merlin's Handbook for Seekers and Starseeds*, and *The Path of the Human-Incarnated Angel and Starseed*. Dr Richard Horowitz appreciates Margaret's allowing the author creative license to adjust some of the Starseed characteristics of beings from different galaxies and star systems as described in Margaret's books for the purpose of imaginative storytelling. Anyone who has ever met a being from these star systems knows that these characteristics may vary from the descriptions in this novel. We therefore apologize for any confusion this may cause to anyone who actually is a **W**alk-in, **I**ndigo, **S**tarseed, or **H**ybrid from Arcturus, Andromeda, Alpha-Centuri, Sirius, the Pleiades, Lyra, or other starsystem and belongs to the W.I.S.H. alliance. If you are a Reptile however, no apology will be forthcoming.

Dedicated to the children of the world,
Mother Earth, and all life which is sacred.

PROLOGUE

There are three kinds of people in this world:

Those who learn by reading,

The few who learn by observation,

And the majority, who have to pee on the
electric fence to learn for themselves.

—Borgafar, 20th century Dolteatharian philosopher

I was sixty-three years old when I finally woke up. To be clear, I always knew I was "different," and although many clues popped up during my life, I never recognized them for what they were.

Astrology was explained to me when I was a boy, but I ignored it. Most of us born with a sun in the twelfth house have difficulty recognizing who we are and where we come from, and so all the strange "synchronicities" that wove throughout my life went largely unobserved. It turns out each such event represented a signpost leading me towards a grand scheme foretold more than a thousand years earlier.

I always had great difficulty believing in things like that.

Such claims were, to me, challenging and somewhat dubious. Tantalizing, yet more like faint whispers of an early-morning dream. Until my sixty-third year, I could barely remember any of my past lives. Only hints and the deep, deep slumber of ignorance. Even when I awoke, it was a lot to grasp. Suffice it to say, mine was not your average childhood.

. . . .

We were in Maimonides Hospital in Brooklyn, New York. The sun *had* been shining when we arrived, but then, just as her contractions started, storm clouds appeared. Pitch-black shadows quickly erased the heavens as if monstrous Lovecraftian things from space had clawed ominous charcoal slashes across the sky. Then, swirling winds and a nor'easter appeared from nowhere, blanketing the streets with more than two feet of snow.

By all known accounts, it was impossible to see even an inch ahead of you. Although changes in the climate had led to sudden new weather patterns—changes to which people had become accustomed, even bored—this was all a bit much. Everything along the Eastern seaboard shut down for more than an hour.

Then, as my head crested, the snow stopped, and when I was born—minutes later, always a thoughtful son—the firmament cleared, and a double rainbow appeared. At least that's what I've been told.

My grandmother held me shortly after my birth. I was tightly wrapped in a mohair blanket. Grandmother was known to have no filter between her brain and mouth and didn't disappoint that first morning.

"He looks like a half-cooked lobster," she said. "A lobster with a gross little tufts of hair." These were the first words to greet me as I exited, fontanelles screaming with excitement, into human existence.

It's true, however, that I was not the best-looking baby to ever emerge from a womb, but when you combine those ice-cold forceps and the clumsy yanking, it tends to leave you with a misshapen skull. Red-faced from the exertion, you *do*, in fact, often look like a half-cooked lobster. My grandmother was simply being accurate.

"This baby," she proclaimed, "is, without much doubt, the ugliest slab of human flesh I've yet seen. Are you sure he's ours, Doctor Wilcox?"

"Quite," my mother's physician replied. "Look at it this way," he said, trying to be comforting. "It can only get better from here."

Grandmother tsked.

"Let's have a proper look," the doctor continued. They judiciously counted ten fingers, ten toes, one head. The puzzled look on my red and misshapen face as I stared up at Grandmother let them all know I would be "okay." The doctor pushed and prodded. "Just look at those clear blue eyes, that royal nose, and the dribble sopping off his chin...a handsome young fellow in the making."

Grandmother, I'm told, left the room.

Mother knew he was, as they say, sucking up to her for money, comparing me to some flash-in-the-pan movie actor, when in truth, as a preemie babe wrapped in a blanket, I could have easily been mistaken for a roasted Peking duck gone bad. Even then, I think, I could intuitively tell this guy was full of crap.

Even so, my birth was something of a miracle. The chemical burden of industrial pollutants and estrogenic compounds men and women ate, drank, breathed, and swam in every day had caused sperm counts to plummet. Those who wanted children often needed the services of specialized reproductive centers—centers stocked with healthy eggs, sperm, and hormones to help those who still could still be healed. Birth rates in 2037 were declining fast, so all of the women who had come to give birth at Hospital Maimonides were treated with great respect.

Especially those with natural male pregnancies and money.

As if to prove this very point, a nurse rushed into my mother's chamber.

"Mrs. Sobel is crowning!" he wailed. "And the baby, a boy, is stuck. Please come quickly!"

Dr. Wilcox sighed. "So many women, so little sperm."

Everyone—including me, I'm told—nodded their heads in agreement. Even when children *were* being born, the female variety vastly outnumbered the males. Perhaps it was Mother Earth's way of restoring balance. Fewer children to destroy the planet.

Grandmother returned to the room as Dr. Wilcox was leaving.

"Doctor, I just want you to know, we *are* grateful for all you've done," she said. "Our family will finance your new IVF wing."

"Thank you, oh, thank you," he gushed.

"And," she continued, "we would be even more grateful if you could provide us with the name of a good plastic surgeon."

• • • •

It was a pivotal time in history.

In 2037, the news feeds were filled with stories of death and destruction. Flooding in low-level areas across the globe led to crop destruction and famine. Heat waves and forest fires made matters worse. Infectious diseases—like West Nile, Zika, and Lyme disease—were on the rise, along with some not seen since the Middle Ages. Even the black plague emerged from flea and rat infestation in major cities. A report published on December 12, 2018, drew attention to rat infestations appearing in Washington, D.C., but local health officials ignored the warning.

"We're used to rats here," they said. "What's the big deal?"

Indeed, people were getting dumber by the minute. You know how you sometimes think, *Are people really that dumb?* Well, it turns out the answer was yes, and although the medical journals in the late 1990s reported the side effects of environmental chemicals, not a single governmental agency anywhere on Earth paid attention. It was as if they *wanted* their people dumb. This was, clearly, not a great time for humans to survive with any quality of life on the planet.

In any case, the synchronicities pointing to my destiny could be found in most newspaper headlines the day of my birth on that cold January morning in 2037. The front page of the *Times* said it all that day:

GLOBAL CLIMATE SUMMIT IN DAVOS

BEGINS TODAY: IS THERE STILL HOPE?

At the time, few believed "monsters" could exist.

PART ONE:
ARRIVAL

CHAPTER 1:

ALIEN REVELATION

"The highest education is that which does not merely give us information but makes our life in harmony with all existence."

—Rabindranath Tagore, 19th Century poet and philosopher

The temperature hit 124 degrees Fahrenheit, breaking all of the records, and there was no breeze to be had.

It was so hot that planes couldn't take off. Overworked air conditioners knocked out the power for three-hundred thousand New Yorkers. The sounds of ambulance sirens were everywhere as citizens succumbed to heat stroke and hyperthermia. Radiant waves of heat rose from concrete sidewalks, and pedestrians tried to avoid burning themselves by bouncing along as nimbly as they could, looking like Mexican jumping beans dancing in a microwave.

Throughout Times Square, misting wands sprayed customers who entered the retail stores to escape the sweltering heat—but there were few customers to be sprayed. No one wanted to be outdoors until nightfall. No one except the one naked woman coated in body paint, making her look like some sort of sexy space cowgirl. She seemed to be out there 365 days a year, twenty-four hours a day.

At 1:58 p.m., at the peak of the heat, the giant signs towering over the square all went blank, then began to flash with the same message:

ALIEN SPACE CRAFT APPROACHING EARTH

STAND BY FOR OFFICIAL UPDATES

Everyone gaped at the signs. Someone chuckled nervously, then another, and another until most of the sparse crowd was laughing. They all thought it was hoax. *Another* one.

This was an Earth generation that had finally become impervious to the media and the stories they spewed, like Elvis sightings, bi-annual impeachment trials, and websites claiming to teach you how to levitate. They didn't quite specify *before* you had clicked on the site what type of instructional videos you would be shown, nor which body part would be levitating.

Alien jokes in particular had become quite popular on Earth, ever since a junior member of Congress had claimed to be from Ganymede—which *everyone* knew had a strict travel moratorium—so no one took this initial report seriously. In fact, when faced with the genuine prospect that some serious "alien shit" was about to go down, society resorted to processing the concept in the safe form of…humor.

"*How can you tell the difference between an Alpha Centuri anal probe and an American beer?*" That was one of the most popular. "*One is a butt light, and the other is wanting to go to Uranus.*" One of my favorites was, "*A guy walks into a bar carrying an atmop on his shoulder. The bartender says, 'Hey, you can't bring that pig in here!' and the guy says, 'It's not a pig, it's an atmop' and the bartender says, 'Yeah, I know…that's who I was talking to!'*"

Maybe ten people on Earth knew what an atmop was, but I loved this joke anyway. In any case, most people figured the report of an alien craft was coming from some hacker, or the lead-in to a new scam.

Then, all the screens went blank again, and footage appeared of the space craft. Uncloaking and growing larger as it moved closer, it looked for all the world like a silver glazed donut with a shiny munchkin wedged into its hole—perhaps a cunning ad to entice people to get off the streets and into a coffee shop. Such places were struggling as changes in the climate devastated the growth of coffee beans.

No one was laughing now.

For years, mankind had been aware that life existed on other planets. Seventeen years earlier, in 2018, NASA's Mars InSight Lander had burrowed into the red planet and found evidence of carbon life forms. Initially seeking to measure heat production beneath the surface, the probe had collected various physical samples and analyzed them. Earth's geophysicists were surprised to find carbon and graphite, mixed with organic molecules arrayed in a repetitive fashion, with base pairs similar to our own DNA structure.

This was hailed, in 2019, as "Absolute Proof of Extraterrestrial Life," and the journal *Science* published the report. They had no idea what was coming. The life forms were dubbed "Martian Moles," named in honor of the 1951 black-and-white film *Superman and the Mole Men*—which ironically highlighted the danger of drilling deep oil wells into the Earth and provided boner jokes for the Silent Generation in their early teens.

It was many decades before aliens or the threat of carbon pollution would be globally recognized, and while these microscopic "Martian Moles" created quite a buzz among the evolutionary scientists, there was a big difference between red dust with an organized base-pair structure and an alien space craft rapidly approaching the planet humans call home.

• • • •

The reaction to this world-changing revelation was a mix of excitement, Wellsian fear, and abject apathy. Most were simply too hot to care or had grown immune to decades of Earth-shattering news that amounted to absolutely nothing.

Nevertheless, before long, media outlets ran nothing else all day and night. Stories varied greatly on the astonishing development depending on the respective readership. The *New York Times* front page was straightforward:

NASA SCIENTISTS CONFIRM:

WE ARE NOT ALONE

The *New York Post* cover adopted a slightly different tone:

POPSICLE THREAT

ALIENS WANT TO MILK

FROZEN HUMAN GENITALIA

The online media took even greater artistic license:

CRUISE TESTIMONY CONFIRMS

SCIENTOLOGY IS ALIENTOLOGY!

The talking heads on the network news programs discussed whether or not it was the start of a *coup d'etat* by a former President whose name they would no longer say aloud, and a once-popular far-right network called it a hoax, a military fabrication, and a "A Deep Democratic Conspiracy Designed to Undermine American Values."

• • • •

Two days *before* the flashing message announced an approaching alien spacecraft, deep in a costly top-secret silo in the mountains of the Red Rocks of Sedona, the U.S. government had begun debating their response to this unexpected arrival.

The United States had, almost a century earlier, taken the lead in the race for alien tech after a spaceship with an "unusual guest" crashed in the Nevada desert in 1947. Thus, proof of advanced alien life wasn't new to those holed up in the Sedona base. A full contingent of Army brass and scientists in Silo 74, as well as another team headquartered in Area 57, already had intimate knowledge of such life—its existence, advantages, and dangers.

The ET Army Command was formed in mid-1947 after a second spacecraft landed in Roswell, New Mexico. The local citizens who were the first to reach the spaceship speculated that it had arrived from the planet Krypton, or that it was some kind of Russian spy craft. Then, when a bewildered Pleiadian stepped out of the craft with four talking dogs that looked a lot like pugs, the locals realized it either had to be the apple pie moonshine from the Arizona Wilderness Brewing Company…or they needed to call to someone higher up. Deciding between the two wasn't as easy as one might suspect.

Between 1947 and 2019, the Arizona Department of Liquor allowed citizens to "give away your homemade liquor to family and friends age twenty-one or older, without requiring a license." This led to the rapid growth of homemade distilleries in Arizona where "prairie organic spirits" became commonplace, and inebriated Arizonians often made phony phone calls to the local authorities.

Once the authorities figured out that it wasn't the moonshine talking, they dispatched someone in response to the call.

Sheriff "Butch" Urp, Wyatt's great grandson, drove out from Roswell Barrack B to the landing site and found the stunned Pleiadian and the dogs next to the spacecraft, singing what appeared to be cowboy space tunes. One of them 'I'm so lonely, I could be an ameba' seemed vaguely reminiscent. Urp listened and reckoned the visitors were friendly enough, but decided to go even *further* up the food chain.

Shortly, a group of black-clad men and women hustled the newcomers into a couple of cars. Others dressed in military fatigues got their spacecraft up onto the bed of Ray Patterson's Dodge Brothers truck and drove them all out to Area 51, a nearby Army base used for training exercises. The MP stationed at the security booth radioed to his supervisor that "a sheriff with a funny new truck and a bunch of giggling dogs" had just passed through.

Against his better judgement, the superior officer at the time, Major General "Rufie" Scott, dressed hurriedly and hustled out to investigate. When he saw the eight-foot-tall bluish crash victim, the "funny new truck," and the dogs, he immediately contacted the Pentagon. Rufie was later promoted by President Harry S. Truman for his "heads-up" thinking and put in charge of the secret military operation for several decades until it was subsequently moved to Area 57, where his son, General Thomas "Tommy Gun" Scott, took over his father's command.

Area 57 became famous among the various branches of the military, and rumors abounded for decades about secret operations performed there. For example, the army food at the base—usually tasteless—became famous in clandestine circles for its quality and nutritional value, with soldiers bulking up and losing unwanted fat. Questions arose like, were those *real* chocolate candies for dessert? And if so, why did they taste so good and why were they so plentiful? The pugs in particular got a lot of crap over that one.

Healthy, delicious food at the base, however, was the first clue that the aliens were up to something. Other advancements included the "lazy bones" tuning device, allowing you to change the television channel from your easy chair—*Amazing!* said one member of the top brass, who no longer had to find his privates to change the channels—along with video-tape recorders, superglue, and the hovercraft invented by Christopher Cockerell, clearly based on Pleiadian anti-gravity drives.

Such evolutions, however, came at a price. Many "unexplained" explosions occurred in the areas surrounding the base, usually and speciously attributed to research being done at Los Alamos Laboratory.

Over the years, most presidents of the United States visited the military-alien installation—in part because of great personal curiosity, but also because they believed an alien intelligent enough to fly a spaceship to Earth probably had "secrets" which might prove useful to the world's superpower. The alien pilot's name was Plamorius, and he came to be known as Commander P.

The first to visit was President Truman, and *his* first order of business was to find out if there was "any intelligent life out there?" Commander P appeared not to understand his question, and the pugs remained silent. Then followed President Dwight Eisenhower, who asked the aliens if there was "any intelligent life out there that could help me win wars."

Still the aliens remained silent.

Finally, President John F. Kennedy asked if there was "any intelligent life out there that could help me *prevent* wars." According to records, Commander P spoke with Kennedy at length.

• • • •

Eighty-eight years after Plamorius' arrival, the ET Army Command was again the hub of frenetic activity. In command were General Tiberius K. Scott, a son of "Tommy Gun" Scott, and Major Bophades Broward.

Years before, a psychological profile of top Army brass revealed these two were a good fit to be playing with aliens deep in caves, having both been captured and tortured during the famous twenty-eight-day Mexican-American Comido War of 2024.

As the history books unambiguously illustrate, the trade wars among Earth's nations had escalated to the point that the price of avocadoes reached twenty-five dollars a pound, resulting in severe unrest among Mexican-restaurant owners. Food fights erupted on the border towns, and two soldiers were captured while eating supposedly "free-range tacos" from a food truck. Scott and Broward were held for nearly a month as military prisoners of war deep underground in a small eight-by-eight room in Tijuana and fed nothing but beans and rice with Corona beer. A television in the room kept playing a DVD with beach commercials in which people stayed thirsty.

This technique was affectionately known by the Mexican rebels as the "Mexican Mal Olor" torture. This diet, combined with watching endless beer commercials on a loop, resulted in a continuous state of inebriation while remaining perpetually thirsty, with a smell impossible to ignore, leading the prisoners to intermittently explode with maniacal laughter occasionally so intense that their abdominus rectus muscles would go into spasm, causing searing pain.

The methane buildup, however, also proved so intense that when Scott managed to steal a cigar and light it, the explosion blew off the door to their cell. Both men escaped.

When liberated and debriefed, General Scott was credited with "resilience," "open-mindedness," and "determination and grit," as well as being a "top tactical strategist." He was deemed perfect for a job where his mettle might be tested in bizarre and potentially dangerous circumstances. Scott's character was reflected in his appearance: six-foot-three with a muscular frame, broad torso and shoulders, firm jaw, thin grey mustache, short cropped gray hair, and exceedingly bushy grey eyebrows.

Major Broward's character profile and appearance, on the other hand, indicated quite a different story. *His* psych evaluation had indicated that he was "gullible," "insensitive," "bullheaded," "foolish," and "arrogant" with a touch of the coyote-trickster thrown in for good measure. Truth be told, his psych evaluation before captivity hadn't been much better. With a nickname of "Nuts," he stood five-foot-seven and was built like a 210-pound bulb of garlic. At only forty-two years old, there was more hair on his knuckles than the top of his head. He was, however, a dedicated soldier who obeyed orders to a tee—even fatuous and immoral ones.

"General!" Broward shouted. "We've received an update. The alien craft is less than one hundred thirty thousand miles from Earth."

Across the room, General Scott remained nonplussed.

"Is that a fact?" he asked, waving his hand to indicate the nearby poker table. "I got four Pleiadian dogs playing cards, smoking cigars, and drinking my whisky...all while arguing about Kierkegaard. One little spaceship doesn't particularly impress me."

All four pugs turned toward Major Broward and mumbled "loser" in perfect unison. One of them held up a recently-emptied glass.

"Could sure go for a cold one," he barked. "Must be one hundred and eighteen degrees out there."

"Yeah, and *this* whisky stinks," growled another. "Where's the single malt?"

"Speaking of stinks..." a third pug laughed and pulled his cards close to his chest while sniffing at Major Broward. "Hey, Major B...feel like playing a round or two with us today?"

The major just straightened his collar. Broward had played cards with Commander P's companions early in their stay at Silo 74, foolishly assuming they were of inferior intelligence. He'd lost just under five thousand dollars in a single day.

"No, thank you," he grumbled. "I...I don't—"

"Relax, Major." The fourth pug grinned to his tablemates. "You look like you wet the floor again."

"The five of you, keep quiet!" General Scott snapped. Contrary to his implied indifference, he was concerned with the extraterrestrial situation as it was developing. Every few months, another alien craft—sometimes two or three—would buzz past Earth. In each instance, his primary duty was to discover if the approaching ship leaned friend or a foe. If friend, the U.S. Army Command would secure another mean-ingless ally. If foe, he had to determine how best to destroy them with-out leaving any trace.

Scott turned to Commander P.

Plamorius had been working with Army command for several de-cades. He hadn't crashed at Roswell in 1947, but he'd subsequently arrived to retrieve the poor bloke who had. Upon learning that his predecessor was deceased, Plamorius stayed on, living at the ET Com-mand Center for some seventy years, maintaining residences in Spain and Avalon, New Jersey as well. Thanks to his superior intelligence, his caring and amiable nature, and his four talking dogs, he was popular with the military personnel.

Seated in an old leather lounge chair, he was, by pure coincidence, reading Tolstoy's *War and Peace*. The book sat in his lap, however, and he was staring off into the distance.

"Commander P," the General called over, "you wanna put that down for a minute and tell us what you think about this damned ship?"

P slowly lowered his book. He was seven-feet-tall, thin, and bony with slate-grey skin, a large cranium, saucer eyes, a small mouth, thin neck, and arms so long it looked as if they could hug you from ten feet away. Indeed, P actually did hug people from ten feet away. The Pleia-dians were a very affectionate group, and when he did so he would—out of the blue—shout "Love fest!" This caught more than one unsus-pecting person off-guard and was a constant source of both discomfort and...humor...on the base.

P had been daydreaming, imagining himself as Romanoff whisking away his lovely new bride, Annaluskha, and saving her from the Reptil-ian invasion. A tear, which had formed in the corner of his eye, trailed down the side of his cheek.

"Show me the lights," he muttered. "There's likely a pattern?"

"Yes, sir!" A soldier working seated at a console ran the recording of the spaceship's lights. "It's a repeating pattern. Red, red, blue, red, red, blue, blue, red, red...seventy-two more combos after that.... Then it repeats. The same eighty-one color pattern."

"It's definitely a message," P said. "Run the recording through the analyzer." The Army sergeant again followed P's orders, and the com-puter screen lit up with a message:

Seeking pizza and ice-cold beer.

Please send Uber Eats immediately.

That is all.

"What in the name of sweet Baby Jesus...." Scott growled. He spun and discovered that the dogs had snuck away from the poker table and hacked again into another terminal. One of them was typing furiously—no mean feat, given the lack of fingers. "Someone get these puny mutts out of my sight!" the general bellowed. "Major Broward, clear that screen and reenter the data!"

The major saluted and joined the soldier at the terminal. Pushing the man aside, he quickly typed in the command, and the message immediately changed on the screen.

CLOSING ON PRIMARY OBJECTIVE

PREPARE TO ENGAGE AGGRESSIVE FORCES

CODE WORD: REPTILE

A silence fell over the room.
A large smile appeared on P's grey face.

CHAPTER 2:

ARCTURIANS

"**T**his is it," he said. "The Arcturian mothership I told you about. The time must now be right, and they've come to assist us."

"Assist us?" General Scott squinted again at the monitor's message again. "With what?"

P scowled. "The Reptilians, of course."

General Scott laughed huskily. "Right…the lizards," he said. "Colossal waste of my time." He peered at the four pugs, who had returned to the makeshift poker table. "Deal me in the next round, boys," he said.

"Don't you see, General Scott?" P persisted, confused at the general's response. "It's the Arcturians."

"And?"

"'And?'" P looked around the room for some help, but there was none to be found. Even the pugs remained silent and just stared. "It's… it's the *Arcturians*. I've told you about them before. They're the most—"

"Listen to me," General Scott held up a hand. "There are, what, a half-dozen or more different alien races on this planet now?"

"At least," P said. "Of which I am aware."

"Have any of *them* been able to help us with our lizard problem?"

"No, but—" P began.

"Then why should we expect these *Arthurians* to be any different?"

"Arcturians," P corrected.

"Exactly." General Scott slumped into a chair at the table. "The damned reptiles are dug in so deep…. Not to diminish your accomplishments here, P, but what's one more alien race added to the mix? I mean, really. You're the smartest damn guy I ever met. What can they bring to the table that you can't?"

The four pugs looked at one another and then all turned toward the General.

"I can whistle Dixie, cite Robert Frost, and drink a *Corona* all at the same time," one said. He cleared his throat. "*Two paths diverged in the woods, and I took the one that smelled the best. Stay thirsty, my General.*"

"Child's play," the second one growled. "*I* can whistle the Pleiadian anthem, drink a Russian mule, and cite Emily Dickenson." He took a deep breath, sipped from a copper mug and proclaimed, "*Dogs are better than human beings because they know but do not tell.*"

"Who's Emily Dickenson?" the major asked.

Ignoring him, the third laughed at his fellow pug.

"An Aranosaur with a speech impediment might not agree with your poetic diatribe." The other two bobbed their heads up and down in agreement. The three-legged Aranosaur was a highly evolved triped with a penchant for poetry. They would often sit in the middle of town squares and beg for money while reciting poetry. If you didn't give them money or food and appeared to not enjoy their poetry, they ate you.

The third pug persisted. "I can whistle 'Someone's in the Kitchen with Dinah' *and* cite Edgar Allen Poe while downing two ounces of Wild Turkey. All at once!" The dogs rarely missed an opportunity to drink *and* show off. This would likely now go on all afternoon. One paw already on the Wild Turkey, the pug reached with his free one and grabbed the Ace of Spades to perch it on his shoulder. He drank and spoke simultaneously, yielding a gargling sound.

"*And the Raven, never flitting, still is sitting, still is sitting, on the pallid bust of Pallas just above my chamber door; And his eyes have all the seeming of a demon's that is dreaming….*" He finished the poem and the drink and took a deep bow.

Everyone in the room clapped.

The last pug chortled. "Oh, gentlemen and ladies, I apologize for my colleagues' beleaguered efforts to impress. I will now eat cherpumple and slumgullion, drink down a Black Bison—raising our glasses to *your* military genius, General—while I lead my associates in a selection from *The Pirates of Penzance*." The four quadrupeds stood in their chairs and began to sing the Gilbert and Sullivan tune "The Modern Major General's Song."

When they'd finished, the room broke out in applause, but the General just glared.

"What was the point of this Broadway production of *Dogs*?" he growled. "Waste of my time."

"While my four friends lack…social skills," P replied, "they make a valid point. Each intergalactic race possesses a unique gift and purpose—as is the case with the different species who populate Earth. It is no different on other star systems. For example, in the far distant galaxy of the Crab Nebulae, on the seventh planet from their sun, beings can telepathically communicate without the need for words or gestures. Supreme quiet reigns and marriages last forever. The Andalusians can cut off their arms and legs and, in salamander fashion, grow back new appendages within days. Bored Andalusian teens tend to do it just for kicks, mercilessly teasing their parents. In turn, parents occasionally cut off male genital appendages, hinting 'not everything grows back.' Not surprisingly, Andalusian offspring are some of the most exceptionally well-behaved aliens in the galaxy." Everyone nodded as they reflected on these unusual gifts.

"And the Arcturians…" P paused, thinking. "Let's just say that if you have *any* hopes of surviving the Reptilian infestation and saving your species from environmental annihilation, this group is the best chance you or I have."

The General snorted something deep in his throat but considered P's words carefully. "What do we know about these guys?"

Commander P tapped at one of the consoles and the monitors filled with images of two alien planets. One box showed the approaching ship moving in real time.

"The two planets are the same one shown twice," P explained. "The first image is the planet Proxima Centauri B, commonly called Arcturus, in the Alpha Centuri star system *before* the Reptilian invasion." The globe had a bright greenish glow, which, he explained, was due to the lush fauna. Even from space, it still seemed to dominate densely populated areas. Plamorius noted that species across Proxima Centauri B had been living together in harmony for millions of years.

The planet appearing on the screen just to the right was quite different. It looked dull, smaller, with brown and dark areas crisscrossing the surface. No signs of visible life could be seen.

"The Arcturians are one of the most powerful Starseed tribes," P continued. "A sacred conglomeration of species, spread across multiple universes and dimensions, who are committed to defeating the Reptilians and establishing peace and harmony across all worlds and galaxies, throughout time and space."

"How does this concern us?" the general huffed.

P pressed on. "The Arcturians, General, are what you might call a superpower—a major player within the Starseed alliance. As if the Roman and Mongol empires had combined forces. To that end, they comprise two distinct…populations. The first are highly evolved spiritual beings with the ability to read minds and feel truth, access hidden knowledge, and move in and out of the third and fourth dimensions, holding consciousness in the fifth and sixth. These very powers have allowed some of the Arcturians to escape lower dimensional realities and avoid harm during dangerous times, including the Orion Wars."

"Just what we need," the general said. "Intergalactic war refugees. We don't need escapees—we need genuine help."

P smiled. "General, their ability to move about dimensions *also* gives them access to hidden knowledge planted by their ancestors deep within the third-dimensional reality. Knowledge regarding the healing of individuals, and entire planetary bodies…knowledge needed to defeat the Reptilians. Sacred and powerful knowledge concealed centuries ago into Earth's rocks, trees, and mountains."

"The answer to defeating the Reptilians…is *here*…on Earth?"

"Has been for a thousand years, General," P confirmed. "Since the Starseed Elders escaped their own various star systems and fled to Earth, one of the most remote planets in this dimensional reality. Why do you think I've stayed here as long as I have?"

"Why didn't you tell us this before?"

"How remote you are?" P asked. "I assumed you knew. If you mean, why didn't I torment you with this 'hidden knowledge,' there was no point. This special information can *only* be accessed by the most advanced of the Arcturian tribe—those they call *Tertons*. The starship now hovering one hundred thousand miles from the Earth contains, by my reckoning, *several* such beings. Those masters who've chosen to be born in difficult times and trained to help bring back planetary balance."

"They've come to save humanity," Major Broward marveled.

"Not entirely." P scratched his chin, choosing his next words carefully. "Their primary goal, I suspect, is to help those from their own tribe—those who were unable to shift dimensional realities during the Orion Wars and escape. Arcturians who evaded the Reptilian invaders in other ways."

"I don't understand," Major Broward said. "How does coming to Earth help save other Arcturians?"

"Because they're already here," the General answered for P.

"Precisely," P said, and he sighed deeply. "Many took incarnation in *human* bodies here on Earth. They look perfectly human…." He stopped and scanned the command center. "Jeff, for instance, is an Arcturian." Staff Sergeant Jeff Pratt looked up, appearing a bit bewildered, and then waved sheepishly from across the room. He was six-foot-ten and had the eyes, nose, and chiseled features of a male model. For the first time the general noticed how golden the sergeant's skin was—he had always assumed it was some form of jaundice.

"Is that the case, Sergeant?" Scott demanded.

"I'm afraid the…commander is mistaken," Pratt replied. "I'm from Iowa." But he frowned as he said it, and the general wasn't convinced.

First things first, Scott thought. *Personnel records can wait.*

"As you can see, they *look* perfectly human, and implanted memories make them believe it," P said. "Yet they've never felt as if Earth was their true home, and they carry the scars of pain and suffering, buried deep in their subconscious. General, there are many Starseed lineages present on your planet: Sirians, Alpha-Centurians, Annunaki, Andromedans, Pleiadians, and Lyrans…not just the Arcturians." When the general gave him a doubtful look, he continued.

"Many of these incarnated Starseed souls have been labeled 'depressed,' 'anxious,' and even 'schizophrenic with delusional components.' Often they are unable to fit in and frequently are drugged with heavy doses of medication to address their 'illnesses'—drugged by the very Reptilians they had once hoped to escape. But these are individuals separated from their true ancestry, beings who are searching for truth, yet remain lost. These are the brothers and sisters the Arcturians have come to retrieve," he said, "and the message is for them."

• • • •

With this new revelation, Army ET Command launched again into planning mode. However, they had to account for the fact the Arcturian message might also be picked up and decoded by scientists, astronomers, and even hobbyists across Earth.

It was.

For many, this was the first proof of "reptile aggression." Speculation began to spread like a California wildfire stoked by Santa Ana winds.

Previously, the only widespread rumor of reptilian aggression had been based on scanty evidence that the U.S. government was performing top secret biological experiments in a level-five biohazard facility on Plum Island, off the coast of Connecticut. As the story went, Nazi scientists from World War II had been given refuge in this secret biological bunker—working with American scientists to create biological weapons that could effectively disable a population while impairing their intellectual and reproductive capacities.

These genetically modified spirochetes, rickettsial bacteria, and viruses were placed inside ticks, which would act as stealth pathogens and "superbugs," highly effective agents of biological warfare. They were the perfect weapon. Too small to be noticed, they delivered an anesthetic to prevent the subject from feeling the bite, and by continuously changing their outer surface proteins, effectively evaded the human immune system, overwhelming the subject.

According to rumors, initial experiments were done on Americans. Unsuspecting subjects would suddenly experience disabling fatigue and brain fog, unrelenting pain, resistant insomnia, and high levels of anxiety and depression. Some would even become psychotic. It was a perfect biological weapon, and to ensure their plan was foolproof, rumor had it that Reptilian CEOs of Big Industry collectively dumped billions of tons of toxic chemicals into the air, food, and water supplies every year for decades.

Then they hired top scientists to deny the effect of the chemicals, which acted as potent neurotoxins and endocrine disruptors. In addition to lowering IQs and impairing reproductive capacity, they led to large numbers of the population developing cancer, heart and lung disease, ADD, ADHD, Autism Spectrum Disorder, and Alzheimer's dementia.

The scientists found that when they mixed these environmental toxins with their "super spirochetes," it would effectively disable any individual and create a mysterious illness that none of the top medical professionals could figure out. Anytime the media tried to discover the origin of this spreading illness, their access to the island was cut off. Military contractors outfitted with AK 47s surrounded the perimeter to make certain no one ever found out what the scientists were really doing.

Conspiracy theorists believed it was a perfect reptilian plan to subjugate the human race.

They were correct.

The only other prior sign of reptilian aggression and most widely shared theory to date was put forth by Dr. Ophidian, a wildlife biologist at the Conservancy of Southwest Florida in Naples. Florida was caught in the grip of a major python infestation, and a youngster named Jimmy Rosen, who'd been playing in his backyard in Manatee County, had disappeared just the week before. The only clue was a large pile of reptilian poo next to his favorite stuffed bear, Pooh.

The headlines practically wrote themselves:

ALIEN PYTHONS INVADE FLORIDA

SCIENTISTS FIGHT BACK WITH
SEX PHEROMONES

Since Florida was, indeed, facing a reptilian infestation, the extraterrestrial angle struck a chord, and the authorities struggled to prevent widespread panic.

"Snakes eating small children?" Tom Barazach of the local Naples police responded. "The only reptiles around here causing trouble are the sixteen-foot alligators near the Glades and swamps around Orlando. People go missing in this area, but it's got nothing to do with aliens and flying saucers." Reporters, however, were quick to observe that he dodged the question of pythons.

Local forensic experts began to investigate the phenomenon. One Florida-based team, comprised primarily of elderly Jewish scientists who had an unusually strong interest in bowel movements, began studying the recent disappearance of small children, as well as migration of snakes and elderly grandparents—two potential food sources for the reptiles—to the sunshine state. The highly trained scatological team, led by Dr. Ophidian, reminded people of the science of reptilian bowel movements and how to differentiate droppings based on stool consistency, color, weight, size, and fiber content.

"Most reptiles pass feces that is relatively distinguishable from that of mammals," Barazach explained on a morning news program. "Herp stools often appear to have distinct parts—the yellow or whitish urates and the brown to black solids, which are often comprised mostly of hair. Lizards expel their fecal matter—urine and stool—through the same opening, so there is a white tip of uric acid crystals, as lizard urine is concentrated.

"Thus, the remains of young Jimmy Rosen were not," he concluded, "made by a python."

This only intensified speculation that Jimmy's disappearance might be the result of this supposed reptilian invasion. Was there something worse in Florida than giant pythons—something far worse than what the media was reporting? Inquiring minds wanted to know.

• • • •

Faced with growing hysteria, General Tiberius K. Scott began to assess how the Arcturian arrival might be used to their advantage.

"Perhaps we can somehow link their goals to our own," the general proposed, scratching his chin. "If we can pull that off, and seven billion *true* Earthlings are saved…"

"The Arcturians would, as you say, 'call that icing,'" P offered.

"You said there were *two* groups of Arcturians here. What's the second?"

Plamorius smiled. "Those Arcturians who could not take human bodies and still landed on Earth some four-thousand years ago. Another species or clan…one far less evolved. As if your *hominins*—the common ancestor of humans and chimpanzees—still walked the Earth, owned homes, and had jobs."

"The Greys." General Scott gasped. "Greys are Arcturians?"

P tapped the console, and a typical grey alien appeared on the giant screen. Short, large eyes, and bulging heads—the Spielbergian type that had been credited with abducting and probing humans and cows for centuries.

"Already far behind in the great cosmic evolutionary steeplechase, they completely shut off their hearts during the Reptilian invasion," P explained. "The ability to feel and know truth—the most essential Arcturian traits—are now lost to them. All the probes and abductions are simply their effort to reestablish balance between head and heart. Their attempts to merge *their* DNA with human DNA is their way of trying to recapture the ability to feel."

"You might have told us this *twenty* years ago," the general said.

P shrugged. "Y'all weren't ready."

"I hate those little buggers," Major Broward grumbled. "I was…" Everyone in the room turned, and he paused to collect his thoughts. "I woke up in my bed fourteen years ago…soon after I arrived in Sedona. Let me tell you, it's given me nightmares…. I don't remember the last time I had a good night's sleep. One of them things was there, coming around to…well, collect my sperm and put something up my nose." He grinned. "I claimed my balls had been blown off by a land mine in '98 *and* that I had a bad cold. Stupid bastard believed me." The grin fell away. "I told him to go next door and visit my wife instead. She hasn't spoken to me since."

Soon after that, Broward visited the local psychiatrist, a Dr. Carl Watersford. The doctor had shown him a spacecraft not fifteen feet from his back deck. Such events were far more common than Broward had been led to believe and the townie response far more blasé. The aliens, the doctor explained, wanted to know if they could come indoors and play some cards.

"Do they really think we're that stupid?" Dr. W had said, grinning. "Everyone around here knows to avoid inviting these guys into your house." Major Broward frowned, feeling regret. While his wife never spoke to him again, he often heard her occasional screams in the middle of the night.

"Oh, Grayson, yes, yes. Probe me again. Do it to me one more time." Broward still cringed when he heard that old song on the radio. Nothing could be more humiliating than being so easily replaced by a Grey.

Silence filled the room, and then P held out his arms as if to embrace the whole room.

"We all have an essential role to play in this multiverse," he said. "The Arcturians arrival comes at a crucial time in your planetary history."

"What's that mean for us?" the general asked, alarm appearing in his voice. "For the human race, I mean."

"It means," P said, and he smiled, "that it's finally time for *everyone* to know the truth."

CHAPTER 3:

IN THE STARS

At that moment, thirty-thousand miles from the Earth, Commander Avorius, Queen Dawn, King Aston, and the Royal Mother Helen prepared to be addressed by Amius, the Arcturian master astrologer.

Their arrival on Earth was rapidly approaching, leading Amius to call this gathering. She stood from her chair and bowed as the royal family entered the room. An elliptical silver table in the shape of a comet's hyperbolic trajectory stood dead center, with magnetic floating chairs around it. The newcomers quickly took their seats.

"I wish to inform you of the astrological significance of this present time," Amius began. "How Earth has evolved to its present state, and what energies we will need to employ if we are to achieve a successful outcome. The sub-group known as the Americans appear to be most ready to receive us. As we hope to work with them and their military, we need to understand their culture and where they come from...in order to understand where they are *going*.

"The birth chart of the nation called the United States—visible on the screens in front of you—shows that Pluto was at twenty-seven degrees thirty-three minutes in the sign of Capricorn. This placement of Pluto in the second house—a house representing values, finances, possessions, home, security, and natural resources—has been reflected in their society from its beginning. Accumulation, materialism, acquisition, the creating of large organizations that are prone to control, manipulation, and domination—including hierarchical structures in government and corporations.

"Even an individual's value appears to be reflected by their finances. However, Pluto *also* represents destruction and re-creation. This forced a complete transformation of American society twenty years ago when Pluto reached its first full cycle and return. This is when Earth's climate emergency began to unfold."

The queen raised her hand for Amius to pause.

"Great Master Astrologer," she said. "Is this how we'll break through the indoctrination that has warped the Earth people's sense of reality? Many are locked into specific thought and emotional patterns by a media that keeps them like prey dangling at the end of a pole."

"Quite right, my precious queen," Amius replied. "As I said, Pluto also represents death and regeneration. *Transformation*. This includes the transformation of their way of thinking. One of the keys to enabling the humans to break free during the Pluto return, my Queen, is their return to 'feeling.' Compassion, with a deeper understanding of themselves and others through the fine instrument of the heart."

The queen smiled. The wisdom of the heart *would* prevail.

Amius continued, "In the year 2021, when Pluto returned to twenty-five degrees Capricorn, the devastating effects on the weather were still in their relatively early stages. It was the first time that this large political unit—the United States—began a passionate restoration of values, abandoning patriarchal views that had contributed to the havoc wreaked on the planet. Americans considered restoring a set of values that were life-giving, care-giving, and co-creative. It was a balanced union between divine feminine love and divine masculine will—something your Highness has advocated for ages amongst our people and for which we are all grateful."

Everyone in the room, except for the Royal Mother, bowed in respect.

"Excuse me, Master Amius," Helen said. "How is it that a backward, primitive civilization—exhibiting massive egos and brains slightly bigger than a pea—would suddenly wake up and smell the dead and drowned blooms on their soon-to-be-flooded planet?"

Amius took a moment.

"It's simple, Royal Mother," she replied. "Fortunately, a Uranian influence came along and guided things in the right direction, just as Earth's women began to exercise the appropriate influence. Climate awareness arose because strong women spoke up and began to fight for the future of their children and their children's children. Earthlings in the early part of the 21st century began to treat *all* life with respect and equality.

"Unfortunately, much damage had already been done," Amius continued. "The early signs of climatic change had been ignored by the patriarchy, and consequences unfolded. The last vestiges of Pluto's destructive power must be addressed if the Earth is to survive with any significant quality of life. Uranus, the modern-day ruler of Aquarius, moved into Taurus in 2019 and stayed there until 2026. The effects during that time helped to wake the sleeping masses.

"Uranus assisted Pluto in shaking everything up—including the Earthlings' ability to receive information. 'Cosmic consciousness,' Earth's people used to call it. Some recalled at deeper levels who they were, breaking free of old patterns. A remarkable achievement, really. Pluto then moved into Aquarius at the beginning of the Earth year 2023—this officially ushered in the Age of Aquarius with transformative technology, a change in consciousness, humanitarianism, and an awareness of planetary interdependence.

"Communities began to work collectively. For example, food and water were at a premium, so new ways of production were developed. Therefore, my Queen, royal family, and Commander, the astrological energies bode well for us and for all who wish to come together and preserve life on the planet Earth. Collectively, we *will* help the people retain their fundamental rights, halting the Reptiles' stranglehold on the planet."

This appeared to satisfy the royals, and they stood to leave. As they filed out, Amius stopped Queen Dawn.

"One more thing, your Highness," she said. "Just before Pluto leaves Aquarius in March of Earth year 2043, astrology verifies that you *will* give birth to a male baby—half-Arcturian and half-human, in the morning of January 25, 2037. At 8:00 a.m., to be precise. This will make him an Aquarian with an Aquarius rising.

"With this zodiacal blueprint, as you've so often witnessed in your dreams, your son will be a savior to this world and to our people."

CHAPTER 4:

A CRASH COURSE IN ARCTURIAN CULTURE

"If an alien came to visit, I'd be embarrassed to tell them that we fight wars to pull fossil fuels out of the ground to run our transportation. They'd be like, 'What?'"

—Neil deGrasse Tyson, American astrophysicist

Top Army brass at the Pentagon agreed it was imperative to accept the alien invitation and to meet the Arcturians directly, in order to size them up—in every way, as they'd been forewarned that Arcturians are all more than seven feet tall.

The military was specifically concerned about letting a new and unknown race of aliens into the United States without a better understanding of who they were. They had stopped plenty of Mexicans, Guatemalans, and Canadians in their time, but this was a horse of a different color. The main risks posed by these other nationalities were, respectively, smuggling fifty-nine varieties of non-genetically modified corn seeds into the country, bringing in 33 percent Guatemalan dark chocolate bars, and bringing in loonies—one-dollar coins, not crazy Canadians—while forcing everyone to finish sentences with "eh." This bastardizing of our language was a well-known risk to anyone who engaged with a Canadian for more than a five-minute conversation.

It was very likely the Arcturians carried weapons of mass destruction as well, and despite upgrades in military intelligence, top brass were rightly concerned we wouldn't recognize dangerous alien technology until it blew us up.

The welcoming team was chosen, consisting of General Scott, Major Broward, Commander P, and the Pugs. They would be joined by Dr. Pedro Hernández Correro and Dr. Antonio Garcia Morales, renowned Mexican scientists who had slipped past the poorly constructed border wall in 2019. Both prominent scientists had received asylum from the 46th president of the United States. The two were credited with the discovery of a broad range of advancements in astrophysics, animal physiology, and the food industry. These included the invention of the first wormless Mexican jumping beans, 100 proof wormless Mezcal, the proposed Correro-Morales warp drive by which a spacecraft could enter a "wormhole" and achieve faster-than-light travel, and an automatic "de-wormer" for dogs.

The plan was to have the alien craft descend somewhere in a remote part of Boynton Canyon in Sedona, and then transport everyone up for a brief introductory cocktail party. They were instructed to don their best military outfits, shine all buttons, medals, and shoes, and make sure no unwanted nose hair was emerging from their proboscis. This proved a difficult requirement for the pugs, who would have none of it.

• • • •

The welcome team stood, waiting in the designated spot in the middle of a large field in the canyon. The sun was just starting to descend and illuminated the tops of the red rocks. Peaks in the distance looked like brilliantly lit phosphorescent matches. Another beautiful Sedona evening.

A pack of coyotes began to howl in the distance, as if alerting the group to the impending arrival. As if on cue, the sky directly above them quivered, pulses of energy rippling the air as if someone had tossed a boulder into a lake. Gold and blue lights appeared in the ripples—the alien spacecraft emerging.

The major got a shiver up his spine and a tingle in his privates. Broward glanced from person to person to pug.

"What if the teleporter doesn't work correctly?" he posed. "And… and we're missing parts of our bodies when we arrive? Or, even worse, body parts are accidently relocated? Our ears and dicks in the wrong place. Or our noses end up where our feet should be?"

"Well," Dr. Correro suggested, "if your feet smell and your nose runs, then they put you back together upside down."

"Hey, Major," a pug asked as the other two chortled. Plamorius held them in a firm embrace. "How will we tell if your nose and dick are in the wrong place?"

"Boys, behave yourselves," P snapped. "We are to meet Arcturian royalty, so keep a muzzle on it." He turned to Broward. "Major, the Arcturians perfected this technology a very long time ago. We're all quite safe." Even as he spoke, a bright light above grew stronger and more distinctly conical, and then they all started to move slowly upward toward a circular opening.

"Whoa!" Broward cried out. "I'm flying!"

"Beam me up, Scotty!" Dr. Correro grinned. "How in the name of red-hot tamales are they doing this?"

"I'm a doctor, not an engineer," Morales replied, though he *was* in fact an electrical engineer. "Things are only impossible until they're not."

"Get hold of yourselves," Scott bellowed in order to be heard above the humming that filled the air. "It's no time to be quoting corny sci-fi." Peering upward, he took in the immensity of the bottom of the Arcturian craft. "Although clearly," he admitted, "we *are* boldly going where no man has gone before."

· · · ·

Before you could say "Saturn's size spectacularly skyjacks the celestial syzygy show," the team was floating in the ship's docking bay. As the bottom of the craft closed beneath them, a hissing sound emerged from the walls of the cabin, pressurizing the chamber. A whirring sound gently vibrated through the room, and a fine mist came from apertures in the ceiling, humidifying the air and making the skin tingle. Plamorius knew that the Earth visitors were receiving a subtle spritz of decontamination spray.

When the mist cleared, a hatch behind them opened up, leading to a u-shaped corridor angled upward out of the airlock. At the very top of the walkway waited an Arcturian wearing elaborate military garb. At seven feet two inches, he was strikingly handsome with long blond hair and a muscular physique, looking every bit of an Asgardian warrior king preparing for battle.

It was Avorius, the head of the Arcturian army and a longtime friend of Plamorius. Their relationship had been forged in fire, shortly after their worlds endured the Reptilian invasion.

"Plamorius," the man said in perfect English. "It's good to see you and your furry friends. It's been far too long!"

The pugs wagged their tails in perfect unison and tried to ineffectively jump out of their commander's arms. He knew how to treat them well, and it was only a matter of time until they would be drinking 100-proof Arcturian absinthe.

"Avorius," P replied, dropping the pugs and stepping into the commander's outstretched arms. "You amazing azygous Arcturian! I am amazed to arrive again aboard your airship." The alliteration wars had begun, P thought ruefully.

It was a long-overdue reunion. They'd both escaped their planets' destruction during the earlier phases of the Orion wars, and each had been part of the resistance movement that stretched across the galaxies, revealing what was happening on different planets and aiding the opposition. Their mission was to liberate the civilizations that could hear and see the truth buried within the darkness.

They were veritable brothers of light.

"May I introduce my American friends to you, dear Commander," P said. "General Scott, Major Broward, Dr. Morales, and Dr. Correro. They represent the country that helped colleagues of mine after a terrible crash and have welcomed me as a guest—a friend—for more than sixty years. We are grateful for the help the Arcturian royal family wishes to now provide in our war against the Reptiles."

Commander Avorius bowed deeply.

"Our pleasure, entirely, and to that end...let us now meet the royal family." He led them up the walkway and toward the main chambers of the spacecraft. As they stepped into a connecting passageway, the walls had a mesmerizing blue-green glow and were lined with labradorite crystals of all shapes and sizes. Such crystals were often used on Earth by "new agers" for grounding spiritual energies and enhancing strength and intuition.

With each step down the corridor, music of the spheres played in the background. Then Avorius stopped and turned to address his guests.

"One thing I should probably tell you. The Royal Helen of Antwar, the queen's mother, occasionally has...what can easily be described as an attitude problem. Do your best to smile and agree with her. Resistance, most assuredly, is futile."

They continued on and arrived at the main living compartment of the spacecraft, a cavernous, platinum-walled chamber with a large floating elliptical table in its center, swathed in a royal magenta-and-gold tablecloth sporting the Arcturian seal. Large, engraved silver goblets and gold silverware accompanied the royal china. Two high-backed maroon thrones floated at one end of the table, alongside a beautifully adorned chair that appeared to be eighteenth century Louis XIV style with legs carved like Roman columns. There the Arcturian king, queen, and the royal mother sat.

To one side, there was a mountain of fluffy, multicolored pillows piled in a corner of the room next to three bowls of succulent treats. *These people certainly know how to handle the pugs*, Plamorious thought.

The Arcturian King was the first to greet their guests.

"Honored Americans and Pleiadians, bring me your tired, bring me your poor. *Live long and prosper!*"

How fortunate that the king hadn't watched episodes of *VEEP*, *Madam Secretary*, and *House of Cards* to learn about American politics, P mused. Yet Antwar had to have observed multiple impeachment proceedings, presidential debates, and State of the Union addresses. That would have told him that Terran rulers usually did whatever they wanted and ultimately had the last word. Nevertheless, he wouldn't want to insult his new guests. The King reflected for a moment, reviewing the cultural lessons about Earthlings he learned from watching *Star Trek Universe* and old science fiction films. As no one had yet responded to his initial greeting, he resolutely continued in a slightly louder voice.

"Klaatu. Barada! Nikto!"

Dr. Correro and Dr. Morales couldn't restrain their joy. The King was a Trekkie and sci-fi enthusiast!

"While we clearly have differences, may we, together, become greater than the sum of both of us," Dr. Morales said, bowing to the King. He stood with a proper Vulcan gesture.

"Yes." Dr. Correro mirrored the pose. "One man cannot summon the future, but one man can change the present!"

The general stepped forward, eying his two enterprising scientists warily: "We are honored, and grateful, to have been invited to meet with you," he said while perusing the interior of the ship. "Your star cruiser has…fascinating décor."

The architectural mix of George Jetson and Louis XIV, the general guessed, revealed a decorator obsessed with comets and their elliptical trajectory—elements of the future, the past, and of cultures across time. Unfortunately, the result was a French-English mishmash that looked like a futuristic amateur production of *Les Misérables* in which Jean Valjean used ray guns to escape.

The general bowed to the entire royal family. Major Broward just looked confused.

The queen stood to address her guests. As she rose, the humans gaped, and P smiled as best his features would allow. She was wearing a maroon-and-black vest over a long Marchessa silver gown which gracefully adorned her seven-foot shapely body. Plamorius had warned them that the Arcturian queen was quite beautiful, but there was an extra radiance emanating from her which they hadn't expected. There was a majestic presence infused with sincere kindness, a softness, and a deep love and care that emanated from her soul. The group was mesmerized. A couple of the humans wiped the corners of their mouths.

"Your Highness," General Scott said, bowing again. "It's a great honor to meet you. Words cannot express our gratitude for the help you are providing in the fight against the Reptiles. We are truly in your debt, and look forward, in return, to be able to help *your* people, those trapped as…" He turned to P.

"Starseeds," P said. The general nodded. Plamorius had briefed him on the Arcturian culture, information embellished by sources like Margaret Doner, whose work brought forth the earliest stories of our ancestors and other Starseeds. These had been described in detail in Doner's books, *The Path of the Human-Incarnated Angel and Starseed*, *Merlin's War*, and *Merlin's Handbook for Seekers and Starseeds*. The general had perused these books as part of his interstellar ET training and was confident he had a basic understanding of these races.

"Right!" General Scott said. "Those 'Starseeds' on *our* planet...allow us to help them in whatever way we can. Let this night be the beginning of a genuine intergalactic friendship."

"Well said, General," Queen Dawn replied. "Commander Plamorius has told us of your generosity in helping *him* after a Pleiadian spacecraft with his friend crashed on Earth. He also told us that he remained an ambassador and has garnered many good friends. Including..." She looked around. "Someone named Major Broward whom he, apparently, hugs quite often. Would that be you, sir? You may want to wipe your chin, I'm afraid."

The whole room turned to the major. He was utterly frozen, staring at the queen and drooling, transfixed by the whole situation—from being on an alien spacecraft to meeting this beautiful woman. It had clearly overloaded his circuitry. He suddenly jerked awake.

"Yes, ma'am...I mean, your Excellent...your Royal Highness. I...I am he, the one they call Broward." No one was sure where this style of grammar came from, but P was never one to miss an opportunity. He saw an opening to wake up the Major and went for it.

"And I am he," the Pleiadian Commander said. "The one they call P, whose mission it is to spread love freely!" P reached out with his long, spindly arms and grabbed the Major from a distance, trapping him in a hug. "*Love fest!*"

The major blushed, and his trance disappeared entirely. "Get your grubby Pleiadian arms off of me!" he yelled. "This is a big night! People might even write about this one day. You're embarrassing me!"

The pugs had spread around the room during the introductions, lounging on pillows, eating some sort of chow, smoking cigars, drinking, and lying on their backs while making pitiful faces, desperately looking to have their bellies scratched. No one was paying them any attention.

"Hey, P, don't embarrass the major," one said. "Only dogs should pant that hard!"

"Apparently, on this spaceship," another said, "girls rule and boys drool."

"I drool, therefore I am," the third quipped.

"Don't fight it, Major," the fourth embellished. "Drooling is your new religion, and a clear path to salivation."

General Scott winced inwardly, and Plamorius released the soldier.

"Please, have a seat at the table," the queen said, appearing nonplussed. "Have some Arcturian absinthe"—she gestured to the drink the pugs were downing eagerly—"and enjoy some Arcturian specialties we've put out for you. These have been specially prepared by the royal chef under the guidance of my dear mother. Speaking of whom...I'd like to introduce to you the Royal Mother, Helen of Antwar."

The Earthlings and P all bowed. So engrossed had they been in the queen's beauty, Broward's drooling, and the Pugs antics, they had forgotten the older woman's presence. They'd also forgotten Helen was an Arcturian, which according to Plamorius meant she could feel truth and read minds.

"Relax, boys," the royal mother said. "My daughter forgets me all the time; I'm used to it. If I didn't show up for breakfast one morning, it would be another week before a search party was sent out."

"Oh, Mother," the queen replied solemnly. "At least *two* weeks."

They moved to the table. As they took their seats, the general pulled rank and instructed Broward to sit beside the royal mother and gestured for Morales and Correro to take seats on either side of her. Plamorius sat next to his old friend Avorius. Then came the king and queen. General Scott took his place between the queen and the major. Strategically, it was the safest spot he could have chosen.

CHAPTER 5:

DINNER WITH A SIDE OF CATASTROPHE

The first course, ironically, was alphabet soup served, Queen Dawn explained, in honor of the English language. The chef put a dash of Arcturian absinthe into it, enabling them all to experience the primary characteristic flavors of the English language: receptiveness with a touch of arbitrary, social, vocalic, and creative zest.

At first everyone ate quietly, the uncomfortable silence interrupted occasionally by loud slurping coming from humans and pugs alike. About halfway through the potage, the major decided he should try and impress the royal mother by spelling something in his soup. He caught her attention and gestured for her to gaze down at his soup, where "MAJOR" floated in the broth. He was quite proud of his achievement and even more so as she responded quickly.

She rapidly rearranged the letters in *her* soup.

They spelled out "MORONIC."

The queen rang a bell then, and several well-dressed Arcturian servants in long white gowns appeared carrying elliptical silver serving platters. She said these were some of the rarest delicacies of the universes and identified each one in turn. Piled high in perfectly arranged geometric patterns of the solar system were Adorbian testicles—deep fried—layered on top of gelatinous Vegan deer cartilage, mini-beetlejuician brains, and Crespian-style crustacean tempura with a spicy eel intestine dipping sauce. From Earth, there were pigs in a blanket and Nathan's French fries. The servants went around the table offering the guests whatever they wished to try. The general was polite and tried one of each.

The doctors eagerly followed suit.

Major Broward, however, was wary of eating anything he didn't recognize. "I'm sorry," he said, "but...but are those...'egg-shaped' things on the plate...what I think they are? They remind me of mountain oysters from a Colorado trouser snake."

"Precisely, Major," Helen replied, turning to him. "We castrated an Adorbian servant earlier today just for you!" He glanced around. The male Arcturian servants went pale, and several could be seen tightly clutching their librarian handwarmers.

"Thank you, but I'll pass," the major said, not sure if she was serious and trying to not appear rude.

• • • •

"Dear guests, our cosmic brothers," the queen began, slowly and deliberately, "it's time to discuss why we have gathered this evening. Our hope is to expand your understanding of the galactic situation. We appreciate how difficult it is for most species to embrace the concept of their own extinction, despite the many examples your planet has experienced. The dodo, Great Auk, Pyrenean ibex, Tasmanian tiger, Baiji white dolphin, Roman empire, Atlantis, and the Olmec civilization, to name but a few." She paused, then continued.

"The Nabatean and Clovis cultures, the Aksumite empire, the Minoans, the Mycenaeans, Khmer Empire, and the Cucuteni-Trypillian cultures all mysteriously disappeared. Denial is a psychological defense mechanism, an ingrained genetic trait found in multiple galactic civilizations designed to avoid worry and physiological stress, especially when the truth is so overwhelming that it cannot be completely understood. Yet the result so devastating as to paralyze you and, ultimately, doom you all."

They all stopped eating.

"In the early part of the twenty-first century, your species had scientific proof of how fast a region you call Antarctica was shedding its ice. The American space administration and the Indian Space Research

Organization provided satellite images spanning decades and showed how increased carbon and methane production was affecting this area faster than other parts of Earth. Simultaneously, parts of the Arctic region, frozen for centuries, were melting and creating local lakes with cold water runoff into the ocean. Your culture's response?" She peered around the table. "Nothing. You did nothing of any consequence."

The look on her face went grim. "Sea levels rose and destroyed coastal towns and cities. Powerful cyclones and severe droughts in Zimbabwe and West Africa had millions facing starvation. Ego-based self-interests and paralyzing fear prevented you from saving yourselves.

"Had you limited global warming, you could have protected several hundred *million* people, blunted the damage done by vector-borne diseases such as malaria, dengue fever, and Lyme disease, and prevented catastrophic damage to yields of maize, rice, wheat, and potentially other cereal crops, particularly in sub-Saharan Africa, Southeast Asia, and Central and South America." Her voice was louder and she stood. "Livestock could have been protected from the spread of diseases and the effects of drought."

She glared at them with an accusing expression, then calmed herself and sat back down.

"What's all this mean?" the general asked, his voice strained. "I'm not prone to statistics and facts."

"It 'means' that the genuine-case scenario for your species," the queen replied, "is *extinction*. The best-case scenario is that you will survive but, due to your inaction, suffer global death and destruction for centuries. The risks to health, livelihoods, food, water, and economic growth were predicted fifty years ago, and now they are happening. Time, my dear, *dear* guests, is of the essence."

"Excuse me..."—the general pushed back from the table—"but what does this have to do with defeating the Reptilians?"

The queen smiled, but it was strained.

"To save your planet and yourselves, we must first finally expose the Reptilians—and their agenda, which includes climate catastrophe—to the entire planet and place the power back with your people. To quote one of your most famous American presidents, Franklin Delano Roosevelt, who apparently understood better than could have been anticipated, 'Let us never forget that government is ourselves, and not an alien power over us. The ultimate rulers of our democracy are not a President and senators and congressmen and government officials, but the voters of this country.' This human understood well that the power to effect change is fully in the hands of the people.

"You must begin immediately if your planet—and those Starseeds living on the Earth—are to survive. The Reptilians stand in the way of such change and promote the opposite every day. This is how they've destroyed and enslaved another fifty systems and planets. Advanced Arcturian technology, along with an understanding of occult spiritual forces beyond your ken, have given us a distinct advantage in this war," she explained. "We lacked this full knowledge of our enemy and his weaknesses when Proxima Centauri B—another name for Arcturus—was attacked, but now we are better armed and prepared."

"You keep using the term 'Starseed,'" Dr. Morales said. "Plamorius has mentioned them as well. What exactly are we talking about here?"

"Starseeds," Queen Dawn explained, "are ancient souls who have lived many lifetimes on other planets in the multiverse. They fled to escape Reptilian domination and wish to share their accumulated wisdom and help as lightworkers in our fight against this darkness. Each Starseed carries deep within their subconscious memories of their invasion, the wars which happened on Arcturus, the Pleiades, Andromeda, the Sirius system, Lyra, Antares, Vega, and the Alpha Centauri star system, to name but a few. Many of these Starseeds are now on Earth, but they do not remember their history, as the veil came down during their latest incarnation. Our goal is to wake them and use the strengths of each star civilization to help defeat the Reptilians."

The room went silent.

General Scott sat back. The ET Army Command had heard many of these facts before—it was not new information. What *was* new was the direct connection between the Reptilians and the queen's offer, which would give them access to sophisticated Arcturian technology.

Queen Dawn stood from the table, and everyone rose with her.

"I would like to introduce you to a highly valued mentor and spiritual guide from Arcturus," she said, "who will be assisting during our time here. Gentlemen, may I introduce you to the very honorable Master Dorje." She pressed a button on her bracelet, and an elderly man stepped into the room. He wore a shimmering silver gown adorned with stars and moons and sported a long white beard. Disheveled hair and bags under his eyes made it look as if he had just woken up. Dorje walked with an unusual cane made out of spiraled multicolored wood with a strange crystal affixed to the top.

Despite his appearance, he had a deep penetrating gaze. A type of knowing, the general thought. There was definitely something, a *je ne sais quoi.*

"Honored guests," the queen said, "please meet the spiritual master who is going to help rescue your world from the forces of darkness." She sat again, and everyone followed her lead.

"It is my great honor to serve her Highness," Master Dorje said, bowing first to her and then the rest of them. "And those she deems worthy—but, as we know from Master Amius's astrological prophecies, it is not I who will be the great protector of this world. No, it is your unborn son, Prince Ian of Arcturus, the Royal PIA, who will fulfill that greater destiny." He smiled for the first time. "I will simply assist."

He continued, "The first order of business is to wake our fellow Starseeds and, in the process, make the entire planet—or enough of it—aware of the Reptilians and their greater agenda across the cosmos."

"And how, exactly, do you plan to do all that?" the general asked, his eyes squinting in suspicion.

"To begin, my new friend…" Dorje turned to the general. "We're going to throw the biggest party Earth's ever seen."

CHAPTER 6:

PARTY PREPARATIONS

"Neither a wise person, nor a brave one, lies down on the footpaths of history to wait for the mobs of the future to stampede over her."

—Bqqzt the Vanquisher, Dolteatharian queen, fifth epoch

By "biggest," Dorje meant the party to end all parties...for Earthlings, at least. Compared to other parts of the universe, it wouldn't even crack the top ten.

For example, on the Pillars of Creation located in the Eagle Nebula, the star queen sends out yearly invitations across the galaxy, each party to celebrate the birth of a different civilization. Since the myth of Adam and Eve exists in most civilizations, attendees dress with fig leaves that typically end up covering their ears because the music is so loud. Talking serpents hang from trees reciting in each native tongue the benefits of a fruit-based diet.

The civilization from the Tarantula Nebula, one of the largest star formations close to the Milky Way, throw fabulous fiestas to celebrate the Day of the Dead—another universal concept. Instead of cleaning and decorating the altars and grave sites, however, for this auspicious occasion, they dig up those relatives with whom they didn't get along with and hang them like piñatas, striking at them while blindfolded.

The last time Messier 33 of the Triangulum galaxy tried to host a themed party, the planet was so badly trashed that the drunken leaders decided it would be a good idea to have the entire world scrubbed from one end to the other with a with a giant pressure-washer. It took almost three hundred years, and by the time they had finished, no one alive knew why they had started.

Careful preparations would be necessary for the upcoming event.

• • • •

The fateful meeting aboard the Arcturian ship eventually wound down, and before a day had passed, the United States brought together its top dogs—no offense to the pugs—to determine their next steps. The gathering included the highest-ranking members of the Department of Defense and members of ET Army Command. General Scott, Major Broward, and Commander P were video-conferenced in via the largest screen in the Pentagon's War Command room.

Also in attendance were the Secretary of State and the honorable ambassadors from Canada and Mexico, who already had begun renegotiations of NAFTA with consideration of tariff-free alien goods. General Pete "Pistol" McDonough, head of the U.S. Space Force, attended. Although McDonough had never actually been in space—or even met an alien—his expertise in playing *Star Conflict*, *No Man's Sky*, *4 X Stellaris*, *Kerbal Space Program*, and *Eve: Valkyrie* had made him perfect in his esteemed position.

They all assembled at the Pentagon, which (except for better monitors) hadn't changed a bit in more than five decades. The *New York Times* described the main situation room twenty years before Wikileaks existed:

> "On one wall are six different screens on which, with
> the aid of computers, many things can be project-
> ed—from the weather in Washington to the position
> of a bomber ordered to strike an enemy position. On
> another wall, draped over for the press tour, is what
> the Air Force brigadier general in charge described

as the 'alphanumeric display board.' It gives the position and readiness of every missile poised to hit the [enemy] bloc.... If in some crisis the Secretary [of war] has to go to the bathroom, there in the men's room...is a loudspeaker with a volume control on the wall so he can keep track of all discussions."

The feed could be reversed, allowing the secretary to communicate with those back in the situation room.

There was also a long corridor known as "the bowling alley" where more than fifty loudspeakers were spaced fifteen feet apart. The appellation was quite accurate, since bored servicemen and women used to roll grenades down the hallway to try to knock over a series of M16 rifles arranged like bowling pins. This game came to an unfortunate end one day, but the name remained.

Finally, in the middle of the emergency conference room reserved only for crises, there stood a fifty-foot-long table around which twenty-plus officials could sit to make decisions on war or peace. Or, when called upon, extraterrestrial parties.

Chairman of the Joint Chiefs of Staff, Ashton Robert Crismer—"Ash," as he was commonly known—presided over the gathering. He had a long and distinguished military career and a reputation for a sharp tongue. He had double majored in Physics and Medieval History from Yale University, where his senior thesis, "How to Cut off a Head with W and Z Bosons and Photons," was followed by his famous "Quarks, Charm, and the Psi Particle."

Beside him sat the Deputy Secretary of Defense, General Robert M. McDougal, and Secretary of Defense John M. Marks, who had surprisingly come out of an early retirement for the event. When the press queried Marks about his choice to re-enter public service, he admitted, "I've worked with aliens before and I feel more-than capable of doing it again." McDougal, on the other hand, was pulled from the Basic School, Quantico, VA, where he'd been serving as the head of the Offensive Tactics Section. No one knew better how to deal with offensive situations than McDougal.

Also at the Pentagon that day were General Ike "Aero" Smith of the Army—a nickname derived from rumors that whenever someone asked him for a special favor, his customary reply was to "Dream On"; Admiral Susie "Squeeze" Morton of the Navy, known to "squeeze" the enemy like a ravenous boa constrictor who hadn't eaten in a month; General Rickie "Tomboy" Tomlin of the Marines, the military poster child who could kick anyone's ass *and* got the new multi-sex bathrooms installed at the Pentagon; and General J.R. McMasterson Jr., the son of the prior U.S. National Security Advisor.

• • • •

For two hours, General Scott and Commander Plamorius reported on the Arcturian arrival and subsequent formal dining event. P explained that the last time the Arcturian royalty had visited Earth had been more than three thousand years earlier—during the days of the Egyptian Pharaoh King P Za-Hut. Based on Plamorius's decades of study regarding Earth's religious history, he'd ascertained that Hebrew slaves had caught glimpse of someone with a big stick making the seas part and knew this guy might be of use in the future.

They befriended the alien called Mitzvapickagoymalchizedekmoses, but decided to call him "Moses" for short. They built the triangular stone structures that, as he explained, were geographically necessary to prevent an Arcturian mothership from "incorrectly" touching down, as one had done in the Northern Tibet in the Kham region. This was centuries before the Arcturian ships had developed advanced radar and GPS capabilities, and they'd had the great pyramids of Giza built to act as a beacon from space.

His audience had no real idea what he was talking about or where the "Kham region" might be, but they decided to humor him.

When the Arcturian ship arrived in Tibet and its occupants first exited their spaceship, they were believed by locals to be holy beings descending from the sky. Some of the newcomers formed monasteries and mated with the local Tibetan women, creating lineages of half-human, half-Arcturian spreaders of wisdom. As far as the sky gods were concerned, the arrangement was fine, since both the wisdom and sex were great, but the food sucked. All they got for their big arrival on Earth was a bunch of dried yak meat—which was so hard that a steel hunting knife could barely cut through it—year-old yak butter smelling like milk left out too long, and thick Tibetan perogies called Mo-Mo's that would sit in the stomach for a week and still refuse to leave.

Listening to P's account, everyone in the Pentagon meeting thought they understood the Arcturians' request for a big coming-out party with an emphasis on great food. Yet such a public display hadn't been attempted in more than three millennia.

Was this a good idea?

Indeed, the last time an alien revealed himself, he parted the Red Sea, caused an endless number of frogs to pour from the sky, and hailstorms had rained down along with golf balls of fire. He'd even told Pharaoh to "let my people go," which was exceptionally confusing, since the Egyptian ruler knew Moses was an alien.

What if the real reason for the Arcturian return to Earth in 2035 was just to have an excuse for a huge gala?

"The Arcturian mothership has come back to help us *and* their own people here on Earth," Plamorius insisted. "They have asked that we go loud and wide with this one. No more redacted X-files and top-secret bunkers. This is to be for *all* eyes, or it will never work." He scanned the room for reactions and found none. *Bloody dense humans.* "The Arcturians are here because the climate crisis resulting from Reptilian infiltration requires a global buy-in of solutions," he continued. "Besides, the Arcturians who escaped the Reptiles during the Orion Wars are trapped here on Earth, suffering, and can only be awakened with a proper shaking."

"What kind of 'shaking' is that?" General Rickie asked.

"They like music, dancing, and good food," P replied.

"So what's the big deal?" General Marks grunted. "Rent out Leonard's Catering Hall in Queens. Nice space. They regularly do big weddings and religious celebrations there, and you know the Jews only attend places with great food."

"A fine idea, General," P said, thinking otherwise. "But the Arcturians will want a much larger and more…*interesting* venue. Something more Arcturian. Numinous. Transcendent. Something, perhaps, like the Louisiana Voodoo Music and Arts Experience during the Mardi Gras. Or perhaps the Life is Beautiful Festival in Las Vegas; Mawazine Festival, the Rhythms of the World music fest in Africa; the Rio de

Janeiro Mardi Gras, or Holi, the ancient music festival in India and Nepal where throngs of people drink bhang before slinging mud, colored powders, and water at each other."

"Before we order this massive smorgasbord and spend a fortune we don't have," General Kelley said, "are we one-hundred-percent certain these aliens are friendly?"

"Friendly?!" Major Broward said loudly. "General, I've had interactions with alien species for some time now, and they are *definitely* 'friendly.' My wife can—"

He started to complain again about the source of his nightmares. To shut Broward up, Plamorius shouted "Love fest!" and stretched his ten-foot arms from across the table to embrace the Major. Those not familiar with the Pleiadian's habits gaped soundlessly at the screen.

The major blushed and squirmed as he sank down in his chair until he was almost out of sight.

"See what I mean?" he muttered.

P released the major. "The Arcturians are allies," he said firmly, "and the mothership now hovering above Earth's atmosphere contains some of the highest evolutionary forms in the multiverse. Those with the wisdom and scientific expertise to help the Earth overcome its self-destructive crisis, as well as the biological warfare affecting the human race's intellectual and reproductive capacity. In fact, they are likely the *one* race who can help you at this time.

"Their civilization is based on an ancient maternal power lineage with roots in a prehistoric, shamanic line. They embody the best of science, wisdom, and magic, woven with compassion. They will be a strong ally in the fight against the dark forces." P cleared his throat before speaking again. "Not all aliens are evil, gentlemen. You don't need to keep them out of your country."

"Any downside?" General Tomlin asked, peering at the screen. "To accepting their help."

"None that I can find," P replied. "Their worst shortcoming, perhaps, is that Arcturians do not know how to lie. There often is no filter between their brains and mouths, and this proves difficult in certain circumstances, as you all might imagine. You may not like everything you hear, but it will be the truth."

The whole room of "top dogs" shifted nervously.

"But what about the *other* races of aliens?" Admiral Morton asked. "Your report indicated there are several here on Earth, including those who may not have the purest of intentions. If you announce this gathering 'loud and wide,' as you say, won't the Greys attend? The Reptilians?"

The chair at the center of the table was reserved for Secretary of Defense McDougal, who had at his immediate disposal a red "secure" phone placed to his right for top secret military matters to be discussed with the President. To his left was a gray phone.

It was time to use the grey phone.

This used to be reserved for "insecure" conversations—i.e. to talk to a military command anywhere in the world—but the phone had been adapted for communication with the "Greys" who were *not* going to be invited to the party. It would be his task to break the news to them. Although the US government had looked the other way for decades, alien abductions could *not* be part of the opening ceremony, and although the Greys wanted to mount a social media campaign to clear their sullied name, Plamorius had made it clear that they were not to be trusted, and under no circumstance should they be allowed to attend.

"We will need to anticipate and expect such possibilities," P admitted, "but this is part of the Arcturian plan. They *want* such enemies to attend. They want the whole world watching."

"Excuse me for a moment," McDougal said. "I need to use the little boy's room." He rose from his large brown executive leather chair and moved toward the exit.

"Here's an idea," General Smith said. "You want the whole world watching? What if we hold it at Devils Tower, Wyoming? Not too far from where you are already in Sedona. *Close Encounters of the Third Kind* filmed their movie there, which everyone is familiar with. We could put up 'ET Came Home!' signs with pictures of Spielberg grinning, putting his arm around an Arcturian."

"Yes, and...no. I don't think that'll work," General Scott said. "The location is too remote, too difficult to get to, and it's the site of a large, explosive volcano."

At that moment a long, low-pitched gastrointestinal eruption emanated from the fifty overhead speakers. The pugs looked around and sniffed at the air.

"Secretary McDougal!" General Scott shouted, even though he was thousands of miles away. "Please turn off your microphone!"

General Smith didn't miss a beat. "Okay, then how about Pine Bush, New York? People in Pine Bush apparently have alien sightings all the time," he said. "They even throw some kind of alien parade every year where everyone dresses up. New York isn't remote. What if these Arcturians landed in a large, open field in Pine Bush and had signs around their neck with hashtag-METOO while they played kazoos and marched in the parade?"

General Scott grimaced and hoped no one saw it.

"There's no parking and not enough land in all of Pine Bush to accommodate the millions who'll want to attend," Admiral Morton countered. "This thing will be bigger than Woodstock."

"What's Woodstock?" Broward asked, looking around for help.

"Now *that's* a great idea," General Tomlin said. "We could supersize the original. Sixty-six years after…Woodstock 2035!" She stretched out her hands, imagining God only knew what. "With all the aliens and weed that'll be flowing…perhaps we could hire a Sly and the Family Stone cover band to do 'I Want to Take You Higher.' Or maybe a Janis Joplin clone could do 'Kozmic Blues.' Perhaps a Leslie West cyborg and Mountain could make a comeback and rock the award-winning grey alien hit 'Waiting to Take You Away.'"

"Woodstock 2035…" P said. "That could be perfect, actually."

Scott gaped but remained silent.

"It's perfect!" The pugs barked from off camera. "Naked, getting high, drinking, and rolling around in mud!"

"Guarantees a large enough audience, and it could alleviate people's fears—or at least distract them," McMasterson said. "Sticking with Max Yasgur's Farm is our best bet. If Greys crash the party, there'll be plenty of animals there to keep 'em occupied."

"I don't think it's a working farm anymore," Admiral Morton said.

"It's still a great idea," General Tomlin said. "But how about if we had it at Watkins Glen, which could accommodate way more people? For those who can't attend, we'll televise the event across the whole world and make a fortune with sponsorships and advertising. We'll tell people that a portion of the proceeds goes to a newly formed nonprofit for displaced aliens. The Arcturians will like that, and people are suckers for those kinda things."

"Yes, and with food and souvenir stands set up there, as well as in every major city around the world, *everyone* could participate," General McDonough said. "We'd rake in enough money to pay for our new satellite defense system."

"We could serve Arcturian ale, intergalactic ice cones, other treats, and sell Arcturian pet space rocks—it worked years ago, and humans haven't shown any signs of being smarter," General Kelly retorted. "Everyone would be encouraged to buy antennae and put them on their heads as a sign of support."

"But General," P said, trying to put a cap on the discussion, "only the atmops have antennae. The Arcturians have heads resembling yours, although quite a bit more attractive."

"Who's gonna wanna see another pretty face?" Scott huffed. "Antennas will work fine."

"As you will," Plamorius conceded, "but please be careful. Most atmops believe *any* creature with antennae are part of their species, and they've been known to…well, secrete powerful pheromones to both attract and dominate."

"Thank you, P, but I think we'll be fine," the General said. "Let's stick with the plans we've come up with today. Woodstock, the antennae, the whole kit-and-caboodle. The ET team will present it to the Arcturians and get their approval. Everyone in agreement, say 'aye.'" The General leaned into the camera so that only his hairy nostrils and part of one eye showed in the Pentagon's giant monitor.

"Aye" resounded across the room.

And so it was determined that the US government would throw the biggest intergalactic bash of all time—on Earth. All they had to do was to find and invite the key guests and prepare for the predicted party crashers.

CHAPTER 7:

A TABLE FOR TWELVE

"If you define yourself by your power to destroy, control others, and gather material wealth and possessions... Then, you have nothing."

—Pre-twentieth century philosopher

A long, winding road led into the Earth village Oak Creek, and on the early evening of September 1, 2035, the dipping sun's rays reflected off rose-colored dust swirling along the sides of that old, paved highway. The sky above was painted in crimson and teal. Another magnificent Arizona evening as the caravan passed rows of 150-year-old cacti, Joshua trees, brittlebush, and prickly pear and pulled up to the entrance of the famous Cucina Divinica.

The Cucina Divinica was a longtime favorite hangout for the aliens living in the area, so the Army brass chose this as their initial Earth-bound meeting site. Before Chef Rocco Ferrari took over the famous restaurant thirty-five years ago, it was the site of a legendary alien-human cowboy bar called My Favorite Martian, where locals and aliens from across the universe would come to share stories and have a drink together. Its main claim to fame, however, was when Elvis Presley showed up in the middle of a hot Sedona summer in the late 1950s, shortly after the alien crash happened. They were having karaoke night, and he walked in when aliens were doing bad impressions of "Santa Bring My Baby Back To Me" and "There Goes My Everything." It's been reported the experience affected Elvis forever, leading to the song "All Shook Up" and production of the movie *Stay Away, Joe*, which was filmed in parts of Uptown Sedona.

The full entourage arriving at the restaurant consisted of General Scott, Major Broward, Plamorius, Dr. Correro, Dr. Morales, Commander Avorius, and the Arcturian king and queen. Three of the queen's servants accompanied her and were holding her two Antwarian atmops, Amori and Audri. No one on Earth had ever seen atmops—creatures looking like walking octopi with antennae—but because the Antwarian breed of atmop is famous throughout the multiverse for its exceptional warmth, playful character, insatiable sweet tooth, and ability to influence lifeforms through their mesmerizing pheromones, glances, and touch, the group felt they would immediately be accepted—at least in Sedona.

Master Dorje was also present. To the surprise of no one, the royal mother and pugs were left at home with a small legion of guards who functioned as babysitters.

When the group arrived, everyone got out of the cars and strolled up the red-and-grey tile path lined by an adobe archway adorned with small gargoyles. The Arcturians, having fought such creatures in the past, eyed the gargoyles suspiciously—in particular, Commander Avorius and all the queen's servants seemed ready for trouble as they gripped large swords sheathed in leather. Several human military police officers flanked the group sporting semiautomatic machine guns.

The arch led to the outdoor patio where General Scott and his honored guests entered the restaurant. There they were met by the current owner, Aavoream Erpicum.

Erpicum was originally from Mintaka in the star system Delta Orionis, twelve hundred light years away in the constellation of Orion. When the Orion wars broke out, he traveled to Earth and became an original maître d' and chef of Cucina Divinica. At six-foot-four-inches tall, with a lanky physique, small moustache, and oversized cranium, he looked like a towering alien mix of Paul Bocuse and Mario Batali on meth doing intermittent fasting.

The major had always struggled to understand Erpicum's particular accent—a bastardized mix of English, German, French, and Spanish he claimed to have acquired while working in the restaurant and learning English for the past thirty-five years.

"Mine Generale!" Erpicum shouted. "It eese a grande plaisir to see your eminence again."

"Thank you," the General replied. "Erpicum…we need your best table for twelve. On the starlight patio, of course."

"But, General…" the maître d's eyes went wide. "Shurely, you can't be serious aboutta getting a gooude table at disss late hour! You should have made reservations."

"Last-minute plans," the General said. "Please, Erpicum…" He added a coy smile. "I *am* serious—and you know I hate it when you call me Shirley." The Army scientists laughed and turned to the royal family to show what a great time everyone was having.

Major Broward stood confused.

"We have *very* honored guests today," the General further explained, hooking his thumb over his shoulder. "Let's get them the finest table in the Cucina."

Erpicum finally looked at the full party waiting to be seated. Plamorius, the General, major and the Army scientists he all recognized, but they were standing next to several tall *extremely* handsome, muscular, well-chiseled men in what appeared to be royal and military garb standing alongside women who could have been daughters of Venus—radiant visions of beauty, grace, and elegance. They caught Eripicum off guard. He'd *never* before witnessed such stunning beauty, despite serving customers from many parts of the galaxy, including the Aldebaran star system, known for its seductive and effervescent seven-breasted women. Erpicum knew beauty but was nevertheless stunned.

Then he then noticed two more silk-clad servants in the back holding some type of creatures. They stood next to an enigmatic-looking man. Erpicum had met many aliens in his day, but there was something distinctly different about this person which made him stand out from the rest of the group. He had an air of pride and wisdom yet seemed aloof and shrouded in some impenetrable mystery.

Wearing a shimmering azure gown speckled with silver stars and purple moons, he was much older than the rest of the group. He had deep furrowed brows, fine lines etched across his high boned cheeks, and a long white beard that made him resemble Merlin or Rumpel- stiltskin waking up after sleeping for a few centuries. The mysterious man also sported Lucchese Men's Baron Gator Western boots while tightly holding onto a walking staff, which clearly did more than sup- port his aged body. An insignia with a strange blue crystal affixed to its top radiated faintly.

"Arcturian royalty," General Scott confirmed. "Visiting Earth on important business, and we want to show them a good time. A *very* good time."

"Ohhhh! Vy didn't you tell mee royal Arcturians ver coming to dinner?" Erpicum lamented. "I vould have prepared a deesh of Anzlea- nian eels covered in Silurian seedweed along with a Pleiadian pot de crème and Martian marscapone Teerameesu for dessert."

"Not a problem," the General said. "This was all very last-minute."

"Give us a moment," Erpicum pleaded, and he hurried off, shout- ing to his staff. They rushed about, several human diners were moved, and then the maître d' came forward again, smiling broadly.

"Right diss way, please."

Whereas Oak Creek locals were used to extraterrestrials coming to dinner, the tourists—who'd heard the rumors of ETs in the area—as- sumed the establishments were putting on a show for them, as if they were dining in at Disney World. A clever PR trick to get people to visit their arid Arizona desert community. After all, who would want to just come see a bunch of red rocks? Thus, all heads turned as the royal party entered, creating a sudden commotion as the diners noticed the unusual entourage and then furiously began snapping selfies and texting photos.

A seventy-eight-year-old woman approached the Arcturian servants.

"How darling! May I take a picture with your cute 'alien pets?'" she asked, tightly gripping her own brown-and-white Chihuahua, Ches- ter. As she marveled at the pair of atmops, a large Spanish bell rang in the background.

"I'd run for the border, if I were you," the major muttered.

The queen nodded to her servants, instructing them to put the atmops on the ground, where the creatures rushed over to the elderly Earthling. Their antennae quivered wildly as they got closer to her, and her little dog, too. One of the atmops, Amori, scrambled up and onto the woman's lap and began making cooing sounds. The other, Audri, began stroking her Chihuahua with his tentacles.

"Be careful not to feed them any sugar," Commander Avorius warned, chuckling as he passed the table. "They can become a little...agitated." Both the human woman and her animal were mesmerized and proceeded to do *whatever* the atmops wanted.

The group arrived at the large round table in the middle of the restaurant, directly under the elliptical hole in the ceiling. The starlight patio was appropriately named, as it had brightly-lit porcelain stars hanging from different parts of the ceiling, while the opening in the middle of the restaurant allowed direct gazing at the stars and constellations.

To the great dismay of the general, the elderly woman began feeding Amori her sumptuous chocolate lava volcano dessert without a second thought, while Audri had her dog happily dancing circles on its hind legs. A sort of *Alien Dancing with the Stars*, he supposed with some alarm.

Major Broward—always uncomfortable around expressions of "fun"—was having none of it.

"Hey, you two mop buckets!" he yelled. "Get back over here and leave the poor old woman alone."

The whole table of Arcturians and humans turned toward the Major with horror and looks of disapproval. Broward ducked his head, realizing he'd made a "major" faux pas—he had broken the first two cardinal rules of Area 57. First, don't piss off an alien until you know what they're capable of doing, and two, don't piss off an alien *pet* until you fully understand what *they* can do.

The rules stemmed all the way back to Edgar Cayce's famous *Alien Planetary Influences and Protocols* (1963), *How to Psychically Resist During an Alien Abduction* (1966), *No Sperm, No Eggs, No Problem!* (1980), and *101 Alien Jokes to Distract Your Captors* (1967). He was embarrassed.

"Oh, I wouldn't do that," the queen advised ever-so sweetly. "Once they're occupied with something, it's best to leave them be." As she spoke, the atmops waved to the Major as he grimaced and sat back in his seat. Sweat glistened on his brow. "They'll settle down," she added.

"Let's just order!" the general growled, causing Broward to dip even lower in his seat, and the entire group opened their menus to examine the large selection of local organic meats and vegetables. Eating clean was already a rare treat in 2035, as the toll of global pollution had made it difficult to find food not tainted with heavy metals, volatile organic solvents, or pesticides. Nevertheless, Cucina Divina had found a way to offset those limitations.

"Maybe get a few apps for the table to start," Plamorius suggested. He'd eaten there a hundred times and knew the selection by heart. "Erpicum, can we please get three each of the Artichoke Beignets, Calamari Perfezionare, Melanzane rollatini, and five Eccezionale Tapas Plates for the table. Also…please provide every table in the room with an Eccezionale Tapas Plate. On us. This is a celebration, and *everyone* should be in on it."

General Scott went noticeably pale but said nothing.

The "addictive" tomato sauce in the Melanzane rollatini was one of Cucina's bestsellers—people kept ordering it even when they were thoroughly stuffed—but the last dish, the Eccezionale Tapas Plate with magic mushrooms, was the big hit. Diners who'd never tasted them before had claimed to have "mystical" dining experiences in the restaurant—the usual explanation as to why "alien life forms" were seen dining in the Sedona area. P made certain the entire room was heartily consuming them before the night was over.

Before long there was a silence in the room except for the "oohs" and "ahs" and "mmmms" escaping from the tables tasting the Eccezionale apps. The Queen gestured to the rest of her party, indicating that it was time to begin the conversation.

"We have reviewed your recommendations regarding where the arrival event should be held and have watched the *Woodstock* film several times now. We especially enjoyed the Grateful Dead's fifty-minute version of "Turn on Your Love Light." Since this festival appears to have been a pivotal moment in your history and a defining moment for the counterculture generation, with the appropriate psychedelic overtones, we feel it is an excellent choice."

Commander Plamorius patted the general on the back.

"We're thrilled to hear that, your Highness," General Scott said.

"We're also delighted with the announcements that went out regarding our arrival," Queen Dawn continued. "We have been monitoring the digital interactions on Earth, as well as the psychic ones, and we're genuinely astounded at how well the Earth people are responding. Based on our prior review of human history, we had thought you were a people who primarily fed on aggression with fear and mistrust of aliens. Except for a person by the name of Steven Spielberg.

"The welcome we are receiving is therefore quite unexpected and quite refreshing," she said. "The excitement and joy are palpable, and it appears many believe that intelligent life has arrived on the planet for the first time in history. While wonderful, this is rather mystifying. Did you not have leaders who were intellectually adequate to fulfill their responsibilities? Indeed, something called a Gallup Poll claims that America has been polarized for decades, and the majority are eager to meet with us and to learn about Arcturian culture and ways to improve life on the planet.

"At the same time, we find odd those who do *not* want to meet us—evidently a color-challenged group with rednecks and white socks, drinking blue-ribbon beer and subscribing to a group called..." She leaned over, and Master Dorje whispered in her ear. "Q. These individuals seem to be more aggressive than the rest—similar to the Reptilian masters we have dealt with on our home planet."

"General Scott," Dorje said, addressing the group for the first time all night. "What is it you think you understand about the Reptiles? You are aware of the Orion Wars, yes?"

"Yes, sir," the General said, glancing at Commander P, his main source on the topic. "We first became aware of our Reptilian problem in the early 1970s, when we realized our governmental systems and major corporations had been infiltrated by *some* type of evil force. We didn't initially know what to call it, but the signs were obvious. Rats began to appear on the streets of Washington D.C., while politicians and business leaders began to engage in reckless behavior for their own personal gain without any thought of others.

"By the 1980s, there was a growing number who believed that a sort of extraterrestrial incursion might be connected to these trends—video was found of these beings revealing themselves on film, including that creepy eye thing they do. When the World Wide Web came, it became a certainty—any fourth grader could type 'reptilian' into Google and witness firsthand dozens of these creatures in our newsrooms, boardrooms, or oval-shaped offices. For years, we've managed to push it off as conspiracy stuff and a few bad eggs. But the situation has expanded beyond our control, and it seems as if the only course of action will be exposing this infiltration and invasion for what they really are.

"Plamorius has told us what these beings did to his planet and to yours, and…it seems like we're the next planet on their damned list."

"Indeed," Dorje said with a nod. "A fine segue, General. We'd like to tell you tonight what happened on Arcturus, otherwise known as Proxima Centauri B. It will be difficult to relive the memories…but you, all of you"—he gestured around the table—"must be prepared and understand the strengths and weaknesses of our mutual enemy."

"Bring it on," the General said as he popped a mint into his mouth.

"First," Dorje presaged, "it is necessary for you to put aside all preconceptions. What I am about to explain to you will *sound* like an improbably wild fantasy, but it is not. It is the deepest truth, though it contains elements that will stretch your imagination. Please keep an open mind."

"An open mind," the queen clarified for her own entourage, "does *not* mean your brain will fall out." The Queen and King had an improving grasp of English colloquialisms but understood that their royal servants did not. A couple already had grasped their heads and glanced around to make certain no grey matter was escaping.

"In a distant galaxy a long time ago," Master Dorje began, "after the Big Bang's hot gases cooled down and solidified into millions of planets, there was a choice that had to be made by the creator being. As matter began to form, different levels of *density* would become necessary to scaffold a multitude of vibrational realities. Physical 'reality' as we know it is just consciousness that has contracted into a solidified version of an idea. Yet there was a second step needed in the creation of multiverses.

"There had to be a way to move through these various densities, and to determine which beings would live on the lowest vibration and which would live within the highest vibration. The easiest and most logical approach was to use the dualistic consciousness that was forming, which could expand into higher states of vibration through love, compassion, selfless generosity, realization, and proper action, or contract into lower states of vibration through hate, greed, fear, ignorance, and improper action. For beings to enjoy creation, they needed to be *conscious* of these emerging physical realities." He paused to allow his words to sink in, then continued.

"It is difficult to enjoy something until you know it exists. It would be hollow to create a universe in which no being is aware of said cosmos. Or, at the very least, extraordinarily boring. Thus, dualism was born.

"Consciousness of self, alas, most easily occurs when there is consciousness of the 'other.' Unfortunately, that also leads to a perceived 'separation from source'—although this is, of course, physically impossible. Eternal mind cannot be separated from its source, as there is no physical density that can impede and limit consciousness's access to its own pure awareness.

"Are you with me so far?"

The General nodded and so did the Major, though he looked dubious.

"So the second step needed in the creation of the multiverses," Dorje continued, "was to find a way to move through these various densities and determine which beings would live on the highest vibration or on the lowest one. The easiest way to do this would be to use *emotions* as the vehicle. The ability to contract or expand via the 'emotional body' allowed consciousness access to *all* states of existence. Therefore, insistence that the world in which we live is the 'only real one' is based on a faulty and limited view. The five senses—which allow us to see, hear, smell, taste, and touch—are non-conceptual and ultimately seen through the filter of the sixth consciousness: our conceptual mind."

The major fidgeted, received a couple of irritated glances, and froze.

"This causes us to interpret events based on our own particular filter, freezing reality into our individually fixed versions, while missing the big picture." The great Arcturian teacher paused, looked around to see how much of his explanation was sinking in, and realized he needed to simplify fast. "It's like this. Life is God's dream, and everything in the dream is an external manifestation of God's awakened mind. Even though we see beautiful flowers, picturesque trees, magnificent oceans, and people who appear to be separate from us, God is dreaming it all. One day, because of free will, we will *choose* to wake up from the dream, recognize our ultimate power and nature, and realize we have never been separated from the source, the creator.

"As consciousness grew, it began to naturally experience *other* dualistic extremes. Consciousness began to perceive male and female polarities, along with happiness and sadness, wealth and poverty, and of course, life and death. Yet none of these perceptions were *absolutely* true. They were only *relatively* true, as per the teachings of one of your leading scientists of the twentieth century, Albert Einstein. Relative or not, one of the strongest emotions to emerge within this dualistic ego consciousness was fear."

He took a deep breath, and his expression darkened.

"The Reptilians would have us all believe that is the case—that we have been separated from the source of creation. This is a disaster in the making. Nothing can impede our access to this pure awareness—a condition with unlimited potential—but the Reptilians have convinced far too many. Fear contracts consciousness, constricting it like an imploding star, leading to even greater density. The more fear there is, the more dense and 'real' the experience of the individual will be, causing matter to sink to a lower tier on the universal vibration."

As he finished, bursts of riotous laughter exploded from numerous tables in the dining room. As if on cue, at another table a three-month-old baby began to wail uncontrollably. Laughter and sadness, perfectly reflecting the tenor of the spiritual teachings on duality.

Also, the magic mushrooms were kicking in.

"Then there *are* other dimensions," Dr. Correro said.

"Ten that we know of," Dorje confirmed. "Nine spatial dimensions and one *time* dimension. These different aspects comprise the universe and the fundamental forces within it. The 'M' dimension, for example, or 'Magical Matrix,' is one we Arcturians have learned to master. Therefore, the three-dimensional reality *you* find yourself living in is only one of these several possibilities. A 'solid' dimension created largely by... fear. The literal girth of fear. And that, ultimately, is the full secret to the Reptilian power here on Earth."

"Fear?" General Scott said, his voice loud. He pounded his first on the table and pointed a meaty finger at the alien mystic. "I'll have you know that we in the military *laugh* at fear. I eat fear for breakfast. We charge headlong into battle with no thought of self, jump out of airplanes with no concern that our parachutes might fail to open, eat off food trucks in foreign countries with no thought of the consequences, enjoy intercourse with prostitutes with no thought of STDs, spend *thousands* of dollars on non-vehicular clutch discs worth thirty-two dollars a pop, with no thought of fiscal responsibility. Hell, we get tubes stuck up our privates without any anesthesia!" The Major winced, as he was privy to such behavior once during a dare, but the General just glared. "So don't talk to me about fear!"

Without warning, an enormous black shadow suddenly appeared. It came from nowhere, just above the middle of their table. Spindly, monstrous arms reached out for the military men as if to pull them back into a black abyss of its nothingness.

General Scott covered his eyes as he quickly recoiled from the table.

The Major fell to the ground and curled into a tight ball. A wet spot appeared in the crotch of his pants. The two of them were shaking and paralyzed with fear.

As quickly as it had appeared, the shadow vanished.

"Does that convince you, General?" Dorje asked calmly.

"About sums it up," Dr. Morales agreed.

"Now that we've settled that theory," Master Dorje said, "are you ready for the good news?"

"Please." The General looked out from between closed fingers as he moved closer to the table.

"There is a most-simple antidote for such fear," the Arcturian wizard said.

"Tactical nukes?" the General suggested.

"The opposite of fear…" Master Dorje said.

"…is love," Plamorius answered. "Love is all you need."

"Quite right," the Queen said, and she smiled.

"In the mental, emotional, *and* spiritual universe," Master Dorje said, "love expands where fear contracts. Love can even expand the mind, leading it into ever more subtle realms. The subtlest and purest of those realms is the awakened consciousness of the true creator. Transcendental love—putting others above self—will eventually lead to liberation from a fear-based reality and help unshackle humanity from the states of mental and emotional confusion you find yourselves in."

"This is how the Reptilians take advantage of the dualism," he continued, "of your separation from the All. With fear. On your planet, it started millions of years ago with the Alpha Draconians, who are the ancestors of the present Reptilians. They were offshoots of the dinosaurs which lived on your planet during the late Cretaceous and middle Jurassic periods. Tyrannosaurus Rex and the Velociraptors were perfect examples of aggressive Reptilian energy. They dominated through power and fear. Although your people think the dinosaurs became extinct after a massive meteor crashed into the Earth, they did not perish. They survived because extraterrestrials living on your planet at that time took several specimens with them and merged their DNA with their own ancestors. The result is the Draconian Reptilians we are all fighting today. They've traveled to different star systems, conquering whomever they meet and using up the resources of the planet while feeding their insatiable desire for power and control."

"Earth," the Queen said, "has become a melting pot for a multitude of displaced Starseeds. All those hoping to find safe refuge from the Reptilians. Unfortunately, the threat has followed them here."

"That explains a lot," Dr. Correro commented with a smirk. "It's not as if we can build a wall to keep them out, either." Dr. Morales shot him a look, but didn't say anything.

"How did you three manage to escape?" the Major asked.

"*Thousands* escaped. Knowing that the Reptilian aggressors were coming, those of us who could made the shift from the third and fourth lower dimensional realms—where we could be easily captured or killed—traveled to the higher fifth and sixth dimensions, but at the cost of leaving behind most of our Arcturian brothers and sisters. Not everyone was trained in this ability or had the power and skill to maintain consciousness at these higher levels. It was only the most evolved of our Starseed tribes who had transcended fear and could shift vibrational realities at will.

"The Reptilian invaders could not see us when we vibrated at higher levels of being. That is how we escaped. Although this dimensional barrier kept some of us safe from lower vibrational corruption, those who could not maintain the higher consciousness vibration were forced to leave and were cast off into space to provide for themselves."

Across the table, Queen Dawn felt herself becoming alarmed at his words. She took a deep breath, calmed herself, and—recalling the instructions she had received as a child—accessed the Arcturian Akashic stored memories.

This deep Arcturian meditative state allowed her to accurately recount details of the deep tragedy which befell her people without falling into blackness and succumbing to the intense grief. After all, she was one of the lineage holders; she had to remember so that the memory would never be lost. Whenever she entered this state, she possessed an uncanny ability to show strength and fragility at the same time. She could relive the pain while keeping her heart open, accessing and sharing the wisdom within the experience.

Emerging from her meditative state, the Queen opened her eyes.

"It was an extremely painful time for us," she said simply. "We were forced to witness the invasion and the ensuing subjugation of our people yet remained powerless to help. These Draconian armies had advanced military forces made up of many different types of species and machines. Advanced robotic killing automatons and Reptilian demons who marched over our lands, slaughtered our people, and tore families apart in a massive intergalactic genocide. Many of our Arcturian brothers and sisters who escaped the invasion carry those wounds deep within their subconscious minds. As do, no doubt, the Starseeds who have escaped from other systems. The Reptilians only kept alive those they thought could serve a purpose."

"Plamorius told us a similar story," the General said grimly, and he turned to Commander P, who'd remained silent the entire time, carefully contemplating each word.

"It proved especially difficult," P said, "for us as Pleiadians, since we had maintained such a blissful existence on our planet. We were inspired artists who lived to create beauty, whether through painting, sculpting, dance, song, or simply loving each other and the natural world. We were a peaceful civilization and had never before experienced violence and hate.

As far as we knew, it wasn't even a remote possibility. Not even part of our vocabulary. Thus, we were unprepared for the pain inflicted by the Draconian Reptilians.

"Our sensitive nature, like that of our Arcturian cousins, made it difficult to face these unexpected challenges. The only reason any of us are still alive and are able to help in the Orion Wars is that our elders had the wisdom and knowledge to assist during our time of crisis. Pleiadian Queens, who could vibrate at a higher frequency. They were able to hold and stabilize a rarefied energy field at higher dimensional levels such that many of our fellow Pleidians could escape and avoid being seen on the third dimensional plane of reality."

"Are there still other Pleiadians living on these multi-dimensional worlds?" Dr. Morales asked. "Why were they captured if the Pleiadian Queens could vibrate at higher frequencies?"

"When news of the Reptilian invasion reached the Queens," P said, "some of them contracted their consciousness in fear, lowering their vibrational energy. Before that point in time, the Reptilians couldn't see us. It's similar to how angels in other dimensions cannot be easily seen by most of the members of humanity."

"Angels actually exist?" The Major shook his head. "I always assumed that was just some fairytale designed to give comfort to the masses."

"Quite real," Master Dorje assured. "Angels were here on Earth in a denser physical form many centuries ago, and reproduced with the more evolved humans on your planet. Their offspring ruled the human race for centuries and were known as the *Nephilim*—and described in detail in your biblical Book of Enoch. Their progeny still exists to this day and are in danger with the rest of civilization. Their angelic parents have been overseeing humanity's fate, waiting for the perfect time to come back and assist their offspring."

"As are many of the Pleiadians," Commander P said. "They are also waiting for a safe time to reappear in the third dimension. It is the same for those civilizations from Andromeda, Sirius, Lyra, and the Alpha Centauri Star Systems, as well as the Annunaki who were invaded. The elders and the more highly evolved of each of these civilizations knew how to shift consciousness and decrease their density to avoid being captured. The most evolved souls of each of these civilizations formed a part of the 'Family of Light' to combat the evil that was spreading in the multiverse from the 'Family of Dark.' Some of the braver souls, however—those who needed to express themselves with a physical incarnation—chose not to live in these dimensions and are now living on your planet and a few others, in hiding. These are the ones we need to rouse to their true selves. You can always spot the Arcturians and Pleiadians living among you, as well as the Starseeds of these other places, because of certain character traits they manifest."

That piqued Major Broward's curiosity. He was intrigued with the idea that people he already knew, apart from Jeffrey, might be from other parts of the galaxy. Certainly, everyone knew someone who was a bit strange. The Major wondered whether his wife might be an extraterrestrial. She'd enjoyed Grayson a little too much.

Inadvertently he stifled a yawn.

"And what would those traits be?" Dr. Correro asked with a wry smile. "What would help us identify these…Starseeds?"

"Elementary, my dear doctor," Master Dorje said. "The Arcturian incarnations on Earth are frequently your top scientists, who appear detached and uncaring, as they have difficulty coming to terms with how they abandoned their bretheren who could not make the dimensional shift. Many are working at top universities as MDs and PhDs, helping to find solutions for the world's most pressing problems. A second group of Arcturians are mystics, living the life of a spiritual adept in religious communities, and can oftentimes be found in Christian, Tibetan, and Hindu monasteries. There, in seclusion, practicing as hermits, they can commune with the divine, practicing and perfecting their religious and mystical arts."

"Pleiadians," Commander P said, "are equally easy to spot. They are the artists and artisans of your communities. Those who are idealistic sensualists who want to have frequent sex and love everything and everyone they meet. I have met a few during my time here on Earth while living on your military base and in my hidden residences, but…"

The Major frowned with hints of disgust as he thought of P having sex with incarnated Pleiadian women and the numerous times he and others had experienced unexpected hugs from Plamorius. He wondered whether any of these were overtures he'd missed.

"The Pleiadians are your classic hippies frequently cohabitating in new age communities," P continued, "as they care for and appreciate all precious life on this planet. They are empowered by crystals and animals surround their homes, as they live in harmony with the trees, flowers, and natural environment. They love everything and everyone they meet, viewing sex as a natural creative expression of their deep abiding affection for all life. You can easily recognize a Pleiadian Queen by her pure heart, beauty, charisma, and great joy."

"And the other Starseeds?" General Scott asked, seeming eager to change the subject. "How can we find them to bring as many as possible into the fold of the intergalactic force we're creating?"

"The typical Sirian-human," Master Dorje said, "descends from the Atlantean civilization that lived on Earth over ten thousand years ago. The mythical stories of 'mermen' and 'mermaids' derive from the Nommos tribe of the Sirian people, who were beings wielding great power. You will oftentimes find members of the Sirian-human lineage working as business and political leaders in your society, holding positions of great power. Tales of the Scottish monarchy and legendary British leaders from days of old derive from Sirian mythology, where each member had influence and authority, sharing responsibility for the betterment of society.

"They usually wear precious gems and crystals all over their bodies, utilizing these stones to access magical power. Modern day psychics, mediums, channels, 'witches,' and 'sorcerers' with supernatural abilities who can communicate with those who have passed on, or with beings in other dimensions are usually of Sirian lineage. Although some are unaware of their ancestry, many remember their true nature, and are able to communicate with Sirian motherships that are sporadically orbiting the planet. Their power and magical abilities will be valuable assets in the fight against evil."

"Sirian motherships orbiting the Earth?" the General asked looking through the skylight at the stars above them. He lamented the demise of the Star Wars defense system, which had been abandoned in part to fund the U.S.-Mexico border wall. "For how long have—"

"For hundreds of years," the Queen explained. "Generations. There are many Starseeds who, like us, have been watching the Earth's progress and the evolution of our half-breed offspring during the past few millennia. We were all waiting for the right time to expose ourselves."

The Arcturian servants covered over their private parts, looking around and unsure what the Queen was saying.

"So that time is now?" the General asked, before adding, "Or you wouldn't be here."

"Precisely." The Queen smiled.

"Finally," Dorje said, "there are four more species you should know of. All displaced by the Reptilians, all hiding on Earth. These are the Andromedans, Alpha Centurians, Annunaki, and Lyrans. The Andromedans are your leading inventors, computer experts, scientists, and architects who understand sacred geometry. These are Starseeds whose innovative technology is light years ahead of the human race. Once they were captured by the Reptiles during the Orion wars, they helped them build sophisticated robots, advanced spaceships with cloaking devices that could move stealthily through time and space, along with genetically manipulated species, that were transformed into 'hybrid power breeds.' Unfortunately, these scientists and architects were unaware of how their creations would be used for the Reptiles' nefarious purposes. Your Nikola Tesla and Albert Einstein are two examples of brilliant scientists of Andromedan lineage that understood complex mathematics, yet whose discoveries were used for both good and evil, depending on the leadership and culture existing at the time."

"And then there the Alpha Centurians," Commander P said. "The centaurs are best known in your mythological tales of Chiron and Sagittarius in astrological lore. These formidable beings who were half man, half horse, fought for truth, integrity, and justice. The Reptiles knew that these powerful warriors, if not permanently disabled, would return one day to destroy them. They therefore used advanced genetic editing which they learned from the Andromedans, to turn them into horses and humans. You can find on Earth and in many galaxies spread throughout the multiverse, the offspring of the Alpha Centurians living as either humanoids or horses. Those whose lives revolve around riding and taking care of horses, as well as the most intelligent and powerful breeds who regularly win competitions, are usually Alpha Centurian."

The Major liked to play the ponies and wondered how much money might be made by gazing into a horse's eyes, looking for such intergalactic intelligence.

"Then Mister Ed—" he began.

Dr. Correro and Dr. Morales both snickered.

"Oh, Wilburrrr," Morales said, neighing.

P smiled. "Your entertainment shows often cloak the truth in what is perceived to be fantasy. A horse is a horse, of course, but, like your 'famous Mr. Ed,' you'll discover that Alpha Centurians speak the truth plainly and freely. These are the societal 'whistleblowers' and those who work on behalf of Earthly animals and endangered species. You'll usually find them working in rescue shelters, the local nature conservancy, or stuck in foreign countries like Ecuador and Russia, seeking asylum for releasing sensitive government information. Who on Earth but an alien would put themselves at risk by publicly releasing a Collateral Murder video or the Afghanistan and Iraq war logs? Indeed, as you are now aware, many of the people you know are actually aliens in disguise."

The Major and General Scott exchanged nervous glances. Who among their acquaintances—even family and close friends—was an alien? Broward had a childhood friend, Donald Fingers, who had six fingers and at eight years old could put together a radio telescope. Then there was Leona Lipgood, a childhood sweetheart who could stay underwater in the ocean for minutes at a time without coming up for air. Or the Major's mother-in-law. She'd clearly been abducted and replaced with a demon from another star system.

What about the Native American friend he'd had growing up by the name of Joseph Running Bear. "Longnose," whose bodily appendage seemed to grow when he was excited? Though they chalked it up to imagination, they used to tease him.

"They are here and living among you," Plamorius said. "The ones you *cannot* see, however, are as prevalent as the ones you can. The Annunaki possess tremendous physical size and extraordinary strength, but the Lyrans do not fit into your other categories of life forms. The ancient Lyran souls decided the best way to escape the harsh realities of the Reptilian invasion was to take different forms. Some hide out in miniature worlds, reminiscent of the tales of your 'wee people' in Ireland or 'Tinkerbell' type fairies found in movies, as they are seeking similar conditions to their own home planet."

"That's not very PC," the Major said.

"Major, I didn't..." Plamorius began in a tolerant voice; then he appeared to drop it. Master Dorje stepped in to clarify. "Let's move on, Major. Suffice it to say, there are realms beyond all human vision that exist on the same plane as your own. One of those is the fairy realm, but these are not the wispy creatures told in your Disney fairytales. These are powerful and fierce beings with magical abilities. When they could no longer tolerate the pain and suffering on their Lyran home planets, they, too, escaped to Earth. They've been called many names in your culture. The wee people, elves, leprechauns, and fairies—all are part of the Fairy realm, which exists as a fifth-dimensional world both outside and inside the Earth. Their home located deep inside the Earth's crust is called Agartha, and they have lived there for centuries, waiting until they can finally be free to reveal their true nature."

"Lyrans coming out at last," the Major muttered. The Arcturian servants peeped at each other and immediately left to check their surroundings to be sure no one was in hiding.

"There is a lot you and your people do not know," Master Dorje said. "Do not be so arrogant as to suppose you understand the intimate workings of the universe. All of these Starseeds on Earth have a purpose and destiny that has led them here."

"The truth is," the Queen said, "for us to evolve to the next level of spiritual awakening, the Arcturian elders must learn to look at their shadow, and face the terrible choice we had to make in abandoning the less-advanced members of our society, and find peace. The Pleiadians have to face their fear and regain their personal power—which initially led to the downfall of their civilization—by acquiring the ability to hold a higher vibration in the presence of darkness. The Andromedan scientists must learn to face both the constructive and destructive aspects of their creations and transcend the ignorance and arrogance that are the sources of their present suffering.

"The Alpha Centurians, on the other hand, must face the enormous rage they hold inside, and discover how to let go of anger and mistrust so they can see goodness in others and love again. And while the Annunaki must demonstrate immense courage to liberate those caught in the Reptilian netherworld during the last part of the Orion Wars, the Lyrans must embrace truth and face the third-dimensional darkness present in our perceived sphere of reality. The most advanced of their tribe have chosen to incarnate in human form by actively contracting their consciousness, thereby temporarily forgetting their true nature and lineage until the time arrives to wake up. All of these beings periodically experience in the dream state the horrific visions of the systematic slaughtering of their people, and many of them already are silently working on behalf of Earth to help with your infiltration and ultimate subjugation.

"And how, exactly," the General asked, "will all of these Starseeds learn their lessons and come together to fight the Draconian Reptilians in order to save us from environmental annihilation?"

"The Arcturian elders," Queen Dawn replied with an assured response, "and wisdom keepers of the different traditions will collectively enter the dream state and communicate with our star brethren. We are going to let them know the time has come to wake up and come together to defeat our collective enemy. To be clear, my dear General and Major, humans will play an essential role in winning this war. The problem each race faced in the past is that they were unprepared and did not have the benefit of strong allies. We know which humans will be your leaders outside the conscripted military. We have analyzed the trillions of base pairs and chromosomal DNA patterns contained within the data sets of your people. The 'ancestry fad' your people experienced was no coincidence. Humans' attempt to understand their ancestry has allowed us to compare it to known genetic profiles of the Starseeds from different galaxies. We now know who amongst you has alien blood and what their role will be in winning the war."

General Scott paused and reflected on the words of the Queen, as well as the stories they had just heard regarding the history of the universe and the Orion Wars. As fantastical a narrative as it might have appeared, the truth no longer seemed stranger than fiction. Especially because the Antwarian atmops had now visited everyone's table at the restaurant, all of whom were high on magic mushrooms.

Amori and Audri had also each consumed several delicacies from the "Lista Della Deliziosi Dolci," which consisted of two portions of *Cassata*—liqueur-drenched genoise sponge cake layered with sweetened ricotta and fruit preserves, with a marzipan shell and colorful candied fruits on top; three portions of *Pasteria*—rich Neapolitan tart with cooked wheat berries, ricotta, and pastry cream, topped with candied orange peel and flavored with orange blossom water; and a *Raspberry Panna Cotta* to top it off—silky smooth chilled pudding layered with fresh organic raspberries.

Commander Avorius had warned everyone about what would occur if the Atmops ate sugar. Alas. The creatures now had everyone in the restaurant mesmerized, and they began forming a long conga line and singing *La Bomba*. The Major grabbed hold at the end of the line and followed along.

Commander P and Commander Avorius looked at each other, the royal guests, and Army personnel. They smiled, and Scott joined them. It was an auspicious launch of Woodstock 2035 and the saving of Planet Earth. The energy was, well, *right*. The Earthlings seemed to be enjoying their arrival and accepting their guidance.

"After dessert," the Queen prefaced, "we'll cover the more... *difficult* matters."

"We're planning a party for two hundred-thousand people, half of which will soon be newly woken aliens," the General grunted. "What could be more difficult than that?"

"The arrival of those we *won't* be inviting," the Queen replied.

"Reptilians!" the General said with slowly rising anger. "And probably some Greys, we assume."

"Of course," the Queen said. "But the Reptilians have more powerful allies. In addition to the Greys, many vampires, zombies and, undoubtedly, demons from the fourth dimension."

"Vampires and zombies?" the General glared. "And did you say…?"

"Demons," the Arcturian Queen confirmed.

"Is that so?" The General slowly re-counted his enemies with the fingers of his left hand, then stared at all those fingers. "And what in the ever-lovin' name of dear God are we gonna do about all that?"

"After dessert," she said again, reaching for her fork.

CHAPTER 8:

LOOSE LIPS

"Loose tweets sink fleets."

—conservative news commentator Carl Tuckerson

Amidst all the other necessary planning—facilities, food preparation, stocking booths with alien souvenirs, including adorable Atmop dolls with super-flexible tentacles, security, and advertising in newspapers and tabloids—additional complications arose in the days leading up to the festival.

The first matter involved the Fourth Estate.

For nearly two weeks, the world's conventional news organizations shared the ET Army Command's news releases exactly as they'd been written and submitted. The problem first appeared with the *Weekly World News*, which featured a daring headline on the front page:

ALIEN BIBLE FOUND!

THEY WORSHIP OPRAH!

Although everyone involved vehemently denied the claim, the *National Enquirer*, a well-known and respected tabloid, exacerbated the problem. Their headlines were known to include "Bigfoot was an Alien: Kept Lumberjack as Love Slave," and the Reptilian overlords blatantly attempted to confuse and mislead the public.

AL GORE'S REAL REASON

FOR STOPPING GLOBAL WARMING!

HE'S A SHAPE-SHIFTING REPTILIAN ALIEN

WHO CAN DESTROY ALL LIFE ON THE PLANET!

With no time for fact checking or developing their own news stories, the ET Command team exploited the unquenchable demand for news about the aliens, rolling out a systematic and steady barrage of official information and "leaks," providing as much as the talking heads could sink their teeth into. It was a technique the Reptilians had employed for decades.

Then, the *U.S. Chronicle* broke a story no one expected.

The newspaper received an anonymous call from an "unidentified source" high within the government, someone who claimed to be intimately involved in the planning the Arcturian arrival and subsequent festival. The headline—conveniently appearing on the July 4th front page—sent everyone reeling.

ALIEN ORGY PLANNED FOR WOODSTOCK

THREE DAYS OF KINK AND MUSIC

Social media just about broke and calls flooded the newsroom demanding to know about their "anonymous source." The *Chronicle* would only reveal that the person had originated the call, had spoken in a gruff voice, and had referred to themselves as "BB Draco."

While this meant little to the world at large, at ET Command, General Scott knew the truth. BB Draco had been the cat of Gentle Weis, a member of the Sirian royal family who'd lived on Earth since 1967 and had died in 2033. The cat, per the file, was still alive but MIA somewhere in South America.

While the newspaper refused to reveal its source, the military conducted an extensive investigation that yielded the number from which the call had originated. Taking the most straightforward approach, General Tiberius K. Scott dialed the number.

A surprising name showed on his screen.

Across the room, Major Broward answered his phone.

Instantly, they knew what had happened.

One of the Pleiadian pugs had stolen the phone and contacted the reporter, primarily hoping to lure Weis's cat out of hiding. It was done at 2:30 a.m., as the Major was sound asleep. When the *Times* reporter called back, the pug panicked.

As luck would have it, Broward chose that moment to talk in his sleep. All the pug had to do was hold the phone next to him.

"So, Mr. Draco..." the reporter said, "What *can* you tell us about the secret plans for next week's Woodstock festival?"

"One of his love fests...he kept hugging me, and then one of them wanted to put a probe up my hoo-hoo," the Major muttered, a hint of drool running down his cheek. "Next door, I said...go see my wife." He snorted. "It's been downhill from there."

The reporter was confused, but pressed on.

"Is this what the aliens *really* want from us?"

"It all starts with a big bang and a lot of gas," the Major said. "An alien orgy after a big meal..."

"I'm sorry?" The reporter's pencil snapped. "Did you say—"

"They want to dominate. To make me, make us...slaves. Something about love."

"Love slaves?"

"Yes," Broward sighed, and snored a bit. "That's...yes. Love slaves."

"And how, exactly, do they plan on doing that?" asked the reporter.

"Something to do with changing vibrators," Broward muttered in his sleep.

"And will they do this to everyone?" she asked.

"Everyone..." Broward said. "Especially the fairies and little people."

The reporter had all she needed, but Broward just kept talking. Out came details of Silo 74, private meetings with the Arcturians, and details of "love fests" Plamorius had told them about—in great detail— after a summer in Ocean City, New Jersey.

It all appeared in the article.

Soon afterward a poster went up throughout the Silo 74 bunker.

LOOSE LIPS

SINK ALIEN SHIPS

The name "Babbling Broward" was scribbled in pen at the bottom, and thanks to the pugs, occasionally the Major would be spotted with a sign taped to the back of his uniform.

Probe me,
I'll tell you anything.

Had this been the *Enquirer*, there might have been plausible deniability. But the *U.S. Chronicle* was considered a reliable, mainstream source of news. The best that could be hoped was for the story to blow over.

The second press mishap involved, ironically, *Rolling Stone* magazine. For weeks, a series of posters and signs appeared on telephone poles and billboards across the country, promoting the connection between the original Woodstock and the new event. There were pictures everywhere of famous 1960s rock stars photoshopped with extraterrestrials.

On Interstate 87, in upstate New York close to the exit for Watkins Glen, there were billboards with Richie Havens hugging a Lyran with a spacecraft hovering in the background. Another showed Roger Daltrey and Pete Townshend asking a Pleiadian, "Who are you?" Melanie had her arm around Commander Avorius above the caption "Beautiful People." Commander P even showed up with his arm around Joan Baez.

Despite the *Chronicle* "exposé," Earth was hailing the festival as "The Great Intergalactic Music and Love Fest" of the 21st century. The Pentagon enlisted top concert promoters to help plan the Arcturian arrival, a prudent move given that the Pentagon had never really thrown a big party before. The most ambitious party ever to take place at the Pentagon had been catered by a fast-food chain in October 2023 and consisted of eight dozen cinnamon bagels with a shmear of cream cheese, two dozen Danishes, and eight cartons of black coffee.

Unfortunately, when one of the primary organizers was interviewed in *Rolling Stone* about the three-day festival about to occur, he was asked to name everyone who would be involved—including those not of this Earth.

"We're open to unique collaborations," he said, meaning the musicians. "Maybe some reunions and a lot of new and up-and-coming talent. This time around, we'll have control of everything…except possibly the Greys."

The public reaction immediately spiraled out of control. For years there had been rumors about the Greys, especially in intellectual circles like the Tsoukalos Institute, but skeptics hadn't been sure of their true existence until the *Rolling Stone* story broke, already supported by pictures in the *Weekly World News*.

This time damage control swirled *within* the military as brass began demanding answers. What would happen if little grey men showed up at the festival and actually tried to collect...samples? What about this supposed "Alien Bible?" As it turned out, such a thing really existed, and Army experts pored over it from cover to cover, flagging certain parts that concerned them. Especially one particular section, the Gospels of "Matthew the Grey," chapter 2, verse 9:

> *And yea, so should you all fall to your knees and lift your*
> *big bulbous craniums and lanky arms up to the sky in*
> *honor of she, the Great Mother, the one called the Big O.*

Should the Army begin encouraging people to obtain a copy of this bible? Would mass producing copies and placing them in hotel rooms worldwide contain the media frenzy? And what about the Greys? Could this leak perhaps bait the Greys to come to the festival?

((######))

Less than twenty-four hours after the article appeared in magazine, another emergency meeting was held at the Pentagon Briefing room.

"What do we do about this?" General Rickie demanded.

"Calm down—there's nothing *to* do," the enormous face of General Scott said from the 3D-screen hovering in the room. "It only adds mystery to the event. Yes, there are conspiracy theories surrounding the Greys. Some deluded scientists believe they're not extraterrestrial beings at all, but dwarfs with elephantiasis and errors of pigment metabolism. Rumors like those are none of our concern. Attendance is already far beyond capacity, and we have the attention and the interest of the whole world. More so, in fact, thanks to the leaks."

"Should we, you know..." The secretary of defense made a gesture and then looked around the rest of the room for approval.

"Eliminate the interviewee?" General Rickie asked. "Cut off the source?"

"Not necessary," Secretary Marks barked. "This gives us a strategic opportunity to bait the Grey bastards and finally get them out of the way."

"Still, it might be best to get a better grasp on what's said," General Scott admitted. "After all, loose lips sink alien ships."

"General Scott," Marks countered. "I don't give a good goddamn whether or not anyone believes the guy. *I* believe him, and he got his information from someone in *this* room. The Greys *are* coming…" He held up a folder. "Our latest intel indicates that they're showing up *en masse* and will try to abduct both people *and* animals." In the background, the pugs grimaced. "So what's your damned plan?"

"Sir," Commander Plamorius began judiciously, "we have an elaborate strategy in place—one which involves a great many troops. Thousands."

"Now *this* is what I want to hear," Marks said. "The reports your branch has—"

P stopped him. "But secrecy and surprise remain our greatest weapon. The enemy, as we know, is spread across Earth. The fewer who know of our plan, the better."

"Be that as it may, Commander, to put the rest of this room at ease, I order you to share as much as you can."

On the screen, Commander P turned to Scott.

The General shrugged. Plamorius turned back.

"For the Greys," Commander P said, "we plan on using life-sized plastic cows and camels as bait. Also, a thousand Marines will be donning animal costumes. The Greys, we know, are suckers for good-looking animals with big teats." Behind him, Major Broward blushed and sank deeper into his chair as the Pugs started to make mooing sounds. "Military escorts are assigned to every performing band and alien guests. The Arcturian ship will land on a pad in a highly secured area directly behind the stage. Bell UH-1Y Venom choppers and Piasecki X-49 Speed Hawks will secure the skyline, and MPs will surround the perimeter of the property with sharpshooters stationed in the trees. Every attendee is required to come through a metal and bomb detector, as well as an infrared scanner that picks up alien physiology."

"We have a scanner that can do that?" General Smith asked.

"Commander Avorius provided us with the schematics. Should prevent unwanted guests from entering through the front gates. After all, some of these species can shapeshift and look human."

"And the Reptiles?" Admiral Morton asked. "Many occupy high-level positions within Earth's governments and major corporations. The public's not yet aware of this infiltration—that these men and women in power are often not all they seem. This enemy will undoubtedly seek to sabotage the event. Even if this new-fangled scanner picks them up, how will we combat them?"

"We have a plan for that," General Scott said. "The Reptiles are known to crave power, and the males of the species in particular are suckers for beautiful women and gourmet food." Those at the Pentagon nodded. "So we've created the *Weinstein Play and Pay Pavilion*. A very special tent provided by Eclipse hotels for those identified as Reptilians. When they arrive through the gates, they'll be tagged with wristbands containing chips which track their whereabouts *and* provide electrical stimulation to their Reptilian pleasure centers. These can be turned on and off at will, by us, if any of them get out of control."

"The technology is amazing," Dr. Morales said. "Any chance a member of our team can get one of those to test it out?"

"I'm sorry, doctor," Plamorius said. "These are highly classified electronics. Only a Level Five clearance is given access."

Major Broward sat up in his chair.

"And what about these supposed zombies, vampires, and demons from the fourth dimension?" General McMasterson asked. "How will we control them if they show up?"

"It involves movies and blood sausages, but," General Scott replied, "in the name of intergalactic and interdimensional security—I'd prefer to say nothing more, sir."

A new face appeared on the screen, and General Scott introduced him just as "Dorje."

"As backup," the newcomer said, "I have prepared a few magical remedies."

"Magical?" General Tomlin muttered. "Can you tell us what they might consist of?"

"I'm afraid they would prove rather difficult for you to comprehend, my dear General," Dorje said. "Only those who have attended the Copernicus-Chiron Magick Academy have the spiritual and occult training to properly deal with the dark forces that exist around us. Without proper training, even discussing them opens up the uninitiated to nefarious energies which can literally suck the life out of you."

Major Broward, who was in the background, partially concurred, although his experience told a slightly different story. He cleared his throat and spoke up.

"I deal with my in-laws on a regular basis," he muttered, "and *I'm* still alive." Though few knew it, the major's mother-in-law was, in fact, the subject of a demonic possession—a singular individual named Yeenogu from the arch-yugoloths, who tortured and killed her victims by sucking the life out of them via unending barrages of poisonous, hateful speech. Broward was almost killed in 2018 when Yeenogu ran after him with an electric carving knife that he'd bought for her for Christmas when the other women in the bridge club received mink coats.

"Very well, Mister Dorje," General Tomlin conceded. "We've all been debriefed about your history and abilities. We trust your paranormal skills and value the Arcturian ability to read minds, if necessary."

The meeting was adjourned.

It was neither the beginning of the beginning, nor the end of the middle. But it was, possibly, the middle of the beginning.

PART TWO:

PARTY TIME

CHAPTER 9:

TO KNOW MY FUTURE

*"The past cannot be changed. The future is yet in your power
and the best way to predict the future is to create it."*

—Abraham Lincoln, 16th President of the United States,
upon discovering vampires were planning to take over
the United States

It was a clear, crisp morning on Saturday, August 15th, the 227th day of the year 2035 in the Earth Gregorian calendar.

On the planet Rigel 5 in the Orion belt, where certain species only have a twenty-four-hour life span, every day is Day One. The Margotians, a race of advanced mathematicians from the star system Procyon, have established their dates based on multiples of Π, i.e. 3.14159265358979323846264, divided by the square root of Stern-Levinson parameters, whereas Anton LaVey and the Order of the Trapezoid—a Satanic cult located near San Francisco in the 1970s—were known to record every day as 6/6/6.

As the sun first rose over the mountains in Watkins Glens, the mist in the fields burned away to reveal hundreds of enormous festival tents nestled amid the brilliant yellow sunflowers and purple loosestrife dotting the landscape. Closer examination revealed large neon signs which offered intergalactic delicacies—everything from Kosmic Kandy to Saturnian Sake Bombs and Martian Macadamia Nut Pies. There were stations for Pleiadian Pepperoni Pizza, which came with a warning required by Army lawyers: *overconsumption may lead to Barrett's esophagus, gastric ulcers, duodenal erosions, Crohn's disease, Ulcerative colitis, gaseous eructation, epistaxis, seizures, and death, as reported by independent Army taste testers who had required hospitalization after daring to eat half a Pleiadian pie in a single sitting.*

In order to cool the palate, there was Arcturian Apple Cider, a bit stronger than the usual varietals, and delicacies designed to please even the most discriminating tastes or, at least, to provide flavorful munchies for those whose endocannabinoid receptors were about to be overly stimulated.

The food stands were interspersed between multiple wooden stages erected around the two-thousand-acre park beneath intricate lighting structures and massive black JBL speakers, which towered over the scaffolding. The August temperatures were expected to reach 121 degrees Fahrenheit, so water stations had been set up to help avoid sunstroke, and portable toilets—the newest aseptic kind with bidets and warm water jets which sterilized *and* soothed with lavender essential oils—were stationed every thousand feet to ensure safety, comfort, and sanitation. These proved a big hit, ultimately causing longer lines than usual.

Bustling crowds—those without tickets to enter—had gathered outside the gates, and many were holding colorful helium balloons in the form of alien heads and flying saucers. Some were dressed as Spock-eared Trekkies. Others dressed as robots from *Westworld*, characters from *Harry Potter*, or were wearing high-tech uniforms from *12 Monkeys.*

Protestors and hate groups had come as well, and they carried signs proclaiming, "ET Go Home!"

The gates opened precisely at 6:00 a.m. Eastern Standard Time, and those who *did* have tickets began filing piecemeal through multiple scanners. It was like Disney World on acid. Old hippies in red and white bandanas and shorts, women of all ages in colorful Indian saris, excited children holding spaceship-shaped balloons, businessmen and women in sharp Calvin Klein suits, babies pushed in carriages, politicians from every state wearing pins with the American flag, as well as honored guests from across the globe, each wearing their countries' finest attire. Every ticketed guest received a badge identifying their seating area—VIP status or the lack thereof—and whether they'd paid for a multi-pass to get to all of the stages and events.

As the crowds passed through the dozens of special scanners, NSA and TSA officers reviewed the images on the screens. It was a predictable pattern.

Human.

Human.

Reptile.

Human.

Pleiadian.

Reptile.

Human.

Cockroach…

Bug aliens, like the infamous Edgar Blattodea (1934–2035), could still occasionally be found living on Earth, despite rumors to the contrary.

The VIP line primarily showed reptiles, and it could be predicted in advance who many of them would be, as they often were chief executive officers or other high-ranking members of influential firms, government representatives—some of whom openly resembled turtles or lizards, or top-ranking members of Big Agriculture, Big Pharma, Big Oil, Big Industry, and Big Finance.

Occasionally, someone passed through the scanners and confused the NSA and TSA agents when the image was neither human nor Reptilian and seemed unrecognizable. The first to present such a challenge was a New York senator who had been secretary of the interior during the late 2020s. As she passed through the scanner images, part human, part horse appeared on the screen.

"Ms. OC, may we see your credentials, please?" a male TSA agent asked.

"Of course," the Senator replied. "Is something wrong?"

"No ma'am, just a routine check." The agent pulled over another to review the screen. They conferred, and the second agent laughed.

"Oh!" he said. "She's an Alpha Centurian and doesn't know it yet. Didn't you review your ET manual, slim? These 'centaurs' are the warriors who fight for truth and justice with few Twitter filters. That's how you recognize them."

While the Senator pondered patiently, the agents slapped a bracelet on her and hurried her through.

"Enjoy the day, Senator." The first agent smiled coyly.

And thus, one-by-one, each lifeform who passed through the scanners received bracelets that were quickly affixed to their wrists. These bracelets were also programmed to track where each guest went during their day, thus identifying not only the Reptilians but any Sirian, Arcturian, Alpha-Centurian, Annunaki, Pleiadian, or Lyran attending the festival, ranking their traits *and* recording their DNA via Arcturian nanotechnology.

The wristlets reserved for the Reptiles were particularly ornate.

"Good morning honored and handsome TSA agent," one attendee said smoothly. The TSA agent was immediately alert, having been trained to spot a Reptile by their overuse of honorifics and manipulative behavior. "What is this amazingly beautiful bracelet I'm receiving today?"

"You have a very good eye, sir," the agent responded. "It's a very special and limited commemorative version of the Woodstock 2035 bracelet. Gold and silver with semiprecious stones in the outline of an Arcturian spaceship. A special gift from the organizers to show their appreciation for your being here. Because of your honored status, sir. Please make sure to keep it on at all times during the event—it's a collectible."

"Well, it certainly is exquisitely stunning," the Reptilian said. "Pleasing...I will treasure it and make sure it never leaves my body."

"We're happy you approve. Now, please be sure you take your seat by 8:00 a.m., sir," the agent directed. "The Arcturian spacecraft will be landing then, and you won't want to miss the event!"

It actually would have been almost impossible to "miss" the landing. The event was being televised across the world on every station on Earth—except for cable networks TNT and HBO, which were showing, respectively, a Rocky marathon and *Game of Thrones* seasons one through eight, minus the finale. The only persons on the planet *not* watching that day were North Koreans, who had been instructed to hide in bunkers waiting for an alien attack and COVID-35, and certain residents of Vatican City, as the Sistine Chapel and St. Peter's Basilica were presently on fire.

Along with the various badges and bracelets, most attendees also received a small purple pack of mushrooms—a special "party snack" for the event. Denver, Colorado, as one of the states leading in progressive thinking, had been the first to decriminalize and legalize the mushrooms back in 2019. "Happy pills" that raised serotonin were no longer considered enough. To announce the new law, greeting card companies in Colorado had made up special cards showing purple Rocky Mountains and mushrooms with the caption, "Here in Colorado, we climb the HIGHEST mountains. We look far past the horizons. We dream, we dare, and we Do (Shrooms)!"

At the festival, the dose was given to "increase the mystical experience" and to help with the rampant depression and anxiety present in most of those who were attending. The majority of people in 2035 suffered with some form of mental disorder. According to the World Health Organization, depression had affected more than 350 million people around the world in the early part of the 21st century, and with the major climate change events during the 2020s and 2030s, more than 3.5 billion people suffered from some type of psychiatric illness.

Although scientists in the 21st century identified a multiplicity of causes, including microbes such as spirochetal bacteria, multiple Bartonella species, virulent herpes viruses, noxious fungi, and parasites, the primary source was the destabilization of food and water supplies in many states and countries across the world. People were anxious over what happened to the planet and were concerned, rightly so, with whether it might get worse.

The mushrooms also would assist in waking up many of the Starseeds who attended the festival. Dr. Chick Harris-Carson from the Imperial College London had explained, "Only by losing the self, can you find the self.... People try to run away from things and to forget, but with psychedelic drugs, they're forced to confront and really look at themselves."

Several thousand invitees were about to meet their true selves.

Growing crowds milled about the various other pavilions where scanners kept track and indicated whether each individual was one of the displaced Starseeds. The ET Command Team had worked with the

Arcturians and Master Dorje to invite many specific guests, including more than seven hundred persons who Master Dorje had identified as leaders in their Starseed tribes.

It was estimated that one in five people on Earth was a Starseed or a close genetic offspring. Playing such odds, twenty percent of those in attendance would, should, or could react to the day's events. While those watching on televisions, phones, and other devices across the world wouldn't get the full whammy-jammy, it was believed the event could still stir an awakening in those ready for such things. By day's end, close to a billion Earthlings could be awakening.

Except for the North Koreans, who wouldn't be permitted to watch the broadcast until the year 2087.

The first order of business, however, remained the collection of information on those in attendance. Thus, the special pavilions—several of which proved especially popular.

There was Hippie Heaven, where customers could buy clothes from the 1960s and 1970s, along with soft plush cushions made with colorful Indian fabrics, saris, fragrant Tibetan incense, and posters of Jimi Hendrix wailing on his guitar. There were wooden percussion instruments on the floor for anyone to play. It was a haven for those in the arts who loved to create beauty and joy through different expressions, whether it be as a singer, dancer, artist, or musician. Pleiadians flocked there in droves. As they did, bracelets buzzed, and purple mushrooms were joyfully consumed.

Arcturian scientists and Andromedan technology wizards filed into the Einstein Quantum Pavilion. Those who had chosen medical careers were pulled into the Arcturian Healing Temple, fashioned after the Aesculapian ancient temples in Rome. Scanners there picked up those who were ill with microbes and toxins.

One of the most popular attractions was Ye Olde Dorje Magick Shoppe. Earthbound mystics from the monasteries and ashrams were particularly attracted to this pavilion. After passing through velvet drapes covered with fluorescent stars and moons, guests entered the white hexagon-shaped tent and a whole magical universe emerged. Tables and booths were spread throughout the enclosure, each offering the latest magical apparatus. Adults and children who aspired to be magicians could purchase everything from whoopee cushions, hand buzzers, and pepper gum to the most-advanced magic wands, some designed for older men which gave them the ability to levitate objects which hadn't risen in years.

There was a well-stocked section on the occult sciences in the back of the tent filled with books by Aleister Crowley, Edgar Cayce, Alice Bailey, Alan Moore, and other occultists of the 19th, 20th, and 21st centuries, as well as posters of dragons and magicians, and the latest 3-D talking Tarot cards which gave readings to passersby even if they didn't ask. No opportunity was missed to separate attendees from their funds.

One reticent Starseed by the name of Augustine, who was actually a sleeping Arcturian monk, walked past the table. The 3-D talking Tarot immediately sprang into action.

"Hey, Augustine! Wanna know your future?"

The man stopped, looked around, and shrugged.

"Sure," he said. "Why not?"

The talking Tarot deck told him to shuffle and lay out five cards in a cross. The monk did as he was told and placed the cards on a velvet-covered table that also held a crystal ball, white candle, bell, and an old leather-covered book. As he put down each card, 3-D images appeared in the space in front of him. The first five major arcana cards appeared in perfect numerical order. the Fool at the bottom; the Magician in the middle; the High Priestess to the left; the Empress on top; and the Emperor to the right.

"Pick one more," the deck instructed, "and place it to the right of the Emperor." The monk chose the final card and put it down. Wisdom appeared in the space in front of him.

"What does this mean?" Augustine asked.

"It means you're about to start a new journey, leaving the past behind," the deck said, "where you will need to make a great leap of faith. You will use your intuition to move forward, as the love of the Great Mother fills your being and leads you to mastery and ultimately wisdom."

When the deck said no more, Augustine continued on his way.

And so it went for Starseed after Starseed who entered each pavilion. Alpha Centurians were attracted to the horse pavilion, which contained life-sized images of talking horses along with magnificent living specimens of Arabians, Appaloosas, Mustangs, Haflingers, Percherons, and Lipezzans. Stories of the life of Chiron were told in books, videos, and paintings.

Lyrans were drawn into tents with multicolored fairy statues of different sizes, miniature homes elaborately decorated with silks and expensive fabrics, along with hanging air moss and exotic orchids perfectly placed among the statues.

Two hours passed, and then the atmosphere underwent a dramatic change. Music of the spheres began to emerge from the massive loudspeakers, and the excitement was palpable. People emerged from the pavilions and rushed to their assigned seating. The music stopped and was replaced by five musical tones: G, A, F, an octave drop, F, C. The tones repeated—G, A, F, F, C—and kept repeating in a hypnotic fashion, growing faster and faster. As they heard the repetition, Baby Boomers and Gen-Xers started to hoot and chortle, chanting the notes as loudly and as best they could in unison. Even the Baby Boomers got in on the action—the ones that could still dance without relying on their canes, that is.

Millennials and Zoomers, on the other hand, looked puzzled, trying to figure out what drugs the old people were on.

((######))

Just behind the main stage, General Scott, Major Broward, and the scientists from the Army ET Command studied the scene, including the landing area. They were stationed in a large green-and-brown camouflage tent with a full console of video monitors receiving input from infrared cameras, drones, and spy satellites continuously scanning the grounds and surrounding woods.

Above the crowd, the U.S. Navy Blue Angels and Air Force Thunderbirds appeared from nowhere and flew in formation over the grounds, doing aerobatics that seemed to defy gravity. They'd disappeared just as quickly, and the crowd roared with delight.

Then another craft with an oblong metallic shape suddenly appeared and zipped through the air in dizzying patterns. Gasps arose from the crowd after they watched the craft perform a series of seemingly impossible movements and then suddenly stop in mid-air and disappear. There was an eerie silence throughout the park.

Was this the alien craft with a cloaking device? Were the Arcturians showing us their military capability? Questions buzzed through the spectators, growing in volume.

Suddenly, the JBL loudspeakers crackled.

"Welcome to the U.S. Military supremacy of 2035," a man's voice said. "Our newest space age X-19 craft can outmaneuver and outsmart any aerospace technology on the market. Feel safe knowing you have X-19 protection!" Everyone sighed in unison, knowing it was just the military showing off.

There was a buzzing overhead as a series planes appeared over the festival grounds. People were mesmerized by the skywriting that emerged out of the blue as a smoke-casted image of the latest smartphone appeared. It was the 22X, the model that replaced the 21X with a new and improved super enhanced neural engine, and an augmented reality feature that allowed users to take pictures of their friends as aliens and upload them to the cloud—specifically engineered for the event. The speakers played "Hit the Road, Mac" as a slogan appeared under the phone:

Think different. We've accomplished

Mission ImpossibleTM and

we're NOT out of this world!

Pinging arose throughout the crowd as phones picked up an advertisement for *Mission Impossible 8: Code Word Reptile*. A loud murmur arose as well as spectators scanned the skies and audience for any sign of Tom Cruise, but the stunt had been vetoed by the producers who were concerned that at seventy-two years old, the actor would irreparably damage himself.

The Army still ended up pulling in a cool $500 million for the largest two-minute PR event of the century.

Once the airshow was complete and silence fell again over the crowd, the General got on the com. "Ranger Post 1, report." This was repeated, over and over, and then after the last scout had checked in and safety was assured, General Scott turned to everyone in the tent and spoke in a strong, booming voice: "We're cleared for landing! Commander P, inform the Arcturians. The rest of you, get ready for a day you'll not soon forget."

Within moments, the silver Arcturian spaceship appeared in the sky and descended silently and slowly over the landing pad. Video monitors followed the trajectory as a combination of 150,000 cheers— as well as some shouts of fear—broke out among the crowd. Chants of "ET, don't eat me, ET. Don't eat me" could be heard among the fearful, along with other, more optimistic exultations.

"Just like Groot, Put Down Your Roots" could be heard chanted by a group looking forward to finally having intelligent life living on this planet. Signs were raised and waved:

Who's Your Star Lord?

Another group drinking Corona and sitting on colorful Oaxacan blankets had a banner writ in bright colors:

I'm an Illegal Alien

Take Me to Your Leader

A group of dairy farmers in blue overalls held small plush xenomorph dolls and their own message:

Who's Laying the Eggs?

Even the Army vehicles decided to join in the fun. Signs were posted on the back of their vans:

Caution: Alien Onboard

That confused the Arcturian servants to no end, although it was explained to them the sign was meant to be humorous and that people on Earth wouldn't actually ram into one another if there *wasn't* a small child in the vehicle.

As the enthusiasm rose to a fever pitch, the Arcturian spaceship set down perfectly in the middle of the landing pad, and the crowd fell unnaturally silent. Platinum-covered stairs extended from the ship. The door slowly opened.

This was a moment humanity had been waiting centuries to reach. Finally, proof that alien life really existed, above and beyond Dennis Rodman, Cher, John Holmes, and Congressman Daniel Sickles. He was the first historical evidence of a Reptilian in Congress, having openly cheated on his pregnant wife with a prostitute, murdered his wife's lover in cold blood, and argued the temporary insanity plea for the first time in legal history while becoming a Congressman and receiving a medal of honor. Only Reptiles could manage such a feat, yet it was still indirect evidence of an alien infestation.

But this arrival was ultimate proof Earth was not alone. Never had been.

Proof that humanity still had a chance of surviving.

CHAPTER 10:

FIRST IMPRESSIONS

"For thirty years, I've held that image in my mind. What I saw was a circular object that looked like two pie plates put on top of each other with a golf ball on top. It was a classic flying saucer. And it shot a beam of something at our warhead."

—U.S. Air Force Lieutenant Robert M. Jacobs, largely ignored until 2035

The first Arcturian to emerge was Commander Avorius, and there were immediate gasps from the crowd, especially the women.

The commander wasn't exactly what they'd planned for in an alien. Thanks to fifty-plus years of Hollywood, they'd expected a short and spindly grey thing with bulging eyes or maybe even something with insect-like armor. What they got instead was the best parts of *The Avengers*: A Thor face, a perfectly formed and muscular seven-foot body of the Hulk, and tight slacks that hinted at parts that were all Iron Man.

Avorius wore his best royal Arcturian military garb, a silk gold-and-maroon shirt, and a large silver sword which hung sheathed at his hip. Thousands of women and men began to swoon.

"Oh, slay *me*, military man," one man cried out. The Arcturian servants listening in the background looked horrified. "Maximus, Maximus!" a female attendee yelled with a big smile on her face. "Is that a large sword in your sheath, or are you just happy to see me?"

Avorius waved politely to the woman and then the whole cheering crowd and was reassured to see the warm welcome the Arcturians were receiving. During his study of Earth literature, film, and social media, he had encountered the English tale of the sword in the stone and was grateful for the woman's reference to his physical prowess and strength in battle.

"Thank you, my lady," he responded. "The last time I pulled it out, the entire legion cheered for hours!" There were gasps from the crowd and several of them fainted. They took him seriously, indeed. Avorius obviously mistook the English reference, and military men were not always known for their wit.

Though he didn't know it, the last military man recorded as having a sense of humor was Army Gen. Tommy Franks as he addressed the Marines prior to the commencement of operation Iraqi Freedom. He was quoted as saying: "*When you boys get home and see a lot of war protesters, go up to one, shake his hand, and smile. Then, wink at his girlfriend because she knows she's dating a pussy.*"

Commander Avorius smiled broadly, continued to exit the ship, and perused the area. His primary goals were to confirm that the landing area was safe for the King and Queen and to gauge the response from the crowd. Seeing that it was safe, he motioned to his guards to come down the stairs and form a perimeter that would protect the royal family and their servants.

For just a moment, though, he frowned. During the Commander's early years, he had failed to protect the Queen only one time—while she was picnicking on Planet Xerius located on the far side of the Milky Way near a spot containing nests of what were called—on Earth—kissing bugs. His research had informed him that on Earth, the insects "were a well-known health menace. They were biting insects prone to chomping on lips—therefore unofficially dubbed the 'kissing bug'—and became a terrifying menace after researchers revealed up to 30 percent of its victims developed life-threatening health problems, including heart disease and sudden death." Fortunately, nothing of the sort had happened to the Queen. Women with collagen lip enhancement procedures were found to be especially at risk, and Queen Dawn was above such artificialities.

As the alien militia and servants descended the stairs and onto the platform, the crowd's reaction shifted from wild cheers to amazement—especially once the King exited the spacecraft, followed by the Queen's mother, known formally as the Royal Mother, Helen of Antwar. Then the Queen herself exited the craft in all of her royal splendor, and the crowd again fell completely silent.

Queen Dawn was absolutely stunning. Whereas the audience might have expected her to wear a metallic space suit, in preparation for this occasion, her retinue had done some serious shopping for the finest accoutrements Earth had to offer.

She wore a gold and silver Prada glittering gown slit to the thigh, with a low neckline, several Cartier platinum and diamond bracelets, a Tiffany platinum round 3.09-carat diamond solitaire ring, high-heeled gold Christian Louboutin shoes, Mikimoto pearl earrings, and a multicolored diamond and emerald bejeweled crown the likes of which no one had ever seen before. Given the average height of an Arcturian, it was a mystery how she had managed to find anything in her size.

Though the Queen was trying to fit in, it was an impossible task doomed from the get-go. In truth, she looked to be a towering supermodel, stylishly dressed beyond the human imagination. The effect on the crowd couldn't have been more profound if she had stepped off the cover of a *Sports Illustrated* swimsuit issue. Not a sound was heard—not even from the native birds—as Queen Dawn of Antwar slowly descended the ramp, her servants carrying a red cape flowing behind her.

The trail of servants continued until the last of the Arcturian retainers exited carrying Amori and Audri, the Queen's atmop pets, firmly wrapped in blankets to protect the crowd—for now—from any conga-line shenanigans. From a distance the creatures looked like well-behaved children, albeit with tentacles.

Finally, the crowd roused again. They cheered and did a stadium-style wave. Some of what resulted were transverse waves, others longitudinal. The Brits at the festival—many of them expats thrown out of the UK following Brexit—went with the famous Queen Elizabeth Windsor wave, partly in Elizabeth's honor and partly to get on the big screen.

The last special guests to exit the spacecraft were Commander Plamorius and his four pugs. Since P was almost eight feet tall, he fit right in and greeted the crowd with a ten-foot wide open-armed gesture that covered half the stage.

"Look, it's a *real* alien," one member of the crowd cried out. "It's about time!"

"And look at those cute dogs!" another yelled. "Aren't they adorable? I just want to take them home and play with them!"

That's all the pugs needed to hear.

"Hey babe!" one yelled, a cigar dangling in his mouth. "You can come play with me anytime."

"Let's start with petting and see where it goes from there," another barked.

"How about a little strip poker?" the third suggested.

"Anyone got a cold canine *cerveza*?"

Everyone within earshot was speechless—even the woman who had started it all. Everyone, that is, except for a lone gentleman in the front row, a bearded debonair LatinX who shouted back.

"The beer is located on the main festival grounds. Stay thirsty, my friend!"

The pugs squinted and growled at the man. Commander P, clearly not happy with the behavior of his pets, turned back and gave them an arcane Pleiadian gesture where the fifth finger on each hand slowly became erect. The gesture, he'd assumed, would be unfathomable for the crowd, but would not be lost on the pugs.

The crowd, however, took it as an opportunity to connect with the alien and decided to raise *their* fingers in a similar fashion, until everyone in the crowd was essentially saying the equivalent of "fuck you" in Pleiadian.

Realizing the humans were ignorant of the gesture's true meaning, Plamorius turned back toward the crowd and raised his two pinkies at everyone, flashing a big smile. That was all the crowd needed.

One of the female hippie humans close to him—a woman wearing a vintage tie-dyed Grateful Dead tee shirt from the 1970s with the saying "Steal Your Orbit" cried out, "Hey, tall good-looking grey spaceman with the cool dogs. How 'bout showing *us* some love."

That was all the encouragement P needed. Recognizing the woman as one of his kinsmen in human form, he extended his long arms to hug her and anyone else he could reach.

"*LOVE FEST!*"

With that he dove into the crowd. Instantly, the Arcturians on stage and Army security went on high alert. Before they could react, however, cries of glee emerged from the throngs of people.

As the initial ecstasy wore off, the Army stood down and the precession continued. Queen Dawn turned and waved Commander P back onto the stage. They reached the platform from which they would address the crowd, the entourage took their respective seats, and the Queen approached the lone microphone.

More than two hundred television cameras—and thousands of smartphone cameras—pointed in her direction as she gracefully approached the puzzling human talking device located in the center of the podium. The eyes and ears of a planet were upon her.

CHAPTER 11:

QUEEN DAWN'S ADDRESS

(Begin Official Transcript)

"**G**reat people and diverse cultures of the planet Earth. It is with immense pleasure that we—the Arcturians and our friends the Pleiadians—are here today to celebrate this momentous occasion as our star civilizations come together for the first time. We come to you in the spirit of love and cooperation.

"You are surely wondering why we are here, why we are finally revealing ourselves to you, and why we did not come *sooner*. First, we want to be crystal clear: we have a singular purpose. Our intention is to assist you in the planetary catastrophe that has come to impact the majority of your planet. You are at a critical juncture in history, and unless you—unless *we*—act, more of your people will suffer. Billions.

"Other planets have gone through similar planetary crises, and over time we have developed the technology and the wisdom to offer you solutions so that you may avoid worldwide destruction.

"We have watched your planet go through the first great climate change culminating in your Earth year 2031. Much of your civilization refused to admit that high levels of carbon pollution altered your planetary temperatures. Some amongst you *still* debate the facts, despite the evidence before your very eyes. To use one of your own expressions, your planetary leaders have been 'fiddling as Rome burned.'

"Earth scientists lamented *twenty years ago* that your oceans were warming at a rate faster than in the prior six to seven Earth decades. Ocean temperatures, as you must know, are the best indicators of climate change, as the majority of global heat is deposited in the oceans. The time for debate is past. Science and rationality, employed with compassion for present and future generations, *must* lead the way forward. If they do not, you will go through the sixth great extinction event in your Earth's history.

"To offer you a better understanding of the situation, we will allow one of our top Arcturian scientists, Professor Satu, to explain in detail."

• • • •

A classically-tall, good looking Arcturian scientist rose from a seat behind the Queen and took his place at the dais. He had a high forehead and long, dark curly hair flowing down to his shoulders. A dramatic symbol of two dragons in a helix, the mouth of one eating the tail of the other, was prominently located on the pocket of his crisp white laboratory uniform.

• • • •

(Resume Transcript)

"Thank you, my precious Queen.

"People of the planet Earth, I bring you greetings from our brotherhood of Arcturian scientists. We are an ancient group of highly-trained researchers who are not unlike your experts who have studied the physical laws of universal science. We have tracked the progress of your researchers, especially the Union of Concerned Scientists, and they have been accurately warning you of the danger to your civilization since almost a century ago, yet you have continued to ignore their warnings.

"Your top Earth scientists began measuring ocean temperatures in the late nineteenth century, as you measure time, and record-setting temperatures began to occur in 2014, with each year's measurement higher than the previous one. As was clearly established by your own scientists, the carbon dioxide that was released had nowhere to go but the oceans and was the source of these changes. Yet many of your global leaders ignored and even refuted the data, which is why you find yourselves on the brink of an irreversibly catastrophic situation.

"In January of 2019, scientists predicted that the melting Antarctic ice could soon submerge the Brooklyn Bridge in the city of New York. Although this level has not yet been reached, more and more lands have fallen below sea level and are partially under water. Warmer oceans led to more intense weather events, including stronger hurricanes and storm surges with heavier rainfall.

"Your governments lack the knowledge and ability to work together efficiently, and your people reap the consequences. Yet you *are* a global community."

• • • •

Satu paused and took a deep breath. It would be difficult for some to hear these truths, yet there was no choice. Arcturian scientists had long ago taken a vow to always speak truth, combined with the unwavering intent of benefitting others. Yet he dared not lose the attention and the sympathy of this global audience.

Since laughter was one of the best salves for soothing wounds among humans, he decided to lead off with a story. What many called a joke.

• • • •

(Resume Transcript)

"A rabbi, a priest, and a scientist go into a bar." People in the audience looked at each other in amazement and chuckled. Extraterrestrials knew Earth humor.

"The bartender looks at them warily as they sit down at the counter and order drinks. After his first sip, the Rabbi hears a deep throaty voice, but he can't identify the sound's origin.

"'Hey, Rabbi! I like that star around your neck!' the voice says. The Rabbi looks around, but he doesn't see anyone and decides to ignore it, taking his first gulp of ice-cold beer. After a short time, the priest takes a sip, and another deep voice is heard coming from somewhere in the bar.

"'Hey, Father! Nice frock!' The priest looks around but can't see anyone speaking to him. He only notices the bartender quietly wiping the bar. He decides to ignore the voice, and they all take another sip of their drinks.

"'Hey, Mr. Arcturian scientist! I like your lab coat and cool symbol!' says the hidden voice. The Arcturian puts down his drink and, confused, calls out to the bartender, who walks over, polishing a glass.

"'Hey, barkeep,' the scientist says, 'what's with the deep throaty voices I keep hearing?'

"'Oh, those are the pretzels,' the bartender replies. 'They're complimentary.'"

Groans emerged from the crowd. "Yes, I have studied your species and know you humans like humor, no matter how base, but I tell you this joke for a reason.

"I would like to first compliment your people on some of the magnificent achievements of the past few centuries. You have significantly developed your intellectual, artistic, and scientific capabilities. Agriculture, iron and steam, cogs and pistons—you have made tremendous progress in building computer networks to quickly analyze relatively large amounts of data. Sent probes to explore other planets and star systems, developed medicines to prevent and treat a broad range of diseases. You have figured out ways to increase food production and combat famine, create farmlands on your moon, and have explored the worlds of subtle quantum physics and string theory.

"These are all significant advances of which you can be proud. However great your achievements, your intellectual capacities have far outpaced your moral development.

"The discovery of atomic particles was magnificent, but it was used for more than advances in energy, medicine, and physics. It led to the creation of atomic arsenals designed to kill millions at the push of a button. Your weapons advanced from crude spears and bows used for hunting essential food to biological warfare and handheld projectile weapons that have murdered innocent generations. You have ignored the most primary of basic truths: You are one world, and you share a basic humanity.

"*Every* person living on your planet wants to be happy, to be free from suffering. Your mistake was thinking you were separate and that the actions of one culture or country would not significantly affect the others. Or, if it did, the end justified the means.

"Denial, materialism, nationalism, shortsighted vision, and lack of consideration for future generations have put your planet at great risk. The climate changes with which you already are coping will soon be *irreversible*. They will cause the catastrophic transformation of your weather and geography. Already, flooding and droughts have destroyed farmland, leading to food shortages. Millions of individuals have been displaced. The sudden and extreme shifts have led to wildfires, mudslides, hailstorms, earthquakes, tsunamis, and increasingly frequent level-six hurricanes.

"These natural disasters have led to a downward spiral of your global economies, as you could not repair the damage fast enough before the next round of destruction arrived.

"The third consequence has been a rise in infectious diseases. Your mosquitos, ticks, fleas, and other insects thrive in higher temperatures, which leads to the worldwide spread of vector-borne diseases. And finally, the fourth major consequence—your excess carbon dioxide warming and acidifying your oceans—has led to decreased diversity of species and a lack of edible food. Simultaneously, the thousands of toxic chemicals and plastics that have been dumped into the air and oceans have entered all of your bodies. This has led to increased rates of autism, attention-deficit/hyperactivity disorder, autoimmune diseases, Alzheimer's dementia, cancer, and death."

• • • •

The crowd gasped, which was exactly the response Satu had sought. If only he had gotten through to them. Enough of them to—

The Queen rose again and approached the dais.

• • • •

(Resume Transcript)

"Thank you, Satu.

"The good news, people of Earth, is that there *are* solutions. All is not lost. You must, however, listen carefully if you are to survive. During your *first* Woodstock music festival, on which we are told this one was modeled, a famous spiritual guru by the name of Sri Swami Satchidananda presided over the event. Then, he addressed a crowd of some five hundred thousand people, and today, as we speak to more than five *billion*, we would like to remind you of his message.

"'My beloved Brothers and Sisters,' he said. 'The future of the whole world is in your hands. You can make or break. But you are really here to *make* the world. The hearts are meeting...the entire success is in *your* hands. The entire world is going to watch this. The entire world is going to know what the youth can do for humanity. So every one of you should be responsible for the success of this festival.'

"In the years that followed that event, one of your other great spiritual leaders, Thich Nhat Hanh, addressed your people in 2019. We echo the words he spoke, and those included in an address to your American Congress in 2003. He spoke of the need to lead with courage and compassion. Nothing could be truer at this point in time. As per the guru you called Thai, we quote: 'When you communicate with compassion, you are using language which does not have the elements of anger and irritation in it. All the energies of anger, hatred, fear and violence come from wrong perceptions.'

"The Arcturian King and I, and *all* of our entourage, are here today to communicate with the element of love, wanting you all to be happy. We communicate to you with the element of compassion, wanting you all to be free from suffering. To wake from such nightmares. Wake to new possibilities, to new realities. For if you can listen with an open heart and an open mind and engage each other with love, compassion, and deep care for your Earth brothers and sisters, we will accomplish great things together.

"Our scientists and mystic masters have solutions for you. All you need to do is wake up to the truth. Future generations will remember this as the turning point in your civilization where rationality, science, and cooperation ruled along with love, compassion, and deep listening—not fear, suspicion, hate, and destruction."

(End Transcript)

• • • •

The crowd roared with delight, although many tears could also be seen flowing from the multitude. They knew the Queen spoke the truth, and it struck deep chords inside of many who were listening.

CHAPTER 12:

THE BEGINNING

S uddenly, from the back of the stage, the Royal Mother, Helen of Antwar, got up from her chair and approached the microphone. The Queen, surprised, turned and whispered in a stern voice.

"Mother, please sit down. I am not yet done."

The Royal Mother, predictably, would have nothing of it.

"I gave birth to you from my royal, perfectly-toned loins," she said, "and because of you, I've suffered with a dropped bladder that makes me pee like a leaking garden hose, a torn vagina that required more stitches than an Annunaki gang leader, and hemorrhoids so bad, the term 'miles of purple Pleiadian piles' was created to commemorate them. So don't you dare try to tell *me* when I have the right to speak."

The Queen had heard these very same complaints from the time of her birth. She turned back to the microphone.

"The Royal Mother, Helen of Antwar, would now like to address the people," she said. "Please let us welcome our Royal Mother of Arcturus."

Cheers arose from the crowd accompanied by a flurry of Windsor waves. Meanwhile, everyone on stage and back at the command center braced for impact.

"Ugly, short people of the planet Earth," the Royal Mother began, "I am truly sorry you all suffer with such inferior intelligence." The entourage on the back of the stage grimaced, putting their hands to their foreheads in unison. The crowd, however, made the same assumption as

113

they had with Commander Avorius and Professor Satu, and roared with laughter followed by wild, vigorous clapping.

The Arcturian retinue looked at one another, perplexed.

"Having examined the various life forms on your planet," Helen continued, "it's clear, the way you've treated your Earth mother reminds me not only of how my daughter has treated me but of one of your more erudite expressions: 'Even a bird with a pea-sized brain knows not to shit in its own nest.' You people are so stupid, if I called you that, stupid people would be insulted."

The crowd continued to laugh hysterically with guffaws growing louder and louder.

"To borrow a few more of your classic, uninspired aphorisms: You are clearly not the brightest crayons in the box, sharpest tools in the woodshed, or...as we say, brightest stars in the night sky. You are beyond lucky to have us here. Even a one-year-old Arcturian knows enough not to poop in its diapers and then smear it all over the house. Or—"

The Queen grabbed the microphone.

"Thank you *so* much, *dearest* mother, for those discerning words." She held it tightly as the laughter faded. Sensing that her moment had past, the Royal Mother returned to her seat, though she continued to stare daggers at her daughter.

"We'd like to end this auspicious occasion with words of enlightenment from our sacred Arcturian priest, Master Dorje. He will further clarify why we are here and what needs be done to accomplish our mutual goal.

Dorje arose from his chair. Everyone's eyes fixated on the elderly person who hobbled to the stage, leaning on a large dark brown, wooden, thick staff topped—and glowing faintly—with a strange blue crystal and insignia. His shimmering azure gown was speckled with silver stars and purple moons. He wore John Lobb black boots—or at least good-looking knockoffs—and his long grey beard was of a Merlin who'd woken up after sleeping for a few centuries.

"Thank you, my beloved Queen," he said, his voice surprisingly clear. "My dear people of the planet Earth, we thank you for the opportunity to speak today about an impending crisis of which you are not yet aware." He paused to let that sink in.

"We, the Arcturians, had a great calamity befall us a long time ago, and we wish to help you avoid the same misfortune. We once were a flourishing civilization, one where harmony, love, happiness, and prosperity reigned. We were a people of peace and had never experienced the horrors of war, nor even considered the possibility of such a thing. Then, one day, our dreams and illusions were shattered.

"A group of alien aggressors known as the Alpha Draconians, or Draconian Reptiles, invaded our planet and slaughtered tens of millions of our citizens. Only those of us who had the ability to shift dimensional realities were able to survive the war, avoiding recognition by our captors. Those Arcturians who did not possess that capacity due to lack of spiritual ability and/or fear were killed, enslaved, or fled to other star systems to fend for themselves." Dorje paused, weighing the importance of how to present the next part of the story. He scanned the audience, and they seemed receptive to his message, so he proceeded.

"Many of our Arcturian and Pleiadian brethren, therefore, arrived on *your* planet centuries ago seeking a safe place to live and escape further persecution. They are among you now, as their offspring have taken human form."

Another pause to let that sink in, and many among the audience began to glace around with uncertainty and, alas, hints of fear.

"Unfortunately, integrating into your society was not easy for us. Many of our Starseeds remembered the old ways, and we were soon labeled 'witches' or 'warlocks' or 'demons' or even 'psychotic' by your various powers that be. We were often executed or locked away by those who did not understand that our magick could be used for good. Taking human form, we went into hiding here on your planet, as did members of other intergalactic civilizations, including the Lyrans, Alpha Centurians, Annunaki, Andromedans, Pleiadians, and Sirians, all of whom needed to escape their Reptilian aggressors. We have been in hiding for centuries, but now is the time for us all to wake up.

"Wake up, Starseeds," he said, his voice rising. "I bring you the terrible news that the Reptilians have come to this planet to destroy it and all people who live here. The Orion Wars are now playing out on the planet Earth and are part of the reason the planet's climate is deteriorating at such a rapid pace. These vile beings have *also* been here for centuries, also taking human form, planning, biding their time, and creating the foundation for their assault.

"Many now hold positions of power in your government, large corporations, and other agencies across the planet. They control your economy. They help to drive your climate change by maligning and undercutting energy-efficient solutions which were—and still are—available to you. It is all part and parcel of their master plan. They *also* seek to control the people on your planet by infecting your brains with highly transmissible spirochetal bacteria, noxious viruses, and environmental toxins. In essence, they are dumbing down the population, making you more vulnerable to domination.

"These beings are ruled by greed, money, power, narcissism, and hate, and if they are not stopped, you will lose your planet and its people…just as we have. But we are here to help stop that from happening. WAKE UP, Starseeds!"

The entire crowd was silent, stunned, listening to his words but many, deep down, already understood the truth of which Dorje spoke.

It was the…Reptiles.

As the realization hit everyone fully—that the infiltrators and invaders were real, systematically destroying the Earth, *and* that they had attended this event in droves—screams abrupted from the crowd. A few at first, then more and more.

Those Reptiles in attendance, both invited and not, realized they'd been found out. Hundreds at the *Weinstein Play-and-Pay* tent leapt from their lap-dance couches and gambling tables. It had finally dawned on them: They'd been corralled among their own brethren.

If the Reptiles already had known who they were, they were not alone. After hearing Dorje's speech, others began to stir. Vampires, ghosts, zombies, demons, and droves of Greys hiding in the woods just beyond the event. Something wispy and dead with enormous leathery wings suddenly fluttered across the stage, accompanied by the stink of sulfur.

Master Dorje waved for the King and Queen to exit immediately and follow him to safety. The fight of good against evil had begun.

CHAPTER 13:

VAMPIRES AND DEMONS AND REPTILES. OY VEY.

*"Never open the door to a lesser evil, for other and greater
ones invariably slink in after it."*

—Baltasar Gracian, Spanish warlock and early Nazi

The scientists and soldiers of Army ET Command watched the monitors as the crowd ran for cover and immediately went into action. General Scott hit the red-alarm button on the computer console and a piercing, high-pitched siren went off three times, blasting through the overhead speakers throughout the park.

It was somewhat unnecessary, though, since some of the invading horde had to pass through the squads of Army Rangers who'd been stationed around the perimeter of the compound. Those who made it through were pursued by soldiers who carried machine guns and, at Dorje's insistence, crossbows with silver stakes.

Scott peered at the carnage unfolding on the screens.

It was time to execute the Hallucination Gambit.

People were only just adapting to the idea there were aliens and slumbering Starseeds on this planet. It had been decided, on advice from the Arcturians, that concepts such as vampires, ghosts, and de-

mons—commonly held to be the stuff of fiction and reality show television—would prove too much to handle. And while the ICD codes
covered being struck by a duck and hit by a spaceship, supernatural
creatures had yet to be addressed. The debate had been raging for years
among federal agencies.

But the cat—or more accurately, the werecat—was out of the bag,
and a justification for the appearance of such beings had to be applied.
The General grabbed the microphone and spoke in a stern but calm,
reassuring voice, the same voice his father had used right before he'd
moved to Spain with Aunt Cassie.

"Attention ladies and gentlemen...and everyone else within earshot. We are experiencing technical difficulties, and our 3-D projectors
are on the fritz. The *illusion* of strange creatures flying around the festival grounds is not real. There is nothing to be afraid of."

The chaos slowed but not enough.

"The magic mushrooms you took when entering the park, combined with the, ah, inadvertent broadcast of *The Walking Weird*, season
fifty-seven, is giving the *illusion* that ghostly demons are breaching the
perimeter. There is nothing to worry about. Please enjoy the experience,
and feel free to buy a zombie doll in the gift shop. You'll want a souvenir of this wondrous experience for you and your grandchildren. The
technical snafu will be under control shortly, and performances will
begin on every stage. Let's get back to the music!"

The Army scientists watched the monitors. *Would this plan really work?*
Yes.

Two things occurred simultaneously.

People started to calm down, and laughter and cheers broke
out among the crowd, along with conversations heard through the
hidden high-tech microphones strategically located throughout the
festival grounds.

"Wow, what a trip!" said a ninety-year-old hippie wearing a red
bandanna, tie-dyed Grateful Dead tee-shirt, and blue bell bottom pants.
"I thought the acid I dropped in the sixties was good, but then, I only
saw people's faces melt into rainbow colored wax. This..." As barbed
demons zoomed overhead and scurried past, he stared with wonder.
"This is so much cooler. Kudos to the organizers of this festival and
whoever grew those 'shrooms!"

His ninety-two-year-old hippie wife, wearing a flower-power tee-shirt and red designer bell bottoms, turned to him.

"Yeah, Sidney…this stuff's cooler than the Kool-Aid we used to spike the water fountains with at school." As a number of demons converged on the couple, all the two did was laugh and dance.

"So far, so good," Morales said. "These people are morons."

Fortunately for them all, many of the people attending the festival belonged to the Lotus Eater culture—a society where everyone just got high all the time on booze, pills, opioids, nicotine, caffeine, and pot, which had become legal in all U.S. states by 2035. Except for Indiana, where the state militia—a former vice-president and his wife, who'd allowed him to fight—had declared war on the federal government.

The second thing that occurred was that, faced with victims who didn't believe they existed, many of the vampires, zombies, and demons didn't know what to do. They were used to prey that fled, not prey that *laughed*.

There was another couple in their seventies—a ruggedly handsome man dressed in a dark blue and white sailor's uniform with a red bandana around his neck with a partner dressed in an Ermenegildo Zegna Bespoke tailored blue suit with a white shirt, Satya Paul design studio Suashish burgundy tie, and Louis Vuitton brown-laced shoes. Demons and ghosts be damned—heads turned when these two humans passed by.

As one of the fiends approached, trying to scare them before feeding on their fear, souls, and spleens, the sailor *mocked* it.

"Oh, you're soooo scary, Mr. Demon man. Who dresses you? Your mama haunt a garage sale of the damned? I mean, no one I know would be caught *dead* in the rags you're wearing."

"It's so sad," his partner pitched in. "Run along and join *Cirque du Tasteless* with that clown uniform. You'll be a big hit!"

The demon, who had once sat on the throne of Angkor Wat and terrorized countless humans throughout the 1100s, stopped short, its black-pit eyes wide, then scrambled away as quickly as it could, and the two men broke out in laughter. Elsewhere on the grounds, vampires abandoned their intended victims and began assaulting the concession stands for their Slim Jims.

Damn, General Scott thought. *We may need to rewrite the manual for hand-to-hand combat.*

In other parts of the park, however, not everyone was so calm. Some young kids were smoking joints and throwing rocks into the tents, knocking down clothing displays. Others—caught up in the chaos—set fire to the air conditioning units and exploded the cooling systems in some of the tractor trailers, wreaking havoc.

"Look at that," Dr. Morales said. "They're bringing outside drugs. They're bringing crime, they're predators, and some, I assume, are good people. But they're cutting into our concession profits!"

Although many were learning to ride the cosmic waves and show "no resistance" to the unfolding supernatural events, others weren't taking it so well. The extreme nature of the day's events and strong emotional experiences were too much. The drugs and demons were finally getting to some people, who began freaking out.

Once the undead smelled fear in the crowd, that was the signal for vampires and zombies to begin attacking vulnerable humans. Fear would incapacitate them, making them easy prey—a classic page from the Reptilian playbook. Those creatures that weren't already in the festival began emerging from the surrounding woods. The first ones to appear were the zombies. Hordes of brain-hungry marauders suddenly appeared at the left gate, shaking the fence in unison until pieces of it fell to the ground. Others began ripping down the makeshift barriers around the glen, and as several got through, screams began to emerge from nearby picknickers.

Two unsuspecting couples lying on colorful blankets at the perimeter of the festival were stoned and enjoying the music with their eyes closed. When they first heard loud groaning sounds, it didn't immediately dawn on them that they faced imminent danger. As the sounds got louder and the picknickers opened their eyes, horror and disbelief overwhelmed them. A few scant yards away, zombies with blood dripping from their mouths and arms outstretched were closing fast.

Only one woman overcame the paralyzing fear. She screamed and jumped to her feet.

"*Help! Help!*" she cried out. "It's the walking dead! *Help! Help!*"

Army Rangers heard her cries and left their posts on long ropes, running toward the screams and commotion, while Arcturian solders at the further perimeter also heard the call and began to run at full speed toward the crowd of vulnerable bystanders.

"Get down!" one of the Rangers yelled. As the woman fell to the ground, he took the crossbow off his shoulder, planted his feet, and fired at the nearest zombie. It was a clean shot right through the eyeball into the rotting brain. As the zombie shuffled in pain, an Arcturian amazon appeared, jumped in the air with the agility of a martial arts master, and cleanly cut off its head with her sword.

The two men quickly took defensive positions in front of the picknickers, protecting them while—one by one—they took down the undead menace. Within seconds, more Rangers and Arcturian warriors arrived on the scene, rapidly lopping off the heads of the remaining stragglers who got through the perimeter. The picknickers sobbed in relief. One of the men refused to let go of the leg of his Arcturian savior.

• • • •

Following the situation from within the relative safety of the Arcturian spacecraft, Master Dorje watched carefully as the situation unfolded. He turned to the Arcturian royalty.

"My precious Queen and King...clearly, we must employ magick if we are to control the supernatural creatures employed by the Reptilians. Although the Army can handle the zombies for the moment and perhaps even the vampires, there are no traditional weapons Earthlings possess beyond mere distraction that are effective against the demons. Normally, we would not want to display our abilities in public for fear of revealing our actual potential. Once they understand what we can do, the Earth Army will surely want to use it for *other* purposes.

"Yet while the festival attendees have the upper hand, that cannot last, and I ask your permission to make an exception. These people are so stoned they will not be able to differentiate reality from fantasy. Please allow me to use Arcturian magick from the old religion. Though banned because of its power, it *did* subdue some of the Reptilian masters and helped protect many of our people from capture during their escape from Arcturus."

Commander Avorius nodded. "The Earth people are not prepared for the onslaught that inevitably must follow, your excellencies. The demons are just getting warmed up, and the vampires will be hungry. The American sausages will only hold them for so long."

"Can you limit our involvement, or at least shroud it from the military and still protect these people?" the queen asked. Dorje thought for a moment, and then a wry smile appeared deep within his beard.

"I know exactly what we need to do, dear Queen, to fulfill your request." He turned to Avorius and whispered to him. The commander laughed and nodded in agreement. He then turned toward the communications officer of the ship and spoke in a stern and urgent voice, the same voice his father used when he went to the Pelios star system to ensure the Bactricans enter into the Federation.

"Please open up a channel of communication. I want to discuss with General Scott our plan of action." The communications officer immediately hailed General Scott. The screen showed Major Broward and a group of soldiers who were preparing to go into battle with enemies against whom they were powerless.

"General, this is Commander Avorius. Based on the present location of our unwanted visitors, we recommend moving Mr. Dunham and Achmed the dead zombie dummy to the eastern part of the park. Then relocate Mr. Copperfield and his giant disappearing Reptiles to the northern gate and Teller and the man-eating tiger to the western end, where the demons and vampires are starting to congregate.

"Finally, if Mr. Robbins were to move to the southern end of the park where the Greys have gathered, he could pickpocket them and remove any stolen sperm and eggs they've somehow managed to collect during the festival." He paused while, in the command center, the general gave the commands.

Then Avorius continued. "At least five separate adversaries require our immediate attention—the Reptiles, demons, vampires, and Greys— and I'm not *entirely* sure about all the zombies, but I believe some are here from Congress. Primarily those Congressional members responsible for H.R. 9, the Climate Action Now Act that did nothing but reduce EPA regulations. Are the Reptilian electrosonic bracelets working?"

The General checked. "Functioning at peak capacity."

"Excellent," Avorius said. "Commence Operation WHMS. Please turn on the monitors in the *Weinstein Play and Pay Pavilion.*"

"Execute!" the General bellowed. "Operation Pickle Tickle!"

The Army engineers manning the computer consoles flipped several red and black switches while everyone else focused on the series of video monitors in the *Weinstein Play and Pay* tent. The Reptiles' bracelets began to glow and emit subtle pulsed electric shocks, charges immediately transmitted to the amygdala of the Reptilian brains. These caused an immediate shift in the mood. Faces previously reflecting pools of disbelief, aggression, anger, and irritation soon morphed into content, happy expressions.

• • • •

A short-skirted waitress took an order from a well-dressed Reptilian woman sharply dressed in a green Chanel suit with a green and brown Hermes alligator bag draped around her shoulder, along with a green emerald-studded beret stylishly placed in her golden hair.

"I'll have the apple pie a la mode, but only if it'sss made with margarine and GMO grown blueberries," the Reptilian female hissed, all of her "S" sounds prolonged and lingering in the air.

Decades before, the Reptiles had convinced everyone margarine was "fit for a king" and that GMO-grown food was not only good for them but led to healthy brain development. It was true if you were an extraterrestrial immune to GMO's documented effects. Humans, on the other hand, had been forced to deal with increased immune system disorders, cancer, allergies, gluten intolerance, ADHD, kidney and liver disease, and infertility.

The waitress adopted a look of consternation, as she knew the kitchen was running low on this specialty. She used her earbud to check on the availability.

"I'm sorry, ma'am," she said with a look of dismay. "We're all out of GMO blueberries. Would pesticide-laden berries work instead? We have crates of some still available."

"Of courssse," the female responded calmly, a big smile spreading across her face. "Bring on the pesssticides! Can never get enough of those delicious toxic treats. Thank you." She'd turned to the male playing blackjack just beside her. "Kindly remove your left hand from my privates, or I ssshall remove it."

"I'm sssorry," the well-dressed Reptilian male said sibilantly, his pronunciation also sounding snake-like. "I asssumed you wanted me to."

"Why would you ever think that, you worm?" the woman said.

"It'sss what woman want." The male looked confused, as if never before confronted with such a question. "They always seem very satisssfied."

"And if someone was faking pleasure?"

"You don't think I could tell the difference?"

• • • •

The Army engineers looked at one another sheepishly and then turned to the general. He nodded to them and gave the sign to increase the power to the bracelets being worn by the Reptiles. Now everyone in the enormous tent would feel the growing effects.

Soft, sensuous sounds started to emerge from all of the individuals sitting at the tables. It reminded the General of the first time he joined the Navy officers during their extended leave in Amsterdam, where the insides of the 1600s Dutch rooms all began to chirp like a chorus of sex workers singing "Need A Little Sugar in My Bowl." The sounds built to a crescendo reverberating throughout the tent. The non-Reptilians inside looked quite confused as to what was happening.

"Ohh…"

"Ahhh."

"Oh God."

"OOOH. Oh God!"

"Oh, ah!"

Women and men alike started to bang their fists on the gambling tables. The sounds continued to grow louder and louder into a seemingly coordinated screaming across the enclosure.

"*Oh god!*"

The Reptiles had found religion.

Once the commotion died down, one of the few humans in the tent turned to the waitress and exclaimed confidently, "I'll have *two* of whatever they're having."

The waitress just walked away, shaking her head in disbelief.

CHAPTER 14:

ZOMBIE SEASON

Operation Pickle Tickle was a huge success. Everyone wanted to know how to get a hold of the bracelets as they would make great Christmas, Hanukkah, and Kwanza gifts for the person who had everything. Concerned with the demand, Major Broward had already absconded with six boxes of them for his own safekeeping.

Now that a large number of the Reptiles present were under control, as was the remaining zombie menace at the perimeter of the park, the general and Arcturian army had to deal with the remaining threats. Throughout the glen, half a dozen bands had taken the various stages and began to play.

The demons never stood a chance.

On Stage 3, a tribute band was playing "Black Magic Woman." They'd been told to stretch the song out as long as necessary and had confirmed the lead guitarist could bend the same three notes for two hours if needed for the stoned crowd. On Stage 4, the appropriately named Zombies were playing "Time of the Season." All of the people *dressed* as zombies, alongside any real ones who had shown up, were already congregating there. The band was contracted to do up to six encores.

Then, on Stage 5, a Mick Jagger lookalike played *Sympathy for the Devil*. He was ninety-two years old and rocking the stage with his tongue hanging out of his mouth—except it wasn't on purpose. He was, of course, performing with a Keith Richards clone, who looked no different than Richards had in any decade. If anything, his genetic engineering made him look a little *younger.*

"One more thing, General," Dorje said. "For the demons, I'd like to teach you to use a combination of some Earth magick combined with a dash of our Arcturian abilities."

"We have Earth magic?"

"Of course, dear General. Just have a little faith, and we will show you how it all works in the field."

Another tool for battle? The General was intrigued. "Wonderful," he whispered to Major Broward. "This Rumpelstiltskin guy is alright. Let the party begin!"

Operation Taurus began at exactly 04:47 hours EST.

Animal sounds were piped from the loudspeakers at the edge of the grounds, and it was announced over the amps that a special petting zoo was opening in five minutes at the far end of the park.

Major Broward spoke up at 4:49. "Sir, I request permission to lead the team in the Watkins Glens zoo area, sir!"

General Scott turned, surprised and impressed. He had always fancied the major a raging coward.

"Request granted Major. Give 'em hell, boy."

"*Hellboy?*" the Major echoed, confused. "You want me to play movies for them, sir?"

"No, numbn…Major. It's just an expression." The General wondered if Broward had snuck out and taken some of the purple mushrooms.

"Just be careful, Major," Plamorius warned. "You know the Greys can be…*tricky* creatures."

"Sir, yes sir," the Major replied. He immediately left the tent and took a small battalion of men with him. They were ready to do whatever was needed to capture the gnarly little horny creatures.

The General continued with preparations, gathering garlic with silver and wood stakes to use against the vampires. The perimeter of the movie theatre was surrounded and cleared of civilians. Operation Mongo was to begin. The Navy seals were dressed in Mama Mia's delivery shirts and carried in a large number of garlic pizzas. The hope was to flush them out of hiding using the pungent pies. The effects weren't limited to the undead, however.

"I would like a pizza with everything on it," Dr. Correro said. "And if they could throw in some stuffed cheesy bread with spinach and feta, that would be great."

No one paid him any mind. After all, everyone knew it was another chain that was famed for stuffed cheesy bread sticks with bacon and jalapeno.

"Let's get hoppin' folks," the General exclaimed. "We have a mission that must succeed. The fate of the world depends on it."

He and his entire command knew that hungry vampires wouldn't stop at just a few blood-sucking adventures at the festival. Once they got a taste of human blood, it would incite their insatiable thirst for more, unleashing a hemophiliac nightmare of grandiose proportions. Epidemics of blood-sucking hermaphrodite Asian bush ticks, *Haemophilus longicornus*, had already invaded the U.S. decades before, leading to regular reports on the evening news with images of people and moose at death's doorstep, shriveled up, dehydrated, exsanguinated chimeras of their former selves.

The ticks and vampires were in global competition.

As for the zombie invaders, they were at the greatest disadvantage, as the 2011 Department of Defense Counter Zombie Dominance measures, dubbed CONPLAN 8888, would finally be put to the test. It was initially called CONPLAN 666, but the Generals felt that would be too confusing for the demonologists.

CONPLAN 8888 had been carefully designed by top military U.S. strategists, as described by a Pentagon spokesperson. It had been met with resistance, however, from the older generals, largely because the only proof of zombies to date had been the threat of "chicken zombies" arising from that unusual incident at the Sanders poultry factory in Petaluma, California. In 2006, the Colonel who ran the company decided to euthanize the chickens by putting them all in the factory garage with the door closed and turning on the engines of all the delivery trucks. It appeared to be effective until the carbon monoxide alarms went off, summoning the fire department. They arrived on the scene just in time to witness haunted hens crawling out the piles of their slaughtered fowl sisters.

Although CONPLAN 8888 was initially based on George Romeo films and the prescient writings of a famous comedian's son, it was nevertheless a carefully-laid-out military strategy thoughtfully divided into four parts. First, a defensive strategy to protect the human race from mind-munching marauders. Second, methods to eradicate the hordes of the walking dead. Third, recommendations on how to restore stability to war-torn economies. Fourth, plans on how to capitalize on the invasion and create a new series for streaming television.

For almost thirty years, the U.S. Army had been jonesing to test it all out. Not to be outdone, the Centers for Disease Control created their own Zombie Preparedness Manual, which they posted to the CDC.gov website.[1] It contained blogs, study guides, classroom exercises for educators, special undead posters, which all the CDC and Army brass had hanging in their offices, as well as packets of "Zombie brain food" to be used only in an emergency. Rumor had it these were the chicken's brains from the Petaluma farm incident.

There was still no master plan for dealing with epidemics of Lyme disease and emerging tick-borne infections worsening every year with global warming, but at least someone had carefully planned for the eventuality of zombie attacks.

Although the zombies inside the park had been docile so far, the Army knew their initial strategy to pacify the undead with music would only work for so long, so anyone going through security who had unexplained breaks in the skin, strange staccato movements, and visible bleeding around their nose or mouth was given a free packet of Petaluma chicken brains. That would keep them happy, at least for a while, but they'd still need to be subdued and ultimately eliminated in a manner that would not raise too much suspicion from the crowd.

The General asked his communications tech to get the Arcturian mothership back on the line.

"This is General Scott again," he said. "I'd like to commence Operations Mop Up and Scheming Demon. We've sent a convoy of our men and women to music stages three, four, and five—where our targets are located. They have begun to congregate there, as you had predicted, Master Dorje. Please meet us and bring the Queen's pets, as we had discussed."

Dorje turned to the Queen. "Your Royal Highness, would it be alright if Commander Avorius and I took Amori and Audri out for a stroll? I think they might like a little fresh air and…some fun."

---

1   For more information, please see: https://www.cdc.gov/cpr/zombie/index.htm.

"Of course, Master Dorje," she said, understanding his full intentions. "Just make sure they don't get into too much trouble."

Avorius scooped up Amori and Dorje picked up Audri. The pets immediately snuggled in their arms, and then the Arcturians opened the spacecraft door and proceeded past the force field down the stairs. The Queen's pets wiggled their tentacles in delight and anticipation of potential and impending mayhem.

A hundred Arcturian troops had gathered outside, with swords drawn. They knew from carefully studying Earth movies that the only way to kill a zombie was to lop off its head and destroy the brains but that such an act might create too much suspicion done publicly, even among super-stoned humans of inferior intelligence. Decapitation was, therefore, the last resort and if employed, had to be done discretely, as it was in the woods at the perimeter of the park.

Dorje, Avorius, and the troops joined General Scott and the Earth soldiers and proceeded toward the music stages located at the eastern end of the glen. Music could be heard from a distance as they approached. Cheers, clapping, and screams of delight were coming from the crowd so loud it almost drowned out the beginning of a song. As they got closer, a guitar wailed as the Latin percussion section, drummers, bass, and synthesizer all rocked in perfect unison to "Black Magic Woman."

The Earth troops and their Arcturian counterparts inspected the field for any demons or devils. They would recognize them by their jagged forms, and demons loved to brag about their way of life. So far, however, no such dead giveaway came from the hordes.

Then an unforeseen difficulty arose.

The soldiers—Terran and Arcturian—found they couldn't resist the hypnotic effect of the music. They began to dance in place and sway in unison, while the Atmops began wiggling their arms in harmony with the song's sweet, sweet rhythm.

By dint of extreme effort, Dorje resisted the effects of the song and watched for any signs of magic. Nothing was out of order at Stage 3 and, although the soldiers protested leaving before the end of the song, the General instructed them to move over to Stage 4 where the musicians were just beginning to play "Time of the Season."

There the search bore fruit.

Although the musical group wasn't made up of brain-eating marauders and looked like normal British humans in black suits, white
shirts, and black ties, the *genuine* walking dead didn't know that. They
got it into what remained of their surviving neurons that the coordina-
tors of the music festival had put on a show in their honor. This impression was enhanced by the fact that most of the audience were dressed
up as zombies—it was difficult to tell the humans from the real thing.

This was fortunate for the humans disguised as zombies among the
zombies watching The Zombies. They wouldn't erupt in panic until the
intruders got hungrier and started to feed on living human flesh.

The stage began to rock to "Time of the Season," cheering when
they heard the lead singer belt out that iconic word: high.

Zombies turned to one another, making slow gnawing sounds.

Then the audience all raised their hands in unison, and those with
flesh falling off were identified as certified targets. Nevertheless, the
military hung back on the periphery. General Scott sent some of his
soldiers to make additional preparations. During the musical interlude
and before the group sang the next verse, Dorje and Avorius put Audri
and Amori on the ground.

"Okay, guys. You know what to do," Dorje said. "Treats are coming. All you have to do is smell out the zombies. They're the ones with
putrid flesh and foul-smelling breath. Form a conga line and lead them
to the edge of the park. We're going to have a big party with delectable
desserts. Let's go!"

The Atmops appreciated fine food and loved nothing more than a
good time. Once free, their tentacles began to swing in the air as they
used their suckers to smell their prey. One by one, they enchanted
and hypnotized the walking dead in the crowd, who started to form
a line. More than once, the *faux* zombies tried to join them, but they
were rebuffed—something that barely registered in their chemically
enhanced condition.

The song continued, along with the swaying, as Audri and Amori
succeeded in getting the walking dead to form a conga line moving toward the edge of the park. The scene resembled a poorly-choreographed
sequel to the "Thriller" music video.

As the zombies moved away from the stage, they approached pic-
nic tables covered with red- and white-checkered cloths and smelled

calf brains laid out in beautiful displays on gold and silver platters. They were also enticed with veal sweetbreads, prion laden human brains, sheep and goat brains with scrapies, plus the brains of cows that had recently gotten through FDA screening after they died from bovine spongiform encephalopathy. This had been a problem since the entire meat industry was deregulated back in 2020, leading to an increase in BSE dementia.

Bad for humans but delicious for zombies.

The undead started to run for the table and clustered there, eating the delicacies. As they did, the Arcturian army approached from behind and lopped off their heads. So intent were the creatures on gorging themselves, they didn't notice as, one by one, their fellow zombies no longer had mouths with which to eat. Even then they moved around awkwardly, arms flailing, looking more like the zombie chickens from Petaluma until finally, amid cheers from the Army and Arcturian troops, they all dropped to the ground.

Operation Mop Up was another notable success.

Given the crucial role Amori and Audri had played in the military endeavor, Avorius pulled out bars of organic dark chocolate from Belgium—one of the few no longer laced with high levels of lead—and broke off pieces for the pets. When he picked them up again, they were purring with contentment.

It was time to put the next and final intelligence operations into play.

CHAPTER 15:

SCHEMING DEMONS

"It is better to conquer yourself than to win a thousand battles. Then the victory is yours. It cannot be taken from you, not by angels or by demons, heaven or hell..."

—Prince Siddhartha, addressing the demon Mara, who unsuccessfully tried to set him up with his incredibly sexy daughter, Desiree

As the first zombie was being decapitated, Master Dorje had already moved on with a U.S. Rangers special ops team and was arriving at Stage 5, where the final song was scheduled to begin.

In front of the stage, a sea of human bodies swayed back of forth with hundreds of people cheering. They held up lights, waiting for the music to begin again. The crowd had just been treated to several rock classics from "Start Me Up" to the celestial music classic "2,000 Light Years from Home," and they were pumped. This was a huge hit. This music was a radical musical experiment for the Stones and of course appropriate for the Intergalactic Woodstock music fest, but what the band didn't realize at the time was that this song held a particularly powerful synchronicity for certain alien Starseeds in the crowd.

The star system and planets associated with the constellation Cygnus were discovered—thanks to Einstein's work on relativity—to be exactly two thousand light-years from Earth. The ground-breaking astrophysical data and discovery of the planet Kepler-76 B with a type-F star had been reported earlier in the prestigious scientific UK journal, *The Daily Mail*.

Some of the Starseeds from this constellation were in the crowd, and even they couldn't figure out why they were all laughing and weeping hysterically during the song. Everyone around them thought they'd just dropped some bad acid laced with MDMA, or ecstasy. They calmed somewhat as the lights dimmed.

The lights went up again as the group took their positions on the stage for the next song. Roaring cheers of delight emerged from the crowd. It was unclear if the crowd was cheering because of the incredible music or because some of the old rockers were, shockingly, still alive and kicking. The lead singer's silver-grey wispy hair was down to his shoulders while the percussionists appeared from a distance to have their drum sticks glued to their hands, giving them genuine "Sticky Fingers." The other singer, also the guitarist, had features that looked like rivers of the Grand Canyon had worn away the first six layers of his dermis. In other words, his clone appeared to be unchanged.

The large projector screen in back of the stage lit up with a large picture of the devil standing in a mass of flames. The lead singer hobbled to the microphone.

"To all of our fans," he began, "dead and alive, holy or sinners… we're dedicating this last one to you, as well as to my good friend Vlad Putin. We met when I stayed in Trump Towers in St. Petersburg. After a show there, we had dinner, and he told me of his love of our music and how he firmly supported the American way of life and our political process. In his and your honor, get ready to rock!"

The crowd erupted in cheers. Meanwhile, appearing seemingly out of nowhere, demons began materializing from the fourth dimension, lining up to get seats in the front row. Large terrifying forms with red, smoking horned heads were followed by demons with pitch-black faces, rotting lips, and curled, sharp teeth, followed by winged bulls, pitch-black ravens, and snakelike demons with thin, scaly faces and revolving eyes. It was like a sitting family photo from Johann Weyer's *Pseudo-*

monarchia Daemonum. They initially appeared to behave themselves and even sat in alphabetical order in the first row: Aamon, Apollyon, Abezethibou, Abraxas, Abyzou, Adrammelech, Aeshma and Agaliarept.

The usher had to move Baal to the second row, as he hadn't learned to read English yet—only Aramaic. Then came Babi Ngepet, Bakasura, Baku, Balam, Balberith, Bali Raj, and finally Banshee, who had reached demonic fame when the American Indians adopted him because of his ability to scare the hell out of white settlers around the campfire in the middle of the night. As everyone settled in, some of the damned used their breath to roast marshmallows on sticks; others popped corn on their heads. The last demon to arrive wasn't quite as docile as the others.

"I am Vinz, Vinz Clortho, Keymaster of Gozer. Volguus Zildrohar, Lord of the Sebouillia," he proclaimed in a booming voice. This just confused the usher, who thought it had to be a joke.

"I don't give a Satanic shit," the man said. "Go sit in row G or we'll have to eject you from the concert." Volguus growled but did as he was told, pushing several demons out of the way. He found a fiend in his seat who refused to move and just ate him.

The band began the song, and the classic percussion started to play. Bongos and high hats began to hit the drums in rhythm followed by the classic bass line and intermittent piano chords. *"Please allow me to introduce myself..."* The demons in the first few rows started to roar, yelling obscenities.

"Fork Faith!"

"Long live disbelief!"

After all, they had reputations to uphold.

The General turned. "Okay, Dorje. You're on. Let's see what you got. Subdue those commie creatures from hell!"

Dorje nodded gravely and turned to the rest of the group. He asked Commander Avorius and his troops to form a semicircle around him. The Arcturian sorcerer clamped his eyes shut, concentrated, and lifted up his arms, drawing a circle of magical protection in the air around the group. Then he began chanting in a firm and deep voice:

Forma Circulus De Lux In Nomine Deus.

Non Est Ergo Nothi Evadere Et Protege Nos!

A ring of bright white fire formed around them, blazing several feet in the air. It looked hot, yet no heat emanated from its flames. Those rangers who touched the fire quickly jerked back their hands, for it was cold as ice.

In nomine Patris, et filii et spiritui sancto,

Vincere daemones ex inferno

The wizard paused to see if the demons were paying any attention at all. So far, so good—they were not. There was no arousal of suspicion. A couple glanced back, but likely just thought it was a Catholic mass being held on the grounds in honor of their attending the event.

Just to be sure, however, he gestured for the Army command to hold up signs they had prepared for the operation.

Welcome Demons!

You Rock!

Humans Drool.

Demons Rule!

Dorje continued. The area around them went dark, but everyone was wrapped up in the music and took little notice.

Dico vobis, magnus amicus et protector. Tueri boni ex hac tellure, a daemonum vires nunc affligere eos. Michael, Michael, Michael.

No one in Army command understood the words Dorje was saying, as they sounded like Latin chants. They did, however, recognize the name of Michael. Dorje turned toward the sky, put his hands together, and called out the name again with a strong, clear voice. His hands began to wave again, forming a second magical circle in the sky, and he began to concentrate on visualizing a crack opening up between the worlds.

Then he shouted with all of his might:

Vetus amicus Michael.

Nos postulo vos. Nunc age!

The sky opened, clouds parting in an unnatural swirl as light rays gashed down through the darkness to form a shimmering halo of light directly above the crowd. Sparks ruptured from the center and Archangel Michael appeared, blazing in a glorious blue-purple fire. Several archangels followed behind him including Metatron, Gabriel, Uriel, Raphael, Selaphiel, and Sandalphon, the angel who assures victory through crisis. Behind them came a swarm of angelic protectors.

Trumpets and horns accompanied the arrival, along with a choir of angelic voices emerging from the halo, singing in perfect harmony with the Stones. Some mesmerized and stoned members of the crowd looked up and swore they heard the newcomers singing "You *Can* Always Get What You Want."

Master Dorje continued in English.

"Michael, great protector and friend, you who have the power to subdue evil and demonic forces, thank you for appearing. I implore you in the name of goodness, love, and compassion. As I open a crack between the worlds, please subdue these demons of darkness and send them back to the fourth dimension. I will hold open a dimensional doorway for you to put these creatures back where they belong. Michael, Michael, Michael, may it be done. Thank you for your assistance, great friend!"

Dorje expected the humans to assume the archangels were a spiritual hoax through which the masses could believe in a greater good and to give soldiers comfort on the battlefield. After all, Michael was the patron saint of the military and those who were ill on Earth.

The truth of the matter was that archangels were present on all levels of dimensional realities. When the heavens, the Earth, and all worlds throughout the multiverses were created, archangels were assigned as messengers to communicate between the denser physical dimensions and less dense spiritual ones, so divine intervention could intercede when necessary. The key, which Dorje intimately understood, was not praying in a conceptual, dualistic mind consciousness and simply uttering some "magical words" from a mystical book or chanting "sacred" words from a religious text.

That level of consciousness limited what was possible. What was *necessary* was entering the non-conceptual meditative space where limitless possibilities exist and then calling the divine with a prayer directed unselfishly toward the greater good and benefit for others, while resting in a place of heartfelt deep compassion.

This could recreate reality.

Dorje finished his words and began another series of gestures. A new opening appeared in the air above them as the archangels hovered near the front of the stage, one after another. Michael remained overhead, anticipating the battle that was to unfold. Each angel picked a demon as their target, ready to strike when the time was right. Once they were sent back to the hell realm from which they had come, Dorje would close the doorway between the worlds.

As Mick continued to sing, the audience grew wilder than ever, stunned by the coolest 3D projection ever produced. Not everyone, however, was enthralled with the performance. Some of the crowd sitting near the demons felt a paralyzing fear come over them as they noticed that there was an unusual heat arising from the "illusory" supernatural gathering.

That fear quickly intensified as some of the flaming marshmallows and popcorn coming off the demons' heads accidently fell on them, burning their skin and setting fire to their clothing. Near the stage, several attendees shrieked in pain and dropped to the ground rolling as their cotton and linen shirts caught fire. The putrid smell of burning flesh filled the air. Bystanders sitting next to them immediately jumped up to get out of the way and screamed, running from their seats.

"They're real! *They're real!*" one young woman cried. "Save yourselves! The demons have come to take us to hell! *We're doomed!*"

General Scott, observing the situation from the perimeter, knew they had to act *fast* before they had a massive lawsuit on their hands. As he mulled over plausible deniability, he turned to Dorje.

"We're all going to be drowning in boiling water, Dorje, if you don't act now. Whatever trick you've got up your sleeve, you better do it fast!"

Dorje nodded and looked up at Michael and his legion of angelic protectors.

"Michael, Michael, Michael. The time is now for you to act, great friend. We implore you in the name of love and compassion. Protect these humans and Starseeds from the malignant forces of darkness!"

Michael smiled, and Gabriel's horn swiftly sounded the battle cry. It was time to send the demons back to their hell realms. The angels immediately flew to the front of the stage and locked their arms around the slick, thorny demon bodies, lifting them into the sky and into the vortex between the worlds.

The audience roared with delight with each and every flight of an angel disappearing through the hole in the sky. Thousands now sang along to the "Ooo, who" in harmony with the band. Each time a demon went through the doorway, they sang "*Oooh*" even louder.

The only exception was a lone person in the back who was clearly disturbed and yelling in a loud voice to their friend. "She's not my girlfriend," he protested. "I just met her and find her interesting because she sleeps above her covers. *Four feet* above her covers! How the hell was I supposed to know she was possessed? I just thought, hey, she drools in her sleep and has some sharp claws."

People around him rolled their eyes at the Ghostbusters reference and sang louder to drown him out.

"Ooo, who...ooo, who."

The loudest chanting, however, came when Michael himself swooped down and subdued Volguus, who had remained sitting and stunned in the seventh row. Volguus was angry—not just because he was missing the rest of the show, but because he felt unjustly treated.

"It's profiling," the demon raged. "I'm calling my lawyer!"

Michael grinned and turned to Master Dorje. "Next time he will think twice before bothering you all." He leaned into Volguus and—in perfect harmony with the last verse of the song—said to him, "Hey Volguus, what's my name? Tell me, baby, what's my name. Tell me, sweetie, what's my name?"

The archangel then flew off into the sky with the demon wriggling in his arms and waved to everyone as he disappeared. The instant he did, Dorje closed the hole between the dimensions and there was silence.

The audience went wild.

The applause reached a crescendo never before heard at a concert. It was louder even than the event in Cuba when they played before five hundred thousand people smoking what everyone thought were Montecristo No. 2 cigars, although the odor wafting through the air was a bit skunkier and more pungent.

Scott and his command team sighed a relief as the battle ended. As one, they turned and stared at Dorje with awe.

Could he make elephants and buildings disappear? the general wondered. *Could he spend three days entombed inside six tons of ice or push pens through his hands without even a mark? Could he shackle himself to the side of a burning car filled with explosives and walk away unscathed?* If so, he'd be a big hit at a USO show—and a formidable weapon against China and Russia in the game of world domination. *The military applications could be wonderful.*

"Thank you," he said aloud. "We are in your debt." He forgot that Mystos could read minds.

"Save it, General," Master Dorje warned. "No debt here. It's a cash and carry universe, my friend, and the battle for Earth is only getting started."

CHAPTER 16:

OPERATION TAURUS

"The chief cause of failure and unhappiness is trading what we want most for what we want in the moment."

—Bertrand Russell, October 30, 1929, after losing his shirt in a bet that he could mathematically predict when the next stock market crash would take place

Weeks before the battle, the U.S. Army had worked closely with the Arcturians to choose the most appropriate names for their secret plans. The naming of an event, everyone agreed, was known to influence the outcome, with many examples in world history.

Operation Pillow Pants, for example, was a military disaster for the allies during World War II after soldiers jumped out of planes over Normandy with newly designed high-tech pants containing inflatable pillows designed to cushion their fall.

The Dingle Campaign for sobriety was similarly a complete and utter failure after attempting to take alcoholics from around the world to a sober living house located near Dingle Bay in Ireland's southwest. The area was home to more pubs than Carter had little pills.

Other examples include the Charge of the Light Brigade, which took place during the Crimean War in 1854 when British soldiers were told to go "half a league, half a league, half a league onwards." A British officer misinterpreted the order from his superiors and went one league further than was necessary, which led to a suicidal charge against the Russians.

Thus, for the operation against the Greys, "Operation Taurus" was selected from among several choices. "Operation Cow" was deemed too confusing for Army astrophysicists, as a cosmic flare called the "Cow" had recently revealed a new way that stars die.

Several generals—all male—also considered "Tittypalooza" because of the penchant the Greys had for cows, but the #MeToo movement was still a thing in 2035, and top female brass strongly objected. In turn, they suggested calling the strategy "Operation Limp Dick," named after General Dick Diddle, who had tried unsuccessfully to use his rank and power to have his way with multiple female subordinates. This name, too, went over like a pork chop at a Kosher wedding.

After more deliberation, "Operation Taurus" was selected.

Once the demon threat had been subdued, Commander Avorius radioed the mothership. Queen Dawn and King Antwar had watched it all on the monitors and were pleased to see Dorje had limited his magical displays to *only* opening up a doorway between the astral dimensions without letting the Earthlings see the full range of his powers.

The Arcturians had meticulously studied the history of military forces on Earth and knew that many had dabbled in developing such psychic capabilities to gain advantages in battle. The best known were the search by the Templars for the Holy Grail and the Nazi's quest for the Ark of the Covenant. Fortunately, the Nazis never discovered the truth behind the Ark, the source of its power, or the secret to a good corned beef sandwich.

Thus, the Arcturians well understood that magick had to be kept pure and only used for the highest good. Should it be mastered by the wrong hands, the results could be catastrophic. The first step in even *considering* sharing such information with these humans rested first in the Earthlings' ability to defeat and appreciate the Greys.

"We are very proud of the work you've performed thus far today," the Queen told the American command team. "Be cautious, however, concerning the Greys. Although they are less-evolved Arcturians, they can still be quite challenging and are devious tricksters. During the centuries of suffering they endured at the hands of their Reptilian masters, they've traveled from galaxy to galaxy, abducting life forms to genetically manipulate their own DNA…and perhaps regain what was lost. They intuitively understand that they lack the wisdom of the heart and cannot ever be complete until both sides of their brains are in synchronistic coherence.

"Unfortunately, the Greys have not yet succeeded, and so they lack the moral compass to understand right from wrong. That left-brain thinking, combined with self-survival Reptilian instincts, mixed with toxic testosterone, create a recipe for disaster.

"Any action they take could lead to destruction and the ecocide of entire planetary systems. If you wish to succeed in changing the dire direction of your planet, your rules of engagement will still apply, but you must intimately know your enemy and what they are capable of—this is essential in the art of war."

General Scott spoke up. "Your highness, thank you for providing insight into our enemy and understanding what we may face *before* we enter into battle. I tried reading Sun Tzu once, and *The Art of War* didn't make much sense. In particular, his basic dictum that 'winning without fighting is best.' How can we accomplish such a deed?"

"We have learned from our experience," the Queen replied, "that the ultimate achievement is to use knowledge and strategy to *avoid* conflict whenever possible. Your fellow Earthman Sun Tzu knew this when he laid out the tactics of winning without fighting and accomplishing the most by doing the least.

"Some of the most highly evolved of our species—ourselves included—used this strategy to escape conflict by moving into the fifth and sixth dimensions. From there, we had to watch our own people suffer at the hands of their captors, and this caused us great pain. The Arcturians are a peace-loving culture and had never before experienced war and the heartbreak associated with it. We now understand that choice is no longer an option. We must be prepared to show resistance and be ruthless—but not in the sense your culture normally understands.

"True ruthlessness," she continued, "is based on more than slaying our enemies. Rather, we must turn ruthlessness *inward* and use it to cut through the ultimate meaninglessness of greed, the attachment to material possessions that underlies most aggression. Entering into battle without understanding this ultimate truth will lead to inferior results."

The General nodded. He had served as a commissioned officer in the armed forces for most of his life, as did his father and grandfather and great-grandfather before him. His great grandfather, Major Phoebus Scott, fought in WWI as part of the American Expeditionary Forces that worked closely with the French and Buffalo soldiers. He received the coveted French *Croix de Guerre* medal yet often spoke of the horrors of that conflict. Despite his legacy, General Scott believed war always should be the last choice and that diplomacy and skill were an officer's best friend.

"Loyal men and women of the U.S. military," the general said, turning to his command staff, "you've served your country well. Over and over again, you've put your lives at risk in battle for the greater good. Today, right now, we need to win this battle to ensure freedom for our people. However, we must try and avoid direct conflict, as per the wise words of our intergalactic friends. We are therefore going to put into action Operation Taurus. You've all been briefed and have studied the battle strategies. Please take up your positions at the edge of the petting zoo on the western side of the glen and wait for my signal."

Then the General got on the festival-wide channel which was piped over the JBL loudspeakers throughout the grounds.

"Ladies and gentlemen! Starseeds…and 'old friends'…the Woodstock petting zoo is about to open. There will be hundreds of GMO sheep, cows, and pigs for all your heavy petting needs. In addition, prizes will be given for the best animals in their classes. Please proceed now to the western side of the park to meet some of the finest animals on the planet. There you'll also find the newest styles of lambie jammies!"

"Lambie jammies" were a ploy designed well before the festival. There were people with nothing better to do than sit at a loom and spin colorful pajamas for their sheep, intent on keeping them warm after they'd been sheared. The Army had figured out how to weaponize this absurd behavior. The pull of seeing the latest in animal fashion would be too much for the Greys to resist.

Additionally, the extraterrestrials loved their good food—Krispy Kreme triple cheeseburgers, Australian battered potatoes with sour cream topped with cheese and bacon, fried watermelon, deep-fried turkey legs, deep-fried funnel cakes with powdered sugar, and deep-fried coffee in a sweet pastry dough topped with sugar and fresh whipped cream. These made the treats at most county fairs pale in comparison.

It was a solid plan that would leave most with diarrhea...or worse. Articles in publications like the *British Medical Journal* claimed that eating fried food was tied to increased risk for cardiovascular death, yet everyone knew the Brits *primarily* ate fried fish and chips. Given the contamination of chemicals that made its way into the fish in the Thames every day, including anti-depressants and seventy thousand lines of cocaine, everyone in the UK *needed* their "sole food" to get their daily dose of dopamine.

What the hell, no one lived forever, General Scott mused to himself.

The general put down the microphone.

"That should get them to come," he said with a grin.

• • • •

"Did they say *petting zoo?*"

"Yes!" his companion said gleefully. "This far exceeds the Intergalactic Species Exhibition we attended on the planet Lyra. All they had were miniature cows, dogs, and sheep. When I went to dissect them, I could barely find the fallopian tubes. Oh, the ecstasy of getting my hands on a soft, full-sized mammalian mammary while I steal a few ripe ovaries and eggs."

The two Greys moved quickly toward the western gate.

• • • •

The Arcturian forces led by Master Dorje joined the Army rangers in pulling back from Stage 5, heading to the western quadrant where the fake zoo had been fabricated. Disguised men and women manned the many food booths here, where concessions awaiting the greys contained treats spiked with sedatives. The surreptitious military personnel all wore white chef's uniforms and tall white hats with a CIA emblem on them. The symbol was for the Culinary Institute of America, a well-established and respected gourmet school in Hyde Park, NY.

A 4-H clubhouse was also set up on the grounds. The motto of the organization, "head, heart, hands and health," was replaced by a sign which identified "the 4-H Club: Hijacked Heifer Hookups Here." All the more likely to entice the horny beasts.

A few younger soldiers in blue dungaree overalls and red-and-white-checkered shirts manned the pens where the animals were located. They resembled typical young agricultural enthusiasts from Dogpatch, USA—except for the bulging tranquilizer guns hidden in their pants.

In case anesthetics didn't work, one of the pens held Army privates dressed in cow costumes—two per disguise. The front section had a microphone in the mouth which would make pleasurable *mooing* sounds, while the back section boasted lifelike large rubber teats filled with a sleeping formula the Army affectionately called "coma compound," a secret mixture of seven trademarked medications mixed in 150 proof vodka. The instant the thirsty Greys tried something frisky, it was *pow*—out like a light.

There was a long and well-documented history of the Greys stealing cows and other farm animals, as compiled in four volumes by J.P.P. Ramsteadder: *How to Lift Cows and Influence People, My Udder Mother, Ruminations on Rumens and Rumps*, and most notably, *Advanced CRISPR Techniques Fore Udder Horny Aliens*. These meticulously describe the first recorded cow tipping and bovine abduction in Babylon, where a poor Mesopotamian farmer watched a large golden calf mysteriously disappear into the sky, thereby resulting in the worshiping of ungulates.

CHAPTER 17:

MOO JUICE

Just as the Arcturians and rangers arrived on the scene to take up their positions in the woods adjacent to the zoo, the first pair of Greys arrived. They were wearing Mickey Mouse ears and holding a volley of colorful balloons, strolling alongside a pair of unsuspecting hippies. The Greys had studied human behavior and believed their disguise would be an effective ploy.

It was a futile attempt.

No human being in their right minds looking to properly assimilate into the human race would buy Mickey Mouse ears and actually wear them in public. Unless they'd stayed at Animal Kingdom Villas and taken advantage of the free dining offer. Those meals were expensive, and the deal was that the only ones who got to eat were the ones wearing the mouse ears. Many forgot to take them off before going through the long lines in the Orlando airport.

As the Greys strolled alongside the hippie couple, the hippie woman noticed them.

"Oh, hello little ones. Are you lost? Did you get separated from your parents?"

The Greys were confused. Was their disguise that effective? They were considered good-looking specimens for their race, but to be mistaken for humans was something new. Perhaps these humans thought they were disfigured midgets who overdosed on colloidal silver to address their Lyme disease and subsequently suffered from argyria?

They decided to play along.

"Yes, I can't find my mommy and daddy," the first said. "I think they are at the petting zoo feeding the cows. Can you take us there?"

"Oh, kind sir and madam," the second added. "We are lost. If we don't suck on some healthy cow milk soon, I fear we may shrivel up and die."

The hippies were confused.

Everyone in 2035 knew natural breast milk had been tainted with more than fifty toxic chemicals regardless of species. Despite a brief return in popularity in the early 21st century, it was no longer was a preferred source of nutrition.

In the 1980s, during an Environmental Protection Agency investigation of California women, it was found that many lived near farms spraying atrazine, chlorpyrifos, and glyphosate. Other chemicals—including flame retardants like PBDE—had been turning up in women's breast milk across the US for decades, contributing to the gradual decline in humanity's intellectual and reproductive capacity.

As the chemical exposure only got worse over the decades to follow, the EPA decided it would be best to create an educational campaign touting the benefits of pesticides, chlorpyrifos, and PBDE. Billboards and commercials could regularly be seen across the country:

Protect your child and show them that you love them!

Eat food with chemicals and PBDE,
Your baby will be flame resistant
and invulnerable to voracious insects!

For some reason, not everyone believed the PR. In retrospect, it turned out that Dr. Benjamin Spock's medical textbooks from years earlier had been correct. It was dangerous to breastfeed.

Despite the warnings, it appeared as if no one cared, especially the hippies who were high on pot, purple mushrooms, and the excitement of being at a Woodstock festival again for the first time in thirty-plus years.

"Yes, of course, children," the hippie woman said. "We'd be delighted." Each hippie took one of the Greys by the hand and happily strolled off toward the animal enclosures, looking to reunite the "children" with their parents.

Exacerbating the situation, the majority of the Greys had been waiting for hours in the woods surrounding the animal pens. They'd only brought along protein bars and granola mix, which wasn't cutting it. More and more converged, until one group suddenly broke off from the crowd and raced toward the pen with the fake cows.

Slowing as they came closer, they cautiously approached the closest cow. It let out a seductive-yet-rather-mechanical *moo*, which provided the necessary reassurance. They entered the pen, and the first Grey approached the mammal.

"Yum, what a tasty female specimen we have here," he said. "Just look at those humps!" The Grey remembered his lessons in Earth history from watching Mel Brooks movies and began petting the mounds in the animal's back, leaning in reassuringly. "You know, I'm a rather brilliant surgeon and have dissected quite a few animals in my time. Perhaps I can help with that hump."

The animal seemed to squirm beneath its own skin, and a muffled voice came out of nowhere.

"What hump?"

The Grey peered around, seeking to locate the source of the voice. Seeing no one, he began to stroke the bovine even more aggressively. Thus, another anxious *moo* emerged from the cow. Finally, the Grey couldn't help himself any longer and approached the tempting teats located beneath the cow. He squatted low, dipped, and started to drink from one of the pronounced nipples. As he did so, another muffled sound came from the creature.

"Mmmmmmmm…"

This encouraged more Greys to partake.

"Oh, do you like it?" the first Grey said. "I prefer the Hershey's chocolate variety myself. Or warm Ovaltine."

Next to him, another Grey looked confused. "Who are you talking to?"

"To you. You just made a yummy sound, so I thought you liked the milk."

"I do, but I didn't make any 'yummy' sound."

"But you did," the first Grey insisted. "I just heard it."

"It wasn't me."

"Well, if it wasn't you, and it wasn't me…"

The voice came again.

"Mmmmmm! Soooooo good…"

The first Grey realized then that it had to be the cow—an uncommonly *appreciative* cow. Glad to be of service, he took up another teat and began drink. Then the tent began to spin. He sought to warn his counterpart, and began to play charades. He put up his long grey fingers…

…and his knees buckled.

One by one, the extraterrestrials put their heads on a pile of hay or a pile of dung, and soon they were snoring happily.

• • • •

The waiting Army commandos sprang into action and carried their captives away to a milk delivery truck waiting just on the other side of the pen. They did this a dozen or more times.

With the faux bovine emptied of sedative, the "lambie jammies" would be used to lure the remaining Greys into additional enclosures. The aliens would reach doors rigged to release sleeping gas the moment any unsuspecting visitor passed through them—hopefully caught up in the lure of high fashion and oblivious to the booby trap.

The Army quickly moved back to an area of the zoo where real cows grazed at hay bales in pens filled with large piles of shipped-in manure. To help lure the Greys, some two tons of manure had been brought in from adjacent cattle farms. No human not enlisted in the military would go to the back of the zoo, as the stench was overwhelming. The stench was so bad that it permeated their Army fatigues for weeks and reminded them of the smell of hundreds of babies with lactose intolerance.

The Arcturians and Army Rangers took positions safely back in the bushes. As they did so, Major Broward suddenly appeared. He didn't see the others waiting behind the bushes and approached one of the pens.

"General," Avorius said. "Has your man got all of his marbles?" This confused many of the Arcturian troops. A muttering arose as soldiers asked one another why their commander seemed to want to play a child's game.

Avorius paid them no mind. "Does the major have a death wish? Given the density of methane back there, passing through at this juncture would be the equivalent of entering a gas chamber. At the very least, it might lead to brain damage."

"Damage or not, I'm going to give him a piece of my mind when this is all over," General Scott growled. Now the Arcturian troops were truly horrified. They put hands over their mouths in disbelief. These humans certainly were a strange species.

Meanwhile, Major Broward stealthily approached the pen, opened the gates to get into the enclosure, and suddenly, the Reptilian bracelet he had stolen went off on his right arm. It was activated by the electrical impulses from the electromagnetic field surrounding the pen. Overcome with ecstasy, the Major giggled as he walked into the pen, ignoring the stench. There the gas went off, and the Major started to laugh hysterically as he made louder and louder moaning noises.

"Oh, ah, ahhh, oooh. Oh God, yes, *yes!*"

"Holy crap!"

The last came as an exclamation from one of the troops as the Major fell into a large pile of cow dung, fast asleep and snoring.

"Do you think he'd mind if we take a few pics?" asked an Army Ranger, trying to suppress the laughter. All of the troops—even the Arcturians—were struggling to maintain control.

"I don't think he'll give a shit," General Scott replied.

The Ranger got up, held his breath, and snapped a few pics but then noticed a pair of Greys approaching from a distance. He closed the doors again, raced back to his position behind the bushes, and waited for their prey to approach the pen.

"Hmmm, what do we have here?" the lead Grey said. "The scent here is utterly intoxicating!"

"Yes," his companion, a female, agreed. "It seems to be coming from behind those doors."

Knowing that Broward still slept on the other side of the entrance, the Army men and women looked at each other—and at the General— to see if they should intervene. General Scott, however, was laughing so hard he couldn't have given an order if his life depended on it.

The Greys proceeded to open the animal pen, releasing the sleeping gas for a second time.

"Look, there's someone already here," the female noted. "And he seems to be having a grand time. I wonder if he would mind it if we probed him…"

As they entered the enclosure, the Major began to wake up. Emerging from a deep sleep, not certain he was really awake, he registered on some subliminal level that something extreme was about to occur. He saw one of the Greys begin to pull at his Army fatigues just as the gas was going off again.

Then he realized what was happening.

The gate also set off the electromagnetic field again.

The major began to groan.

The sleeping gas finally took effect. The two Greys fell asleep with their arms around the major. One by one, the rest of the extraterrestrials followed suit, until the ground was littered with grey bodies.

One of the soldiers, thinking quickly, took out a piece of paper and a magic marker. He quickly scribbled something on it and ran over to the animal pen, holding his breath to avoid the gas. He placed the sign around the Major's neck:

> Probe me, and I'll
> tell you all about
> alien threesomes!

When posted, the photo went viral on social media and received more than eight hundred million shares on various platforms. It retained its position at the top for a full decade until a post by Cambridge Analytica revealed the most spectacular alien orgy of all time hosted at a high-level political gathering in Italy. According to the news media, several 2045 U.S. presidential candidates were caught up in the scandal…their political careers ended but their social lives ensured forever.

• • • •

Master Dorje remained silent during this last phase of the military operation. He reflected on the foolish human behavior he just witnessed involving the Greys and the major.

Suddenly, he was struck by an obligation to comment on the wise teachings of an ancient Indian philosopher by the name of Saraha whom he had studied while living in Tibet over a century ago. Perhaps an Earth mystic's wisdom could help enlighten everyone regarding their childish behavior. He stood and addressed the troops.

"Those who hold to reality are as stupid as cows," he told the assemblage. "But those who hold to *unreality* are even more stupid." Everyone looked at each other to see if they understood what the Master was talking about.

Evidently, no one had a clue.

Dorje shrugged. There was no time to waste on philosophical reflection. It was, rather, time to address the vampires. The last and most dangerous part of the Battle of Woodstock.

CHAPTER 18:

VAMPIRE CAMP

"Nothing in life is to be feared, it is only to be understood. Now is the time to understand more, so that we may fear less."

—Marie Curie, after putting a bar of highly radioactive materials in her front pocket before touring the countryside of Transylvania

The Arcturians and U.S. Army commanders regrouped back at a tent set up as a mobile surgical hospital, where the first order of business was to have Major Broward take a shower. No one could stand to be around him except a few of the local barnyard animals.

In honor of his "love of the Greys" and to cover over the pungent aroma emanating from him, Broward received several bottles of Obsession by Calvin Klein as a gift from his troops.

While the Major was in the makeshift shower outside the tent, cursing loudly while vigorously trying to scrub off hardened cow dung deeply embedded in almost every crevice, casualties began rolling in from the festival. People on stretchers with IV bags hanging from steel metal poles began to fill the triage area. Many had bites on the neck, interspersed with what appeared to be bullseye hickeys spreading over the victims' bodies—the first telltale signs something was awry.

The Army's doctors were stumped. The same victims complained of migratory pain, fatigue, headaches, and memory loss.

The most challenging cases were those festival guests speaking in eastern Slavic accents, hallucinating wildly about their need and ability to fly and claiming they were invisible in front of mirrors. These guests were immediately strapped down and placed in a special ICU.

Commander Avorius pulled together ET Command and those American troops set aside for the vampire mission. They gathered in an open space outside of the MASH tent.

"We, the Arcturians," he said loudly enough for all to hear, "are not at risk from these creatures, as our blood will not satisfy their thirst and they cannot overpower us with their might. However, they pose a great risk to the human military personnel and all the guests at the festival—far more so than the zombies or the Greys."

General Scott listened attentively. Although he'd begun the day not particularly trusting of extraterrestrial advice—Commander P notwithstanding—there was no denying that they produced results. As for vampires, he'd been given numerous reports he'd found confusing and difficult to swallow. Besides, reading had never been his strong suit, so for this mission he relied more on classic vampire movies like *Dracula*—the Bela Lugosi, Christopher Lee, and Gary Oldman versions, of course—*Interview with a Vampire*, and *Love at First Bite*. He'd avoided seeing *Twilight*, as it clearly was a chick flick, and *Van Helsing* because he didn't understand why the hairy guy didn't use his claws on the bloodsuckers.

The Brides of Dracula provided some extra incentive to continue his research, over the course of which he gathered that the creatures could hypnotize people and turn into animals, especially bats and wolves. Their primary weaknesses appeared to be stakes and garlic, so he thought about bringing in Chef Rocco as a special consultant.

The thought made his stomach growl.

"Commander," General Scott said, seeing an opportunity to avoid further reading. "Could you please explain in greater detail—to the troops, I mean—some of the challenges we face here? We've faced the Taliban, Californians, and other sorts of insurgents in the past, but I'm afraid our military may be unprepared for this particular adversary."

Avorius frowned and shot him a disparaging look but obliged.

"As the reports we shared suggest…" There was that look again. "The vampires' heightened senses will present your first challenge. They have formidable night vision and can detect scents over great distances, even several miles. This, as our plan dictates, might be used to our advantage. The most alarming of their skills, however, is their ability to morph into different forms. They might transform into a familiar of your species and bypass your intuitive defenses with their mesmerizing charm. In your culture, there are stories of such beings—tales that have more truth than you might suspect. I believe you call them 'Black Widows.' They mate and then kill."

"Commander Avorius," Major Broward said, choosing his words carefully. "What is the best way to protect ourselves against these creatures of the night? Would it be possible…that is, might it be…could we—someone, that is—already have become married to one?"

It had always struck him as strange that his wife's Sicilian mother wouldn't eat the spaghetti with white clam sauce tossed in olive oil and garlic. The old…woman *claimed* she was allergic, but who'd ever heard of an Italian being allergic to garlic? No sir, it was highly suspicious.

For that matter, why won't she walk in front of mirrors, instead insisting that we cover them? Here, again, she had a reason—or was it an excuse? She claimed it was because her last plastic surgery had been a botch job, but the major wondered if she'd even had the procedure. If she had, it didn't look as if it had done any good.

And what about those bottles of "V8" in the fridge?

It's enough, he thought, *to make anyone suspicious.*

"My dear Major," the king said, "I have been blissfully married to my wife for the last one hundred thirty-four years and have learned a few things along the way. The one word of advice I'd like to offer is to always remember that your wife is the most important person in your life, and you should always treat her like a queen. Even," he said, looking to his wife, "if she isn't. If you treat her so, you might be surprised at the results. And *always* remember to compliment her on her shoes and hair."

The Queen nodded in perfect agreement. She turned to the King, and he blew her a kiss.

"Thank you, your Highness," the Major said. "In the first few years of our marriage, I accidently commented on my wife's hairdo after we were walking through windy streets in Chicago. I'd suggested that it looked like two chickens fighting to the death and wanted to take bets on which one would win. A fight ensued shortly afterward, but I was the one who lost. I will do my best in the future to appease my...beloved, Dorothea Allesandra Angelo Bianca Sofia Nicoletta Vito Broward."

"All very well, Major Broward," the Queen said. "And now, if you don't mind, we have one last word of advice before you and your team go into the battlefield against this formidable enemy. One thing vampires have in common is their disinclination to tell the truth about who and what they are. Remember that everything you see and hear will not always be as it appears. That is what got your species into trouble earlier in this century, when the fake media and Reptilian masters tried to sell you a bill of goods, convincing everyone that fossil fuels and red meat were essential for a healthy, growing economy and planet. You must look beyond the superficial *exterior* of people to understand who and what they are and what they *truly* want. Then, and only then, will you and your people remain safe."

Murmuring arose among the human troops as the words struck home. They'd been fooled before and suffered grave consequences. Their entire planet had been damaged—perhaps irrevocably—and they would not let it happen again.

The King gestured to Commander Avorius, and the Arcturian soldiers brought out several large boxes. To start, everyone was given a crucifix to wear around the necks, adorned with rather pungent garlic cloves. The Army's top intelligence officers had considered several other options, including handing out yin-yang symbols. These were vetoed when they remembered the famous "undead trials" in Romania in January 2024. The yang or "light swirl" didn't dissuade the vampires, and indeed they seemed to be intensely attracted to the yin or "dark swirl" associated with blackness, the night, and obscurity.

The Star of David or "Shield of David" was also considered a possibility, as the six-pointed star was held by Kabbalists to be a protection against evil spirits. Unfortunately, all that resulted was vampires dressing up like delicatessen workers in food trucks, pulling in the soldiers with bagels and lox, potato knishes, and Kasha Varnishkes.

Next, the troops were each blessed with holy water. A group of Catholic priests had been flown in from all over the United States, Canada, Ireland, the United Kingdom, and several other countries. According to Church officials, they all had firsthand experience of vampiric activity with minors, and the priests' close proximity to minions of darkness would be an asset.

Finally, each of the soldiers was immunized against the paranormal virus responsible for transforming human DNA into vampiric building blocks. The early messenger RNA vaccine trials had been a success, and those who were subsequently bitten didn't fall prey to the vampire's spell of the undead.

Doctor Morales had spent days locked away in secret underground medical facilities working side by side with Arcturian scientists. The extraterrestrial cryptozoologists had been working on variations of this formula for a long time and believed it would be as effective as human vaccines had been in helping to prevent chicken pox or measles. Instead of protecting patients from getting an incredibly itchy rash or a case of shingles, however, they would be protected from becoming a walking demon of the undead.

When it came his turn, Major Broward refused the injection.

"Has it been tested yet? They say vaccines aren't safe!"

"Given the speed with which we had to develop it," Dr. Correro admitted, "tests were not possible. Also, the FDA wouldn't allow us to experiment on live human subjects. We begged, but they still said no. We begged again but to no avail. We tried one more time, but *niet*." His face showed his exasperation. "Then we tried the jails—what's a few death row inmates to spare? There, the concern was that if the vaccine didn't work, and the prisoners became 'undead,' they'd run out of space for inmates who'd never, ever die."

"But is it *safe*?" Broward asked.

"We're confident it will work," Correro replied. "We've replaced the mercury, thimerosal, and aluminum in your usual vaccines with colloidal silver. Vampires *hate* silver. If they try to drink your blood, it will taste like crap and burn and paralyze them at the same time. It won't kill them as efficiently as a wooden stake through the heart, but it will slow them down enough that they will be defenseless and easier to eliminate."

• • • •

Major Broward remained unconvinced. When his wife Dorothea Allesandra Angelo Bianca (also known as Dottie) was pregnant with their first child, she had researched the safety of vaccines and found conflicting research. Some of the scientific literature showed more neurodevelopmental disorders and allergies in children who were vaccinated than those who weren't and had concerns that the vaccines would make their child dumber than a box of rocks.

The Major disagreed with his wife's assessment but was swayed by his wife's decision without taking a harder look at the science and potential benefits. And in this case, he realized, the benefit might be to avoid becoming an eternal blood-sucking member of the vampiric undead.

Early in the 21st century, there was a worldwide anti-vax movement, as major laboratories worked on vaccines to prevent epidemics of Lyme disease, Ebola, Alzheimer's, and Parkinson's disease. Anti-vaxxers ignored the basic science, including facts that vaccines were among the most successful public health interventions of the previous century.

However, Dottie insisted there *were* valid concerns among parents, and she didn't want her child to become a "walking zombie." Since actual zombies had become a well-established public health issue, it was enough to make any parent nervous about potential harm to their child. And no answers were being given by the medical establishment.

The value of vaccines became especially apparent in the year 2028, when the Earth's temperature climbed to 1.5 degrees Centigrade above baseline temperatures due to a catastrophic set of feedback loops that released large amounts of carbon dioxide and methane from previously frozen "permafrost." That caused an increase in flooding and water-borne diseases, significantly increasing the number of fungal, tick-borne, and mosquito-borne illness. More than ever, safe and effective vaccines were needed.

Not all parents had kept up with the emerging science, and when some did try to understand why vaccines caused illness in some unlucky individuals, they ended up with a conundrum: there was conflicting data.

For example, scientific studies which appeared in medical publications like the *Journal of Neuroscience* and the *Journal of Trace Elements in Medicine and Biology* discussed potential autoimmune effects from adjuvants like aluminum in vaccines and that in many cases, no long-term safety studies had been done to properly evaluate the risks. That was enough to put doubt in anyone's mind—*even if* people wanted to pore through the research.

The key solution to the problem of neurodevelopmental delays and disabilities finally emerged in the year 2035, when scientists discovered that some individuals had adverse reactions to vaccines due to a primed, overactive immune response and poor detoxification pathways. The problem wasn't due to *just* the vaccines, per se, but rather to their interaction with hundreds of toxins and harmful microorganisms, especially in young, developing brains. Toxins that had been dumped into the environment for decades by CEOs of Big Industry. When these were combined with stealth bacteria, parasites, viruses, and nutritional deficiencies, the toxins led to health disasters with unbridled inflammation in some individuals.

Some, in fact, did act like "walking zombies."

So based on the science, apparently the Major had nothing to worry about. He wasn't a three-year-old with Lyme disease, parasites, and nutritional deficiencies. It was safe for him to take the vaccine.

"Don't worry so much, Major," Master Dorje said. "You won't need to rely entirely on the vaccine. I will be putting a magical sacred sphere of protection around everyone during your time in battle. The vampires' dark magic won't be able to penetrate this circle, as it emanates directly from the pure essence of divine source. You will be protected and can be fearless in your actions on the battlefield."

"But has the magic been tested?" the Major protested. "Is it safe?"

The Arcturian Mage shot him a hard look.

He shut up and took the shot.

"Before entering into battle with a formidable foe," Dorje said, "the warrior must be prepared physically, emotionally, mentally, and spiritually. The physical is the easiest—that requires discipline in training and treating the body as a temple. For you, Major, that would mean healthy food, proper exercise, yoga, Tai'Chi, and getting adequate sleep."

I guess eating that bag of Doritos while lying on the couch playing Gears of War 3 *until four in the morning doesn't count*, the Major mused.

"Emotional and mental stability, on the other hand," Dorje said, "require learning equanimity and adopting proper motivation. Although you are taught in your military to withstand harsh training in order to develop resilience, centuries ago, Krishna taught Arjuna in the *Bhagavad Gita* advice for the warriors before going into battle. His guidance was to adopt desireless action—the highest form of action motivated not by human ego, but by that which makes one an instrument of the Divine Cause.

"You must not let the fruits of your action be your motive, Major Broward. True heroism is to work tirelessly for the benefit of others who are oppressed and let go of the outcome. The vampires are a result of black magic. To counteract their power and spells, your highest motivation must be a spirituality that is grounded in the light. This is why these creatures cannot stand direct sunlight and the light of day, as their darkness is exposed to a power that is greater than their evil.

"A spiritual warrior fighting the elements of darkness needs to learn that the self is something different from the body and can never be harmed. If you take that knowledge with you into battle and align your Earth consciousness with Divine will, your actions will be inspired with a truth and power that cannot be defeated."

Holy shit, the Major thought. *No one taught me this stuff at Archbishop Peter Paul Catholic School.* The only lessons the boys learned were not to tug on girls' pigtails, fling spitballs when the nuns turned to write at the blackboard, or use the crucifix as a sword.

Except for the time Sister Saint Bernard, who they called Sister Nun-of-It, came into the room, put a chalk mark on the blackboard, and told everyone that they were that mark and that if they sinned, God would take an eraser and wipe them off the face of the Earth.

"And besides, Major," Dorje said, "we've set traps for those vampires, whether you understand these teachings or not."

CHAPTER 19:

OPERATION VLAD

"**P**repare for battle!" Commander Avorius exclaimed as darkness fell.

General Scott got on the com and let his troops know they were about to commence Operation Vlad.

"Today's enemy is prepared to defeat us at all costs, and I must warn you again…the vampires are cunning creatures of great strength and deception, so *do not*, and I repeat, DO NOT under any circumstances engage them at close quarters, or they will surely make mincemeat out of you. In the process, they might also just rip off your head or an arm for fun.

"If you get a clean shot, do not hesitate. Any 'fog of war' here should come only from their ability to vanish literally into thin air or turn into a bat. Do *not* friend them on Facebook or Snapchat, no matter how interesting their posts or videos. The only introduction you want to make to vampires is to introduce to them to holy water, your silver sword, or a stake through the heart. Feel free to lop off their heads and put a baptism candle in their mouths before they burst into unholy flames.

"It's your choice, really."

After that rousing pep talk, everyone went into action. The blood drive tents that had been manned by Marines posing as doctors and nurses began to hang tainted plasma on the IV poles to give the enemy the impression they'd just hit the motherload.

At the same time, teams of specialists arrived just ahead of the night. Funeral home directors laid out their finest oak, hickory, maple, teakwood, rosewood, and mahogany caskets. Highly trained Columbia University psychotherapists sat across from couches, waiting for their next clients to arrive. There were those among the undead who felt guilty about having to take life in order to survive. Those with such remnants of humanity left inside of them enjoyed therapy to help relieve their guilt and shame. It was especially effective among the Sicilian vampires, who carried tons of Catholic guilt to begin with.

Finally, Army Rangers entered the woods, donned their night vision goggles, strapped high tensile crossbows across their chests preloaded with thick silver arrows, and prepared their portable flame throwers.

The game was on with festival patrons still on site.

Two hundred Army Rangers stealthily surrounded a Quonset hut movie theater that was preparing to let out the crowd from the double feature *Dusk Till Dawn 4* and *Daybreakers*. They sent in their first undercover pizza delivery boy, a Navy Seal carrying six large garlic pizzas, whose pungent aroma could be smelled from miles away.

As he entered the doorway, he bellowed in a loud, booming voice, "Mongo delivery service. Anyone here order six large double-stuffed-crust, double cheese, double garlic pizzas?" He shuffled into the main area and looked around to see if anyone heard him. As he did so, the movies let out and the aroma wafted in the direction of the vampires, leaving the darkened theaters. Faces immediately filled with disgust, clearly identifying the enemy.

"Who the fork let loose with that ferociously fragrant fomenting fart from Hades?" one of the vampires asked.

"He who smelt it dealt it!" a vampiress cackled in the back.

"That sucker smells like the dregs of my sewer system when it backed up into my sister's bathtub!" another exclaimed.

"Enough lip, guys," the "delivery man" yelled. "Who's paying?"

The vampires approached slowly, holding up articles of clothing to cover their mouths and noses. Step by step, inch by inch, they approached—some actually wore cloaks. Old habits die hard.

The SEAL held still as long as he dared. Finally, he dropped the pizzas on the counter and ran outside as fast as he could, screaming as convincingly as possible.

"Oh, don't hurt me, please don't hurt me. I was just doing my job. It's not my fault that the kitchen screwed up! I promise it won't happen again!"

Thirty-plus vampires chased after the young man. Ten feet from the movie theater they hit a tripwire, which released a series of silver stakes that came up out of the ground. Several of the vampires were impaled immediately. The ones who evaded the first line of attack were subject to Army sharp shooters. Silver arrows punctured their hearts, and they started dropping like flies whose wings had been pulled off. SEALS immediately finished them off with wooden stakes.

"Die, you commie, blood-sucking vortex of misery!" one of the sharpshooters yelled. He'd recently learned that phrase from his younger sister, who lived with their elderly Italian grandparents on the Jersey Shore.

"Take the last train to Transylvania, and I'll meet you at the station," another sharpshooter said, monkeying around.

It wasn't going to be that easy with the rest of the group.

When the vampires still inside the makeshift theater saw what was taking place outside, they turned into bats and started flying away like geese escaping to Miami Beach for the winter. The sharpshooters, realizing their prey would soon be out of range, drew their boom sticks and double-barreled shotguns filled with silver shotgun pellets and let 'em fly. Half of the bat colony fell dead-dead to the ground. *Thump. Thump. Thump.*

Troops with flamethrowers raced in and burned the battered bat bodies to a caramelized crisp. As the surviving vampires flew to the East, they regrouped back in the woods.

• • • •

The vampire village had been built on the western side of the festival, knowing that as the sun set in the west, the vampires would retreat there. It was tucked in a clearing in a remote part of Watkins Glen, an area where citizens were unlikely and guards were stationed at checkpoints to ensure civilian safety.

Here, too, were the blood drive tents. The Red Cross sign could be seen conspicuously from a distance away, brightly illuminated with flashing red neon lights. The funeral parlor, which sat adjacent, similarly boasted a large casket opening and closing on a prominently lit sign with a dark figure emerging. These were sure to attract the predators.

To up the ante, the military placed a small amount of blood at the entrance to each tent; the vamps would smell it from miles away. Therapy tents were placed at the far end of the village square for those who weren't hungry or were content with not getting the latest model casket and suffered from extreme vampire guilt.

The flying escapees landed and strolled as nonchalantly as they could into the camp, peering around curiously. A "nurse" and funeral parlor director stood at the entrance to each tent. The first vampiric couple approached the Red Cross sign.

"Can I help you, sir and madam?" the nurse asked. "Are you here to donate blood? There are hundreds of our fellow Americans bleeding out even as we speak."

Although the image of humans bleeding out seemed highly appealing to the vampire couple, they kept their focus. They were dressed in brand new Armani suits—a dead giveaway—and Berluti handmade shoes.

"No, we're from the FDA," one lied. "And we want to, ahhhh…*ensure* the safety of your blood products. There have been some reports of relapsing fever, Babesia, Bartonella, *Anaplasma phagocytophilum*, tickborne encephalitis, *Ehrlichia ewingii*, Colorado tick fever, *Ehrlichia chaffeensis* and rickettsial infections. We're concerned these are making their way into the blood supply and are here to, ah, check it out."

The duo looked very official.

"I see. Of course, come on inside," the nurse agreed. "We're happy to assist important people like you in any way possible, so that we can protect the American public." Having been thus invited, the couple entering the tent instantly had smiles appear on their faces. Several IV poles with blood products hung from the shiny metal poles.

"Hmm, those look a bit deli…er, *suspicious*," the first said, identifying himself as Mr. Black.

"Yes, I agree," the woman, Ms. Noir, said. "We should test those samples hanging from the poles. Nurse, could you please give us two bags of those fine-looking red liquids? Please place them on the table over there and we'll proceed as quickly as we can, so you can continue the good work you're doing here."

The couple located a pair of beakers on a nearby supply bench. Placing it on the table, they opened up the Baxter ViaFlex plastic bag and poured the dark red contents into a large glass. Drool dripped along the edges of their lips.

"We need to test your IV fluid bags as well as their contents," Mr. Black explained in an official tone. "The industry that produces IV fluid bags has been bothered for years with fungal impurities resulting in moldy plastic containers. These are produced in Puerto Rico, which still hasn't recovered from the 2017 hurricane. The pharmaceutical company which makes the bags was found to not be at fault, but we are required to check all aspects of your operation and ensure the highest standards of safety."

Climate change had hit the vulnerable island four more times since Maria. Visitors were subjected to an eerie sight, seeing water up to people's knees as they leisurely strolled through the streets, shopping and going about their daily lives.

The vampires carefully poured the red liquid into their flasks, held them up to the light, and stirred.

"Looks dirty," Mr. Black said seriously. "We'd better perform a taste test to ensure its acceptable for human consumption." Ms. Noir nodded her agreement.

The nurse looked questionably at the two FDA scientists. "I thought only Tibetan doctors tasted body fluids for health purposes," he said. "Is that the only way to tell if the blood has been affected?"

"Yes," Ms. Noir replied. "We have gone through extensive training, making us certified sommeliers and blood tasting aficionados. We can even turn blood into wine." That alchemical ability was, of course, the final confirmation that these people were not who they appeared to be. The two proceeded to take a taste of the blood.

"Hmmm, kinda smoky with hints of grapefruit, cranberry…and a hint of syphilis."

"I agree," Mr. Black said. "And I think some remnants of metal in the background. This poor bastard probably ate too many large fish with mercury poisoning." As he uttered these words, the two vampires started to realize something was terribly wrong. They rapidly began to turn dark green and grabbed at their necks as they began choking uncontrollably.

Something they'd eaten clearly wasn't kosher.

At that moment, the nurse took a wooden stake from beneath his lab coat and thrust it through the heart of the first vampire, then the second, followed by a swift decapitation. The creatures burst into unholy flames, and their ashes were quickly gathered up. The plan was to present them to the president as a trophy of a successful mission. They'd be safe there as long as no one opened up the containers and sneezed.

That happened in 2063 when a nosy house sitter by the name of Phillip and his curious cat Felix were accidently nuked from 10,000 feet after inadvertently opening up one of the containers, releasing toxic vampire ash and setting off a nuclear chain reaction. It wasn't a complete disaster, however, since as was the case in Chernobyl and Fukashima, the fruits and vegetables in the surrounding area were now six feet long and each melon and zucchini were able to feed a family of ten.

CHAPTER 20:

A-TISKET, A-TASKET, A GREEN AND YELLOW CASKET

Meanwhile, the funeral home next door was doing a booming business. Vampire couples strolled through the tent and enthusiastically studied all of the caskets now out on display. Draped maroon curtains separated each coffin from the next for privacy.

"Sir, could you please explain the advantages of *this* model?" one patron, who called himself Mr. Cuspid, asked.

"Oh, I'd be happy to," one of the carefully disguised Marines replied. His name tag identified him as "Loman," and he was impeccably dressed as a casket salesman. "Here is one of our finest models. The coffin and lid are made of solid Brazilian mahogany, and the top raises up easily with our specially patented hydraulic lift. If you purchase today, it comes with a guaranteed fungal-free dirt bottom. You will be getting a forty-eight by forty by thirty-six-inch double-wall Gaylord box with lid from ULINE thrown in with this offer if you buy your coffin in the next hour."

"That's quite an offer we can't refuse," Mrs. Cuspid said with the hint of an accent.

"May we try it out for size?" Mr. Cuspid asked.

"Of course!" the salesman exclaimed. "Take your time, and be sure it fits your needs. After all, this is a purchase to last an eternal lifetime."

Chortling at the remark, Mr. Cuspid climbed into the box and smiled. It smelled of newly cut dead trees.

"C'mon in and join me," he urged.

"Here?" Mrs. Cuspid said, blushing her husband's second-favorite shade of crimson. "In front of everyone?"

"Absolutely. No one can see us."

The maroon curtains offered just enough privacy, and Mrs. Cuspid climbed into the coffin on top of Mr. Cuspid.

"Is it acceptable if I'm on top this time?" she asked politely.

"Sure, sure…sweetheart. Just don't scream or make too much noise." He then closed the coffin lid.

Much to the vampires' surprise, as the lid closed, multiple wooden stakes burst through the bottom of the coffin, impaling the two. The coffin immediately dropped into its platform and the bottom opened, depositing the bodies into a hastily erected industrial furnace below. The hydraulic lift then brought the coffin back up for the next set of unsuspecting shoppers.

Loman quickly wiped the spikes clean.

• • • •

Others attracted to the camp were not, alas, genuine vampires. Many were simply Goths—people in black attire with pale faces, over-done makeup, and black hair. The military had to figure out how to get these unfortunate civilians out of harm's way and take care of the remaining vampires.

Major Broward watched from the outskirts and decided it was time to be a hero. He would show Dorje he could be courageous in the face of danger. After all, he knew he was protected with Dorje's elliptical sphere of light surrounding him, and the civilians lacked such protection.

What could go wrong?

The Major strolled out of the woods and went into the middle of the town square. He suddenly began to yell at the top of his lungs.

"Red hots here. Red hots here. Come and get it. Free Vampire therapy in tent number thirteen! Come and get it with your red-hot-blooded therapist!"

Most of the vampires turned, curious to see who this dimwit was, although a few started moving toward the therapy tent. The rest began to assemble around the Major, and the humans knew enough to avoid the scene that was unfolding. While the Major distracted their targets, the military personnel quickly grabbed the Goth teens and brought them to safety. Not all of them were happy to be removed, though, and one shouted "Beetlejuice" three times.

A stately woman in the crowd surrounding the Major suddenly took several steps forward to greet this unusual specimen. Her name was Vera Vampiress, but people called her VeeVee for short. She was voluptuous and wore a low-cut black gown slit to the waist with high-heeled, red spiked shoes. Her nails were a bright ruby red, as were her lips. She was the most seductive woman he'd ever encountered, and the major could feel himself being pulled under her spell.

"Are you a doctor?" VeeVee asked in a forlorn voice. "I have a rare disease called porphyria. It causes vampire-like symptoms such as an extreme sensitivity to sunlight and excessive hairiness. I have to shave and use cocoa butter lotion several times a day, and that bikini area of mine is *still* a jungle."

The Major imagined himself as an explorer entering uncharted territory.

"Can you help me?" VeeVee continued. "You're one of the medics from that tent over there, aren't you? Could we go somewhere private, and have you examine me? Maybe you could solve the mystery of my light sensitivity."

The Major looked at her and wondered how his wife would feel about him playing doctor—but it was too late. That fleeting thought disappeared as quickly as it had arrived, as did most of his thoughts, and he was hooked. He went through a list of differential diagnoses in his mind that might make his actions seem plausible. Migraines, Lyme disease, Porphyria and, well, "being a vampire" were the first few to come to mind.

"Yes, of course," he said. "I would love to…be of service to you. Yes, indeed, I promise to service you to the best of my ability." Service to humanity was, after all, one of the philosophical tenets Master Dorje had mentioned. He was only being a good Samaritan and following the intimate laws of nature.

• • • •

While the Major was leaving with VeeVee, a dark-cloaked man of Native American heritage walked into the therapy tent to see the psych intern who was stationed there. He was nervous and led off with a classic joke he learned from his Uncle Ahanu.

"Doctor," the man said. "Sometimes I think I'm a teepee. Then, I think I'm a wigwam. Then, I think I'm a teepee. Then, I think I'm a wigwam."

"Your condition is clear," the psych intern responded, understanding instantly. "You're two tense." As she pronounced her diagnosis, an Arcturian soldier came from behind the man and splashed him with holy water. He started to scream in pain as smoke began to rise from his body where the water landed. This was no ordinary human with PTSD from dysfunctional parenting. The soldier drew her stake and ran it through his heart, while using her silver sword to decapitate the vampire. His head rolled as he went up in a cloud of unholy fire and smoke.

As the screams died, everyone assumed the "cure" had been a success.

• • • •

Before he could get far with VeeVee, Major Broward realized that a small mob of vampires had started to encircle him.

"What *is* that scent you're wearing?" one of the other females asked. "It's haunting, and I can't stay away."

"Oh…it's cow dung mixed with Calvin Klein," the Major said proudly. Then it struck him that Obsession might not be the right cologne to wear for the occasion. Throngs clustered around him, yet he was deeply under their spell. A tall, handsome bloodsucker emerged from the dark shadows, naked from the waist up which showed off his powerful pecs.

"It's Vlad," someone hissed.

"Oh hello, handsome," the Major said, babbling away, mindlessly remembering his Army training on monsters, having watched *Young Frankenstein* and *The Bride of Dracula*. "You're a good looking fellow. People laugh at you, people hate you, but why do they hate you? Because…they are *jealous*. Do you want to talk about sheer muscle? Do you want to talk about the Olympian ideal? And listen to me, you are not evil. We know you didn't rig those American elections. You…are…*good*."

Taken by surprise, Vlad started to cry, and the Major hugged him tenderly. Suddenly aware of what the American was doing, the vampire pulled away and yelled in a loud, booming Slavic accent.

"That's my gal you're diddlin' with, comrade! Now you shall pay with your life!"

• • • •

That was the cue for Dorje, who had been waiting in hiding and emerged from one of the tents holding Audri and Amori. Dorje wore a white flowing gown and a large magician's hat, holding a large brown wooden walking stick with a crystal affixed to the top that emanated a faint blue light.

"Hey, big guy," the Master said, adopting a persona based on Earth's movies. "Why don't you pick on someone your own size?" He put the Atmops down, and they started to run into the center of area. The vampires were confused, especially when confronted by someone who would challenge the great Vlad.

Music suddenly filled the square as guitar chords C, F, and G began to play a lively, familiar tune.

"La Bomba."

The vampires fell under the spell of the atmops, and a conga line ensued, led by Amori and Audri. One by one, the vampires sauntered out of town Pied Piper style, happily dancing and singing. Once they got to the edge of the "village," the Arcturian troops came out of hiding and shot them with volleys of silver arrows followed by stakes and quick decapitations.

The last two who remained were Vlad and VeeVee. Dorje moved to the center of the square and gestured for the duo to follow him, ignoring Broward's forlorn expression. Thinking they had found an easy victim, the vampires prepared to attack. The space wizard suddenly raised his arms and began to chant in a deep, sonorous voice.

"*Sol soles. Ast clare in nocte, et perdere malo, qui esset, non nocere ad homines. Mitte eis in perpetuum ex hoc loco!*" A large bright sun suddenly appeared in the middle of the square, blinding anyone who even caught a glimpse of it out of the corner of their eye.

The vampires screamed as smoke began to emanate from their bodies.

"I warned you to pick on someone your own size," Dorje said. He turned toward a cache of wooden stakes brought in by the Rangers and, using his powers of telekinesis, made them rise, then streak through the air and penetrate directly through the hearts of the creatures. Only then did the sun begin to diminish until it was no worse than midnight construction on Route 87 traveling to upstate NY.

The vampires were gone.

They'd disappeared in the holy fire. Only smoke and ash and silver arrows lying on the ground were left as proof of their having been there. Any ghouls and mortal minions that remained raced off for cover.

"What happened?" The Major blinked, shook his head, and tried to focus.

Despite everything, Dorje was proud of Broward. The Major had overcome his fear and tried his best to help the other humans in need.

"You did good, Major," Master Dorje said. "If it wasn't for you, we might have had a few more civilian casualties today. Just do me a favor. In the future, stop watching so many old movies, and please don't wear any more cologne. You almost lost your head."

They had completed the most difficult part of their operation, accomplishing a great deal this day. Dorje turned to the group.

"Remember, everyone," he said, his voice serious, "what you witnessed today must be kept secret. The rest of humanity cannot know the truth about these beings of darkness and the power wielded by the proper use of magick."

In fact, he was buying time, keeping everyone in one place. Amori and Audri returned. Dorje signaled the atmops to clear the memories of all of the humans who were present. Within a matter of minutes, the two hypnotized the entire group, leaving them all smiling blissfully. Slowly, they gathered their equipment, leaving it to civilian contractors to deconstruct the festival structures. Everyone returned home, content in the knowledge of their first successful mission: throwing the most spectacular party in human history and saving a large chunk of humanity.

Their next mission: save the entire planet.

CHAPTER 21:

MAGICK FOR BEGINNERS

"Impossible is just a big word thrown around by small men who find it easier to live in the world they've been given than to explore the power they have to change it. Impossible is not a fact. It is an opinion. Impossible is not a declaration. It is a dare. Impossible is potential. Whatever you believe you can accomplish, do it, for action born of deep unwavering faith and right motivation has magic, grace and unlimited power in it."

—Fourth Countess of Maracord, the Invincible, Fifteenth-Century Sirian Crone, close advisor to Joan of Arc

The Pentagon briefing room was understandably abuzz. It had been five days since the success of Woodstock 2035, and the military teams had gathered to debrief, gloat, and politely make demands.

The world had changed irreversibly since the alien music fest. New enemies and dangers were known to be real, and they challenged global security in ways humans were completely unprepared. If it hadn't been for Dorje and the Arcturian capabilities, all would have been lost. The use of "magick" could perform miracles and overcome seemingly insurmountable dark forces.

And the American military knew it.

The Queen and royal family understood that the opposite was also true—misuse of the occult powered by the wrong motivation was dangerous and could yield devastating results. Therein lay the dilemma, Queen Dawn knew. How could the Arcturians share the essentials of magick yet ensure that they would not fall into the wrong hands?

Gathered around a large oval table in the National Military Command Center were the chairman of the Joint Chiefs of Staff, along with other military top brass. General Scott, Major Broward, and the ET Army command were present via a video feed from the Silo 74 command center, along with the Arcturian Royal family who sat in the background alongside Commander P, Commander Avorius, and a few of his troops.

Secretary of Defense Marks spoke first. "Your highnesses, Commander Avorius…we are extremely grateful for the assistance you provided against the various creatures who were lured out of hiding by the festival. Without a doubt, you assisted humanity at a most perilous hour." He held up a piece of paper. "In doing so, you helped garner the best Nielsen ratings ever recorded for a live musical event not featuring Taylor Swift."

Soft applause spread throughout the chamber.

"It was our great honor," Queen Dawn replied. "From what we have been told, there has been renewed interest in civilians joining the military, as well."

"Affirmative," Secretary Marks acknowledged. "More people than ever want to join up to cream demons, vampires, and decapitate zombies. There are lines out the door at recruiting centers across the United States. If we'd known years ago that there would have been this kind of interest, we'd have changed the posters to show Bruce Campbell carrying a sword, flame thrower, high-tensile crossbow, and semiautomatic weapon. There's the problem with the Feds, though, who passed a law obliging people to get a comprehensive identity check before we sell them military-grade weapons." He laughed. "What's this country coming to?"

"Yes," the Queen said. "I can only imagine how challenging that must be for you. The world is indeed a difficult and dangerous place to live in."

"It *is* difficult, your Highness," General "Aero" Smith said. "However, not as difficult as it would have been if our military faced these foes without your assistance. And so, your Highness, we would like to know…"

He sat up in his chair, lighting his cigar.

"How can we train our armies to access the power and skill your military has developed? To be frank, we don't like to rely on outsiders, and we now know of the formidable enemies who pose a clear and present danger to the United States and the global community. Humanity's future lies in the balance. Can you train us in the ways of the Arcturians so we can effectively protect our own people and all those Starseeds who wish to live in a world in balance? Far more than the Arcturian Starseeds need our protection."

"*A world in balance.*" The words struck a chord with the Queen. She'd witnessed tremendous suffering at the hands of the Reptiles. One day there was peace and prosperity, and the next, her kingdom was torn apart by war. If these same Reptiles were successful in continuing to toxify planet Earth, causing irreversible damage to its ecosystem, the humans would end up suffering the same fate her people had. *And yet…*

"General," she said, "it's not simply about our willingness to share our military knowledge. We *can* train your soldiers in the Arcturian philosophies, sciences, esoteric, *and* magical traditions. However, these powers are not meant for everyone. They require *very* special individuals, and your human candidates would have to pass a series of tests before even being allowed to begin. There are secrets held in these teachings that, if they fell into the wrong hands, could hasten your destruction…not prevent it.

"In addition to their military training, Commander Avorius and his troops have studied the mystical arts with Master Dorje. This required several *years* of intense dedication before they were fully competent on the battlefield. Only a very few Arcturians are skillful enough to know whether a battle can be avoided and, if not, which methods should be implemented to reach the best outcome for *all parties* involved. This means considering your enemies and recognizing that they, too, are suffering. These teachings are not simply about 'winning' and 'losing.' They are beyond such dualistic extremes.

"And so," she said, "these teachings above all others must be held in the strictest confidence by those whose motivations are peace and harmony."

To her chagrin, the members of the military command seemed genuinely confused by her words. On the video monitors, heads shook side to side in disbelief.

The only goal they understand is winning at all costs.

"You believe," she said, "that the Reptilians among your corporate leaders and heads of state are simply evil, doing everything for their own gain and reaping the rewards of their aggression. But I assure you, these beings are ignorant and far from happy. They search for meaning in material things that are by their very nature impermanent while ignoring the consequences of their actions, which will only lead to suffering and eventual rebirth in one of the eight hot or cold hell realms after they pass.

"Since the shortest time in these hell realms is twenty-five thousand of your Earth years, the Reptilians' suffering is guaranteed. They may have won some battles, but they have lost the war without even realizing it. However, due to interdependent causes and conditions, everything that you do ultimately affects everything else in the universe. Once you grasp this, you will see that there is another, more effective way to deal with your enemy. Not just making war. Finding common ground. They are like you. They are searching for the same things you are. Peace. Prosperity. Contentment. Happiness. Security.

"If you can show them a way to attain that, which is possible only through higher spiritual practices—transcending ego's limitations, accessing transcendental wisdom, and considering others before yourselves—then you have accomplished two pivotal goals: you have turned your enemies into your friends by showing them the true path to peace and happiness, and you have avoided unnecessary war and suffering amongst your own people.

"Such skillful action and impeccable use of body, speech, and mind requires that a candidate has embodied the finest human qualities," she said solemnly. "Anyone or anything else will result in failure."

"Your Highness," General Tomlin said, "some of the finest men and women in the world serve in the U.S. military. I'm sure we could administer whatever screening process you require. The only real question today is 'When could we start?' Clearly, time is of the essence."

"General…" Dorje replied. "I will confer with our royal family and get back to you concerning the time frame for any such 'entrance exams.' Just remember, these exams and training are not for the faint of heart…or mind. We will begin with the best recruits you pick, but only those with the highest level of physical, mental, emotional, and *spiritual* development will be allowed entrance into the final program.

"Once the training is complete," he continued, "these men and women should become your future leaders in all areas of society, not just in the military. They should engage in your political process. Their wise council should inform your decision-making to help ensure that the Earth does not fall back into the ignorance and darkness that now engulfs it. Those chosen must agree to a lifetime of commitment. Embracing the Arcturian Thresholds of Knowledge never ends. We will only agree to train you and your people in Arcturian wisdom and magick if you promise to follow the guidelines we outline."

At the Pentagon, the generals looked at each other around the table, and murmurs of approval were heard. They had no choice, Queen Dawn mused, but to accept the terms of the Arcturian family.

A vote will be taken, but there can be only one outcome.

Secretary of Defense Marks banged his gavel on the table, and the murmurs stopped.

"All in favor of accepting the Arcturian terms described for instructing our finest in the ways of Arcturian magick, raise your hands and say AY."

"AY!"

The vote resounded clearly and fervently from all members of the Joint Chiefs of Staff.

"Are there any opposed?" the Secretary asked. There was silence.

"It's agreed," Marks said, banging his gavel twice. He turned back to the video com. "Master Dorje and your Highnesses, we await your list of requirements so that we may begin to screen our best and brightest. We need to—"

"In the meantime," the Queen said, "it is imperative that we evaluate *how* to limit the power of the Reptilian invaders who've led your world on a path of destruction. Earth is experiencing some of the early effects of climatic devastation. The melting of mountain and Arctic glaciers, resulting in the loss of potable water and rising sea levels, has wiped out many of your communities. Your people can no longer go outside in the warmer weather without strong protection because the rise in global temperatures has led to an increase in tick and mosquito populations which spread deadly diseases.

"Your loss of biodiversity and destruction of pollinators and wild-life habitats has resulted in twenty-five percent of your species becoming extinct. Intense heat waves and associated droughts are leading to heat strokes and worldwide food insecurity with massive climatic migration, overwhelming your borders. You now have to live with an uncertain future from unpredictable weather patterns, where your people regularly experience frequent tornadoes, hailstorms, wildfires, and level-five hurricanes.

"You must act *now*, and decisively, before it is too late, or the Reptiles will succeed in wiping out most of your species and dominating the Earth.

"We will host a conference of top scientists and world leaders in a global, comprehensive climate summit. You must discuss collectively, as a world community, what can be done to stop and potentially reverse the damage that has already put the Earth in peril.

"We have chosen Davos, Switzerland as the location for this critical gathering. I suggest that in advance of the meeting, your leaders establish a set of priorities and values, to determine what you hold most dear for you and your future generations. The United States initiated a Global Change Research Program decades ago. We suggest that your leaders consider and reflect on a number of questions..."

The room of generals leaned forward.

"Ask yourselves..." the Queen continued, "What do you value? What is at risk? What outcomes do you wish to avoid with respect to these valued things? What would you expect to occur if you do not act—in other words, how bad could it get? You must also identify thresholds or tipping points with regard to any given region, sector, or population group." The Queen paused as she measured her words carefully. "All these considerations boil down to a single, simple question for you all to ponder: *What keeps you up at night?* The entire world is depending on your ability to act in a responsible and dependable manner. Your future is in jeopardy, as is that of my son, who will be living on your planet.

"Think carefully before you act."

• • • •

General Kelley was kept up at night by his snoring wife who kept eating dairy that resulted in blockages of her sinuses.

"Your Highness," he said, "although I cannot speak for all of our people, many among us are ashamed at how our ignorance has led to the widespread destruction we now face. Many things we allowed have served our Reptilian infiltrators. Years ago we gave too much power to the corporations, and our Supreme Court supported that mistake. The materialistic concerns of a powerful few Reptilians outweighed the needs of the masses. Short-sighted vision without foresight and far-reaching goals led us into disarray.

"The egotistical concerns of the few must give way to the global good," he continued, "or there's no chance we will survive as a race—certainly not with any significant quality of life. The first two major climate shifts have led to devastation, all because we didn't adequately value and care for what we had. But we who are here today are prepared to make whatever changes will be required."

"That is good to hear," Queen Dawn said. "The first step is to acknowledge your mistakes...acknowledging your ignorance. When a sufficient number follow your example, you will receive the requirements for entrance into the training program."

Murmurs of agreement were echoed by the group in Silo 74, while a few smiled and glanced in the direction of Major Broward. He shot back a look and gave them an arcane Italian gesture that everyone surmised he must have learned from his mother-in-law.

General Smith spoke up.

"Your Highness, although I agree with my colleague, I wish to make clear the military's position here. We will of course follow your advice, but it's not our fault that the Reptiles have infiltrated all strata of society and caused planetary destruction. We take our orders from the President of the United States and have made clear our stance on climate change. It's not our fault that our leaders have ignored the advice of our top military strategists."

The Queen began to reply when her Royal Mother stood up to address the assembly. Based on past performance, General Kelley braced himself, as did several of his associates.

"Some your leaders must have been intellectually impaired and thoroughly corrupt, to say the least," she began. Groans arose from the Arcturian contingent, and the Queen and King rolled their eyes. Helen of Antwar continued, "We have studied Earth history and have been to many star systems before coming to Earth, where we hoped we would find equally intelligent life on *this* planet. We clearly were wrong.

"For the past forty of your Earth years, your planet has been getting hotter and hotter. Seventeen years ago, in 2018, your NASA and NOAA scientists made it clear that the five years prior were the hottest one's ever recorded. But did you listen? The average global temperature has risen about 1.6 degrees Celsius, as you measure it—roughly three degrees Fahrenheit—in just a century and a half. Your own Paris Climate agreement set a limit of 1.5 degrees Celsius, and you've just breezed past that."

General "Tomboy" Tomlin spoke up in response. "Royal Mother, we were aware of the problem. There have been *endless* congressional committee hearings on global warming, so it wasn't a surprise to us."

"Then why has it taken so long for your people to—what's that phrase you use—'get your asses in gear?'" Helen demanded. "Did you ignore the information simply because you didn't like the schlub who delivered it to you? One of them was elected as your president, although apparently he found a way around science. Perhaps too many of your leaders were busy whacking around little white balls when they should have been at work.

"One of your representatives actually called the hearings 'a breath of fresh air.' Clearly, he hadn't got out of Colorado to see Los Angeles, Delhi, Beijing, or even the forest fires in his own damn region. Does any of that sound like a global call to action?" The Royal Mother looked around the room. Not seeing enough horrified looks, she continued.

"Unless you people are looking for free saunas or an early trip to hell, you're in for a rude awakening—in the form of *worsening* droughts, wildfires, floods, and food shortages for billions of people. You will, however, be able to cook pizzas outside on stone sidewalks. Probably not enough to justify your short-sighted position…even for those who *like* pizza. I sincerely hope those leaders who got you into this mess get what they have coming, like the Supreme Moron of the Century award. In the immortal words of your ancient American philosopher, John

Wayne, 'Life is tough. It's tougher if you're stupid.' Or that movie guy Jack Nicholson—I like him—who said, 'If you're going to be a smart ass, first make sure you're smart. Otherwise, you're just an ass.'"

She sat down, and for a long moment no one spoke. As veils of denial were lifted, everyone realized they weren't going to get many more chances to get it right.

"Royal Helen," Secretary Marks said. "Thank you for your...honesty. We will adjourn this meeting and get back to you and the Royal Family about our plans on moving ahead, both with getting recruits for the Magic Academy and our plans for the Davos summit. I would like to thank everyone here today." He paused and looked thoughtful.

"I also would like to order a pizza with Pleiadian pepperoni. If the world is going to get that hot, we may as well get used to it."

CHAPTER 22:

INNER DEMONS

Once the meeting was finished, the Arcturian royal family, Master Dorje, Commander Avorius, Commander P, and his pugs convened with the ET Army command in the Silo 74 video conference center.

"Your Highness," Dorje said, bowing deeply to Queen Dawn. "I would like to begin to put together a list of prerequisites for the recruits to the Academy. The existing requirements for an Arcturian's entry into our Copernican-Chiron Magick Academy would be different than those for the humans, as our civilization is intellectually, physically, emotionally, and spiritually much more advanced. What, realistically, would be the most important qualities for a human to be considered?"

The Queen didn't answer immediately, and the Royal Mother took the opportunity. "To begin, they can't be douchebags. That will eliminate the vast majority."

"Thank you, Mother, for that blistering insight," the Queen said, a smirk playing across her features. She turned her attention to the mystic. "They must possess mental fortitude and a moral compass that will enable them to distinguish between right from wrong and to act accordingly."

"Of course," General Scott said. "Many of the men and women serving in the Armed Forces have proven time and time again they know what's right and what isn't."

"What if they have indiscretions in their past?" Dr. Morales asked. "Appearing in blackface, belonging to the Klan or the Oath Keepers, or storming a government building? Would any of *that* eliminate them from the program?"

"It's thorny," Dr. Correro said. "A lot of influential people have done things that would make them targets for groups like Me Too. It doesn't seem to have limited their success in business or politics, but if we use those benchmarks for acceptance into our program, we may not have *any* candidates."

"If you ask me," one of the pugs said, "the primary requirement should be the ability to play hours of beer pong and then succeed in getting through complex military maneuvers on the obstacle course."

"I disagree, brother," a second pug said before anyone could stop him—or was it her? "They need to be able to play King's Cup, in honor of the royal family, while remaining sharp. If a Navy recruit pulls the ace and has to do a waterfall, the endurance needed to drink that much will clearly identify the superior warrior."

"But what—" the General started to say.

"Oh, poodle poop," a third pug said without missing a beat. "The most important trait will be their ability to play 'Straight Face.' Many of these humans will be going on to politics after the war. They'll need to keep a straight face while being thoroughly stoned and proposing new laws. Just look at H.R.44—the Guam World War II Loyalty Recognition Act, H.R.82—The Baby Switching Prevention Act of 2013, H.R. 107—the Environmental Protection Act of 2027, which decreased the toxicity but increased the total number of pollutants dumped into rivers, and finally H.R. 229—the Voting Expansion Act of 2035, which allowed Uber Eats to deliver food and water to those waiting outside at polls for hours in 118-degree weather in the scorching sun. Those bills were introduced into the House while their proponents kept a straight face. It's phenomenal when you think about it."

General Scott frowned. Perfectly valid legislation, as far as he was concerned. Who *really* knew what happened on Guam out there in the middle of the ocean with no one watching? As for the Infant Protection and Baby Switching Prevention Act of 2013, it seemed entirely prudent. What if animals got into a hospital and bears abducted young babies, replacing them with cubs? Would anyone really notice the infants had more hair than usual and snorted? Would clever doctors chalk it up to adrenal hyperplasia with hirsutism? And who cared about a few more chemicals in the rivers or if someone had to deal with extreme heat without food or water? He lived through several wars where he and his platoon had to go for days without anything to eat or drink.

Builds character.

He opened his mouth to object.

"Your Highness," Plamorius said, "I've been living among the humans for several years now and believe I can identify candidates who would be perfect for the program. Apart from the qualities you have identified, there are those with love in their hearts who only want to do the right thing. I have hugged quite a few in my time and felt their warmth. Doesn't the quality of love trump all?"

The Major grimaced. How could the quality of love determine if someone were fit to serve in the armed forces? Wouldn't *hate* be more appropriate?

Commander Avorius must have seen his expression. "Dear Major," he said as if he was a parent scolding a child. "It might seem to be counter-intuitive to include love as a prerequisite for serving, but love of family, love of country, and love of freedom are essential qualities for a good general on the battlefield. As the Queen so powerfully elucidated, love is also necessary to call upon and use the power of the Family of Light. Hate and revenge simply lead one down the path of the Family of Dark, and although there is power in that force, it's the primary reason your world now finds itself in crisis."

"Love is one of the most powerful forces in the multiverse," Dorje agreed. "Whether we are dealing with inner demons or outer ones, we must all come to terms with the negativities within us and surrounding us, especially when we are faced with a series of ongoing battles. Many times, the inner demons are responsible for the manifestation of the outer ones. As above, so below. As within, so without. This sacred law cannot be transgressed, no matter which world you find yourself on."

"Master Dorje," the Major said, "I've been dealing with demonic possession in my wife's family for decades. Are you suggesting that if I were to just love my mother-in-law, I could emerge victorious? Last time I tried that, she spit on me and yelled something to the effect of 'Oddio, annagia porco miseria,' which, according to my wife, translates into something like 'Bugger off, you miserable pig.' I'm not sure your technique is for everyone."

Dorje smiled. "Some things remain the same no matter where you go. Your relatives are no different than the Queen's, dear Major." The Royal Mother raised an eyebrow and shot the mystic a quizzical glance. "All psyches demand the transformation of inner demons," he continued quickly, "so that individuals can come to terms with their own fears, temptations, ignorance, and aggression. If they fail to do so, they will not be able to succeed in the outer world. It is logical.

"One must first triumph in conquering one's inner demons before gaining the ability to subdue the external ones," Dorje added. "Any initiate in the Copernican-Chiron Magick Academy must first pass through the First Arcturian Threshold of Knowledge. Our own Arcturian lineage holder—Machig Labdrön—has clearly established feeding your demons as an essential first tool of magick."

"What exactly does 'taming and feeding demons' have to do with environmental destruction?" Dr. Correrro asked. "Wouldn't giving those buggers food just make them stronger?"

"Master Labdrön confirmed the universal need to transform our demons," Master Dorje replied. "We all suffer at times from our personal demons of confusion, anger, self-hatred, trauma, longing, or loss. Collectively, the force of those demons creates enormous damage on Earth, including war, racism, hunger, and illness, as well as environmental devastation. To address these forms of suffering, humans will have to face greed, hatred, and delusion at their root. No amount of political or scientific change will end these sufferings unless mankind also learns to work *with* their demons, individually and collectively."

Helen nodded in agreement, and Dorje breathed a sigh of relief.

Even General Scott nodded, remembering the famous quote by Mahatma Gandhi: "Be the change you wish to see in the world." He began to understand how transforming the negative energy of emotions could be essential for troops on the battlefield. If one didn't have control over their thoughts *and* emotions, then success was almost an impossibility.

• • • •

"I am sure we will find many fine candidates," Major Broward said. "Our Army and Marine boot camp are second to none in creating physical stamina and prowess. In the intelligence community, rigorous mental and emotional training allows individuals to be subjected to torture and emerge psychologically intact." He remembered his own CIA training and credited it with his ability to survive years of marriage.

The group began to disperse. The pugs went over to the poker table, and the Major and General Scott joined them there. The pugs dealt out the first hand, and everyone lit up cigars, reclining in their chairs while sipping on Arcturian absinthe. It had been a busy week, and a bit of rest and relaxation was due.

They had a long road ahead of them.

PART THREE:

ARCHANGEL

CHAPTER 23:

A ROYAL BIRTH

"He is most powerful who has power over himself."

—Seneca

Two years after the Battle of Woodstock, during the early morning hours of a cold, blizzardy January, the royal prince arrived. That would be me.

Amius was summoned to the Queen's side. Queen Dawn had just given birth and wanted the master astrologer to interpret my chart and the signs that had just appeared. Especially since this was far from a normal birth.

My mother had chosen to remain on the planet Earth and felt that to be properly accepted into human society, her child should have some human DNA mixed with Arcturian. The thinking was if I were a pure-bred Arcturian, the other children might not want to play with me because they would know I could always read their minds and win all the games.

My parents had things planned for me far beyond child's play. Eleven months prior to my birth, my mother called up the New York Genetics Laboratory and inquired as to their newest technology. While Arcturian science is far more advanced than Terran, it had never even considered the merging of alien DNA with a human. Indeed, some found the idea quite distasteful.

Nevertheless, my mother persisted.

The most extensive study of CRISPR-Cas9 mutations ever published in the medical journals allowed scientists to create the first prediction tool for gene editing. Even so, my nature would present interesting challenges. Arcturians possess twelve strands of DNA, not two, and the hope was that this prediction tool might help make the genetic editing more reliable. After all, my parents didn't want me to come out with two heads like a Pleiadian atmop or end up having my penis coming out of my skull. "Dick head" was a term my mother had learned from observing Earth children, and she didn't want me to suffer that fate.

There was another major decision to be made concerning my human side. Whose DNA would I use? A world-class athlete? Maybe a talented musical prodigy? Perhaps a descendant of Einstein, so I might form the first quantum string quartet?

After great deliberation, Mother decided that Jewish DNA from a world-class physician would be perfect for me. Why? Because, as she understood it, Jews generally only have two possibilities growing up in the United States: to became a lawyer or a doctor. She discounted the law because I was to be brought up to be ethical and responsible. Plus, she knew from her dreams I was destined to become a physician.

There was also the fact the Jews treated their women well. My mother was concerned that after living on this planet for many years I might pick up some bad habits and treat women disrespectfully, as had some "shmucks" she encountered. The Queen also focused on learning Yiddish terms and insults in order to get along with the other mothers. She therefore got trained from a Jewish yenta down the block who would come over and make latkes while teaching her the essential terms.

It was quite amusing listening to her lessons. No, it was shekel, not schmeckle, when discussing money—although the other women would often laugh thinking about playing monopoly with a man's schmeckle. In that my mother was prophetic, as Parker Brothers later released a "Jewish version" of Monopoly with different game pieces.

The most important decision, however, was how to protect me if they gave me Jewish DNA. The Jews had been persecuted for centuries—would that be my fate, also? And what about the Moyle? Some wise, sadistic rabbi decided centuries ago that the best thing to do when you were born Jewish was to cut off part of your penis.

Really?

That's the *first* thing your wise people could think of? How about celebrating with a beer? It's no wonder they roamed for forty days and forty nights in the desert. The children were trying to escape going under the knife.

It was like, "*Oh hello mother, good to see you, what's that bearded guy doing? Is that a knife? Why—*

"*Oh no. This old guy with a tremor? YOU HAVE GOT TO BE KIDDING!*"

So there were difficult decisions to be made.

It wasn't easy finding a doctor to do the necessary gene editing. The geneticists of 2036 were afraid of the backlash if the experiment went awry—the last doctor to attempt such a complicated procedure had been He Jiankui of the Southern University of Science and Technology in Shenzhen, China. Having a healthy child in 2037 was certainly not a given, and he had stunned the world by creating the first genetically modified babies, saying that editing the genes would protect them from certain illnesses.

The thousands of environmental toxins dumped into the environment by the Reptiles had been shown by 2036 to affect proper neurological development, contributing to autism and overall decreased intellectual capacity. Even prenatal exposure to cannabis, a common herb used for nausea and PTSD, might affect the developing brain. Women were regularly ingesting chemicals in their food and water, getting them in cosmetics they were applying to their skin and breathing them in. The list included exhaust pollutants, volatile organic solvents, perfluroinated chemicals, heavy metals, and pesticides—especially atrazine, which was shown to lead to birth defects and epigenetic changes that would adversely affect future generations.

The Reptilians' master plan would affect present populations and ensure the demise of future ones.

The solution for my mother came early in the pregnancy, as she found ways to protect me during gestation on this toxic planet. Getting clean food and water without chemicals was possible for the few lucky ones like our family, who had the resources to afford such luxuries. Inflammation from multiple sources would be trickier, though.

• • • •

After the DNA splicing and implantation, my mother consulted Doctor Menla, the Arcturian master physician who had remained on Earth with the royal family.

"Are you often nauseous?" Dr. M. asked, carefully doing a bedside exam on the Queen, palpating her gentle bulge and listening for the new baby's heartbeat.

"I am, as a matter of fact," Queen Dawn exclaimed.

"And are you regularly visiting your mother or eating her cooking?" the doctor asked.

The Queen smiled. "No, my mother has been leaving me alone for the moment. I think she's binge-watching a human series called *Lost in Space*, where people are stranded on a strange world where bizarre alien life forms and dangers surround them at every turn. It reminds her of our experience here on Earth. In fact, the phrase 'Danger Will Robinson' seems to emerge from her royal chambers every time my father tries to get close."

"That's strange, my Queen," replied Dr. M. "I didn't even know your Royal father was on our craft. I thought he had decided to stay at his royal residence on Rigel V."

The Queen's father, the royal Sid was rarely seen. "Oh, he's in hiding," Queen Dawn said. "I've heard he's binge watching something called *Big Mouth*." Then she became somber. "Doctor, what if the baby doesn't come out normally? Although that never happens with Arcturian children, I've heard some of the Earth children need to be pulled out using a strange device called a forceps, where they yank until the malleable skull fits through the birth canal. I don't want my son to look like a Remulan."

Several Remulans had been stranded on Earth years earlier, tasked with conquering "the Wilderness Planet at the end of the Noctolium Solar Chain." When they, too, became pregnant instead of conquering the Earth, they decided to adapt and blend in, similar to the Queen's situation. To all reports, they had been met with mixed success.

"If your royal vagina lacks the ability to push with the needed force, we can use that device. If that is the case, may the forceps be with you. Regardless of the method, there are a few basic rules to help ensure the royal prince comes out happy and healthy." The Arcturian physician continued, "First, make certain you are getting plenty of rest, exercise, and sleep, as well as eating a diet free of chemicals and pesticides. I will get you a prenatal multivitamin with high dose methyl folate and will prescribe N-acetyl-cysteine, six-hundred milligrams twice a day, along with five hundred milligrams of liposomal glutathione twice daily. This will ensure that you're able to keep removing the fat-soluble toxins regularly entering into everyone's bodies on this planet and should help prevent any neurological complications."

• • • •

Over the next nine months, apart from my premature arrival, the pregnancy progressed normally, and I came out ready to greet the world on January 25, 2037.

At the Maimonides Human-Alien Birthing Center in Brooklyn, it was such a momentous occasion to have the first alien-human child born into the world that the hospital administrators decided to rename the birthing center in honor of me, the Queen's first child. It had previously been called the Sadie and Herman Gluck Pre-Pubescent Pregnancy Pavilion, but a generous donation given by my grandmother made sure the name was changed so no one could make fun of the place that I was born.

Regarding the circumstances of my birth, as they say, "He got stuck in gluck after a hearty fuck." Actually, only the Royal Mother was allowed that honor, following the minor inconvenience of my head not fitting through the birth canal and coming out a bit misshapen. That led my mother to sob uncontrollably for a few minutes, although according to grandmother, I did *not* have a big head, and it was my mother's fault for having a small vagina.

Otherwise, it all went without a hitch.

Arcturian astrologer Amius was well prepared, pulled out her computer, and put in the date, the exact time I emerged from the womb at 8:15 a.m., and the precise location of the Maimonides Birthing Center. She noted the planets in their signs and the relationships between them—there were a lot of squares, trines, quincunxes, and sesquiquadrates. Even *before* my birth, Amius had foretold who I would be—a potential, with all humility, world savior. But nothing had prepared the master astrologer for whom I, the prince, *had once been.*

She waited until the nurses had siphoned off the cord blood stem cells and then rushed to the Queen.

"Your Highness!" she said in an excited whisper. "It is just as you foretold in your dreams. This child *is* destined to help the people on this planet—but it will not be an easy path. He comes in with the mark of Chiron, the wounded healer, who is one degree from his sun in the twelfth house. Still…I have even bigger news." She inhaled deeply. "*Much* bigger."

"Please, Amius." The Queen cradled me closely. "What have you discovered?"

"He is also, without a doubt," the astrologer said, eyes widening, "an incarnation of a legendary thirteenth-level Arcturian master physician, a priest of the old ways. One we know by the name of Master Ian. An elder of the Antwarian clan who lived thousands of years before the Reptilian invasion, a revered healer with access to hidden magical knowledge—knowledge he planted deep in this third-dimensional reality within sacred objects, preparing for the healing of individuals and planetary bodies when the time was right." She took a deep breath, exhaled, and continued. "Knowledge concealed many centuries ago within Earth rocks, trees, and mountains when Ian first travelled to this galaxy. I believe he's come back to rediscover these treasures and help the Earth and our people."

A single tear trailed down my mother's fair cheek. Those Arcturians still in the room, including my father and grandmother, knelt at her bedside.

"My son is a *terton*," she said.

"It appears so, your Highness," Amius said. "He carries the wounds from our past and is here to now help transform them. Please look at his birth chart and see for yourself." While Master Amius continued, the Queen, who had studied astrology as one of the basic Arcturian sciences, reviewed the chart. "As I look at the transits and placement of the planets, there are several outstanding features.

"First, you can see he has two homes, Arcturus and Earth, as Gemini the twins are located in his fourth house of home. He also has a grand water trine with Venus in the first house in Pisces, the Moon in Cancer in the fifth and Neptune in Scorpio in the eighth, which indicates he will be extremely sensitive, possessing a highly developed Arcturian intuition and emotional sensitivity. Not only will he be able to feel truth, as do most Arcturians, but he will be able to access *universal* truths with great compassion. This is represented by his Venus in Pisces in the first house as well as his sun in the twelfth next to Mercury, which illuminates all that is hidden."

"This *is* wonderful," the Queen said. "But will he *fruitfully* bring our highest Arcturian ideals of love and compassion to others and help this planet? If, as a Chirotic healer, he will suffer…will his suffering be worth it?"

"Yes, your Highness," Amius assured. "His Uranus in the sixth house ensures this service will take place in medicine as he brings new, revolutionary ways of healing to this planet. These will not only help heal others, but his Neptune square Sun, Chiron, and Mercury in the twelfth and Uranus in the sixth indicate the healing will come from a deep spiritual penetration of the great mysteries of life and death."

A serious look appeared on Amius' face.

"Yet I must caution you, my Queen. As wonderful as this news is, there is one very difficult aspect. The newborn prince will go through many dark nights of the soul to know the truth. His Pluto and Jupiter in the seventh shows that his relationship with others will be highly contentious as he fights for truth."

"Thank you, Master Amius," the Queen replied, maintaining a stoic expression. "I have one last question. What do you make of his Mars and Saturn at the midheaven conjuncting his north node?"

"Excellent question, my Queen. There will be a strong focus on education, higher learning, expansion of the mind, religion, and medicine. It also looks as if he'll be doing quite a bit of foreign travel. I think it best if you start to train him in different foreign languages while he is young and his mind is malleable."

After hearing the reading of my birth chart, my mother Queen Dawn resolved to name me Ian in honor of my previous incarnation. She became determined to encourage the positive character traits laid out in the chart but also help me modify and transform some of the potentially negative ones like Mars and Saturn at the midheaven in a fire sign, trining Pluto, and Jupiter in Leo, another fire sign. She knew she might have a little fireball on her hands and would have to watch out—especially with my grandmother regularly spending time with me.

At around thirteen months, I was old enough to walk and speak—a late bloomer by Arcturian standards. My mother finally put my spiritual education in the hands of Master Dorje. My nursemaid, Viviane, a French au pair, would care for me during the early morning hours and teach me French, which explained why "Ooh-la-la" was the first phrase to come out of my mouth. This dismayed my grandmother, who would have preferred something like "Bubby" based on my newly acquired DNA.

I was then taken to the Copernican-Chiron Magick Academy, where Dorje was in the process of training the other recruits in a recreated Arcturian temple.

CHAPTER 24:

ASPIRATIONS

As promised following the Battle of Woodstock, Master Dorje *had* opened a new training academy on Earth. The prior Copernican-Chiron Magick Academy was established on Arcturus in the Earth year 1023 in a remote mountain region known as Orablaelus. It was a magnificent 108-foot temple constructed from local granite, iron ore, and semiprecious stones surrounded by ultra-translucent windows. It was the site of all higher spiritual teachings on Arcturus until its destruction during the first wave of the Reptilian invasion in 1524.

The United States Army, Navy, Air Force, and Marines each sent twenty of their finest candidates, all of whom had passed a maddening multitude of initial entrance exams. For almost a year, the twenty-four remaining Academy candidates had trained with Dorje. The others had voluntarily terminated by the second month and not yet been replaced as Dorje reworked the entrance exams.

At thirteen months old, I would sit on my small throne—also useful for potty training—and observe the ongoing exercises, which consisted of not only strength and resilience training but also yoga, stretching, Tai-Chi, and Chi Gong. Then there were all the mental exercises Dorje taught regarding discipline, mindfulness, and right action that would lead to calmness and clarity of mind—essential traits in order to be successful in battle.

I would therefore do the mindfulness exercises with the troops, sitting upright in the proper posture and following my breath in and out so that my half-blooded princely brain was able to focus. I found these exercises very calming, and they cooled the fire that oftentimes I felt burning within. It was especially potent because of the sacred surroundings of the academy—incense with copal filled the temple's main room that had thirty-five-foot-high ceilings, columns painted with sacred symbols in multicolored pastels, and a shrine at the front of the temple with images and candles to honor all religious traditions found on Earth.

• • • •

"Recruits," Dorje said one day. "Today we are going to discuss some of the basic tenets of magick and how to begin to realize our potential. How can we purify and overcome our ignorance? The obscurations coming through the 'ego' and our five senses. How can we do that in the easiest way possible to become stronger in body and mind and achieve our goals?"

Everyone in the temple looked perplexed. This lesson definitely wasn't taught in any school they had yet attended, even military academy. The closest they ever got to this type of training was watching the *Karate Kid*.

"Master," one recruit yelled—his name was Marty. "I know. 'Wax on, wax off.' 'Paint the fence.' 'Sweep the leg.' Right?" This brought laughter.

"No," the Master replied, smiling, "but you've identified some chores for *you* to do after class today." The recruits laughed again. "Come over here," Dorje continued. He made a sharp motion over Marty's *dan tien*, his solar plexus chakra associated with energy and willpower and disrupted his energy field using the mind and power of focused intention. I had seen this before. Dorje had just cut the man's source of energy without ever touching him. "Come at me with all you have," the Master said, backing away. "Surely an old man like me can't possibly take on such a young, strapping specimen."

Marty ran full speed at the Master, beginning a front roundhouse kick and knee strike. Dorje raised his hands and blew in the recruit's direction several feet before he arrived. The Marine's own energy flung him onto the mat several feet away. Everyone gasped as Marty lay splayed out on the mat.

"Fear does not exist in this dojo, does it?" Dorje asked. The recruits weren't laughing anymore. "So how did I do that?" The recruits shook their heads. "I used his own energy against him," he explained, "but to learn such abilities, it took many years of training. So for those of you who lack patience and perseverance, please get up and leave now."

No one moved. In months earlier, some students would have left, but Master Dorje had narrowed it down to those who were truly worthy. A calm and profound stillness came over the room as they realized the power they had witnessed and to which they would soon be privy.

"Purification takes place in four stages," Dorje continued. "First, you must acknowledge your defilements. Anger, pride, grasping at conceptuality, and/or holding onto aversion to that with which you feel repelled. These are some of the first imperfections you must overcome."

"And how can we do that, Master?" Genine asked, raising her hand. She was one of the Navy recruits. "I feel repelled by some of the men who are in this room today, ogling me like I was a piece of chuck roast on display at a meat market." Genine was five-foot-seven with long blonde hair and a striking figure. It was clear to everyone that testosterone was flowing in the air around her.

"Ah, you have very few filters like an Arcturian," Dorje said. Everyone laughed except for Zach, who was sitting next to her. "The simplest and most direct way to achieve purification starts with our creating aspiration prayers," Dorje explained with a firm voice. "My great teacher Master Tai Situpa in his twelfth incarnation revealed that one way to purify and overcome ignorance is to have the strong desire to do what is right...or at least to do one's best. Even if in the beginning, we don't know the way to accomplish our goals, with proper aspiration we will discover methods to fulfill them. We must first start with writing down our aspiration prayers and reading them daily. When we strengthen each aspiration, our subconscious mind knows which path to follow naturally."

Andrew, who was one of the top cadets from his graduating class at West Point, reflected for a moment and then raised his hand.

"Master, can you give an example of why strong aspirations are so important? Isn't it obvious all of us want to succeed? Want to serve our country and do the right thing? Why write down goals we already know and are conscious of?"

Dorje contemplated Andrew's words and searched for the best way to explain. He thought back to his own training with Master Tai.

"Let's take the example of a farmer," Dorje said. "If he wants to grow a prize-winning crop, he must first begin with the right ingredients: the proper seeds and the soil to support and nourish the seeds. Then the farmer must care for the seeds when adverse conditions arise—too much sun and wind or not enough rain. If the growing conditions are not optimal, or if he harvests the seed too early, he will not obtain the full fruit of his labor. Without knowing the proper time to harvest, we will not obtain the best result."

"Our culture has a famous saying," Andrew said. "'As you sow, so ye shall reap.'"

"This is true," Dorje responded. "But can you be certain about the quality of the seed you wish to plant and whether the soil can support it? If the soil—or in our case, the mind—has impurities of anger, ignorance, pride, aversion, and greed, will it support the proper nourishment of the seed…our aspirations? And if the seed itself has not been carefully chosen, are you sure it will grow into the desired crop? If you plant seeds of wheat, you will not get corn." He paused, then continued. "We are looking to plant seeds that grow into more than an average crop but rather, the most beautiful and nourishing ingathering that will provide sustenance not just for a few but for billions in years to come. Do you understand?"

Andrew nodded with the rest of the class.

"Your world must awaken now and reach its fullest potential *if* humans are to survive with any significant quality of life on this planet. You are now going through your sixth mass extinction in Earth's history. There have previously been five: the Ordovician-Silurian Extinction, the Late Devonian Extinction, the Permian-Triassic Extinction, the Triassic-Jurassic Extinction, and the Cretaceous-Paleogene Extinction.

"The last one eliminated the dinosaurs sixty-five million years ago through volcanic activity, asteroid impact, and climate change. It ended three quarters of the life on Earth. Only the Alpha Draconians and their ancestors survived, with very few small mammals remaining. In the case of the current extinction event, one quarter of the diversity of your current plant, animal, and insect species have already disappeared by 2038, and scientists estimate a third will be gone by 2050. That leaves you twelve more years to try to stop the evolutionary clock."

Other than his voice, the chamber was utterly silent.

"Unless there is a radical shift in the way the world and its leaders think and act, once you cross the threshold, inexorable suffering waits on the other side. Due to the intense heat and solar radiation, people will be forced to live during the day in underground chambers like the Morlocks in *The Time Machine* or perish from heat stroke. Food supplies will be scarce, since most growing fields will have either been scorched by wildfires or flooded, and pollinators will be gone, making plant and vegetable growth nearly impossible. Most will have to rely on raising chickens and rabbits as sources of protein as they live off scraps in underground pens, while some humans will try to scrounge for polluted fish in the ocean, where they will succumb to rogue pirates and high levels of radiation.

"Clean drinking water will only be available through advanced home purification units for those who can afford them, as community recycled waste facilities will be scarce and mostly inoperable. Unpredictable weather patterns, the rising sea level, and storm surges will destroy coastal communities and lead to almost a billion climate refugees.

"Working hospitals stocked with medicine will be a rarity and, as insufficient numbers will be around to bury those who die, it will lead to disease outbreaks not seen since your Middle Ages. As parts of the world become uninhabitable, global powers will invade surrounding countries in the attempt to survive and gather precious resources. This is what surely awaits you unless decisive action is now undertaken."

He paused and scanned the faces of those before him.

"We, therefore, have to do something to help those who are suffering and who surely will be suffering. Such action requires great magick born of only the very purest intention, and so we pray and create aspiration prayers. 'May I be able to act to relieve the suffering of others; may I have the wisdom and knowledge to proceed in the right direction so that the greatest number of people may benefit.' Simple prayers with purity of heart and intention will be heard in the universal matrix of love and wisdom. The universe supports such intention and responds accordingly."

His voice dropped and became more ominous.

"Be clear, however. This is from the heart *and* the mind. It reflects in part the meaning of your world's Serenity prayer: 'God, grant me the Serenity to accept the things that I cannot change, the Courage to change the things I can, and the Wisdom to know the difference.' The development of such wisdom is based on proper aspiration and that aspiration is in turn based on not just asking that we ourselves may benefit but that *all* beings may benefit, enemies and friends alike."

Dorje pointed to a glass jar and wore a wry smile.

"Each of you will write down your aspiration prayers and place them into this jar by the end of the day. This will tell me if you understand the beginning steps of wisdom that enable us to see clearly what is right, what is appropriate, and what is essential. I will see you all again at zero-eight-hundred hours tomorrow. Class dismissed."

• • • •

The group stood, bowed to the master as he left the room, and then began chatting amongst themselves. They remained in the room and wrote out their aspirations on recycled paper. One by one, they then walked to the front of the room, dropped the prayers into a jar, and retired to their rooms. Some took only a few minutes, while others stayed in the room all day, contemplating the question and response.

Even I, Prince Ian, staggered across the room with a full heart and a fuller diaper and scrawled as best I could on one of the sheets.

• • • •

At midnight, Dorje opened the jar and read the aspiration prayers. He then knew which recruits would proceed to the next level of training.

CHAPTER 25:

A SOCRATIC DIALOGUE

"Do the thing we fear, and death of fear is certain."

—Socrates, teacher and Alopekean Starseed

Persons of the Dialogue

MASTER DORJE

RECRUIT ANDREW

RECRUIT GENINE

RECRUIT LARRY

RECRUIT MORGANA

RECRUIT MARTY

RECRUIT ROBERTA

RECRUIT SAM

RECRUIT ZACH

PRINCE IAN

The recruits arrive for their training at eight o'clock in the morning. Each takes their cushion and sits on the floor of the temple, meditating undistractedly in their seven-point posture while awaiting the Master. The temple is more than half empty. Questions and the thick smoke of copal incense hover in the room.

ANDREW
Master, where are the other
students?

MASTER DORJE
You are the only remaining
apprentices of the twenty-four who
were here yesterday. The others did
not understand and follow my
instructions. I asked everyone to
write down your highest aspiration
prayers. Only those present today
exhibited the proper motivation and
faith to continue in the program.

ANDREW
I don't understand! These other
recruits had adopted the highest
military codes of honor. Core
values of loyalty, duty, respect,
personal courage, honor, integrity,
and selfless service.

MASTER DORJE
This is true, recruit Andrew, but
there were two ingredients missing
from most of the responses. The
first was motivation that was not
broad enough to encompass all of
life as we know it. The motivation
we are talking about must be
limitless. Only then may we attain
mastery of the highest forms of
magick to transform the world. No
one can be left out. Not even our
enemies.

MORGANA

And what was the other ingredient,
Master Dorje?

MASTER DORJE

Some of the recruits wrote from
their minds and not their hearts.
Anyone can parrot "sacred" and
lofty words. The wisdom *we* seek
is the wisdom of the heart. Even
the little prince knows this.
Master Ian, please tell us what
you learned last night during your
bedtime story.

ZACH

Are we to learn of three little
pigs now? Goldilocks? Is the Big
Bad Wolf a badly behaving Reptile?
Is the ugly troll under the bridge
now online, needing to be crushed
because of their posts? How is a
one-year-old going to teach us
about magick?

MASTER DORJE

How is it, Zach, that the source of
your learning concerns you so? What
would you like to say, Prince Ian?

PRINCE IAN

First, I just made a big number two
on my throne. And here is my other,
very simple secret that only with
the heart can one see rightly. What

is essential is invisible to the
eye. *L'essentiel est invisible pour*
les yeux.

MASTER DORJE

Prince Ian's French au-pair has
been doing more than just changing
his diapers. The quote is from
Antoine de Saint-Exupéry's beloved
tale of a pilot and a young alien
prince. The tale of a young prince
visiting the Earth was chosen by
Queen Dawn as one of the early
fables told to Prince Ian, as
it mirrored his own life and
experience. It would, she hoped,
give him a basis to relate to the
new and challenging conditions he
would face and allow him a simple
way to relate to people and magick.
What our own young prince read
last night is as relevant to our
purpose as any military and magical
treatise you will study.

To help your world, you must first
understand the nature of human
adults and their difficulty in
perceiving what is important. To
understand who we are and where we
are going, we must first understand
where we have come from. The
parable of the *Little Prince* is the
parable of your world. Just as in
the book, if you do not pull out
the weeds overrunning the surface
of your planet the moment they are

recognized as such, the roots will
have gone too deep, leading to
catastrophic effects.

                MASTER DORJE
Does anyone here remember the six
foibles of humanity as described in
the book?

                ROBERTA
I do not, Master. Only that I loved
the book.

                MASTER DORJE
There are six planets with only one
life form living on each. These
include a king with no subjects
giving orders that require no
effort, as they are in harmony with
the laws of nature. There is a
narcissistic man who only wants
praise and admiration although
there is no one around to whom he
can compare himself. An alcoholic
who drinks to erase the shame of
his drinking, a businessman who is
only enamored with materialistic
concerns, a lamplighter on a planet
who wastes his life following
orders with no meaning, and an
elderly geographer who has never
gone anywhere or witnessed the
things he chronicles. Was it true
then, and is it true now?

                    MARTY
Master, it is relevant now. You
taught us yesterday that, without
purification, it will be impossible
for us to reach the ultimate goal
and that first, we must acknowledge
our defilements. We must look inside
and face our shadow.

                  MASTER DORJE
Excellent, Marty. In fact, my
instructions for you today are to
shine the light on your darkness,
to uncover the truth which has
been hidden in the recesses of
your minds and our collective
unconscious. It is easy to see the
darkness outside of ourselves. It
is more difficult when it is hidden
in our minds. The transformation we
seek must come from integration of
the darkness and the light so that
when you do finally come face-to-
face with the Family of Dark, you
will be prepared. Evil has taken
many forms and controls minions
across this and multiple universes.
The Reptiles are only one
manifestation of this destructive
power.

Evil's greatest weapons are fear
and doubt. Fear is one of the six
great emotional afflictions, and
the Reptiles have been using it
to control humans for centuries.
Usually, when we experience

different disturbing emotions—
whether they be the ego's self-
clinging as a "true" independent
entity, desire, fear, hatred,
greed, anger, or impatience—a great
number of thoughts arise, which
often leads us to perform negative
actions. To quote the words of one
of your famous thinkers, Napoleon
Hill, "Fears are nothing more than
a state of mind." Only by examining
and understanding our own shadows
can we survive the onslaught of
disturbing emotions.

LARRY
How shall we start, Master?

MASTER DORJE
After examining fully and honestly
where we are now and what positive
and negative qualities we have
adopted, we will begin the first
step on an ancient path that has
been traversed by many masters who
have come before us. One master in
this particular lineage, Khenpo
Gangshar, was an Arcturian *terton*
who lived in Tibet during your
twentieth century.

The area where he lived in Kham was
in great turmoil as the Chinese
invasion was just beginning, and
Khenpo saw the need to transmit
enlightenment teachings in a fast

and effective manner so the general
populace could more wisely deal
with what they were about to face.
There was no time for a three-year
meditation retreat, the usual path
for those who wish to tame and
understand the nature of the mind.
They needed stability and peace of
mind…and *fast*.

Those citizens who applied these
very teachings and remedies awoke
during that terrible time and did
not suffer.

MORGANA
Master, if these powerful teachings
have been available, why didn't
we know about them until now? Many
of us traversed a spiritual path
before joining the Academy. If
there are others out there who have
achieved the ultimate result, then
why haven't they come forth and
declared themselves so they too
could teach others?

MASTER DORJE
These teachings have only been
passed down from master to disciple
for the past eighty years.
Fortunately, I was present in Tibet
during those times and was one of
Khenpo Gangshar's disciples.

                    SAM
You visited and lived on the Earth
almost a century ago?

                MASTER DORJE
Oh yes.

                MORGANA
And lived in monasteries in Tibet
with fellow Arcturians?

                MASTER DORJE
Most certainly.

                PRINCE IAN
This guy has been around the block.

                DORJE
The first time I met Khenpo
Gangshar, I was studying with one
of his masters in Kham in the
1950s, and word emerged that the
Khenpo had woken. Arising from
meditation on a snowy February
morning, the Khenpo was in his
monastery gazing out the window
at the mountains in Tibet. He
suddenly noticed that the top third
of the mountain peaks had melted.
Early signs of global warming were
present even then. He felt a cold
shiver as he rested his mind to
understand the significance of what
he had just witnessed, and then he
recognized this was an extremely

inauspicious sign and that his
homeland was soon to be invaded,
people killed, and teachings
destroyed. The looming pain was
unbearable.

While meditating on the pain and
suffering his people were about to
endure, he had a heart attack,
causing him to suffer a fatal
arrythmia. As he lay dead on the
cold stone floor, a large black
raven suddenly appeared on the
windowsill and looked directly at
the Khenpo for some time. The bird
then flew from its perch and landed
beside Khenpo Gangshar's head,
pecking at the top of it, where the
energy channels enter and leave the
body.

Within seconds, the Khenpo came
back to life. He sprung into
an upright posture and, having
completely awoken, recognized the
full nature of his mind. A sudden
and full awakening had occurred,
a great gift that had come out of
Master Gangshar's deep compassion
for others. He gratefully accepted
the gift and knew exactly what
to do with it. He shared his
methods with others to ripen their
evolution in a very fast and
effective manner. He might not be
able to change the course of events
or prevent the destruction of his

homeland, but these teachings would help prevent others from suffering the consequences of the crisis they were soon to face.

                GENINE
No wonder you understood human nature so well.

                MASTER DORJE
The reason others, including myself, have not taught these particular teachings is that once the invasion commenced, there was a danger of exposing one's knowledge to the authorities. Such knowledge might easily have been used for the wrong purposes, and so the teachings needed to remain hidden. Until now.

Khenpo Gangshar was an Arcturian *terton* who discovered these mind treasures, and it is your good fortune to have all made it to this stage of the training. Understand, however, once you enter onto this path, it is a path of absolute power, a power to be wielded wisely. If you abuse it, the negative consequences will be multiplied manyfold. If you diligently follow it with just enough faith to follow my instructions each day, you will discover treasures you had not

suspected were yours. It will be
as a poor man complaining that he
has no money, yet his house was
situated directly over a gold mine.

                MASTER DORJE
Before I begin to transmit these
teachings, we must first develop the
proper *motivation* to benefit all
beings throughout time and space.
It is for their benefit we study
here today. Reflect on this. Only
then can you learn to access the
power of the light. To do this, we
must confront the darkness and fear
that live inside each of us. Fear
and courage, light and dark, as
well as good and evil are all part
of a spectrum of dualistic thinking
and feeling that point to something
much more profound and true. We
must transcend the dualistic mind
to see the ultimate truth.

                GENINE
Master, what is that truth?

                MASTER DORJE
It is simple. Life is like a dream,
nothing more, nothing less.

                LARRY
I'm sorry. Did you say life is like
a dream? Are you implying that what
we are experiencing right now is
not really happening?

PRINCE IAN
*"Row, row, row your boat, gently
down the stream, merrily, merrily,
merrily, merrily, life is but a
dream."*

MASTER DORJE
Excellent, young prince. You are
learning your magick lessons well!
Oh, life is happening, recruits,
but not the way you believe
it's happening. Let me ask you
a question. If in a dream you
are being chased by monsters and
you suddenly wake, sweating and
fearful, but happy you are safe,
were the monsters real? Were you
ever really in danger?

MORGANA
Of course not.

MASTE DORJE
Well, it's like that.

ZACH
Then what we experience in our day-
to-day lives has the same reality
as the dream state? I can touch
and feel things while I'm awake—
that tells me it's real. And I can
ask others to confirm the reality
of what I am seeing, hearing, and
feeling. How can this be so?

MASTER DORJE

When you take a human birth, you
come in with dualistic perception
which acts as a veil—one that
prevents you from seeing the whole
truth. Humans experience everything
in opposites. Good/bad, happy/
sad, man/woman, life/death. Yet
there is another way to experience
your reality, and by calming the
mind, you can access this absolute
truth. The final wisdom we seek lies
beyond the extremes of relative and
absolute reality. *Therein* lies the
ultimate source of our power.

I've previously quoted for you a
great Indian master by the name
of Saraha: "People who hold to
reality are as stupid as cows.
People who hold to unreality are
even more stupid." This refers to
letting go of extremes in beliefs
or perception in order to see the
truth. Let me give you another
example. Although the human brain
exists and has a color and form
and location in physical space,
it is not the same for the mind.
You can't say that the mind truly
exists, since it has no color or
form, and no one has ever seen it.
Yet you can't say that mind doesn't
exist, as it is the basis of all
you are experiencing.

The true nature of mind lies
between existence and non-

existence. It can only be
experienced non-dualistically.
When we look directly at mind non-
distractedly and the thoughts and
emotions that arise from it, we
can see that they have no color
or form, do not exist anywhere in
space, and lack any solid reality
or true, absolute existence. That
is their empty nature. Yet they
continually arise, and we can be
conscious of their existence. That
is the clarity aspect of mind. Mind
is the inseparable unity of this
clarity and emptiness, and we can
recognize its absolute nature and
hence, full power, by resting non-
distractedly and non-conceptually
without effort in meditation. That
is why Saraha says, "Homage to the
mind, which is a wish fulfilling
jewel."

It is by working with our mind
and its afflictions that we can
see the ultimate truth. When
thoughts and emotions arise, and
we look directly at the mind
without distraction, we see they
are simply waves in the ocean of
consciousness, waves which dissolve
back into formlessness.

                ROBERTA
Master, if I've understood
correctly, everything comes from
the mind, and by understanding its

true nature, we can access a power
and wisdom not normally accessible.

                MASTER DORJE
Yes. As per Master Norhla: "The
most important thing we need to do
is to recognize the essence of the
one who thinks. Everything that
exists is created and generated
from mind itself. Happiness and
suffering, as well as notions of
birth, sickness, old age, and
death all come from mind. They are
relatively true but not absolutely
true. There is nothing that is
outside of—or vaster than—the
mind. Recognition of the mind's
true nature results in full and
complete awakening. When the
mind recognizes itself, what is
revealed is primordial wisdom and
transcendental qualities that
cannot be experienced by our
ordinary, dualistic perceptions."

                SAM
Then our primary goal is to have
our mind recognize itself?

                MASTER DORJE
These instructions you are about
to receive were given in 1957
before Master Gangshar got sick.
At that time, he was teaching in
Surmong monastery where he shared
a prophecy. There were already

difficulties in Tibet for the
Arcturians who settled there. He
said the fighting and war that was
about to break out would increase
if his people were to struggle,
and it would be non-virtuous
motivation borne out of hatred and
jealousy. Likewise, if we acted
upon such motivation and killed
others during the war, it would be
harmful for this and future lives,
resulting in a deterioration of
the wisdom teachings. What should,
therefore, be done?

The Master said to do things in
accord with The Great Way; to be
patient and compassionate with a
kind heart and to free ourselves,
looking at the nature of the mind
with these special instructions.

                MARTY
How many people applied these
teachings, Master? The ability to
be patient with a kind heart while
witnessing the tragedy of senseless
killing seems almost an impossible
task.

                MASTER DORJE
You are correct, Marty. There was a
window of opportunity to practice
these teachings, and thousands
applied them during that time.
The Master stated that during the
first quarter of the year, things
would get worse as war broke out,

but during the fifth, sixth, and
seventh months, we could go to the
"secret lands." Which we did. These
lands are not outside of us but
inside our minds. His words are as
appropriate now as they were almost
one hundred years ago.

Understand, this was something new.
Prophecies of the secret lands
had been made before by many great
Masters, but the meaning remained
hidden and few truly understood it
until Master Gangshar came along.
What were the instructions?

To get to the secret lands, first we
would come across a great river. We
might try different ways to cross the
river, but there was only one way to
cross. Along the banks, there was a
great tree. We had to chop it down,
but we could cut only at the root of
the tree and not with an ordinary
tool. The instructions were to find
a crystal axe there at the banks
of the river, chop down the roots
of the tree, and then have it fall
across the river to become a bridge.
That was the only way to get to the
other side.

ANDREW
This story reminds me of Zen
koans I learned long ago, which I
tried to solve. Master, wouldn't
a crystal axe break if we try and

cut the roots of a mighty tree? It
would seem to me that one would
need a special weapon to accomplish
such a deed.

                    MASTER DORJE
Excellent point, Andrew. I am quite
pleased by this question. The
key is not to take the words of
the prophecy literally. It is not
possible to have a river we cannot
cross. And does there exist a tree
that can't be cut? This teaching by
Master Gangshar was symbolic. Signs
and symbols pointing to the truth.
Does anyone know what the great
river represents?

                    ROBERTA
I think I know, Master. There's a
famous quote from Rainer Maria Rilke
that reminds me of the great river:
"May what I do flow from me *like a
river*, no forcing and no holding
back, the way it is with children."
Is he referring to acceptance and
not resisting the flow of life to
understand the Great Way?

                    MASTER DORJE
Excellent. It is true that non-
resistance and flowing with
circumstances may provide a way to
swim properly in the river. But
will that get us across?

MORGANA
I do not know.

ZACH
Nor I, Master.

PRINCE IAN
I think Winnie the Pooh had the
answer.

SAM
Dear Lord…

PRINCE IAN
Winnie said, "Rivers know this:
there is no hurry. We shall get
there someday." Now I'd like a
glass of ginger tea, please.

MASTER DORJE
Ah, young Prince, excellent! But
it is a bit more complicated than
that. It is true we *will* all arrive
at the other shore eventually,
whether we rush or take our time,
but in this case, we are still
pointing to something else. Anyone?

GENINE
I think I may know. The quote by
Kabir, "As the river surrenders
itself to the ocean, what is inside
me moves inside you." This points
to the notion of surrender and
oneness. Water here represents the
inseparability of consciousness.

ANDREW
And in *Siddhartha*, the river
symbolizes not only the journey
toward enlightenment but also
the realization of enlightenment
itself.

MASTER DORJE
Also excellent responses. Each
contains some kernel of truth, yet
the great river we are discussing
here is something else. What
exactly is the great river? Master
Gangshar was referring to the
great river of suffering we all
face in our lives. It is filled
with negative emotions and adverse
circumstances arising from our
previous actions. How, then, can we
cross this river?

Alongside the river is the tree,
which represents clinging to the
ego or self. We need to cut it
down, get rid of it. Then once we
cut it, we can *use* it. We bring it
to the path and cross the river of
suffering to arrive at omniscience
and freedom.

Wisdom is the crystal axe. Wisdom
is the lack of self. The only place
you can find it is at the root
of ego clinging, as the self has
no essence. If you see its true
essence, we can use the crystal axe
and wisdom to realize selflessness

and get across the river of
suffering to arrive at ultimate
knowledge and finally experience the
three wisdom bodies—the emanation
body, the enjoyment body, and
the unchanging body of boundless
clarity and emptiness. These all
result from completely cutting the
root of ego clinging, the ultimate
source of our suffering, which
will bring innumerable benefits to
yourself and those around you.

                LARRY
I still don't fully understand,
Master. I have an obvious question,
the elephant in the middle of the
room, I suppose.

            MASTER DORJE
Ahhhh, so that's where I left him!

                LARRY
Master Dorje, Reptilians are
attempting to dominate the human
race and the planet's resources.
There is scarcity of clean food,
potable water, and medicine for
the sick. How can meditation on
the nature of our minds change
the course of what has happened
or will happen? Isn't external
action more important than internal
examination?

MASTER DORJE

A good question, Larry. You must
accept that the mind is the basis
of all experience, good and bad.
You must always remember the mind
can either be a powerful ally or
enemy depending on whether or
not you have tamed it. It is as
it is told in the story of *Le
Petite Prince*: The fox desires
to be tamed and teaches the
prince how to do it. Once tamed,
something considered "ordinary"
suddenly becomes special. The
mind's ultimate nature is that of
unlimited potential. All things are
possible. We can effect significant
positive change in the world, which
is now being destroyed, once we
have realized that potential.

MORGANA

Many of our saints and mystics
have attempted such journeys, and
only a few have succeeded. These,
however, resulted in miracles.
Some powerful female Christian
mystics, including St. Catherine of
Siena, Joan of Arc, Hildegard von
Bingen, St. Teresa of Avila, and
Thérèse of Lisieux, all attained
a level of divine communion and
realization, but it took *years*. It
was ultimately innocence and great
devotion that helped them transcend
conceptual experience. Thérèse

of Lisieux specifically believed
that children have an aptitude for
spiritual experience, which adults
should model.

                    PRINCE IAN
Hear hear!

                    MARTY
There are similar stories of *male*
mystics like Padre Pio, whose
path was also one of prayer and
unification. Those close to him
attested to extraordinary gifts
including the miracles of healing,
prophecy, reading minds and hearts,
the gift of tongues, levitation,
bilocation, forgoing sleep and
nourishment without ill effects,
and even possessing pleasant-
smelling wounds of the stigmata.
Yet to achieve his state, Padre
Pio encouraged people to let go of
emotions like sadness and suffering,
as sadness would prevent the Holy
Spirit from acting freely. If I
feel an emotion like sadness, how
do I quickly release it? Such
feelings seem to remain even when
I *try* to let them go. It's as if
these emotions have a power beyond
my control.

                    MASTER DORJE
If an emotion arises, where does
it come from? Where does it stay

and where does it go? When thoughts arise, where do they come from, where do they stay and where do they go? Look, see what you see, and then relax and rest without distraction in the clear, empty spacious essence of mind. Do this over and over with proper motivation until you have seen the ultimate truth. Then dedicate the merit for all sentient beings, limitless through time and space. That is the instruction for today and for every day.

ZACH

My mind has difficulty, Master, staying in one place. My attention wanders to other objects, so it is difficult to look without distraction. What do you suggest I do?

MASTER DORJE

I suggest that before you attempt standard-insight meditation on the nature of the mind, you *first* stabilize your mind with calm-abiding meditation. Spend five minutes three times a day watching your breath go in and out of your nostrils, and each time your attention wanders, bring it back to the breath. Practice this until you have some stability. Later, I will teach you other techniques to

enhance your practice and correct
common errors.

MARTY

Master, since people are being so
honest, there are days I have so much
stress and worry that I feel like I'm
losing my mind. What can I do?

MASTER DORJE

Have you ever "found" your mind?
You can't lose that which you never
found. Have you ever actually seen
your mind? Does it have a color
or form? Does the mind *come from*
anywhere or *go* anywhere? No. Mind
has no form, no color, and no
substance. The inseparability of
this emptiness and mental clarity
is the primordial, continuous
nature of mind. We simply recognize
it by resting non-distractedly,
non-conceptually, and without effort
in the meditative state. Oh, Major
Broward, we were just wrapping up.

• • • •

Major Broward walked in on the class just in time to hear the last train-ee's question and wasn't sure why he couldn't lose his mind, living with his wife and mother-in-law. He hadn't been there for the entire lesson, but somehow he felt strangely reassured that insanity was not immedi-ately in his future.

He also liked the sound of accessing a state of consciousness in meditation and resting non-distractedly, non-conceptually, and with-out effort. It sounded easy, and there was a peace and assurance that had gently washed over the group that he could feel. Dorje sensed his interest.

"Let's finish with a five-minute sitting meditation," Dorje said. "And now that your minds are calm and stable, I will explain to you one last important teaching before we all leave the temple to retire to our chambers."

He waited as the group sat quietly—long enough that Broward wondered if he'd forgotten what he was going to say.

"A Regent protector of the multiverse is one of the highest and most sacred of responsibilities. You can all be proud of being here and of what you have and will accomplish. I would like to leave off with a quote from my sacred Master Tai Situ: 'First of all, you should have full unconditional faith and trust in yourself, that is number one. Not in your ego but in your awakened nature, your primordial wisdom, your essence.'"

"You will soon be called upon to fully awaken Earth's Starseeds," Dorje continued. "Remember to have full unconditional faith and trust in yourself. You can all do this—and your world is depending on it."

CHAPTER 26:

RETURN OF THE LIVING DEAD
(AND OTHER IMPENDING HUMAN-ENDING CALAMITIES OF EARTH'S 2040s)

"If you look into your own heart, and you find nothing wrong there, then what is there to worry about? What is there to fear?"

—Confucius

Following the Battle of Woodstock, there was relative peace between the years of 2037 and 2038. Exceptions included continued political battles over environmental regulations despite links of environmental chemicals to Alzheimer's disease, autism, autoimmune disease, heart disease, and cancer.

There were legal challenges to force food manufacturers to voluntarily remove heavy metals and pesticides from baby food due to children's diminishing IQs and ongoing fights to remove women's reproductive rights, legal battles over which pharmaceutical company should be held responsible for the latest narcotic, and court battles over using AK-15s for shooting squirrels.

Also, there were rare sightings of vampires and demons in Washington D.C. lobbying for Big Oil. The Reptilians and their various allies were temporarily pinned back and speciously powerless during this short period of time. However, in the summer of 2039, it became evident that this was no longer the case.

The first hint of trouble were the zombies.

A news article appeared in the *NY Post* on February 8, 2039:

FATAL "ZOMBIE DEER" DISEASE
COULD SPREAD TO HUMANS

A fatal neurological disease that turns deer into zombies could spread to humans, health experts are warning. The sickness, called chronic wasting disease (CWD), affects deer, elk, reindeer, and moose and causes the animals to dramatically lose weight and walk in repetitive patterns.

Other symptoms include loss of fear of humans, stumbling, and listlessness. As of January, twenty-four states—including New York—had reported CWD in free-ranging deer, elk, and moose, according to the Centers for Disease Control and Prevention, leading to several outbreaks of infected human zombie populations across the country.

Experts from the University of Minnesota stressed at a hearing Thursday that the disease should be treated as a public health issue, the *St. Paul Pioneer Press* reported.

"It is probable that human cases of CWD associated with the consumption of contaminated meat will be documented in the years ahead," Manny Sickerholm, the director for the University of Minnesota Center for Infectious Disease and Research Prevention, told lawmakers. "It is possible that the number of human cases will be substantial. Anyone who walks around

in circles, stumbling with listlessness, should therefore immediately be shot on the spot."

Shortly after the statement was appeared, the University of Minnesota released a statement indicating
that Director Sickerholm had been removed from
its faculty.

The article caused notable concern among agencies that dealt with
alcoholics, who often walked in circles, stumbling with listlessness.
When the CDC was asked to remark, they declined to comment.

Dr. Sickerholm was among experts who had researched mad cow
disease and its transmission to humans, first discovered in 1996 as
Creutzfeldt-Jakob disease. He'd compared CWD with the mad cow
phenomenon, noting that for some time, experts didn't believe any
such condition could spread to people.

Then the zombie phenomenon manifested at the music festival at
Watkins Glen, forcing everyone to take the threat much more seriously.
Scientists came to believe CWD was passed on through proteins called
prions, present in body fluids like feces, saliva, blood, or urine, and
could remain in the environment for a long time—meaning other animals remained at risk even after an infected elk or deer had died.

The panic that ensued was quickly subsumed by increasing reports
of vampire sightings, horrific stories of demons returning in the form of
political lobbyists, and rumors of the Reptiles returning to power. This
last was substantiated as EPA regulations regarding the health of the air
and water supply continued to be degraded over time by the loosening
and eliminating of prior regulations in order to "stimulate the economy." All despite the Arcturians' fervent warnings.

This allowed the industrial complex to dump increasing amounts
of environmental toxins into the air and water, while air pollution from
raging fires across the globe put increasing amounts of fine particulate
matter into the atmosphere. A perfect Reptilian plan to kill off and
dumb down the human race.

These new risks prompted the national security advisors at U.S.
Homeland Security to invite the top world scientists and physicians
to convene in Brussels for an emergency meeting of the Centre for In-

ternational Governance. The Americans wanted an unbiased group of scientists and physicians who would not be swayed by prior ineffective environmental policy.

Their research, opinions, and public voice had made a difference in the world during the past decades by bringing clarity and innovative thinking to global policy-making by working across disciplines in partnership with the best peers and experts. This allowed them to become one of the few groups that created benchmarks for influential research and trusted analysis.

They were also formed by Canadians, and who didn't like the Canucks?

CIGI now faced challenges which required expanded resources. Having never dealt before with a zombie apocalypse, the spread of vampirism, or demon infestations, they decided to invite the Army ET command along with their Arcturian royal guests.

Including me, the royal prince.

The Army and Arcturians possessed unique, first-hand experience. Scientists who had participated in the fourth national climate assessment were invited, as were representatives of the Department of Commerce and National Oceanic and Atmospheric Administration. The world was at a crucial turning point and now, more than ever, they needed to come up with innovative solutions.

• • • •

The meeting was to be held on June 3, 2039, a Tuesday morning, in downtown Brussels. It was delayed until 10:00 a.m. when many of the participants took a side trip to see the Manneken Pis pee orange-colored beer into a fountain near the main square.

The peeing boy is a two-foot bronze statue, a replica from the 17th-century original. No one could say *why* the statue was erected, but since the Belgian people had created more than five hundred beers in a variety of colors and flavors, no one questioned it, either.

Being a little prince, I especially liked it and asked how I too might urinate orange. I also wanted to know if my father, King Antwar, would make a statue of *me* peeing and put it in our home. It only seemed fair. As a good father should, he agreed, and the statue became the basis for the famous Arcturian microbrewery brand "Get Pissed."

At two and a half years old, it was hardly accurate to call me a "little prince." I was already four and a half feet tall, which alarmed the doctors at the Ian Antwar Pre-Pubescent Pregnancy Pavilion but caused my parents tremendous happiness. They had been afraid my human DNA might stunt my growth, yet I was only a slight bit shorter than the average Arcturian child.

Leaving the statue, the royal family and a contingent of scientists strolled the cobblestone sidewalks of the Grand Place where we were greeted by flower vendors with fragrant purple and yellow freesias, multicolored roses, variegated birds of paradise, and red begonias, which filled the wooden carts. Restaurants buzzed as people sipped their double expressos, drank their Belgian beers, and noshed on crudités and salami with various cheeses and nuts.

I looked up, and noticed a statue of what appeared to be Archangel Michael on top of the Hôtel de Ville. I asked mother what he was doing up there.

"Michael is the patron saint of Brussels," Queen Dawn explained. "Look at the feet of the statue. That shapeless demon represents the Devil himself. Saint Michael was the first defender of the Light against the Dark, and the building he adorns is the *only* original building left in the Grand Place. All of the others were destroyed during various wars. Michael's sovereignty and protection safeguarded his seat of power, and the people of Brussels have depended upon his protection."

Dorje had told me that Michael played a role in subduing the demons at the Battle of Woodstock, so I mentally thanked him and asked the archangel to continue to protect the people of Brussels—as well as my father, mother, and all the other good people on this planet. I also asked him not to allow the weeds on *this* world to grow as they did in the story of the Little Prince.

As I opened and connected with Michael, I felt a warm loving energy and tingling sensation suddenly wash over my body and heard a clear voice resound in my head.

"*Welcome, old friend. My protection is here with you now and always. Just call when you need assistance.*"

My mother looked over and smiled, knowing what had just occurred.

We walked back on the grey patchy cobblestone streets adjacent to the Grand Place, passing stores filled with jewelry, antique shops, cafes, and restaurants. Street vendors sold different local specialties. The frites with mayonnaise in newspaper cones already were my favorites, along with the Vigaufra waffles, the sweet aroma wafting into the streets. I wasn't allowed to eat the *manons* or Godiva or Neuhaus chocolate that I ogled but was allowed to taste one of the waffles, tucking some into a pocket to feed to Amori and Audri later in the day while no one was looking.

Just before Boulevard Léopold III, where NATO headquarters was located, there was a Tibetan shop displaying multicolored flags, brightly colored thangka paintings, and various gold and silver statues. The statues were painted in colorful hues of red, green, blue, and yellow with white cloths draped around the bases. One statue particularly caught my eye: a thin young man wearing unusual clothing holding what looked like a flaming sword in his right hand and a book in his left. I asked Master Dorje who the man was and what book he was reading.

"Excellent questions, young Master," Dorje exclaimed. He was wearing a large white hat and carried his walking stick. "This is Manjushri, the bodhisattva of wisdom who possesses awakened intelligence. In his right hand he holds the flaming sword of compassion, which cuts through desire, attachment, and ignorance. In his left he holds the book of the Prajnaparamita, the teachings on emptiness and the non-dual nature of ultimate reality. Manjushri is an awakened Arcturian master. Perhaps someday you will meet him if you come to school here. Your mother has already explored the admission process to the Free University of Brussels medical school. Your French lessons may soon prove quite handy."

It pleased me to hear that I might be coming to Europe to study. I liked the old buildings and fun food.

"Also, were you to come here, you would be protected by Michael," Dorje added. "You seem to have struck up a friendship with him, no?"

I nodded and smiled.

"That is excellent, young Prince," Dorje said. "I've spoken with Michael, as well, and he will help initiate you—not only into the secrets of medicine but also the great mysteries. There are Arcturian-Tibetans living in downtown Brussels who will be some of your teachers, along with the Freemasons who have built your medical school. The Rosicrucian order has established a strong foundation here. Their studies on philosophy, medicine, mathematics, and alchemy are all preserved in their European libraries, transmitted by way of the Arabic people from Egypt.

"Thousands of years ago, select schools there were formed to explore the mysteries of life. Throughout history, a number of prominent persons in the fields of science and the arts—including Leonardo da Vinci, René Descartes, Baruch Spinoza, Isaac Newton, and even Benjamin Franklin and Thomas Jefferson—have been associated with the Rosicrucian movement, greatly influencing Earth's modern society. You will be in good company as you learn traditions which offer people a way to realize their own infinitely powerful and divine nature."

Dorje pulled out some American money and showed me pictures of Franklin, Jefferson, and Tubman. He also pointed out the eye above the pyramid on the U.S. dollar, explaining that it represented the eye of Providence and God watching over humanity.

"Michael will guide you in your studies," Dorje said, "and show you the common threads among the different Earth religions. He is one of seven archangels, the only one mentioned by name in the Bible and Torah, while also being mentioned in the Qur'an as a protector against evil and a warrior of God. He will be invaluable in fulfilling your destiny."

I pondered Dorje's words as we walked back to the NATO headquarters, getting pieces of the sticky waffle stuck in my teeth. Everyone kept talking to me of my future destiny, but all I wanted was to get to the bathroom and pee. All that orange soda had finally caught up with me.

And then, just as I was heading toward a public bathroom located on the cobblestone side street next to the Grand Place, a strange event transpired—the nature of which has led to ongoing debates to this day among Starseed and human historians alike.

A bolt of lightning struck the town clock tower, causing, Dorje said, an apparent glitch in space-time phenomenon. Stone statues on the tops of the gilded structures surrounding the Grand Place suddenly began to move. Glancing around, I realized the only other witnesses would be those exiting local bars after an evening of what could only be described as "incredibly usual Belgian debauchery."

Several stone statues of gargoyles and demons stained with pigeon droppings began to move in place, spread their wings, and then climb down the sides of the walls of the sixteenth-century structures to congregate at the entrance to the Rue des Chapeliers, blocking pedestrian traffic and any entrance or exit from the Grand Place. Not only was this supernatural demonstration considered highly unusual for Belgium, but even more disturbing, no one could get to the public restrooms after consuming inhuman amounts of beer.

This drove home to me the gravity of the situation.

Then, in a daring feat of courage, some of the brave Belgian citizens who likely also needed to pee stepped up and interacted with the gargoyles directly, asking if they needed any help—perhaps directions to the Manneken Pis or the public facilities. The gargoyles, who miraculously spoke perfect French, English, and Flemish, said they did not.

A gentleman named Monsieur Fou attempted to push past us, and my father stopped him to ask what was being said.

"They told us they just wanted to see the royal family and a young prince who was passing by to pay their respects," he replied. "As any good Belgian citizen who honors my king and queen, I thought that seemed like a reasonable request. Now if you will excuse me, I need to find a *badkamer*."

This reminded me of my own situation, but that was quickly forgotten as the stone creatures began to approach our group. As they approached, they began to make menacing sounds, drooling and spitting Fanta-colored liquid in our direction. I was mesmerized—not so much scared of the demons but incredulous at how many statues in Brussels had Fanta-colored liquid coming out of them.

As the demons slowly approached, Belgians hung out of their windows, drinking beer and watching the event. Dorje planted his feet and lifted his walking stick. It began to glow, and he created a white circle of light around our family through which the demonic forces apparently could not penetrate.

Then in an instant, the statue of Michael that had stood atop the Grand Place for centuries began to move. In an unexpected display of blazing light the archangel flew from the top of the building down the alleyway, placing himself in front of me. As he remained floating in the air, Dorje began to speak in an unknown language, conversing with the demons.

Michael swooped over, scooped up the demons one after another, and placed them back on top of the ancient stone buildings around the Grand Place. With each he voiced a magical incantation that turned them back into stone.

CHAPTER 27:

READY, SET, *GO!*

When the commotion had calmed down, I smiled and turned to my mother, father, and beloved teacher, Dorje and let them know I still loved Brussels and couldn't wait to come back for a visit and to attend school here.

The queen and king beamed with great pride. Their son was an inspiration! Nothing fazed him. Not demons, nor fear of the unknown. As they took my hand, the whole group strolled to NATO headquarters a few blocks away. As the Arcturian entourage arrived at the front gate, military officers greeted us and asked for proof of identification. I would have thought a group including several seven-foot-plus Arcturians in royal garb with military escorts would have given it away—but we showed our green cards, anyway.

When I asked Dorje why the cards were green, he explained it was a joke on the humans' part. In their society, red meant "stop" and green represented "go," although those with green cards were still being stopped at the borders. I asked if it had anything to do with the "little green men" I had heard us called, and he commented that the Arcturians were certainly the antithesis of "little."

While accepting his explanation, I thought the humans had a strange sense of humor.

Our group proceeded to the council chambers to take our seats.

This, I had been told, was the second CIGI summit in Brussels, and it was a prelude to the third Davos International Climate Change

Summit soon to take place in Switzerland. Mankind was at a crucial tipping point and time was quickly running out. Decisive action by world leaders would need to take place at this conference based on up-to-date scientific assessments of what was happening on the planet. Either we came together and addressed the climate emergency head on, bringing our best and brightest people to the table, or nothing substantial would be done, as had been the pattern for years—not a great idea, since it would be equivalent to jumping off cliffs like lemmings, rushing an entire civilization to its climatic death.

Ecocide. Nothing less.

Having witnessed the devastations which took place during the first and second great climate change events, it was no longer a question of knowing what suffering looked or felt like. Everyone knew. This was no hoax. Rather, it was the largest existential challenge mankind had ever faced. Without coordinated action and cooperation among countries, those few who survived would do so without any significant quality of life. We'd all fall like dominos.

My human side caused me to consider myself part of a race that seemed hellbent on racing toward extinction. It was a sobering realization.

Two out of three people in the United States—likely more—suffered from one or more chronic health conditions, and it would be difficult to fight the Reptilians and their destructive agenda when you couldn't get out of bed. The science and solutions were there. Now it was up to my other people, the Arcturians, to come and offer assistance. Especially me.

I was here to save the world.

And I couldn't wait to get started.

PART FOUR:

ECOCIDE:
THE PLAY

ECOCIDE

(aka: The Global Climate Summit)

A Play in Three Acts

By Prince Ian

Cast of Characters

Fabian Morningstar: U.S. Dept. of State

David Ardent Thomas: National Oceanic and
    Atmospheric Administration

May Boeve: executive director of 350.org

Major Bophades Broward: U.S. Army
    Extraterrestrial Command

John Burrows: Professor of Physics of the
    Ocean and Atmosphere

Joyce Carr: U.S. National Science Foundation

Alicia Corusca: U.S. Department of
    Transportation

Dr. Pedro Hernández Correro: U.S. Army
    Extraterrestrial Command

Ashton Robert Crismer: chairman of the Joint
    Chiefs of Staff

David Dixon: U.S. Dept. of Health and Human
    Services

Antoine DuBois: Ambassador from France

Dr. Alexander Milt: quantitative ecologist
    at the University of California, Santa
    Barbara

Cynthia Friend: director of the Rowland
    Institute

Simone Givens: Director, Tufts Univ. Center
    for International Environment and
    Resource Policy

Michael Piper: science director for the SeaDoc
    Society

Philip D. Gingerich Jr.: Department of Earth
    and Environmental Sciences, University of
    Michigan

Carlos Pérez: Ambassador from Mexico

Aleksander Anderson: doctor from Harvard
    University

Carl Greenspan: U.S. Agency for International
    Development

Ayaan Nguvu: professor of mechanical
    engineering at MIT

Jack P. Holloway: Harvard Professor of
    Environmental Science

Feodora Chernyshevsky: researcher at the
    Technical University of Munich

Mark Z. Jacobson: Stanford professor of Civil
    and Environmental Engineering

General Pete "Pistol" McDonough: Director of
    the U.S. Space Force

Mahbruk Malek, PhD: University of California,
    Berkeley

David Rogers, PhD: University of California,
    Irvine

Dr. Antonio Garcia Morales: U.S. Army
    Extraterrestrial Command

Alexandra Ocasio-Cortez: U.S. Senator

Kasper Moth-Poulsen: Swedish professor of
    chemistry and engineering

Don Redenbacher: Chair, U.S. Global Change
    Research Program

General Tiberius K. Scott: U.S. Army
    Extraterrestrial Command

Emmanuel R. Varma: professor from the UIC
    College of Engineering

Jack Smith: Ambassador from Australia

Thomas Davies: Ambassador from UK

Alvin V. Terry: Augusta University department
    of Pharmacology and Toxicology

Dr. Robert Ira-Hansen: Citizen scientist,
    climate researcher

Haotian Wang: Department of Chemical and
    Biochemical Engineering, Rice University

King Antwar: Arcturian Royal Family

Queen Dawn: Arcturian Royal Family

Prince Ian: Arcturian Royal Family

Master Dorje: Arcturian Mystic

Helen of Antwar: Arcturian Royal Mother

Professor Satu: Arcturian scientist

Emily Bissell: American social worker and
    activist

Stephen Hawking: English theoretical physicist

Kermit the Frog: Famous green amphibian

The Little Prince: Explorer from asteroid
    B-612

Elon Musk: Visionary entrepreneur

Will Rogers: Cowboy philosopher

Tecumseh: Native American, Shawnee

Theodore Roosevelt: U.S. Past President

Roger Waters: English songwriter

Master of Ceremonies

Scene
A large auditorium at NATO
headquarters in Brussels, Belgium.

Time
The present.

ACT I

SETTING: The year is 2042. At the center of the stage sits a large oval wooden table. The NATO symbol is clearly shown in the center of the table. A large video screen hangs overhead flashing the multicolored flags of member nations.

AT RISE: The Arcturians enter and walk around the table to see where they are sitting. They then sit in the audience in a specially erected royal circle, stage left. The MC enters from stage right.

> MASTER OF CEREMONIES
> "Ladies and Gentlemen. Please
> turn off your cell phones, as the
> performance is about to begin.
> Also, please take your digital
> communicators out of your pockets
> unless you consciously want to be
> sterilized. For those patrons of
> the theatre who have been dumbed
> down by environmental toxins and
> vector-borne diseases, please
> be aware that both fictional and
> non-fictional characters will be
> portrayed in *Ecocide*. If dead
> people therefore appear on green
> horses during the show, it is not
> a cause for concern nor a need

to call your doctor. Enjoy the performance!"

Curtain goes up. CHORUS enters.

CHORUS

In fair Davos, where mountains kiss the sky

A third time, accord salvation a try

Heralds and heroes from every land

Starseeds and humans now lending a hand

Working to rescue a world from itself

Not an easy thing to do, my friend

Yet if we fail, could well be our quick end

The Reptiles revealed, their allies scattered

World torn, Mother Earth frayed, worn and tattered

Defeated not yet, the world still warming

The seas still rise, Neptune's anger storming

As if Woodstock 2035 had not mattered

We sit bewildered, beleaguered, and
battered

Chronos demands solutions, the end
inevitable

Yet masters of a destiny not yet
inescapable

For the students are learning at
Dorje's Academy

The magic of honing aspirations
'til finally

All awaken to our deepest wisdom
and power

Coming together to watch humanity's
flower

As the Starseeds finally wake from
the dream

Transcending separation, suffering,
and low self-esteem

Knowing their truest selves and
capacity

With hope afoot and faith's true
alacrity

The stars shall align for the
health of all kin

We listen, then act; we might even
win

*(Enter Dr. Redenbacher. He is 5 ft. 6 in., balding,
and wearing thick black glasses, sporting a thick*

*white beard. His crisp white shirt and light blue
tie are offset by a wrinkled grey suit.)*

                    REDENBACHER
Welcome to the *third* Global Climate
Summit. I am pleased to open
today's meeting with a greeting to
the many member nations who could
attend and to our honored Arcturian
royalty who have generously
sponsored the entire event. It is
a great honor to have you all here
today.

(Bows his head to King and Queen.)

The open sharing, consideration,
and even debate of information and
ideas is surely critical in the
endeavor of saving our world. I
know that many of you here today
are concerned about our climate
crisis, but I must emphasize,
most of us now on this planet are
not alarmed enough. We are at a
critical juncture of time, and
humanity lacks the imagination and
foresight to understand that human
civilization as we know it is in
grave danger.

*(As Redenbacher calls each of these out, eight
children—all from different parts of the world—come
onto the stage with a dead albatross around their
necks. The birds are numbered one through eight.)*

                    REDENBACHER

There are many reasons for this.
One: Scientists have been working
with climate models that have
been evolving over time. As this
is a highly complex field with
innumerable variables, they have
been slow to communicate the dire
risks during the past few decades
until their scientific conclusions
were substantiated. That tone
changed in 2021 with the IPCC
report, which was a "Code Red" for
humanity. By that time, significant
damage had already been done. Two:
Humans have difficulty imagining
their own extinction. Denial
is an ingrained psychological
defense mechanism that prevents
us from contemplating the worst-
case scenario. Combine that with
disinformation campaigns by major
energy corporations, and we have a
perfect scenario to deny the truth.
Three: Advances in science during
the past century have convinced
the masses that any problem, no
matter how dire and complex, can
be solved. Four: There is an
inaccurate assumption that the
worst effects of climate change
will be felt in other parts of
the world, not our own backyard.
Five: Nationalism and boundaries
between countries and pitting
one civilization against another
have eroded trust and impaired
coordinated efforts to come together

and fix the problem. Six: The time
paradox, where although the effects
of climate change have been slowly
experienced over centuries, these
effects are now accelerating due to
tipping points, rapidly reaching a
point of no return. Seven: Climate
denialism is still rampant among
segments of the population and
has led to political polarization
with restricted agendas that
have impaired progress. Eight:
The industrialized countries who
out of ignorance, have raped the
Earth in the name of materialism
and economic growth, have lacked
compassion for those countries now
suffering the worst consequences of
our climate emergency.

(Redenbacher removes the dead albatross [labeled
#1] from the first child.)

                    REDENBACHER
Today, we officially rid ourselves
of "timid language" and any
reticence to speak the truth as
clearly and honestly as possible,
even if that entails a certain
element of coarseness. To that end,
I invite to the podium the esteemed
humorist, citizen scientist, and
climate researcher, Dr Robert Ira-
Hansen, who has written about these
very issues for years without the
"politeness" too-often found in
science journals.

(Dr. Robert Ira-Hansen approaches the microphone. Bright, motivated, strong yet deeply fearful for humanity's future. He wears a black suit, white shirt, and black tie.)

IRA-HANSEN

Thank you, Mister Speaker. What I
am about to explain to you is not
fake news with alternative facts.
I am about to paint a dire picture
that accurately depicts humanity's
future if we do not come together
and rapidly institute the solutions
you will hear about today from our
esteemed scientists. Since I will
not have time to read you many
of my climate essays on subjects
being discussed here today, when
you have a moment, please refer
to your handouts, which contain
some of my most prolific writings.
I would especially ask you to read
the epic 400,000-word poem on the
sinking of Venice called "Mama Mia,
St Marks E-vaporetto"; the 278,000-
word literary essay on the sinking
of Holland called "No More Lands
in the Netherlands," referred to
by literary scholars as "Where
Have All the Flowers Gone?"; my
two-volume poem on the sinking of
Miami called "The Florida Keys Are
Under the Seas: Dolphins Fans Have
No More Lands"; the highly quoted
haiku on New Jersey: "New Jersey
no more. Tomatoes, Blueberries,

Gone. Gambled with Atlantic
City"; the two scholarly essays
on the sinking of Indonesia and
surrounding islands dubbed "Parta
Jakarta Aint No Morta" and "Bora-
Bora, I Used to Adore Her," as well
as the 298-verse sonnet about the
flooding of lands in Texas entitled:
"Houston, We Have a Problem."
Finally, for those who are pining
for the return of good ethnic food,
please order online my ambitious
three-volume book culinary series
on the disappearance of Mumbai,
Bangladesh, and Delhi, subtitled
*Where Can You Now Get Good Indian
Food?*

*(Everyone on stage was shocked with such raw
expressions of truth. Many wondered whether Dr.
Hansen had Arcturian blood. There appeared to be
little filters between his brain and mouth, and
he read their minds. Some were in fact wondering
about where to now get good Indian food.)*

                    IRA-HANSEN
This is the reality of the world
in which we live. We have sat by
and watched the flooding of lands,
homes, and crops. Millions of
climate refugees were forced to
flee their homeland to find clean
food and potable water, and many
lost their lives in the process.
We have stood by and witnessed
wildfires destroy tens of millions
of acres of land across the

globe, including The Amazon, the
"lungs of the Earth." For the
first time in history, the Amazon,
instead of being a carbon sink, is
releasing more carbon dioxide and
methane into the atmosphere than
it is absorbing. We have allowed
hundreds of thousands of people
to die from heat exhaustion and
heat stroke, along with billions
of animals and marine life who
have succumbed as temperatures
continue to break new records each
year. Not to mention those who are
now ill from regular exposure to
environmental toxins and spreading
vector-borne diseases. These
unfortunate people now suffer with
cancer, cardio-respiratory illness,
neuropsychiatric problems, and
dementia. Inhaling large amounts
of small particle pollutants from
wildfires with regular ingestion
of pesticides, heavy metals like
mercury and lead, and toxic mold
from water damaged buildings
have led tens of millions to
suffer from a chronic fatiguing,
musculoskeletal illness. When mixed
with brain-invasive spirochetal
infections like Lyme disease, which
have been in epidemic proportions
for decades, you have a perfect
storm to dumb down and disable
the human race. The Reptiles have
fooled you and are destroying our
planet. It is time to wake up. Over

fifty years of denying the effects
of climate change, environmental
toxins, and vector-borne diseases
have put our human race squarely in
the midst of a sixth extinction.

*(The scientists on stage have looks of consternation,
while loud murmurs can be heard arising from the
audience.)*

                    IRA-HANSEN
The prior Paris Agreement had set
a climate goal of limiting global
warming to 1.5 degrees Centigrade
above pre-industrial levels. We
recently blew by that goal and hit
1.6 degrees Centigrade, when we all
experienced the devastating effects
of the second great climate change.
Now the planetary goal is to limit
us to two degrees of warming,
which used to be the threshold for
preventing a catastrophic event.
However, we have already built in a
two-degree warming. The last time
the carbon dioxide levels in the
atmosphere were above 420 ppm—which
is where they are today—was during
the Pliocene era some three million
years ago. The world was around
three degrees Celsius warmer than
pre-Industrial temperatures of the
late 1800s, and sea levels were
at least thirty feet higher. That
would put Miami, Houston, New York,
and Bangladesh under water. Unless
you plan on putting these cities

under waterproof domes to survive
at the bottom of the ocean or have
CRISPR techniques for humans to
grow gills, I suggest you rapidly
institute the climate solutions we
will hear about today.

*(The temperature in the theater rises precipitously
as steam pours out from vents surrounding the stage.
Specially formulated chairs with sprinkler systems
located in the headrest and feet begin to spray a
fine mist as speakers project the sound of rising
seas and massive tidal waves hitting a shoreline,
destroying homes, with people screaming.)*

IRA-HANSEN

Remember that the Earth experienced
five extinction events in the
past. The worst event was 252
million years ago when carbon
pollution warmed the planet by
five degrees and ended most life
on Earth. Almost every extinction
event resulted from massive CO_2
and methane release from melting
permafrost. That is what is
happening now, as we see more and
more 100-degree Fahrenheit days
in the Russian tundra. There is
presently twice as much CO_2 and
methane trapped in the permafrost
than is in the atmosphere, and when
methane is released over short
time periods, as it is now, it has
a warming effect thirty to eighty
times greater. We are releasing
these heat-trapping gases at a

rate which is at least ten times
faster than during the Pliocene
era. Humanity is rushing toward its
sixth extinction event.

(Enter Stephen Hawking and Elon Musk.)

HAWKING
This is exactly the reason I
suggested colonizing other planets.
The science is clear, and we
are rapidly reaching a crucial
tipping point and heading toward
an anthropomorphic apocalypse.
Emissions reductions alone cannot
prevent a climate disaster. We need
to examine other solutions, like
geoengineering to cool the planet
and buy us time or looking at
colonizing other worlds.

MUSK
The thousands of Space X
communication satellites now
orbiting the Earth have confirmed
the acceleration of change in the
Artic. The permafrost has melted,
speeding up the pattern of thaw-to-
methane release. We are just about
out of time.

REDENBACHER
Thank you, David, Stephen, and
Elon. I would now like to have
Ms. Joyce Carr of the National
Science Foundation give the initial

assessment of where we are now.

(JOYCE CARR enters stage right—she has a look of consternation on her face. She pulls the microphone closer and opens up a large, brown manila envelope, pulling out a stack of papers.)

>   CARR
> It is with great urgency I address
> you all today. Twenty-four years
> ago, in 2018, it was the fourth-
> hottest year on record, and it's
> been getting hotter *every* year
> since. As per David Ardent Thomas
> from NOAA's global monitoring
> branch, this warming trend 'very
> much resembles riding up an
> escalator over time.' This trend
> must stop. If it gets worse, we
> could all choose to live in caves,
> ride donkeys, and eat only cricket
> patties, but it won't matter. The
> escalator will continue to rise *no
> matter what we do.*

(Prince Ian, hearing the words of Ms. Carr, turns to his mother, Queen Dawn.)

>   PRINCE IAN
> Mother, I would like to meditate in
> caves, ride a donkey, and eat some
> chicken patties. That sounds like
> fun!

(Enter CARL GREENSPAN, U.S. Agency for International Development, wearing a blue suit, white shirt, and red tie with a small American flag on his left

lapel. Deeply furrowed brows reflect concern. His rapid entrance stage right conveys deep urgency.)

GREENSPAN

Ms. Carr, I thought our scientists estimated several more *years* before we would reach such a critical threshold.

CARR

That, unfortunately, is the problem. They were only estimates. The realities are far more frightening. Erratic rainfall has adversely affected crop production. The warmer atmosphere retains more water vapor, leading to prolonged droughts, wildfires, and significant downpours once the water *is* released. Crop production has also been affected by the plummeting bee population, and Arctic temperatures continue rising faster than the overall global temperature rise. The ice sheets are all but gone now in the summertime. Expect more flooding, food shortages, and the continued displacement of tens of millions of people. It *will* prove to be an economic and humanitarian disaster.

GREENSPAN

We were also all under the impression the situation had stabilized in the Arctic regions.

*(Enter stage left DAVID ARDENT THOMAS, head of
NOAA's global monitoring branch in Asheville, North
Carolina. He is stressed and looks like an unhappy
Santa Claus with a white beard, red tie, and black
suit that looks like he slept in it. Which he did.)*

ARDENT THOMAS

I can answer that. The Larsen B ice
shelf collapsed several decades ago
due to a series of unusually warm
summers, and now the Larsen C ice
shelf on the Antarctic Peninsula,
where an iceberg the size of
Delaware broke off a quarter century
ago, is increasingly unstable.
Larsen C's importance cannot be
underestimated. It buttresses and
reinforces the glaciers behind it
and prevents ice streams in the
rear from flowing faster into the
ocean, raising sea levels. Other
ice shelfs in Antarctica—like the
Ross shelf, which is the largest in
the world—is also melting and like
Larsen C is becoming unstable. If
it were to collapse, the resulting
flow of glacial ice could raise
global sea levels by up to sixteen
feet. A study published in the
scientific journal *Nature* more than
twenty years ago found other ice
sheets, such as Greenland's ice
sheets, "contain enough water to
raise global sea levels by twenty-
three feet—and have been melting
at an 'unprecedented' rate, 50

percent higher than pre-industrial levels and 33 percent above 20th-century levels." By 2012, the rate of ice loss had accelerated to nearly *four* times what it was only ten years before, and by 2038, it had accelerated by a factor of ten. Now there's almost nothing left of the Arctic ice floes during summer months. We may be past the point of no return.

(Queen Dawn stands and raises her hand.)

                    QUEEN DAWN
And how is that affecting the rest of the world?

                    ARDENT THOMAS
Melting ice sheets mean rising sea levels, and almost *half* of the world's population lives in areas vulnerable to rising seas. Ice influences ocean currents and the jet stream, and so we have also seen a slowing of the AMOC, the Atlantic Meridional Overturning Circulation, increasing the severity of the storms and polar vortices as well as heat domes that have plagued the United States and Europe. If the AMOC were to completely shut down from global warming, this could lead to catastrophic results, including an ice age in the Northern hemisphere,

significant sea level rise, and droughts and food shortages for billions of people in West Africa, India, and South America by disrupting monsoon season. For the moment, less ice has led to record-breaking *heat* spells across the globe from the notorious "*albedo effect*." Less heat reflected from the ice means a warmer ocean, causing more methane to be released, leading to heat waves such as the 120-degree days in Australia. On that continent, large swaths of their human and wildlife population die as the extreme heat and wind have completely dried out their fields. Wildfires continue to destroy homes and wilderness, causing power grids to break down. Wild horses, flying foxes, koalas, sugar gliders, possum, galahs, and yes, kangaroo, are extinct or nearly so. Male animals become infertile from their testicles overheating, mares don't become pregnant, and piglets and calves are aborting from the heat. Tens of thousands of fish die per day and decompose on the surface of the water, similar to the massive fish kill in Canada years ago, where billions of marine life perished. It's a smelly, bloody mess.

(Master of Ceremonies enters from stage left)

MASTER OF CEREMONIES

"Ladies and gentlemen. Please be
aware, no animals will be harmed
during this production. They are
dead already."

(Men on stage and in the audience all take out fans
given to them upon entrance to the theater and
use them to cool their privates, while dozens of
dead birds, fish, piglets, and cats fall from the
ceiling onto the stage and audience.)

                    IRA-HANSEN
We are heading toward an
uninhabitable Earth by the end of
this century, which will not easily
support life as we know it. Animals
are already dying off in droves.
Letting Fluffy the cat out for a
bathroom break in 120-degree heat
might be the last time you see her.

(He pauses and takes a drink to calm himself. A
single tear forms in the corner of his eye. His
pet cat Fluffy was missing, and he suspected the
worst.)

                    IRA-HANSEN
The situation is rapidly
deteriorating. We are releasing
a massive amount of carbon and
methane stored in the permafrost
because burning fossil fuels are
warming the planet. The permafrost
contains twice as much carbon as
is in the atmosphere, so as it
is released, it is accelerating
global warming. The Artic has seen

80-degree warmer days in the last
two decades. It resulted in us
almost losing all the agricultural
seeds stored in the "Doomsday"
Svalbard seed vault in Norway
several decades ago. The seeds
were humanity's backup to make
sure our agriculture would survive
in case of a catastrophe, but the
vault was flooded shortly after
being built because of rising
global temperatures melting the
permafrost, which is no longer
permanently frozen. As it melts,
the permafrost is evaporating
partially as *methane*, which is
thirty to eighty times as powerful
as CO_2.

*(MAJOR BOPHADES BROWARD turns to PRINCE IAN after
listening to the talk.)*

                MAJOR BROWARD
Methane causes global warming to
increase at a faster rate than
normal? I guess I should adjust my
diet.

*(Ushers walk down both aisles spraying atomizers
containing a solution of garlic and rotten eggs.
PRINCE IAN lets out a silent-but-deadly one. The
Major, fortunately caught up in his thoughts,
doesn't notice where it came from.)*

*(Australian AMBASSADOR SMITH enters dressed as a
Koala.)*

SMITH

The Organization for Economic Cooperation and Development has
released a scathing review of
Australia's environmental policies,
one which reflects on all of us.
As reported, Australia has made
progress replacing coal with
natural gas and renewables yet
remains one of the most carbon-
intensive OECD countries. Sadly,
all major countries have missed
their emission targets.

(DAVID DIXON from HHS hurriedly enters from stage right, fidgeting with government reports. He has short, cropped hair and is wearing a blue suit, blue shirt, and multicolored tie. He has a look of concern and sweat on his brow.)

DIXON

Mr. Chairman and Queen Dawn, the
United States also has missed our
emission targets. Just seven years
ago, New York experienced a record
124 degrees, and now that's a
common occurrence with the average
summertime temperature, even in the
Northeast, of 115 Fahrenheit, some
days hitting over 130. In parts of
Arizona and Texas, those summertime
temperatures have reached 140 or
greater, and it's impossible to
stay outdoors for more than a few
minutes. Once the temperature in
the human body gets above 104,
or forty degrees Celsius, the

results are dehydration with severe
fatigue, muscle and abdominal
cramps, nausea, vomiting and/or
diarrhea, headaches, dizziness,
fainting, and confusion. Once the
temperature exceeds *105* Fahrenheit,
the body starts to shut down. We've
issued health warnings across the
United States, as have the European
and Australian governments. Despite
those warnings, large numbers of
our youngest and elderly have
succumbed to heat stroke, with the
most vulnerable dying.

*(All characters on stage swoon and collapse from
the intense heat. Ushers run in from stage left
and pour water on them from jugs.)*

                    SMITH
(from floor)

The problems we face are not just
due to climate change. There are
more adverse health consequences
arising from the Reptilian agenda
and global pollution. In Australia,
we've seen the bleaching and
destruction of the Great Barrier
Reef, and in the Caribbean, the
coral reefs are now completely
gone. Massive fish kills, oceanic
dead zones, red tide…these
phenomenon are due to industrial
pollution and toxic chemicals in
the rivers and oceans. Radioactive
waste from Fukushima has leaked

into the ocean for decades. From
swirling plastic garbage in the
Pacific Ocean to microplastics,
pesticides, and heavy metal toxins
getting into the fish, we have
poisoned our waterways. Since 1970,
more than *half* of all the world's
marine life has died.

SMITH
(rises with rest of cast)

We are committing ecocide.

CHORUS
Ecocide. The most heinous crime
possible committed out of greed,
ignorance, and denial. Habitable
life on the planet is being
destroyed.

DIXON
Mr. Chair, our evaluation has
led us to similar conclusions as
our Australian delegate, but we
have examined the physiological
consequences of chemicals
getting into our bodies. In a
recent analysis reported by the
Environmental Working Group,
we have found 1,4-dioxane, a
carcinogen, in the drinking water
of nearly one hundred ninety
million Americans and thousands
of personal care products. This
chemical has been linked to

cancer, liver and kidney damage,
higher rates of pregnancy loss,
stillbirths, premature births, and
low birth weights. This is only *one*
chemical among the *thousands*. The
Reptiles are effectively poisoning
us.

(The back screen of the theater projects successive images of billowing smokestacks, industrial plants pouring out pollutants into oceans, thick smog hanging over Delhi, Beijing, and Los Angeles, piles of garbage heaped up on landfills, dead fish in the thousands on beaches, and skull and crossbones signs over toxic waste barrels lying on their sides. Fade to hospital cancer wards with sick people on IV chemotherapy drips.)

(Enter Monsieur DUBOIS, Ambassador from France.)

                    DUBOIS
These chemicals are found in
everything from pesticides to
cosmetics, food, and children's
toys. They negatively affect the
workings of the endocrine system,
which includes the pituitary
gland, thyroid, adrenal glands,
ovaries, testes, and pancreas. They
exacerbate the world-wide epidemics
of obesity, cancer, and diabetes.
The biggest concern, *n'est-ce pas*,
for the French men is that their
testicles will not work so well,
and we will not be able to make
love to our beautiful Frenchwomen.

*(Everyone nods, including the audience. This is a
big problem. No one knows if France can survive
such devastation. Men, including in the audience,
take out their fans again.)*

                    DIXON
          Small particle pollution—
          microparticles easily inhaled from
          sources involving combustion, such
          as power plants, motor vehicles,
          and smoke from spreading wildfires—
          has been linked to twenty percent
          of the cases of dementia, as well
          as an increased risk of asthma,
          COPD, heart attacks, and premature
          death.

(Enter Mr. PEREZ Ambassador from Mexico.)

                    PEREZ
          In Mexico City, where we have
          some of the largest air pollution
          in the world, brain biopsies of
          animals and children who have
          died prematurely have shown
          Alzheimer's dementia-type changes
          at an early age. We have tried to
          address the dumping of chemicals
          into our environment but lack a
          comprehensive plan and government
          support. Our industries have faced
          the high costs of converting
          factories to clean energy sources.
          Also, we haven't been able to get
          the proper building supplies from
          the United States because the wall

is preventing anything from getting
through.

*(Actor-director ROGER WATERS enters in a long
leather coat carrying a megaphone. Neo-Mexicans
with shaved heads march behind him. Pink Floyd
plays in the background.)*

                    WATERS
Tear down the wall! Tear down the
wall!

                    DIXON
Peer-reviewed studies have shown
incontrovertible evidence that
these chemicals are linked to ADD,
ADHD, Autism Spectrum Disorder,
Autoimmune illness, and Alzheimer's
dementia, affecting *millions* of
citizens in the United States
alone. The Reptiles have succeeded
in dumbing down our population
and decreasing sperm counts while
engineering a worldwide rise in
vector-borne diseases such as Lyme
disease. The resulting infections
are making it into millions of
bodies and brains as the tick
populations continue to soar
higher each year, affecting higher
cognitive functioning, causing
chronic fatigue, joint and muscle
pain, and sexual dysfunction.
Monsieur Dubois, I'm afraid with
the epidemic of Lyme disease in
France combined with widespread

exposure to environmental chemicals
acting as xenoestrogens, the French
people are doomed.

*(The French ambassador grows angry hearing the
words of the American journalist. The implications
are staggering. Also, he's already sipped on a
little too much wine.)*

                    DUBOIS
          Enough! You...you empty-headed
          animal-food-trough wiper. I fart in
          your general direction.

*(Everyone is shocked. Not because of the
ambassador's language, but because as drunk as he
is, he actually remembers lines from Monty Python.
PRINCE IAN looks at the Major and farts again in
his general direction. The Major looks confused.
Ushers walk down isles again spraying atomizers
with garlic and rotten eggs.)*

*(The French ambassador pulls out his cell phone,
calls the minister of health, and speaks rapidly.
It is a national emergency. France immediately
decides to name a day alerting citizens to the
crisis and actions required. It is decided. Baiser,
Enculer et Sucer, Putain la vache! Day. The cast
builds a barricade on stage, marches in place,
and waves banners. Enter THOMAS DAVIES, the UK
delegate.)*

                    DAVIES
          Ladies and gentlemen, since Brexit
          in Great Britain, we no longer have
          the resources to clean out—or even
          monitor—such chemicals. However,

there are advantages. Since
pharmaceutics like Prozac and drugs
like cocaine are showing up in
the Thames in greater and greater
quantity, we have many more happy
people living in Britain.

                    CHORUS
Of course, the birth control pills
also showing up in the water might
be a problem for anyone wanting to
have children, affecting both female
hormones *and* lowering men's sperm
counts with xenoestrogens.

(John Burrows, the representative from Center for
International Governance Innovation, races to the
top of the barricade.)

                    BURROWS
Distinguished guests, we must
work together! There must be
a comprehensive approach to
completely phase out coal mining
and lower carbon pollution,
decrease toxic chemicals in our
waterways, and reverse the negative
effects of these chemicals on insect
populations while stemming the
increase in vector-borne diseases.
We *can* build bridges from knowledge
to power. To that end, we must
convince our leaders to review the
science and cooperate!

The ROYAL MOTHER, HELEN OF ANTWAR stands to speak.
QUEEN DAWN quietly buries her head in her hands.

ROYAL MOTHER
Are you people members of the
I-Don't-See-Anything Society?
Choices have been made by your
leaders, by those in this room,
and you chose to deny the truth.
Claiming that scientific uncertainty
warranted a do-nothing approach,
while life as you know it could
be wiped from planet. Has anyone
considered why they call it
"science?" You had the chance to
adopt a Green New Deal *decades ago*.
Instead, the deal you chose was
brown, and it *stinks*. You polluted
Earth's rivers and oceans, toxified
its air and water, and created
imbalances in Mother Nature—who
now seeks a fitting revenge. Now
is the time for you to critically
look into your heart and consider
all of the facts. As my Grandson
Prince Ian would tell you, it is
only with the heart that one can
see rightly. His future—all of your
futures—are up to you and your
leaders. Tomorrow, you will come
with solutions and to-do lists and
do what has to be done. My grandson
will be living here on this planet
for the foreseeable future. If
anything happens to him, I will
hold you all responsible, and
believe me, I can make your lives a
living hell. Just try me.

(As his grandmother speaks, PRINCE IAN decides to

give the atmops some of his leftover waffles. He
quietly instructs them to go around the room and
project a song into everyone's minds. It's one he
heard while listening to American songs from the
1980s, and it stuck in his head.

(Everyone starts to hum the song. They don't know
why. MAJOR BROWARD, of course, is the first to sing
it out loud. He stands and begins. NOTE: RIGHTS TO
SONG PENDING. PUBLIC DOMAIN 3023.)

(Once he gets past the first verse, everyone stands
and joins him, loudly, emphatically, and largely
off-key, singing while putting their arms around one
another, swaying side to side. COMMANDER PLAMORIUS
stands up in the audience and yells.)

                    COMMANDER P
          LOVE FEST!

(People hug each other and cry. It has been a long
day for the humans, and there is a lot for them to
consider.)

                    PRINCE IAN
          I just hope they make the right
          decision and that the waffles and
          fries are still around when I go to
          medical school here.

               (BLACKOUT)

               (END OF SCENE)

ACT II

SETTING: The Davos Congress Center, 2042. There are six chairs in a row with tables behind a podium and microphone. A large banner welcomes the world delegates with the words "Global Climate Summit. Committed to Improving the State of the World." There is also a large banner high above the stage with the words "Broecker Global Climate Summit."

The center's catering facilities, which are top notch, provide Swiss specialties that include cheese and chocolate fondue, dark chocolate squares, raclette, and Rösti.

AT RISE: A program guide walks up and down the aisles and hands out Swiss delicacies and today's program. People in the audience make oohing and ahhing sounds. The MASTER OF CEREMONIES enters from stage right to announce the morning session.

                    MASTER OF CEREMONIES
          Today's session will be divided
          into multiple segments, each with
          breakout rooms that will focus
          on separate aspects of climate
          change. Be certain you are in the
          right chamber. Top scientists
          and researchers from around
          the world will discuss their

findings and potential solutions
for global environmental and
ecological degradation, rising
carbon emissions, and improving
energy efficiency. Global leaders
will address ways to continue to
transition to a green economy
considering increased global
competition for resources and
social discontent resulting from
mass migrations.

This morning session will focus on
energy efficiency and decreasing
carbon emissions, which as we all
know is the heart of the problem.
The afternoon session in this
chamber will present a brief
overview from each of the morning
groups with potential solutions.
Everyone attending, please hold
your question and answers until the
end of each session.

(The Arcturians enter, followed by armed guards
with machine guns in white bodysuits and white
facemasks. Barricades are set up around the stage.
Protestors line up behind the barricades holding
various signs of climate protest. Some are half-
naked women with body paint written across their
breasts: "SOS. Save the Planet!" The Arcturian
guards try to convince the activists to put their
clothes on. PRINCE IAN asks his mother if the
women are cold.)

(PRINCE IAN, PROFESSOR SATU, QUEEN DAWN, KING
ANTWAR, THE ROYAL MOTHER, and MASTER DORJE are
assigned special seats for VIPs in the front of the

room but again sit on the side of the auditorium since no one, especially smaller-statured Swiss people, could see over the Arcturian seven-foot-two-inch heads.)

(A woman resembling SENATOR OCASIO-CORTEZ opens the meeting. Her hair is in a knotted braid, and she is wearing a sharp green double-breasted suit and boots with a monogramed heel and stylish earrings.)

                    MC
As a congresswoman from New York, the senator had sought to pass a comprehensive Green New Deal for more than two decades. Political stalemates halted the sweeping legislation required to make the United States carbon neutral by 2040. Countries across the world followed suit. If the United States was unable or unwilling to make the sacrifices necessary to become carbon neutral, why should they? The result was the next Great Climate change—increased flooding, nor'easters, die-offs of coral reefs, forest fires, mass extinctions, heat waves, earthquakes, and more. Global leaders refused to face facts and watched the Earth run headlong into a dire future.

Mother Earth was in trouble. Her children had given her agita, and she was fighting back. Several key

reports helped convince the world
governments that climate change
was not only real but also a threat
to all of life as we know it. The
first was a paper by Phillip D.
Gingerich, whose son is our keynote
speaker.

(Enter PHILIP D. GINGRICH JR. He is fifty-six years old and lanky with short-cropped hair, wearing wire-rimmed glasses, a dark blue suit, blue and white striped shirt, and red tie. He has an erudite air. He is head of the Department of Geology, Biology, and Anthropology at the University of Michigan, Ann Arbor and is holding a published scientific review.)

GINGERICH JR.

Thank you for inviting me here.
My father's environmental review
published decades ago in 2019
had been lost among hundreds of
thousands of peer-reviewed papers
published every year in the
scientific literature. Once the data
in his paper on prior extinctions
was compared to rates of present-
day carbon dumping and extinctions,
he knew that life on Earth was at
risk. As the Arctic permafrost
thawed and released a third of
the one-point-eight trillion tons
of carbon trapped in Greenland's
ice sheets, the methane rapidly
heated the planet. It was getting
difficult to remain in denial that
we were cooking ourselves like meat

in a hot soup. With the first Great
Climate Change, people were woken
out of their refusal to face the
facts.

(QUEEN DAWN rises and addresses the audience and committee members on stage.)

QUEEN DAWN

I tried to explain to my son at
five years old the situation the
planet was in. I didn't want to
worry him but knew that he had to
understand the science, politics,
and choices that had been made if
he was to help this planet avoid
the fate awaiting it. I put it in
terms of the planets the Little
Prince had visited in the story by
Antoine de Saint-Exupéry and the
need to not "let the weeds overrun
the planet and destroy it." In this
case, it was the Reptilian masters
who controlled most of your top
positions, making the decisions on
climate change.

They were the politicians bought
off by special interest groups,
influential businessmen and women,
CEOs of large corporations
including Big Oil, Big Agriculture,
Big Finance, and Big Pharma,
deciding the fate of the planet.
Money, power, and fame were more
important to the Reptiles than the
welfare of future generations. At

five years old, Prince Ian found it
difficult to understand how people
were capable of destroying their
own species. I tried to explain the
situation to him in terms of the
women who had helped me understand
Earth culture:

"If you never pay attention to your
Mother Earth and ignore her, this
is what happens. But don't worry
about me. I'll be fine. Even though
you polluted my air and water
with poison so I can't breathe or
take a drink, I'm happy to die a
slow and horrible death while you
go on vacation with your *schikza*
wife and have a good time. When
I'm done with my death throes, for
my funeral, I would have liked
real flowers, but since all fauna
has been destroyed on the planet,
plastic ones will have to do. Just
take whatever money is left in my
bank account to pay for the funeral
service, although banks don't exist
either and I don't have much left.
Besides, our family plot is covered
with twenty-three feet of water.
But as long as you can still take
those expensive family vacations,
I'm happy to have provided for your
every need for centuries."

*(PRINCE IAN turns to his mother and, in a whisper,
asks her what is going to happen now.)*

QUEEN DAWN
We are here today to discuss
possible solutions, and our own
Professor Satu and Master Dorje
will provide a broader scientific
and political perspective based on
our experience with the Reptiles
and climate change on Arcturus.
We are not here to criticize but
rather to share our collective
experience for your benefit.

(THEODORE ROOSEVELT enters on a green horse.)

ROOSEVELT
It is not the critic who counts;
not the man who points out how
the strong man stumbles or where
the doer of deeds could have done
them better. The credit belongs
to the man who is actually in
the arena, whose face is marred
by dust and sweat and blood; who
strives valiantly; who errs, who
comes short again and again because
there is no effort without error and
shortcoming; but who does actually
strive to do the deeds; who knows
great enthusiasms, the great
devotions; who spends himself in a
worthy cause; who at the best knows
in the end the triumph of high
achievement and who at the worst,
if he fails, at least fails while
daring greatly so that his place
shall never be with those cold
and timid souls who neither know
victory nor defeat.

(ROOSEVELT exits and the spotlight focuses now on OCASIO-CORTEZ. She is composed while adjusting her glasses as she begins to speak.)

                    OCASIO-CORTEZ
Distinguished leaders, scientists,
guests and Arcturian royalty…
welcome to day two of the third
Global Climate Summit. Our meeting
today is about tackling hard
truths, and is held in honor
of Wallace Broecker, Columbia
University geochemist and
pioneering climate scientist who
died several decades ago. Dr.
Broecker was the first to put forth
"unpopular" views on global warming
and man's role in it. Therefore,
in his honor, we would like to
officially name our gathering "The
Broecker Global Climate Summit."
We're also announcing three annual
cash prizes of one billion dollars
each from Queen Dawn to be given to
the country and researchers able
to solve the most pressing climate
issues before us. Each year at
our annual climate change summit,
we will announce gold, silver,
and bronze winners as well as the
countries who walk away with the
grand honors of saving the planet.

                    PRINCE IAN
A science Olympics featuring *mental*
gymnastics in the laboratory worth

billions of dollars while also
protecting the environment. Cool.
That could buy a lot of waffles and
fries. I may want to participate....

OCASIO-CORTEZ
Our keynote speaker for the
morning is Philip D. Gingerich
Jr. from the Department of Earth
and Environmental Sciences and
Museum of Paleontology, University
of Michigan at Ann Arbor. His
father was the author of the
study "Temporal Scaling of Carbon
Emission and Accumulation Rates:
Modern Anthropogenic Emissions
Compared to Estimates of PETM-
Onset Accumulation." A real
mouthful, yet Gingerich's research
corroborated scientific exploration
done by Elizabeth Kolbert in her
2014 nonfiction book *The Sixth
Extinction*. It concluded that human
behavior is on the verge of causing
a mass-extinction—the sixth in
the history of the planet and the
only such event caused by human
beings. Can you please explain to
the audience the essence of the
research? As a non-scientist, I find
it quite complicated.

GINGERICH JR.
Thank you, Senator. Although it
sounds complicated, it's actually
quite simple. Using radioisotopes,

we can determine the geologic time
scale of layers in the Earth's
crust with known events on the
planet and know the absolute age
of rocks and other geological
features, including which life
forms existed during different time
periods on Earth.

*(As he speaks, magically animated skeletons of
various dinosaur breeds cross the stage. On the
back screen, large mountains, palm trees, and
tropical fauna become visible, including a flying
pterodactyl.)*

                    GINGERICH
Although the best-known geologic
era was the Jurassic period, there
have been others marked by changes
in the composition of geological
strata which indicate *major*
paleontological events, including
mass extinctions. Although there
are many theories concerning the
demise of the dinosaurs, including
vaping, poor lifestyle habits, and
asteroids, it's been determined
there was a massive release of
carbon dioxide which led to a rapid
global warming event.

*(Tyrannosaurus with small arms are seen attempting
to vape and eat Pleiadian pepperoni pizza. They
all drop dead. An advertisement for flavored vape
oil flashes across the screen above stage.)*

GINGERICH JR.
Of the *five* prior extinctions, the
Paleocene-Eocene is one of the most
recent, a global warming event that
killed 97 percent of life on the
planet. We are, today, emitting
carbon some nine to ten times
faster.

*(Human families enter from stage right and stand
on a raised platform in front of images of burning
forests in Alaska, Greenland, and the Amazon with
piles of dead animals along the banks of dried-up
rivers in Australia. An advertisement for Foster's
beer appears in the background. The screen splits,
showing people in Greenland frolicking in melting
ice floes coming from glaciers on the left. Screen
on the right shows people on a beach in Thailand
running for their lives as a tsunami approaches.
Ushers run up and down aisles throwing buckets of
water on the audience. Those who did not buy the
souvenir Ecocide ponchos in the lobby before the
performance are very unhappy.)*

OCASIO-CORTEZ
We would now like to open the
session with a question for each
of our five panelists. The first
question revolves around the
feasibility of attaining a carbon
neutral environment in the next
decade.

*(Projection screen in the background shows power
plants emitting billowing clouds of pollution.
Images of Delhi, Los Angeles, Zhengzhou, and other
major cities flash in succession with people wearing*

masks. A heavyset man is seen playing golf on a smog-filled course, unwittingly hitting people in the head with golf balls who subsequently fall down, unconscious. Clouds of thick smoke begin to emerge from vents surrounding the theater. Ushers in the aisle hand out handkerchiefs for attendees to cover their mouths. An advertisement for Kleenex tissues flashes on the screen.)

> OCASIO-CORTEZ
> Mr. Holloway, can you speak to our
> need to attain these goals and how,
> if possible, we can attain them?

(Jack P. Holloway stands with some difficulty. He is in his nineties, thin and lanky with wire rim glasses, a white beard, and hair. He looks distinguished in a black pin-striped suit, a white shirt, and red crisscross tie. Nevertheless, he appears exhausted, frustrated, and scared.)

> HOLLOWAY
> If the planet follows its current
> trajectory, by century's end, Earth
> will be almost unrecognizable.

(He chokes up and takes a sip of water before continuing.)

> Thanks to the Reptilians, far too
> much of America's energy *still*
> comes from fossil fuels. Replacing
> them with sources that do not
> emit greenhouse gasses will cost
> trillions of dollars and increase
> energy costs for millions of
> families. Still, the economic

trade-offs are worth it. Saving
trillions on potential catastrophe
by *spending* trillions to prevent
it. An aggressive transition to
non-carbon energy begun decades ago
could have achieved *zero emissions*
by midcentury. We've missed those
deadlines and all those which
followed and now have paid the
price. The longer we wait, the
bigger the price tag.

                    OCASIO-CORTEZ
Would you support a full transition
to electric automobiles?

                    HOLLOWAY
Absolutely. While powerful oil-
industry groups led by the Reptiles
have in the past engaged in
stealth campaigns to roll back
car-emissions standards, we must
support a full transition to such
vehicles. The United States began
a partial transition over a decade
ago, but only half of the 375
million cars on the road are now
electric, and other countries have
not followed suit.

*(Ferraris, Lamborghinis, Bugattis, Mercedes AMGs,
Ford GTs, Chevrolet Corvettes, Tesla roadsters,
Aston Martin DBS Superleggeras, Porsche 911 GT2
RSs, and McLaren Sennas pull into the theater
and surround the stage. Some are real; others are
projected on the back screen as smiling drivers*

*climb out and charge their cars from solar chargers
built into the forestage.)*

OCASIO-CORTEZ
Mr. Jacobson, would you speak to
our ability to reach net-zero
greenhouse emissions across the
economy within the next decade?

*(MARK Z. JACOBSON, Professor of the Department of
Civil and Environmental Engineering from Stanford
University, stands to speak. He is a distinguished
seventy-seven-year-old wearing a blue pin-striped
suit, white shirt, and red-striped tie. He is famous
for his article in the journal One Earth outlining
clean energy roadmaps for 143 countries.)*

JACOBSON
My research directly influenced
California laws requiring the state
to commit to 100 percent carbon-
free energy by 2045, and with only
three years to go, we're on track
to do that. The target of net-zero
greenhouse emissions across the
country could also be achieved by
that date based on the urgency and
speed of climate change, and you
don't need any miracle technologies
to accomplish it. But first, we
need to create millions of high-
wage jobs through a massive clean-
infrastructure build-out.

*(Pennsylvania coal miners cross the stage. Their
heads sport solar-powered beanies with electric
fans. An advertisement for Solar City flashes on
the screen above.)*

                    JACOBSON
          Labor unions have been resistant,
          though, fearing that high-paying
          or plentiful jobs in the renewable
          energy field won't be as plentiful
          as those in oil and gas.

                    OCASIO-CORTEZ
          Ms. Simone Givens, as director
          of Tufts University's Center for
          International Environment and
          Resource Policy, is creation of
          such jobs feasible? After all,
          we have to create jobs for those
          individuals in the coal and oil
          industry *and* attract people to this
          growing field.

*(SIMONE GIVENS is bright and cheery, wearing a red
blouse, thick bobble earrings and necklace, and
black horned rim glasses and sporting a short bob
haircut. She has an air of confidence and optimism.)*

                    GIVENS
          The creation of these jobs is
          very much a reachable goal. Going
          back to 2019, there were about
          750,000 Americans working in the
          renewable energy industry compared
          to 3.8 million in China and 1.2
          million in Europe. Now in 2042,
          that number is only two million.
          There is no reason why we couldn't
          double or triple those numbers
          in the U.S. and across the global
          board. The bigger challenge will

be overhauling the transportation
and buildings sectors. Both require
major financial investments and
regulations. Although President
Biden pushed for EVs to make up
half of U.S. auto sales by 2030, we
did not meet that goal. The United
States government needs to spur
electric-vehicle development in
both the private and public sector—
with incentives and new taxes. We
will not be able to achieve our
goals without building into the
economy a much higher cost for
emitting greenhouse gases—such as
an "exponential carbon tax"—scaling
it upwards for the worst polluters.

                OCASIO-CORTEZ
Ms. McBride, as policy director
at the Brookings Institution, can
you speak to what it would take
to enact such a carbon tax? Is it
feasible considering the political
and economic climate and given the
recent U.S. Civil War between red
and blue states, which ended less
than a decade ago?

*(ANGELA C. McBRIDE has short blonde hair, magenta
lipstick, and is wearing a blue suit and white
silk blouse. She has an air of optimism.)*

                McBRIDE
Very feasible, Senator. An
exponential greenhouse-carbon

gas tax would need to be imposed
on only a few thousand taxpaying
entities, specifically corporations
and municipal plants that have
ignored stricter EPA regulations
and allowed them to pay minimal
fines. Just focusing on those
few companies would target the
vast majority of United States
emissions. Carbon credits could
also be given to families who
remain under the allowed limit of
emissions.

(A happy family randomly picked from the audience
before the performance enters stage right and
stands at the front of the stage. They wave.)

(Enter stage left nuclear physicist MAHBRUK MALEK.
He has thick black glasses and is wearing a black
suit, white shirt, and yellow polka-dot tie. He
has an air of confidence.)

                    OCASIO-CORTEZ
Dr. Malek, can you speak to the
naysayers? There are some who feel
we're not being realistic about
the environmental consequences
of constructing high-speed rail,
manufacturing zero-emission
vehicles, or retrofitting our
buildings because the sheer amount
of carbon dioxide emitted into
the atmosphere while retrofitting
alone will be significant. Can we
use renewable energy sources to
power the plants involved in this
transition? Is that feasible?

                    MALEK
It is feasible. If we cover an area
of the Earth 418 kilometers by 418
kilometers, or roughly 260 miles
by 260 miles with solar panels,
it will provide more than 21.75
terawatts of power. This area is
68,000 square miles. The Great
Saharan Desert in Africa is 3.6
million square miles and is prime
for solar power because it has sun
more than twelve hours per day.
That means only 15 percent of the
Sahara is sufficient to cover all of
the energy needs of the world in
solar energy. There is no way coal,
oil, wind, geothermal, or nuclear
energy can compete with this. The
cost of the project will be about
ten trillion dollars, a one-time
cost at today's prices—rather small
compared to other spending in the
world.

*(Smiling Bedouins on camels enter holding up large
solar panels. The camels spit at guests. Another
advertisement for Kleenex appears on the screen.)*

                 OCASIO-CORTEZ
If the world's governments come
together and collectively work
on this project, could it be
accomplished quickly? If the costs
were spread out over the global
economy, no one country would have
to foot the entire bill.

*(The main screen shows world leaders holding
hands in a sign of support. Reptilians are off
on the side brooding; one is strangely orange-
colored, like an Orange Julius. Above them, in the
background, a green elliptical wave sweeps across
a 3-D projection of the globe which grows and fills
the entire screen.)*

                    MALEK
Yes, Senator. Global cooperation
could allow this to happen within
just one to two years' time.
China, already the world's largest
solar producer, has for more than
a decade *increased* the number
of large-scale solar farms. The
United States could become almost
completely energy independent and
not rely on fossil fuels if we
built solar panels in the Mojave
Desert.… My fellow speaker Elon
Musk did the calculations decades
ago, and his conclusion was "if
you wanted to power the entire
U.S. with solar panels, it would
take a fairly small corner of
Nevada or Texas or Utah." There
will still be a need for liquid
fuels—likely hydrogen produced by
the electrolysis of water. We, of
course, would need the political
parties in the US to finally call
a truce and stop warring to
accomplish this. Sometimes they
appear to forget why they were
elected.

(Senate and Congressional leaders dressed in blue donkey and red elephant football outfits race onto the stage. They tackle each other, spitting, cursing, and arguing with a referee. On the sidelines watching are kids with guns, women dressed as handmaids, and a plethora of people with blood-stained bandages.)

MALEK

People would need to be educated
on the energy efficient options
available, and afterwards, a
national referendum representing
the will of the people could bypass
political stalemates and help move
such action along. This may be the
only way to stop the evil Reptilian
CEOs who still control major
industries.

(Projected on the back screen are young children in bathtubs filled with bubbles, gleefully playing with rubber ducks and miniature nuclear submarines.)

OCASIO-CORTEZ

Considering the nuclear disasters
that have already happened—
in Chernobyl and Fukashima,
for instance—would you agree
transitioning to full solar energy
in such areas makes more sense?
And if so, is there a way of
transferring the energy efficiently?

(The main screen flashes images of nuclear bombs going off and massive tidal waves destroying surrounding countryside and coastal communities.

Fade to farmers holding up pictures of six-foot tall radishes in Chernobyl, and Japanese fishermen smiling as they catch an eight-foot-long radioactive fish. The children marvel as their bathwater glows bright green in the dark.)

                    MALEK
There was a plan in Europe to build
a massive solar farm in the Sahara
to provide fifty percent of Europe's
power by 2050. It collapsed as the
costs involved in transmission of
solar power remained higher than
the cost to build the solar panels.
Japan had worked on the "world's
largest" floating solar farm, a way
for countries close to waterways
to build out solar platforms and
not rely on transmission across
long distances. More efficient
photovoltaic cells continue to be
needed, though they have improved,
and some good solar batteries are
already available which can fill
the gap. We need an international
energy alliance—a plan for world
leaders to work together.

(An image of the Tesla Powerwall battery is projected on screen, lighting up a house at night in western Australia. Men wearing cowboy hats drinking Foster's beer around a campfire are laughing. Kangaroos jump and crocodiles slither in the background.)

OCASIO-CORTEZ
Then large-scale solar farms in the
deserts combined with floating solar
farms would provide an immediate
solution far less expensive than
the trillions of dollars needed to
deal with the damages of global
warming.

(PRINCE IAN turns to his mother and asks
permission to raise his hand and ask the panel
a question. She, of course, agrees. The prince
raises his hand.)

(Ocasio-Cortez recognizes Prince Ian from his
pictures in the newspapers and tabloids and gestures
for him to come forward. Famous tabloid headlines
about the Prince flash on the back screen as he
stands: "Half-Alien Human Finds Headless Body in
Topless Bar"; "Future Alien Doctor Saves Britain's
Most Obese Woman Who Ate A Fridge." Finally, the
tableau at the opening of the summit: "Prince
Ian To The World on Climate: Kiss Your Asteroid
Goodbye.")

(He stands and goes to the front of the stage and
the microphone.)

PRINCE IAN
Grüezi Mitenand. I have a question
for the panelists. Reading Earth's
history and science, there are
around three and a half trillion
trees on the planet. While that
may still seem like a lot,
deforestation decreased that number
from six trillion a hundred years

ago. Trees take up the majority
of the carbon dioxide and help
produce oxygen. So even if we
lower our carbon footprint, we'll
still need to absorb the carbon
dioxide already warming the Earth's
atmosphere to prevent further
damage. Every human being needs
seven or eight trees of their own
to survive.

(A group of children comes onto the stage and plays with self-abandon. A row of eight healthy trees takes position around them. A logo for Eden Reforestation Project is in the right lower corner.)

PRINCE IAN
Although forest products companies
plant three quarters of a billion
trees annually, about 2.5 million
trees are cut down every *day* for
beef farms and industrial use.
So if there are now approximately
eight billion people on Earth,
and each one were to plant ten
trees every year of different
varieties in addition to the
billion trees planted annually by
forest companies—*and* if we lowered
our beef, paper, and industrial
use—wouldn't it take about forty
years to recover the roughly three
trillion trees destroyed and get
back to the prior six trillion
trees on the planet? Couldn't we
involve *every* family in the world
in a common and worthwhile cause?

(A headline appears on the main screen.)

INDIA PLANTS 50 MILLION TREES IN ONE DAY,
SMASHING WORLD RECORD

> PRINCE IAN
> The Reptilians created this problem
> through big corporations, but
> there are many groups that could
> coordinate such efforts, looking for
> volunteers in communities across
> the globe to beat the world record.

(Logos flash across the back screen, including the Nature Conservancy, Plant for the Planet, Community Forests International, The International Tree Foundation, and Trees for the Future.)

> PRINCE IAN
> It could be a contest. The country
> and organization to succeed with
> planting the most trees on its
> continent gets the grand prize of
> one million dollars while surviving
> the climate crisis.

(Everyone is stunned. Was this five-year-old half-human, half-alien scientific prodigy coming up with a simple mathematical and scientific solution? Humans had tried tree planting campaigns but never of that magnitude. It certainly could be part of the answer. Tree planting contests where every human and Starseed on Earth is involved?)

> OCASIO-CORTEZ
> An interesting idea, Prince Ian. A
> worldwide tree-planting campaign.

Naturalist societies and large
charitable foundations like the
Gates, Clinton, Gaga, and Bloomberg
Foundations might support such an
endeavor. This could be part of the
solution. Thank you, young prince.

*(The morning session is ended, and lunch is
brought on stage. The cast and audience enjoy
cheese fondue with crusty baguettes and pieces of
apple. Swiss delegates mill throughout the theater
pouring alcoholic and non-alcoholic drinks for the
cast and audience while filling up the fondue pots.
Women dress in classic Swiss Herdsmen's outfits of
bredzon and short blue jackets made of cloth with
sleeves gathered at the shoulders, along with men
wearing leather shorts with large brown leather
boots. Almost everyone has smiles on their faces;
though some without smiles appear to be lactose
intolerant. Ironic to attempt to solve pressing
climate issues while indirectly contributing to
the problem.)*

(BLACKOUT)

(END OF SCENE)

ACT III

SETTING: The Davos Congress Center, 2042, later that same afternoon.

AT RISE: A giant coffee cup fills most of the stage and reaches the top of the theater. The cup opens at various times as the performers speak and as the audience comes up for a cup of coffee and some Lindt Swiss dark chocolate. Climate change, deforestation, droughts, and plant diseases have put the future of chocolate and coffee at risk, and the vast majority of the cocoa beans and coffee species on the planet are extinct. As the play is performed, the audience can stand around and slowly sip their java brew while eating small squares of their precious dark treats. The chocolate and coffee addicts among the group wonder if this is one of the worst effects of climate change after loss of the butterfly population.

(A door in the side of the cup opens. Enter twentieth-century prophets EMILY BISSELL and WILL ROGERS.)

                    BISSELL
        Great thoughts speak only to the
        thoughtful mind. But great *actions*
        speak to all mankind.

                    ROGERS
          Even if you're on the right track,
          you'll get run over if you just sit
          there.

(Exit)

*(Enter MAY BOEVE, executive director of 350.
org and a formidable force in the environmental
movement for decades, organizing action around
climate change, helping college campuses reduce
fossil fuel use, and organizing protests outside
the White House. She is in her fifties and has
blonde hair, a ruddy complexion, and award-winning
smile. She is wearing a grey suit and purple top.)*

                    BOEVE
          Before we begin again today, I
          would like to announce the winner
          of the Rachel Carson Environmental
          Conservation Award. Rachel was the
          first scientist to warn the world
          about the environmental impact of
          fertilizers and pesticides. This
          year's award goes to…

(There is a pause as she opens the envelope)

                    BOEVE
          …the Nature Conservancy. They
          have protected millions of acres
          of land and thousands of miles of
          river with conservation efforts in
          sixty-nine countries. We thank them
          for their tireless efforts over
          several generations, helping to
          preserve our quality of life and
          environmental diversity.

(A representative for the Nature Conservancy emerges from the cup to accept the award. It is just like the Academy Awards, except no one thanks their agent or wears Dior Haute Couture.)

> BOEVE
>
> I would now like to introduce Professor Satu, an eminent visiting Arcturian scientist who will explain the climate challenges the Arcturian people faced on their own world. Professor?

> SATU
>
> Good afternoon. On our home planet Proxima Centauri B, we faced similar problems leading up to the Reptilian invasion. Expansion of populations and economies across our various kingdoms and clans required increased energy production, and we needed to access affordable technology to grow the economy while reducing emissions. Regrettably, none of our clan leaders were willing to curb local population growth or work together. The result was devastating. Unchecked population growth exhausted valuable resources, and the Reptilians took advantage of our lack of coordinated efforts. They shapeshifted into Arcturian scientists and leaders and easily divided and conquered. Greed, stubbornness, pride, materialism,

ignorance, and a refusal to work
together ultimately led to our
demise. Similarly, here on planet
Earth, the unwillingness of your
world governments to work together—
out of denial, ignorance, and
economic competition—has led you to
the brink of disaster.

(Satu exits. A group of men and women file onto the stage and take positions around Boeve.)

                    BOEVE
Each of the morning chairs from
different committees will now give
a brief summary of their work with
potential solutions to address our
global environmental degradation.
We will begin with Ms. Corusca
from the U.S. Department of
Transportation.

(ALICIA CORUSCA is a bubbly, smiling forty-three-year-old from the Harvard Kennedy School Center for Public Leadership. She works for the DOT, has long brown hair, and is wearing a blue top and black blazer.)

                    CORUSCA
The transportation, building,
and industry sectors have all
seen sizable emission increases
in the past four decades,
faster than previously thought
and with devastating results.
Fortunately, we were able to buy
precious time and lower average

global temperatures by cooling
the planet through two primary
means: solar radiation management
using millions of square miles of
oceanic solar radiation reflectors
created by Harvard physicists,
while scientists from the Center
for Climate Repair at Cambridge
University coordinated the
spraying of aerosols of sulphate
particles into the stratosphere
to restrict solar radiation from
reaching the lower atmosphere.
Solar shading to slow the melting
of the Himalayan glaciers as well
as seeding clouds with sea salt to
brighten them and reflect sunlight
back into space have also had
partial success in helping to cool
the planet, but it only bought us
so much time as carbon pollution
increased. To continue making
progress, we propose using more
clean, renewable wind-water-solar
energy for building and industry
and more efficient high-speed
transportation across all sectors.
This was outlined earlier today by
our esteemed speaker Dr. Jacobson,
working with researchers from The
Institute of Transportation Studies
at the University of California,
Berkeley.

*(An image appears on screen showing the scientific
journal One Earth. Children on solar-powered anti-
gravity hoverboards go to school.)*

CORUSCA

This paper evaluates solutions to
global warming, air pollution,
and energy insecurity for one
hundred forty-three countries and
provides Green New Deal energy
roadmaps. Wind-water-solar, or
WWS, reduces global energy needs
by 57.1 percent, energy costs by
61 percent, and social costs by 91
percent while avoiding blackouts,
creating millions more jobs than
lost, and requiring little land.

*(The main screen shows millions of square miles
of oceanic solar reflectors from space with a
volcano erupting in the background. Planes fly
overhead, spraying sulphate particles into the
stratosphere. A high-speed monorail train carries
smiling travelers in the foreground. An ad for
Disney's Epcot Center appears on the top right of
the screen.)*

BOEVE

Thank you, Alicia. Now we will
hear from Victor Sokolov, UCI
associate professor of Earth system
science, who will speak to the
ability of a country as large and
technologically-developed as the
United States to meet 100 percent
of its electricity demands with
only renewable WWS.

*(VICTOR SOKOLOV is in his late sixties with short
greyish speckled hair, wearing a grey suit, white
shirt, and black striped tie. He is upbeat.)*

SOKOLOV

During *our* committee's morning
session, we examined how we could
have all countries around the
world meet their full energy and
electrical demands via solar and
wind power. Our team analyzed
forty-six years of hourly U.S.
weather data and determined we
could reliably get close to one
hundred percent of our electricity
from these sources.

*(A windmill rises from the top of the coffee cup.
Stuffed bird replicas of extinct species fall from
the ceiling.)*

BOEVE

And Dr. Sokolov, do we have the
ability to improve the efficiency of
solar cells? Could you speak briefly
about our capacity to accomplish
this?

SOKOLOV

Any third grader can tell you that
green plants and algae efficiently
convert solar energy though
photosynthesis. Scientists in the
Physical Chemistry Department at
FAU have replicated this very
process as closely as possible and
revolutionized solar technology.

BOEVE

Mr. Nguvu, has your group addressed
the newest technology to store such

energy? I understand MIT engineers
have come up with a conceptual
design for a system that could both
store renewable energy and deliver
that energy back into an electric
grid.

*(Mr. Nguvu, professor in mechanical engineering
at the Massachusetts Institute of Technology, is
sixty-five years old, dark-skinned, and robust,
sporting a grey goatee, short, cropped hair, and
thin, wired-rimmed glasses. Wearing a black suit,
pink shirt, and purple tie, he is smiling and
assured.)*

                    NGUVU
That's true. We previously
developed a technology called "Sun
in a Box."

*(A man stands center stage in front of the cup and
opens a box. Blinding sunlight emerges. He can't
see and stumbles and falls to the ground. Stage
left, stage right, and throughout the auditorium,
lights come on intensely for several seconds,
blinding people before going to black.)*

                    NGUVU
As you can see, we had a few bugs
to work out. Our prior design
took heat generated by excess
electricity from solar or wind
power and stored it in large tanks
of white-hot molten silicon, then
converting the light from the
glowing metal back *into* electricity
when it's needed. It was vastly

more affordable than lithium-ion
batteries at the time and cost
about half as much as pumped
hydroelectric storage—the cheapest
form of grid-scale energy storage
to date.

Recently, going back to 2039, we
developed a more advanced system in
which the excess electricity was
transferred to small lightweight
graphene supercapacitors, which can
store as much energy as lithium-
ion batteries, charge and discharge
in seconds, and maintain their use
over tens of thousands of charging
cycles. Both of these processes can
be paired with existing renewable
energy systems such as solar cells
to capture excess electricity
during the day and store it for
later use. In theory, this is the
linchpin to enabling renewable
energy to power the *entire*
worldwide grid.

*(Androids powered by graphene supercapacitors
suddenly appear and walk on stage and down the
aisles of the theater, offering treats to the
scientists and audience. Oohs and aahs arise in
waves.)*

                    BOEVE
Professor Moth-Poulsen, could you
explain the method you've developed
to store solar energy by creating a
molecule that offers a way to trap

heat from the sun and release it
upon demand?

*(KASPER MOTH-POULSEN is a seventy-year-old Swedish
professor of chemistry and chemical engineering.
He wears thick black glasses and has on a black
suit and open-collared white shirt. He has a strong
Swedish accent.)*

                    POULSEN
Yes, Ms. Boeve. It involves an
energy-trapping liquid molecule
made up of carbon, hydrogen, and
nitrogen. When hit by sunlight, the
molecule draws in the sun's energy
and holds it until a catalyst
triggers its release as heat in a
storage system that promises to
outperform traditional lithium-
ion batteries by five to ten years.
It can be applied to home windows,
a moving vehicle, creating solar-
powered cars, and even used in
textiles and clothing.

*(An image appears on screen of happy families
driving in their solar-powered cars pulling into
idyllic homes. Children get out of the car and
plug their smartphones into solar-powered vests
while their solar-powered android dogs bark with
delight. A giant moth flies overhead, attracted
to the gigantic cup's light. The symbol of Moth
Photovoltaic Industries is projected onto the cup.)*

                    BOEVE
Thank you, Professor. Now that we
have discussed ways to create and

store renewable energy, we will
discuss other ways to reduce the
CO_2 warming our planet. Mr. Wang,
I have read your report from this
morning. Could you please explain
to our distinguished scientists
and guests how we can reduce
carbon dioxide levels apart from
the global tree planting campaign
presented earlier?

(BOEVE looks over at Prince Ian with a smile. The
Prince blushes as his mother tries to hide her
pride.)

(HAOTIAN WANG is assistant professor of the
Department of Chemical and Biochemical Engineering
at Rice University. He is a bright forty-five-
year-old Chinese scientist with black hair wearing
a blue suit, blue-and-white checkered shirt, and
dark blue tie. He adjusts his thick translucent
glasses as he speaks.)

                    WANG
The process is very simple. We've
learned how to transform CO_2, which
in large amounts is toxic to the
environment, into carbon monoxide,
a key commodity used in a number of
industrial processes. Thus, we are
able to capture the CO_2 released
into the atmosphere and transform
it into useful products.

(A smokestack from a large industrial factory rises
from beneath the stage and blows smoke out of the
top in the form of happy faces.)

                    BOEVE
This is a monumental achievement.

                    WANG
Thank you, but much of the credit
must go to my colleague, Cynthia
Friend. Her paper published in
Nature Materials decades ago led
the way to our being able to
produce more efficient catalytic
reactions. Nearly one-third of
the world's energy is devoted to
the chemical industry. Catalysts
increase the rates of chemical
reactions, and our technique has
allowed us to revolutionize the
speed, efficacy, and environmental
impact of this process. We've
employed nanoporous silver-
gold alloys to make chemical
processes more efficient by either
speeding up catalytic reactions
or enabling them to take place
at lower temperatures. There is
a huge carbon footprint left by
many of these chemical processes,
some of which are more than one
hundred years old. We also can use
catalysts to transform dangerous
greenhouse gases like methane into
methanol for use in biofuels and
transportation.

*(Back screen shows a factory producing lightweight
flying cars at record speed. Scene fades to the
Indianapolis 500-Winged Wheels Championship Race.
Everyone on stage shakes their head and smiles in
unison. The group is making palpable progress.)*

                    BOEVE
Dr. Varma…your report indicates
that researchers from the
University of Illinois at Chicago
have proposed a design solution
that could bring *artificial leaves*
out of the lab and into the
environment. Your research would
seem to piggyback on that of Mr.
Wang.

(EMMANUEL R. VARMA is a happy-go-lucky Indian professor from Bombay. He is rotund and balding, wearing a grey suit and white shirt. He has a strong Indian accent and bobs his head back and forth while he speaks.)

                    VARMA
Precisely. Our improved leaf would
be at least ten times more efficient
than natural leaves at converting
carbon dioxide to fuel. We have
improved on Mother Nature!

(A forest of artificial trees with massive photovoltaic leaves is seen on screen with children playing under the canopy. Shiny green leaves fall from the ceiling.)

                    VARMA
Prior designs for artificial
leaves that had been tested in
the lab twenty years ago used
carbon dioxide from pressurized
tanks. In order to implement this
design successfully in 2042, these
devices need to be able to draw

carbon dioxide from much more
dilute sources such as air and flue
gas—the gas given off by modern
"clean" coal-burning power plants.
Burning coal produces about fifteen
billion tons of carbon dioxide
each year and 70 percent of world
steel production depends on coal
feedstock. Although much of the
world is trying to get off coal,
we must find ways to decrease its
impact while transitioning to
cleaner fuel sources.

(*Projected images show cows and buffalo defecating in the streets of India while people gather the dung to make dried animal biofuel cakes. Image shifts to the same people burning the cakes in campfires. Methane and carbon dioxide levels rise as a carbon-monoxide leak comes from a power plant. Chickens run around outside the plant and fall down dead. Birds fall again from the sky. Carbon monoxide alarms go off. Just as people in the audience appear ready to panic, Varma speaks again.*)

> VARMA
>
> Please don't panic. The process
> is safe. As water passes over the
> artificial leaves, the "membranes"
> pull carbon dioxide from the
> air. An artificial photosynthetic
> unit inside the leaf converts
> this carbon *dioxide* into carbon
> *monoxide*, which can be siphoned off
> and *carefully* stored to be used for
> various synthetic fuels. According

to our calculations, three hundred
sixty leaves would produce close to
a half-ton of carbon monoxide per
day, and oxygen is produced, which
can either be collected or released
into the surrounding environment.
This process can also help lower
methane, nitrous oxide, and carbon
dioxide, the three most important
threats to the atmosphere and ozone
layer.

(Oxygen masks fall from the ceiling and people breathe easier. Some contain nitrous oxide, and certain audience members begin to laugh uncontrollably. Once the laughter dies down, Ms. Boeve continues.)

                    BOEVE
Feeding the world's populations
will become more and more important
as we continue to lose habitable
land. Alexander Milt, can you
please explain to the audience
the work that you and your team
did while you were at Rutgers
University?

(DR. MILT, a quantitative ecologist at the University of California, is an ebullient forty-five-year-old scientist with thick brown hair wearing a blue suit and white shirt. As he stands to speak, it becomes apparent that he is holding an extremely large fish with two heads.)

                    MILT
Worldwide, our fisheries remain
under extreme pressure, with many

stocks over-harvested and poorly
managed. An overall reduction
in yield has occurred over the
past one hundred years. About 60
percent of the fish and shellfish
populations studied saw losses as
a result of the ocean warming and
acidification, while only 2 percent
of the populations increased in
that time. Those that did increase
were fish in the Pacific exposed to
radioactive waste from Fukashima
during the past thirty years with
genetic mutations. This has led to
enormous fish with multiple heads,
three eyes, and razor-sharp teeth.

(The sound of the ocean is played in the background while unsuspecting surfers suddenly scream as giant mutated fish attack their surfboards. It is Jaws on steroids. The pungent smell of rotten fish comes from atomizers sprayed by ushers walking up and down the aisles.)

Certain species, such as black
sea bass along the northeastern
U.S. coast, have thrived in the
warmer waters, but with continued
warming, those gains will evaporate
as even *those* fish reach their heat
threshold. Some regions have been
particularly hard-hit, like the
northeast Atlantic Ocean and the
Sea of Japan, where fish populations
have declined by as much as 75
percent. The Atlantic cod, the
mainstay of fish and chips, also

saw a 64 percent decline. Some 3.2
billion people worldwide rely on
seafood as a source of protein.

*(Images of starving Brits waiting on-line for fish
and chips fade to Japanese people eating glowing
sushi. Images fade to photos of bleached coral
reefs and starving polar bears.)*

        BOEVE
Isn't it also true that the fish we
are harvesting from the ocean are
now increasingly polluted with not
only radioactive waste but also
plastics and heavy metals? Dr.
Piper?

(The image of the Great Pacific garbage patch
appears on screen. MICHAEL PIPER, a senior wildlife
veterinarian and science director for the SeaDoc
Society, stands to speak as ushers hand out recycled
plastic garbage bags. Piper is thin and in his
seventies with short white hair, wearing a blue
checkered shirt and black tie.)

        PIPER
Distinguished scientists and
guests, the coral reefs and their
biodiversity have been completely
wiped out on the planet. One
example is the "sea star wasting
disease" that is the largest
disease epidemic ever observed
in wild marine animals. It has
killed so many starfish along the
Pacific Coast that for five decades,
scientists and scuba divers report

seeing none. The sea urchins those
starfish once ate are proliferating
with abandon. Whole rocks once
covered in sea stars are now
covered in urchins, which in turn
eat kelp. Countless species live
in the kelp forests, and kelp is
a major player in lowering ocean
acidification and carbon dioxide, so
it's setting off a cascade akin to
clear-cutting large forests.

(Spiny rubber sea urchins fall from the ceiling.)

                    PIPER
We have also severely polluted
our waterways with pesticides and
sewage, killing off other sea life.
A quarter century ago, twenty-three
million salmon were dead due to
toxic algal blooms in Chile, and in
2038, we saw more than one billion
dead shrimp, crabs, and thousands
of manatee wash up on the beaches
in Florida. As you can imagine,
spring break did not go so well
that year.

*(The back screen shows college kids trying to walk
around dead animals on the beach while violently
coughing.)*

                    PIPER
Episodic outbreaks of algae-
produced toxins make headlines
every few years when stricken
marine animals wash ashore. These

deaths have been linked to a
"smoking gun" called domoic acid,
which is produced by some types of
algae, causing deaths of marine
birds and mammals. The Southern
California coast is a hotspot
with some of the highest—if not
the highest—concentrations ever
reported. This is a condition
generically called "red tide." We
have now employed winged underwater
robot gliders to predict where
harmful algal blooms occur.

*(Images appear of robot gliders following red tide
as dead fish line the beach. People start to cough,
tear up, and choke.)*

                    PIPER
The substance accumulates in
shellfish and moves up the food
chain, where it attacks the
nervous system of fish, birds,
seals, and sea lions. It can also
cause amnesic shellfish poisoning—
otherwise known as ASP—in people,
with symptoms that include rapid
onset of headaches, abdominal pain,
cramping, nausea, and vomiting.
Severe symptoms include permanent
short-term memory loss, seizures,
coma, and shock.

(Prince Ian turns to his mother.)

                    PRINCE IAN
Could those symptoms also be due to
Grandmother's cooking?

(Queen Dawn motions for him to be quiet. People stumble onto the stage as ambulances pull into the theater with sirens blaring. Medics rush out. The people hold their heads and fall unconscious. They are quickly carried off stage. Advertisements for Dubai's Lotus Evora ambulance, Limo luxury ambulance, Tokyo's super ambulance, Mercedes-Benz Citaro ambulance, and the famous flying arctic ambulances are projected on the screen.)

> BOEVE
> Sobering findings, indeed. Dr.
> Anderson, could you please speak
> about the other toxins that have
> shown up in the seafood and what
> effects they have been shown to have
> on human health?

(ALEKSANDER ANDERSON of Harvard is a ninety-two-year-old Danish MD who is balding with grey hair, thick, bushy eyebrows, and thin, wire-rimmed glasses. He is wearing a bright blue suit, blue and white striped shirt, and red tie. Slowly, he stands to speak with a Scandinavian accent.)

> ANDERSON
> Thousands of environmental
> toxins have gotten into citizens
> worldwide because of unbridled
> Reptilian power. Environmental
> chemical exposure contributes
> to the ongoing explosion of
> neurodevelopmental disorders and
> declining IQ in children, affecting
> at least two in six children
> in the U.S. and hundreds of

millions more worldwide. The most
common manifestations are Autism
Spectrum Disorder, Attention-
Deficit Hyperactivity Disorder, and
Tics. The culprit? Environmental
toxins, particularly heavy metals.
Adding to the concern, scientists
and physicians are increasingly
seeing children with *multiple*
neurodevelopmental disorders and
greater levels of emotional,
behavioral, and educational
impairment. The Reptiles have
been dumbing down our population
for decades, and if they are not
stopped, there will be no one left
to combat their evil machinations.

*(A crowd of children rushes down the aisles and
through the audience, rocking back and forth, many
throwing tantrums. Audience members try to calm
them down. As the children continue to weave through
the audience, the main screen shows young people
of all ethnic groups exhibiting profuse sweating,
rashes, anorexia, fatigue, irritability, apathy,
light sensitivity, tremors, and more. The image
fades to a child playing with a broken antique
thermometer, delighted as he plays with the silver
molten metal.)*

ANDERSON
Essentially, these environmental
toxins are causing brain injuries
and loss of function across a
generation of children and adults.
Rising mercury and arsenic levels
in the fish population are in part

contributing to the problem.
Plastic also now accounts for up to
90 percent of all the pollutants
in our oceans, with evidence of
microplastic contamination in
our lakes and rivers and thus
our beverages and food supplies.
When most Americans drink a
glass of tap water, they ingest
environmental pollutants linked to
cancer, nervous system damage, and
fertility problems.

(Image on the screen shows bald people getting chemotherapy, stroke victims in a neurology ward, and scientists at an IVF clinic trying to coax a sperm to fuse with an egg.)

(Ushers hand out glasses of tap water. Audience members look suspiciously at the beverage and are hesitant to drink.)

                    BOEVE
Dr. Chernyshevsky, you have come
all the way from Russia. What
are the broad physiological
effects of these chemicals? Why do
microplastics and these chemicals
in our oceans, rivers, and water
supplies pose such significant
health risks when combined with the
toxins Dr. Anderson was describing?

(DR. FEODORA CHERNYSHEVSKY, a Russian scientist, stands to talk. She is in her early sixties with grey hair down to her shoulders. She wears a white lab coat and blue top and has a strong Russian accent.)

CHERNYSHEVSKY

Exposure to plastic additives can
disrupt the endocrine system,
triggering insulin resistance,
early puberty, and endometriosis.
Insulin resistance increases the
risk of strokes and heart attacks.
Plastics can also cause birth
defects, reduce sperm production,
and impair learning and memory,
while estrogenic chemicals have
been linked to various forms of
cancer. It is an environmentally-
driven healthcare disaster—we
are dealing with massive-scale
exposure to *thousands* of chemicals
every day, yet most people are
unaware of the danger. On land, the
lifetime of plastics is estimated
to be in the range of centuries,
and because we have no way to
easily get rid of them, they will
continue to accumulate in our soil
and water. China has used plastic
"mulch" to grow crops, which now
covers *fifty million* acres of the
country's agricultural land, an
area equivalent to half the size
of California. Other countries in
the Middle East, Europe, and North
America also use plastic mulch.

*(Farmers walk out, throwing different kinds of
plastic garbage onto the stage, while on the screen,
images appear of farmers walking through fields
doing the same. Ushers hand out plastic flowers.)*

CHERNYSHEVSKY

Some 15 percent of global oil
production is used in plastic
manufacturing, both as the raw
material and for energy to power
the process. While plastic is an
incredibly versatile material
and has a lot of advantages
over other materials, we must
drastically reduce the amount of
plastic we are introducing into
the environment—no matter what the
Reptilian propaganda may tell us.
The companies need to shoulder
responsibility, and it's up to
us as consumers to become more
responsible in how we use, reuse,
recycle, and dispose of plastic.

*(Ushers walk through the aisles with recyclable
containers, collecting plastic bottles, forks,
spoons, and flowers.)*

BOEVE

Agreed, Dr. Chernyshevsky, thank
you. This morning we heard from
Dr. Terry, department chair of
Pharmacology and Toxicology at
Augusta University. He clearly
outlined that microplastic
particles contain hundreds of toxic
substances with known or suspected
carcinogenic, developmental, or
endocrine-disrupting impacts,
including organophosphates. When
you combine the effects of heavy
metal toxicity described by Dr.

Anderson, along with the hormonal
disruption from plasticizers,
we're dealing with a perfect
storm for disabling the human
population, creating a massive
health care crisis across the
globe. Thank goodness scientists
have finally created and produced
a bioplastic polymer that can be
produced from marine microorganisms
called polyhydroxyalkanoate, which
completely recycles into organic
waste. That gives us new options.

*(BOEVE picks up a water glass with purified, alkaline
water and takes a big, slow sip, smiling at the
audience. An advertisement for MXL-9 Life Ionizer
appears on the back screen)*

                    BOEVE
Then the Reptiles have succeeded in
altering the minds of the world's
population, striking at those who
are most vulnerable—our children
and future generations?

                    ANDERSON
Indeed, they have.

                    CHERNYSHEVSKY
Yes, absolutely.

*(Suddenly, there is a stirring in the auditorium.
Several members of the audience unexpectedly
shapeshift into slimy green Reptiles. They stand
and begin to shout and threaten the speakers,*

pulling plastic 3-D guns from their pockets.
Pandemonium ensues with screams from the audience.
People start to jump up from their seats and run
for the exits. As shrieks and cries for help fill
the auditorium, police and security guards on hand
rush to the scene. MASTER MYSTOS immediately stands
and places a ring of protection around the Royal
family. He speaks in a loud and commanding voice.)

                    MYSTOS
     Oh, evil beings of darkness. Your
     master plan for world domination
     has been unearthed, and you are
     powerless here!

(Mystos taps his staff three times on the ground and a
blue-green light radiates from it, surrounding each
of the Reptiles in a sphere of magical subjugation.
They attempt to escape but are immobilized and
defenseless. Gasps arise from the crowd with looks
of amazement as they witness the magical display.
The Reptiles are trapped and are led out of the
auditorium by the police. The audience members
begin to calm down and slowly return to their
seats, murmuring, with looks of shock and wonder
on their faces. Scientists on stage shake their
heads, finally accepting that reptile aliens have
actually invaded the planet. There is a palpable
shift in mood in the theatre with sighs of relief.
People feel a newfound hope. Extraterrestrial
assistance and scientific solutions exist to save
the planet.)

(Enter BUDDHA, a fat and happy version who the
audience will recognize.)

BUDDHA
No one saves us but ourselves.
No one can and no one may. We
ourselves must walk the path.

(Buddha exits.)

(Enter TECUMSEH, Native American Shawnee leader wearing a feathered red cap, a red coat with blue lapels, and a bone necklace with turquoise jewelry.)

TECUMSEH
When you rise in the morning, give
thanks for the light, for your
life, and for your strength. Give
thanks for your food and for the
joy of living. If you see no reason
to give thanks, the fault lies in
yourself.

(Tecumseh exits.)

BOEVE
We would now like to finish up our
session for this afternoon and hand
the microphone to two of our most
distinguished guests, Master Dorje,
one of the great protectors of
Earth, and distinguished scientist
Professor Satu from Arcturus.

(Prince Ian waves to Dorje and Professor Satu as they rise from their chairs and make their way to stand in front of the giant cup.)

SATU

Distinguished world leaders,
scientists, and honored guests…as I
confessed earlier, we on Arcturus
faced many of the same political,
economic, and environmental issues
you face today as we rapidly grew
in our technological prowess
and expanded our population.
We, too, experienced increased
global competition for resources
and concomitant water and food
insecurity. We also did not realize
the full consequence of using up
our planet's resources at a rapid
rate as our society grew. It was a
dark time in our history, and our
situation resembled closely the
World Wars and frequent fighting on
your planet.

*(Screens flash images of prior wars from Troy to
Los Angeles. Death, destruction, and sorrow are
evident in the people who are shown.)*

SATU

Our precious King and Queen helped
to temporarily put an end to our
clans' fighting and unite the
people on Arcturus. We were either
going to work together and solve
the environmental and political
problems, or we faced the only
other option: global destruction.
Huge financial resources had been
devoted on Arcturus to maintaining
our armies and arsenals, so we
collectively agreed that when peace

prevailed, we would funnel our
resources instead into scientific
solutions for the survival of our
planet. A global treaty was enacted
and enforced.

*(Image of world leaders at a conference table
signing a peace treaty and shaking hands appears
on the back screen.)*

Then came the Reptilian invasion
during the Orion Wars. They killed
off our people and took control
of our few remaining resources,
using them for their own needs.
And now you face the same fate. If
you can effectively deal with the
Reptilian leaders who control your
corporations for material gain and
power while polluting the planet,
you may survive. It will require
prioritizing your material comforts
for the greater good of future
generations. Many Starseeds from
other planetary systems are also
here, and they need to be awakened
to help you in your fight. I would
therefore like Master Dorje to
explain to you our strategy. Master
Dorje?

*(Dorje steps forward. His long beard and flowing
white robe brush the floor as his walking stick
begins to glow a deep blue. The audience stands and
shouts of "Dorje! Dorje!" emerge from the crowd as
everyone claps loudly and enthusiastically.)*

DORJE
You are at a crucial point in
Earth's history as you have heard
today from your own environmental
scientists. In order to preserve
some semblance of Earth's quality
of life, you will need to do two
things. First, you *must* address
the Reptilian leaders and their
agenda, those who have been putting
money, power, and fame above health
and humanity's future. Secondly,
we must, as a group, awaken the
Starseed lineages here on Earth.
They come from worlds that have
suffered as you do, they have lived
on your planet for centuries,
and so they are invested in your
future. Woefully, as they fled from
their star systems to come here,
the Reptilians followed.

*(Image are shown on screen of star cruisers with
hyperdrives fleeing to Earth. John Williams music
plays dramatically in the background. In the
theater, imperial guards of the New Order, with
white helmets and breastplates, parade down the
aisles.)*

Still, there is good news, as
these Starseeds have abilities far
beyond your comprehension, and they
can help in your fight against the
Family of Dark. I will soon hold a
sacred ceremony to fully awaken the
Starseed lineages. We must all come
together now for the greater good.

PRINCE IAN
Mother, would it be okay if I spoke
to the group again before they
adjourn? I have a few things I
would like to say.

(Queen Dawn nods and hits the button on her console, then raises her hand. She is recognized by May Boeve.)

QUEEN DAWN
Distinguished leaders and
scientists…before we finish our
meeting, my son, little Prince Ian,
would like to say a few words to
you all on behalf of our people and
the children of the world. Little
Prince?

("Little" PRINCE IAN, now five-foot-eleven, looks around the theater. Everyone has a big smile. Not only because a five-year-old has the chutzpah to speak to a large group of adults but also because his mother had dressed him appropriately for the occasion in green pants, an Arcturian royal maroon shirt with the Antwarian seal, a green tie, and a green beret. He looks like a mix of the jolly green giant and a cute, well-dressed Keebler elf or, perhaps, a large stalk of broccoli with legs.)

PRINCE IAN
I address you today on behalf of
all of the children of this world.
I love living here on your planet.

(The children seen earlier of all different cultures run together throughout the theater. They play with abandon, unaware of the dangers rapidly approaching.)

                    PRINCE IAN
Since we arrived, you have all been
very kind to me and my family.
Today, you have come up with
solutions for the dangers that so
urgently threaten this beautiful
planet. Another Little Prince faced
the same problems years ago. He
lost his beloved rose because no
one paid attention to the weeds
growing on his planet. I do not
wish to see the same mistake made
here.

*(The LITTLE PRINCE from the book by Antoine de
Saint-Exupéry emerges from the cup. He wears a
green outfit and red bowtie and appears sad. A
caption scrolls across the cup: "What is the secret
of what is really important in life?" The Little
Prince hugs the people on stage and then stands
beside Prince Ian.)*

                    PRINCE IAN
We, as children of the world,
do not have the power you have
as adults to make the changes
necessary to ensure our safe
future. But I would ask you to see
through the eyes of love and act
accordingly. As I was taught by my
mother, "It is only seeing with the
heart that one can see rightly."

*(The deep bass tones of a beating heartbeat fill the
theater. Images are projected of loving families
across the world, displaying different colors and
cultures. Tears are shed by those on stage.)*

In the name of love for your
children, grandchildren, great-
grandchildren, and all future
generations, please don't allow
this beautiful world to be
destroyed. Your hearts will suffer
greatly if you know you could
have done something to prevent
the tragedies about to unfold but
did not. The solutions you've
heard today may require courage,
perseverance, and sacrifice, but I
ask you to please do whatever you
can to make this right. In the name
of love—love of the beauty of this
planet and love of life itself—
please do the right thing. Be
green. Think green. Act green.

*(Someone hands PRINCE IAN a guitar, and he begins
to sing for the group Kermit the Frog's song about
being green. Rights to include song in production
are still under review.)*

*(There is roaring applause as people pull out
tissues and handkerchiefs. His mother smiles
approvingly and begins crying as well. People rise
from their seats and approach the Royal family to
thank them.)*

                    PRINCE IAN
Someone has to speak up for the
children. The question is, will you
do what is necessary in time?

                (BLACKOUT)

                (END)

PART FIVE:
THE AWAKENING

CHAPTER 28:

REACHING FOR THE STARS

"Every great dream begins with a dreamer. Always remember, you have within you the strength, the patience, and the passion to reach for the stars to change the world."

—Harriet Tubman

"We're going on a long and difficult journey," Master Dorje said. "Please pack hiking gear, a sleeping bag, your ceremonial robes, and enough food for two days. Meet me outside the temple within an hour—and no questions, please. Time is of the essence," he added. "Bring all the magical implements you've been training with. We'll be meeting up with a few friends."

It was before dawn, and the sky was clearing from a powerful storm the night before with rain, snow, and hail. Marty, Genine, Zach, Andrew, Morgana, the other remaining recruits, and I, Prince Ian, were trying to figure out what the Master had up his enormous sleeve. Still, as ordered, within the hour, we gathered again outside the temple, where six large pink Jeeps with oversized tires were waiting.

Native Americans sat in the front drivers' seats. We recognized these men as members of the local native Navaho, Dine, and Arapaho tribes who occasionally visited Dorje. The guides smiled at the recruits as everyone threw their packs into the backs of the vehicles and climbed in. It was still dark except for the faint reflection of a full moon on the surrounding trees. A sense of foreboding and excitement filled the air.

"Master," Andrew said quietly, fishing for info. "You know I get a bit car sick with sharp curves and high altitudes…. If we plan on going up into the mountains, can I have a barf bag so I don't vomit all over Zach?"

Everyone laughed except Zach.

"That won't be necessary," Dorje replied. "We're only climbing a few hundred feet." Before Andrew and Zach could get out relieved smiles, he continued. "Any nausea will come later."

Andrew grimaced.

Everyone grimaced.

That wasn't exactly the reassuring answer he had been looking for.

The caravan headed south on highway 89A into Oak Creek Canyon, past the Oak Creek Trout farm and general store. As the vehicles wound the serpentine paths through the mountains, the dawn flushed far in the east. The outline of Sedona's irregularly-shaped peaked rocks could be seen high above the canyon, the red mountains soon etched in multicolored horizontal patterns and large black streaks flowing down its sides, as if Mother Earth's mascara had run.

When the Jeeps crossed a bridge, the sound of the river below was deafening as the waters had surged following the storm. The temperature had suddenly dropped in the middle of the night as hail and snow fell, covering the red roads with patches of white slush while large red mud puddles accumulated along the sides. They glided through town, an eclectic mix of cowboy and yoga, and after two more miles of multiple roundabouts, the Jeeps turned off onto route 179, heading toward Boynton Canyon.

The long shadows of dawn made it difficult to make out the full terrain. After about a mile on the paved roads, going past modern adobe-colored homes sporting solar panels, with electric cars in the driveways, the Jeeps turned onto a bumpy dirt road and began to climb. It was then the recruits finally realized where they were and where we were going.

The Jeeps were headed to the holy site of the Amitabha peace park and stupa, a place where Native Americans still had land for sacred ceremonies. We had been there three months earlier for the winter solstice, attending a medicine wheel ceremony as initiates into the Huichol, Peruvian, and Native American traditions. It was now the spring equinox, and the energies were propitious for planting new seeds.

That is why we were here.

As the vehicles approached the site, state and local police cars—as well as black unmarked vehicles—stood on both sides of the road with a barricade blocking our entrance.

What in the name of Borgafar the Bad is going on here?

"ID please," a solemn state police officer said as the lead driver pulled up to the barricade. Everyone produced identification and handed it to the officer. She moved from Jeep to Jeep, carefully reviewed the documents and, seemingly satisfied, handed them back and radioed ahead.

"Dorje and his group have just arrived," she said into the ancient Motorola walkie-talkie. "Let them through."

The guides nodded to the officer, thanking her, and slowly pulled away. As they drove up the dirt road into the parking lot, several Tibetan lamas and Native American elders appeared from behind swirling juniper trees, holding up their hands and waving.

"Ah ho!" Michael Cooley yelled, walking toward the Jeeps. A local medicine man, he wore long moon-disc earrings with turquoise and silver bracelets along with traditional Native American ceremonial garb: a headdress of eagle feathers, a maroon-embroidered chest plate with elaborate silver and turquoise designs, and a shirt sporting red, white, and black Navajo patterns laced with medicine wheels.

One by one we exited the vehicles, grabbing our belongings. Everyone remained perfectly silent as a lone owl hooted in the distance. Suddenly, a black and white speckled roadrunner with spiked hair dashed across our path.

Was that an omen? I wondered. Knowing Dorje, I also wondered if a wily coyote wasn't too far behind.

Reaching the edge of the parking area where Michael Cooley waited, we each held out our hands, forming a cup. A local Tibetan lama in ceremonial garb with dark maroon robes and a large yellow triangular hat poured saffron-flavored water into our palms.

"Welcome," Michael said. "And please take some of the saffron water and wash your mouth with it before entering this sacred site."

We swished the sacred substance in our mouths to begin the ritual of purification, then spit it onto the ground and waited for further instructions. Michael motioned for us to follow toward the east. The group—Morgana taking the lead—began the slow and purposeful climb through the woods as the rays of the morning sun gently illuminated the way. The circuitous dirt path leading toward the stupa appeared more vibrant than the last time.

Was there something in that saffron water?

It was as if Dorje had summoned a phantasmagoric display of native plants for the occasion. Vivid assorted colors of Castilleja species, Sago palm, cat caw acacia, kaleidoscope abelia, desert broom, Arizona cliffrose, and blooming Point leaf Manzanita all dotted the land ahead of us as if beckoned by the Master to magically point the way toward the ceremony. It was an enchanting and mystical display of Mother Nature.

There was also an abundance of silver leaf nightshade and lavender vinca minor, both highly poisonous. Akin to life, they appeared beautiful but if inappropriately tasted, led to death.

Is this also an omen of things to come, or are our minds simply exaggerating the meaning of the signs? The group emerged from a clustering of pinion and juniper pines with stunning crimson spires, arriving at the Amitabha peace stupa, and immediately felt the immense power of the spot in which we stood.

It was one of the oldest forms of sacred architecture on Earth, dating back to the time of the Buddha 2,600 years ago, mostly found in the East where Buddhism first took root and flourished. A stupa was considered to represent the Mind of Enlightenment, built to avert war, end famine, and promote prosperity and well-being. Its sole purpose is to bring benefit to all living beings.

Are we here for a special healing ceremony?

Multicolored flags of white, green, yellow, red, and blue hues sporting black mystical symbols and pictures of spiritual masters riding wind horses flapped from the top of the adobe-colored stupa, greeting the group. Stretching out in a 360-degree circle, they fluttered in the wind and sanctified the sacred space, sending blessings in every direction. The initiates then walked up to bronze prayer wheels covered with Sanskrit symbols of the six-syllable mantra, turning them. Michael Cooley motioned with a quick rotational hand movement to walk three times in a clockwise rotation around the stupa, purifying any remaining negative energy and creating positive conditions for what was to come.

There was another important fact that might explain why we were there. Today was also a sacred day in the Tibetan calendar known as *Lhabab Duchen*, when the Buddha descended from Tushita heaven and all actions were multiplied ten-million-fold. On such sacred days, Dorje explained, one needed to be *especially* careful with our body, mind, speech, and actions.

After the third round of circumambulation we were motioned by Dorje to climb to the top the hill. There were dozens of large white tents purposefully arranged in a sacred geometry, set up as circles within circles surrounding the medicine wheel located in the middle of the sacred site, reflecting the togetherness of the people without beginning or end—symbol and reality simultaneously expressing the universal harmony of life and nature.

Fires burned outside each of the tents where large clusters of individuals all appeared to be waiting for us to arrive. It wasn't just the local native Navaho, Dine, and Arapaho tribes represented—those who'd driven us here. Far from it. Other major figures from world religions and faiths seemed to all be congregated for the ceremony. Pope John Christian the 6th, Rabbi David Cooper Jr., Ma Amritapuri—endearingly addressed as "Amma" by her devotees—His Holiness The 17th Gyalwa Karmapa, His Eminence Tai Situ Rinpoche, Imam Feisal and Sufi leaders, heads of the Sunni and Shiite Islamic movements, Master Jia, a Taoist hermit, leaders and adepts of the Zoroastrianism movement, and many more.

Zoroastrian followers being here was particularly interesting considering the beliefs behind one of the oldest Earth religions and what was now happening on the planet. Zoroastrianism was the first world religion to be founded by an inspired prophetic reformer and influenced the Abrahamic religions of Judaism, Christianity, Islam, and even Mahayana Buddhism. Zoroastrianism bequeathed the concepts of a cosmic struggle between right and wrong, the primacy of ethical choice in human life, monotheism, a judgment for each individual after death, the coming of a Messiah at the end of this creation, and an apocalypse culminating in the final triumph of Good at the end of the historical cycle. Their presence was highly unusual.

Is it a coming apocalypse, I wondered with a shudder of fear, *that requires such spiritual force to be present in one place?*

Many of the major North American tribes were also present in the outer circle of tents, creating circles within circles within circles. There were eighteen tribes, including the Apache, Sioux, Iroquois, Shoshone, Shawnee, Osage Nation, the Ute, Lakota, Omaha, Pawnee and Modoc people, Sac and Fox Nation, and others. Every tribe and their respective spiritual leader appeared to be outside of a tent holding eagle feathers and rattles in their right hands and sacred ceremonial drums in their left, waiting for the medicine wheel ceremony to start.

Grandfather fire kept close watch, as did Father Sky and Mother Earth. Master Dorje's influence was clearly greater than anyone suspected, and *now* we understood the need for such secrecy and security. This would have been a tempting potential target for the still deadly Reptiles, who had been called out at Woodstock and Davos but still maintained many top positions in business, controlling precious resources. With that realization came awareness of the men and women in black positioned in the surrounding red rocks with ET Army Command in the outer perimeter and Commander Avorius and a group of Arcturian warriors strategically stationed around the inner perimeter.

Was that General Scott and Major Broward in the distance attempting to blow smoke signals with their cigars? Is that P and his pugs wearing Native American outfits and smoking a peace pipe? The pugs seem unusually…calm.

The Copernican-Chiron Magick Academy recruits were humbled and inspired. Tears welled up in the corners of Zach and Genine's eyes. Andrew put his hand over his heart and went to his knees. Marty began to breathe in and out deeply, as instructed by the master to ground the energy and let it circulate through his chakras. The other recruits fell into prayer as the gravitas of this event became apparent. For the past year, Dorje had been preparing them for this exact moment, and finally, it fell into place.

We were going to call to the ancestors, God, the brotherhood and sisterhood of light, and all the spiritual guides and protectors of the various religious lineages to fully awaken Earth's Starseeds.

"Now go around the outer circle," Dorje instructed, "and present your ceremonial tobacco and sage offerings to the leaders of the different tribes. Then proceed around the inner circle and offer your folded white scarfs to all the different global religious leaders as a sign of respect. Once completed, please return to the medicine wheel so we may commence the healing ceremony."

The recruits opened their brightly colored woven yarn ceremonial sacks and, in precise military fashion, walked up the hill to pay respect to the tribal leaders. Then we moved to the inner circle and walked from tent to tent, opening the folded white katas, extending our arms, and bowing with the sacred offering. We placed the white scarves in the hands of each religious leader, who in turn placed them around our necks, blessing us and our efforts. Tears flowed like tributaries from a swollen Mississippi River. Before returning to the medicine circle, each recruit approached Commander Avorius and his troops and bowed, giving thanks for the assistance the Arcturians were providing.

Michael Cooley waited for Dorje's students to return.

"Ah ho!" he shouted. "Please take a position around the medicine wheel." He'd noticed the tears of joy and reverence. "And if you could all stop blubbering like hungry babies, we would all be extremely grateful."

Master Dorje chuckled, and the sniffling turned into laughter as the medicine man's humor broke the spell. We moved into the sanctum of the outer part of the medicine wheel, built from large, irregular red rocks that were piled on top of one another in a circle. This created both a physical and spiritual container. The innermost circle where initiates stood to enter the sacred mysteries was created from smaller multicolored red and rose rocks, then larger irregularly-shaped white rocks were arranged to connect the inner and outer circle and form a cross marking the four directions. Initiates would stand in any of the four quadrants marked by the cross or stand within the inner circle depending on where they were on their spiritual journey.

Once the recruits were in place, Michael Cooley smudged himself with white prairie sage and then smudged each of the members of the circle. He began with the tops of our heads and slowly moved down and around our bodies, using an eagle feather to blow the smoke over and around us until every negative emotion had been removed. The five elements were invoked in the ceremony to bring balance and harmony. The white abalone shell in which he carried burnt sage represented the element of water; the herbs and resins represented the earth, the feather and the wind created from it represented air, and the flame which ignited the herbs symbolized fire.

White prairie sage was known to dispel negative energies and had psychoactive properties due to thujone, a chemical that enhanced intuition and spiritual healing while facilitating contact with the souls of ancestors and other realities.

Michael chanted an ancient song of gratitude and blessing, first in his native language and then in the English translation by E. Barrie Kavasch:

Creator, Great Mystery

Source of all knowing and comfort,

Cleanse this space of all negativity.

Open our pathways to peace and understanding.

Love and light fills each of us and our sacred space.

Our work here shall be beautiful and meaningful.

Banish all energies that would mean us harm.

Our eternal gratitude.

CHAPTER 29:

EMAHO!

Once the preparatory cleansing was finished, Michael put down his implements and addressed the entire group.

"Sacred brothers and sisters who've gathered here this dawn," he began, "we thank Great Spirit for the opportunity to walk the good Earth together in friendship and care. We are all brothers and sisters inseparable from the mind and heart of Great spirit. This circle, by its very nature, is *inclusive*. We can no longer live as if we are separate entities on this planet. Whatever one person or country does affects all the others. The circle also ensures we are seen as equals in the Creator's eyes and brings us all together in that larger context, reminding us *now* it is time to share our resources and blessings for the good of all.

"Such acts will not only bring happiness to those around us, ultimately resulting in our own happiness, but this is, candidly, the only way for us to now survive as a species. I thank all of you who have gathered here today as we speak to our Creator with one voice and one intention. To live in love and harmony with all creatures large and small, blessing all those we touch, to bring healing and balance once again to our ailing Mother. Just as we would honor and care for a sick parent whose kindness and protection allowed us as children to grow into caring strong men and women, our Great Mother, Mother Earth, desperately needs our help.

"We are grateful to Master Dorje and our Arcturian and Pleiadian brethren who have helped assemble us in one place so that the power of each of our respective lineages may lift up our voices to the heavens as one powerful prayer resounding clearly throughout the universes.

"All this week, we have performed the preliminary rituals and purifications. Can we talk? Performing that sweat lodge ceremony last night, when it was *already* 114 degrees in the shade, reminded me that now the only two seasons here in Arizona are 'hot' and 'hotter.' It was so hot Satan took the night off, bees took off their yellow jackets, cows gave evaporated milk, chickens lay hardboiled eggs, and the water sprinkled on the glowing rocks created holy water because we'd boiled the hell out of it. By the way, who was the joker who tossed firecrackers in the fire pit?"

Everyone laughed. The Medicine Man had performed his job admirably.

"In any case," he said, "we are ready. May our ancestors come and assist us in this, the sacred task set before us today." After several moments of silence and meditation, he continued. "Would the initiates please take their respective places in the medicine wheel? You know where you are in life and what is needed for you to progress on the spiritual path. Today you have arrived at the truth stage. When aligned with spirit and connected to internal wisdom, your walk around the medicine wheel will be rewarding, although not without trouble and pain."

The initiates entered into the outer circle of the medicine wheel, and the Master pointed out which spot to stand on. I stood by and watched, wondering whether Dorje and I were going to be inside or outside the circle. I hoped I'd be within the inner circle, which represented the great mysteries, and wouldn't you know it, that's exactly where Dorje told me to go.

In the East stood Andrew. The East represented beginnings, endings, and renewal, returning back to our origins. Reflected in the color yellow, it was represented by the fire element, sunrise, emergence of light, leading to enlightenment. Genine stood in the South, the place that received maximum light as the Sun journeyed through the sky and peaks. Represented by the color red, it was associated with the water element, emotional intelligence, free-flowing emotions, addressing our inner child and core wounds with childlike trust and innocence.

Marty took his place in the West, a place of sunset where the sun went down and light returned to the dark. Represented by the color black, it held energy and required introspection, as it symbolized a transition phase often known as the "dark night of the soul" where the shadow aspect within us required confrontation if we were to progress emotionally and spiritually, building knowledge and wisdom. Power could only be properly mastered when the light and the dark both were seen. And finally, in the North stood Zach. A place of rest, remembering, and contemplating the death state, and what we accomplished as a child, youth, *and* adult so as to experience the fullness of self, leading to wisdom and logic represented by the color white and element of air, mental energy.

Once the four initiates were in place, Dorje summoned Morgana and the other recruits. The initiates were to take *their* respective places in the middle of each of the four major directions. Morgana took her place in the Northeast, a place of learning to control and direct spiritual energy. Larry took his place in the Southeast, a place representing the self with our gifts and aptitudes, including those passed on by our ancestors. Roberta stood in the Southwest, representing our dream reality and doors of perception, the place on the medicine wheel where acquired beliefs could influence and distort pure perception and where lucid dreaming can take place. Finally, Sam stood in the Northwest, symbolic of the law of Karma, allowing one to accept the various lessons, joyous and challenging, taught by life every moment of each day.

Dorje took his place at the very center of the wheel standing beside me. The center represented the sacred mysteries, indescribable divine essence, universal spirit, the unity of clarity, wisdom, and emptiness inseparable from supreme omniscient and omnipresent divine consciousness, sometimes known as the *dharmakaya* or "totality." All that ever was and all that ever will be.

Once everyone was in place, the Peruvian shaman standing next to Michael led the invocation, which had been translated from the Andean Codex into English by J.E. Williams.

To the East, the place of insight and rebirth, I send a
prayer.

To the West, the place of death and wisdom, I send a voice.

To the North, the place of clarity and cleansing, I offer respect.

To the South, the place where Amaru, the serpent spirit, dwells and teaches healing and the spiritual powers of plants in the green place of reproduction and regeneration, I sing a song.

To the Four Winds, I cast my spirit, open my heart, release my soul, and surrender to my destiny.

Grant me the wisdom to understand the sacred in nature.

When the invocation was complete, Dorje spoke.

"The Arcturian elders and wisdom keepers of the different religious traditions will now collectively use our combined spiritual power to enable you to enter the dream state and communicate with our star brethren. Woodstock was the first nudge of enlightenment for the Starseeds. This dawn, we shall let them know the time has come to fully wake and come together to defeat our collective enemy. Listen now to the drums and rattles resounding throughout the canyon. Let their sound and the prayers of the spiritual masters carry you on your spirit canoes to the predetermined destination you have all seen in your dreams."

A silence fell, and as the recruits settled in, huddling in blankets, their breath slowed, creating gentle billows of steam in the crisp morning air. The drumming and rattling commenced in unison as the ceremony began. Deep-pitched booming and high-pitched maracas echoed throughout the canyon like rattlesnakes woken up during a violent thunderstorm. And then, just as the sacred ceremony was getting underway, the weather began to change. Dark clouds formed over the ceremony with lightning bolts and thunder in the distance. As the ominous darkness approached the ceremonial campfires, it spread overhead and began forming a large black circle over the canyon, growing bigger by the minute.

The chanting continued as the shadow became so large it eclipsed the light from the risen sun, and only the burning campfires of the prayer circles lit the surroundings. It was an eerie sight. Everyone looked up at the shadow, recognizing what was happening.

Evil had awoken.

As if a spiritual five-alarm fire bell had gone off, Dorje sprang into action—as did all the religious leaders, men, and women surrounding the tribal campfires. They turned to face amorphous forms, which appeared from within the menacing dark shadows above. Rattles and drums, along with chants in different voices, intonations, and languages, became louder and louder to drive away the approaching forces. Just as all the spiritual leaders were calling to the forces of light and mustering their combined strength to fight off their attackers, they finally saw the face of their enemy.

Large, shimmering, green Reptilian heads formed from out of the darkness with blazing red eyes. The King and Queen of the Reptiles had decided to come and crash the party.

"WHY WASN'T I INVITED TO THISS LITTLE GATHERING?" the Reptilian King boomed. "That's not very sssporting of you. I am told I can be the life of the party." The Reptilian Queen shook her luminous green head in agreement.

"Yesss, you sshould have ssseen the lassst Halloween party at our home," she said in a deep booming voice. "It was a blasssssst. The King told everyone to bob for APPLESSS, BUT neglected to mention they were floating in SSSEARING hot oil."

Thunderous laughter from the King and Queen echoed throughout the canyon. Shivers ran up and down the spines of the group. Reptilian humor was an acquired taste, and Dorje knew of their tactics.

"What is it that you want here, oh King of Darkness?" Dorje yelled. "Are you hungry? I hear all the good food is in the base of an active volcano located quite a distance from here. I'm happy to tell you where to go."

"I didn't come for the food, oh Wizard of Foolsss," the Reptilian King replied. "I came to sshow YOU your future. You all seem to be ssssso interessted to know what fate awaitsss you... I thought it would be easier to simply sshow you ssso you don't waste your time."

The darkness above the King and Queen began to part, and vivid images were projected overhead. Terrible visions. Homes destroyed by level-five hurricanes and tornadoes. Earthquakes rocking cities with gaping holes in the Earth engulfing entire towns. Acrid black smoke and cries of fleeing, burnt animals. Hailstorms destroying crops with starving families and dying people lying in piles on the sides of roads. Tsunamis wiping out seaside villages as people fled in fear.

Millions of refugees marching across barren land with hungry children in tow. Wars between neighboring countries fighting for food and water as slain men and women lay strewn across blood-stained battlefields. The images were shocking, macabre, terrifying. Cries of anguish echoed throughout the canyon as scene after scene unfolded.

But Dorje merely...*smiled*.

"Your feeble attempts to place fear in our hearts and minds are useless," he said. "We know well of your power, but you underestimate ours. You are no match for our combined strength and will." Dorje knew it was a perfect time to show the recruits how powerful the group actually was. The mage lifted his hands above his head and chanted in ancient Arcturian to form a circle of blazing light above them all.

"Brothers and sisters!" the Master magician boomed. "It is OUR time. Let us come together and show our Reptilian friends what love, prayer, and devotion—as one heart and one mind—can do!"

Hoots and howls emerged from the group. Rattles and drums boomed even more strongly as their sounds echoed from the canyon walls. Within seconds, light filled the space, and the abysmal darkness began to dissipate as a magical shimmering doorway formed overhead. Angelic legions and fierce spiritual protectors in fiery forms poured out, surrounding the Reptilian King and Queen.

The images continued, but the scenes suddenly changed. The wars and pollution and suffering faded. The waters grew calm. Fields were fertile, forests green and healthy and teeming with animals. There were bustling cities and smiling families. The enemy was no match for the combined power of the group.

Dorje turned to the Reptiles.

"Do not return again," the star-magician warned. "Unless you want us to show you the *full* power of humanity working as one. This was only a taste of what is to come if you dare come back. Begone, King and Queen of Darkness!"

The forms of the giant Reptiles began to writhe, pain distorting their features, and they disappeared into thin air as if they had never been there. The sun emerged from behind the clouds. A profound silence and peace came over them all. They knew now that they *could* win such a battle, not just today but again in the future. With that realization and renewed confidence, screeching, howling, and hooting filled the canyon once more until it was deafening.

The recruits looked at one another in amazement. The master had prepared them for such a day, but they hadn't envisioned such a show of force and spiritual power.

"Ah-*ho*," Michael Cooley yelled. "Enough lollygagging. Our break is over. Time to get back to work!" Laughter broke out again. "You've now seen what the power of Great Spirit can do when we work as one. Let's wake up our sleeping brethren. Take your stances in the medicine wheel. It's time to locate and free Earth's supreme Starseeds."

Rhythmic drumming and chanting once more filled the canyon, and the rattling vibrated them to the core. Listening carefully to the sound, each of the initiates called to their spirit guides and entered their spirit canoes, setting off for their respective destinations.

In the East, Andrew and his spirit bear set off to find Starseed Elders and give them the courage and conviction to wake up. In the South, Genine paddled while her spirit owl flew in the first of eight directions to bring divine messages of awakening. In the West, Marty and his eagle brought love and divine protection to all who were still asleep and afraid. In the North, Zach and his spirit buffalo made offerings to Wakan Tanka to ensure successful outcomes for all of the other members of his tribe.

In the Northeast, Morgana and her black-tailed deer brought compassion and mystical energy to shift the dreamer's perception. In the Southeast, Larry and his spirit wolf brought humility and wisdom, reminding the elders of their leadership roles. In the Southwest, Roberta and her thunderbird, aligned with the sounds of thunder and lightning, brought energy and alignment. In the Northwest, Sam and his mouse (despite Sam *not* being happy about his selection of spirit animal) assured others of their survival as a species with endurance, adaptability, and focus.

As the group set out to find the seven elders of the seven Starseed tribes living on Earth, at the center, Dorje and I traveled together with a spirit turtle named Venus de Milo who was sitting on my lap. She represented truth—the truth that binds all things together. We set out in the dreamtime to journey to the temple of the Akashic records, to speak to the Archangel Metatron and access past, present, and future knowledge. This would allow a deeper understanding of probable futures and ensure the best possible chance of success.

• • • •

The drums and rattles continued for hours, eventually greeting the setting sun and echoing throughout the night. Then a strange and wonderful phenomenon began to manifest. Local animals began to congregate at the outskirts of the ceremony, as if dream manifestations were becoming real.

It started with a lone grey wolf, who howled in the distance and then appeared on the mountain ridge. Minutes later a black-tailed deer sauntered around the campfires looking for food. A great horned owl landed on the branch of a nearby juniper tree, and as if Great Spirit didn't want to leave anything to chance, an Eagle appeared in the sky and landed on top of Dorje's tent. It perched there until the last part of the ceremony, then flew away.

As dawn crested the red rocks to the east and the drumming ebbed, the initiates began to emerge one by one from their dream states.

Wide eyed and barely awoken from their altered reality, they all began to cry again. They had been successful. Each of them now sat around the campfire and, taking the talking stick, spoke of their journeys and what Great Spirit had them see and do. Across the globe on all seven continents, each of the initiates had been drawn to one of the seven elders of the seven Starseed tribes and their families living on Earth. They were told in the dreamtime that each of these Starseed Elders and their children held knowledge that would prove to be key to defeating the Reptiles. Thanks to years of Dorje's training, they had contacted the elders and members of the Arcturians, Alpha-Centurians, Annunaki, Andromedans, Lyrans, Sirians, and Pleiadians and successfully awakened them.

With the announcement of the last civilization, Commander Plamorius let out a shout:

"Love Fest!"

He sat with members of the ET Army Command, many of whom were still sleeping alongside the fire. When he embraced them all, it may have been the first time in history that Major Broward didn't care.

• • • •

Morning dawned, and as if the prior signs *still* hadn't been enough, a double rainbow suddenly appeared in the sky above the canyon. Great Spirit had heard and answered their prayers.

Once everyone had been roused, Michael concluded the ceremony.

"It has been an honor and privilege to spend time with all of my sacred relations here today in this place of power. From the bottom of my heart, I thank you all for making the long and difficult journey to get here. The signs have clearly appeared, and they are good."

There was a long pause—what many called deep meditative silence.

"Each of you has received a consecrated medicine shield, which has been blessed by every member of the spiritual community who partook in our sacred ceremonies. Please keep this as a precious reminder of our time here today. As you return home, please share this gift with your people. Ask them to reflect daily on those qualities that will bring blessing and honor: love, wisdom, honesty, respect, generosity, courage, and humility. Please also ask your people to reflect on those Reptilian values which have led us down the path of darkness: fear, ignorance, pride, cowardice, greed, dishonesty, and disrespect.

"We must guard against these qualities if we are to preserve and protect our way of life, and all the two-legged and four-legged who walk the Earth." Michael looked at us all and let loose one final loud and joyous cry, yelling resoundingly, "*Emaho!*" This reflected their magnificent achievement and deep, abiding compassion for all living creatures.

As the medicine man finished his last exhortation, drums and rattles and piercing joyful shrieks echoed loudly from the canyon walls again, and every campsite celebrated for what seemed an eternity.

Then Dorje turned to the recruits with a smile.

"You have done well, my young apprentices," he exhorted. "You now understand the importance of your spiritual training and why the inherent difficulties you undertook were necessary for success. Get your bags and tents and let us stay here for several more days, fasting and resting in meditation before returning home. We must prepare for the next stage of the journey. We will soon be meeting and protecting the Starseed lineages and their elders as we prepare to enter into a momentous final battle against the Reptilian overlords on Earth."

The Awakening ceremony had concluded.

It was time for Earth's first meeting of the Starseed Council of Elders.

CHAPTER 30:

THE STARSEED COUNCIL OF ELDERS

"I've been asked about UFOs and I've said publicly I thought they were somebody else, some other civilization."

—Commander Eugene Cernan, Commander of the Apollo 17 Mission

They all had the same dream.

On the night of August 22, 2042—or the *morning* of August 23rd, depending on your view of such things—seven families from seven different Earth continents living in different time zones all reported waking up after having experienced the exact same vision.

At first, there was nothing that connected them except for the fact they were all renowned "doctors" with various degrees in different disciplines.

Then news reports emerged from different parts of the globe that each of these seven individuals woke with the precise names and locations of the other six dreamers, even though they had never met. The mystery continued.

The media famously referred it to as "Synchronous Slumbering Visions and Revelations."

They came from different walks of life with dissimilar back-grounds and different physical characteristics. Because they all were doctors, intelligence agencies investigated, trying to determine if they all had Jewish mothers. They did not. Indeed, there was a doctor of medicine, a doctor of philosophy, a veterinarian, a PhD geneticist, biologist, mathematician, and astrophysicist. In other words, they weren't all real doctors, or "doctor" doctors, as my mother's yenta friends would say.

• • • •

Dr. Malcolm I. Antware was a strikingly handsome seven-foot-two-inch man from New York. He grew up in Rego Park, Queens and had an uneventful childhood. At age four he wanted to be a magician, and his first act was sticking nails through his hands, so he ended up visiting the Elmhurst hospital emergency room quite often. After his parents convinced him to abandon that particular career, he wanted to be a rabbi.

He would pray day and night and could easily quote scripture from the Zohar, the Tanya, the Mishnah, Torah, and other sacred texts. That all stopped once he hit puberty. His mother sat him down and told him he had one of two choices: becoming a doctor or a lawyer. When not assiduously studying to get into college to eventually go to medical school, he would drive to the local quarry and—for no apparent rea-son—start to "dig things up from the ground." It was unusual behavior, even for a child from Queens.

Malcolm continued this even after he opened his medical practice, got married, and started a family. What no one—including Malcolm—realized was that he was an incarnated Arcturian master, a terton, a magician treasure hunter. After he awakened, he would be the one to unearth from the rocks and mountains the *Reptilian Book of Death* and the *Arcturian Book of Everlasting Life*. Centuries earlier, these sacred volumes had been hidden in the ground by incarnations of Arcturi-an tertons, myself included, waiting for the day that their successors would return and uncover them when the time was propitious.

. . . .

Dr. Elisabeth Centaure, from Paris, was a French "tomboy" who grew up in the outskirts of the ninth *arrondissement*, working in her family's *boulangerie*. She refused to eat their light and flaky buttery croissants with fresh gruyere cheese, perplexing local doctors, as this had never happened to a French-speaking person before. "Betty" *also* refused to wear young women's fashionable clothing or makeup, a mortal sin in Parisian circles.

Even more extreme, she vehemently refused to shave her legs or arms or underarms at all until the hair became so long, it grew into what the locals would soon refer to as "petites forêts." She was beautiful, yes, but as the hair grew onto her chest, neck, and jaw, she looked more like a circus performer from the nineteenth century, further exacerbated by her unusual interest in dogs and horses. Clearly different from the interests of young testosterone-laden French teenagers.

Her parents brought her to local specialists on more than one occasion to consult French endocrinologists and check her hormone levels. All tests returned "normal," but her behavior was so unusual that not one renowned Parisian medical doctor—including the famous French physician, Dr. Christian Perronne, known for diagnosing unusual behavior oftentimes as a result of Lyme disease—could explain it.

Centaure spoke the truth plainly and freely, picked fights with local bullies, rode and spoke intimately with horses, and studied, assiduously, to become a veterinarian. Eventually she married and bore two children, all the while holding various jobs at human and animal rights organizations.

Then came the fateful night of "the dream."

. . . .

Dr. Mutambe Pleadus from Abidjan, located in the Cote d'Ivoire Africa, also had a love for all creatures. He cultivated an ability to speak different languages, including French, Agni, and Baoule—both Kwa languages from the south—and variants of Mande and Senofu from the north. A large, lanky child, he exhibited a propensity for making music and wanting to hug everyone and everything. This confused his parents, who were PhD geneticists, as they could find no scientific reason as to why he celebrated everything with different rhythms and melodies, including singing and dancing about 21ˢᵗ-century aberrant weather patterns.

Mutambe especially loved "Love Is Like a Heat Wave" by Martha and the Vandellas, "Stormy Weather" by Lena Horne, "Walking In the Rain" by the Ronettes, "10,000 Nights of Thunder" by Alphabeat, "50 Words For Snow" by Kate Bush, "A Hard Rain's A-Gonna Fall" by Bob Dylan, and "A Year Without Rain" by Selena Gomez & the Scene.

Like his parents, Pleadus became a PhD geneticist, and by the time he was thirty, he was married with two children and renowned in his field as the only person to be able to freestyle rap songs about genetic base pairs and their phenotypic expressions.

• • • •

Dr. Samuel Sirus from Brisbane, Australia was, growing up, likewise quite an enigma to his parents and local community. As a Queenslander whose Aboriginal grandparents had lived in the big city for several generations, having been dispossessed of their land—ostensibly "disconnecting" him from his original culture dating back over forty thousand years—he had an all-consuming interest in biology and ecology with a propitious knowledge of the Earth sciences.

At two years old, Samuel began to study math and science while his peers were outside playing with mud. By the time he was six, he'd already organized trips to the outback and ran a highly profitable business he called "Aboriginal Roots." While other children were trying to sell cold lemonade on hot summer days for pennies, Sam assiduously managed a highly-profitable environmental organization and was recognized as a scientific savant.

Once he assumed leadership of the expedition venturing out into the outback, Sam was known for his brightly colored clothing *and* the way local Aboriginal leaders honored him. Whenever he undertook a three-day weekend excursion, or more dangerous walkabouts far from the comforts of modern civilization, he would wear a copper plate snugly around his neck, an ancient Aboriginal breastplate of studded bones given to him by a local tribal chief, along with brightly colored gemstones along his upper arms, wrists, and fingers.

He also wore this costume during "corroborees" where local Aboriginal leaders would "miraculously" appear from out of nowhere and join in the evening prayer circles. Sam was permitted to lead the chanting and dreamtime stories as didgeridoos, clapping sticks, and drums echoed in the background. By the time he was sixteen, he had received a PhD in the biological sciences from the University in Queensland, with an honorary degree in religious studies. In 2042, he was forty-two years old with a family and—like Malcom, Betty, and Mutambe—had exactly two children.

• • • •

Gail Lyra from Amdo, Kham, Tibet possessed a four-foot-nine-inch frame and had a reputation for being a tiny, fierce warrior. For her, animals were to be hunted for food and clothing, and she preferred to wear animal skins. No Polartech super down jackets with the patented triple insulation and electronic solar powered heat lining for Gail.

She had no interest in music—no fancy wireless headsets, and she didn't even own a basic iPhone 25X model that could play the latest 6G, 3-D music videos. In what was perhaps one of the most shocking features of her childhood, she avoided online video games.

Instead, Gail lived high in the mountains and would often stare at the heavens while wondering about distant civilizations. During her rare appearances in town, she would only visit the local library to borrow volumes on astrophysics, which she would stuff into her backpack and then trek back up the mountain. There, in her cave, she would study and memorize them all by candlelight.

Eventually her prodigious talents were recognized; she was pulled out of the cave by Chinese officials and given a full scholarship to Qinghai Normal University. She studied there as an undergraduate before going on to receive a PhD in astrophysics at Tibet University. During this time, she gave birth to two children—one boy and one girl.

• • • •

Although Peruvian and Andean tribes generally were of short stature, Diana Anki Alvarez of Lima was born with tremendous physical size and grew to a seven-foot-six-inch height. She was recruited to play on the Peruvian-Andean national basketball team, where she dunked over Lebron James' head in such a spectacular fashion as to warrant reproduction on a poster.

She also brought to the team impressive analytical and mathematical skills. Diana could instantly assess an opposing team's defense, positions, and shots, and advise coaches when to go back and forth between a one-on-one defense or zone, as well as who at any given point during the game had the best probable shot from three-point range. Under her leadership, they won every game and were so successful that the 2037 American Olympic basketball team, coached by an aging James Harden, cried "foul." The Peruvian team seemed to know with uncanny accuracy each American play, such that they *had* to be stealing signals.

However, video playback clips from the games revealed no wrongdoing. All that was seen was everyone huddling around Diana with computers and whiteboards, busily analyzing data.

Diana received a full scholarship and earned a PhD in mathematics at Pontificia Universidad Católica del Perú, after which she founded her own successful international cybersecurity firm. She started a family and had two children—a boy and a girl.

• • • •

Even before the Awakening, a woman of Diana's size and stature, wearing a seven-pointed ox-horned hat and "melam," was predicted in ancient texts to liberate those who had been caught in the Reptilian netherworld during the last part of the Orion Wars when fires and floods had consumed the land.

It was years, however, before historians studying the *Reptilian Book of Death* finally realized that Diana perfectly fit the description of the Annunaki woman described in ancient Akkadian texts of the second century BC. The deities in the Annunaki tradition wore an ambiguous substance called "melam" which "covered them in terrifying splendor," giving humans who witnessed it "physical tingling of the flesh." She also was predicted to be the one who would stand before the seven judges of the Underworld and convince them to let the Earth survive.

In the standard Akkadian Epic of Gilgamesh, c. 1200 BC, Utnap-ishtim—the immortal survivor of the Great Flood—described the An-nunaki as seven judges who set the land aflame as the storm approached. Later, when the flood came, Ishtar, the East Semitic equivalent to Inan-na, and the Annunaki mourned the destruction of humanity.

Yet in the *Reptilian Book of Death*, the Annunaki princess and hu-manity faced challenges set before them after the Second Great Climate Change and Reptilian rebellion. The seven judges corresponded to the seven continents and seven Starseed families, and only the princess would be permitted to petition the judges; if humanity had enough positive qualities to be allowed to survive. Maite, the God of Death, would weigh the scales for or against humanity.

As per Krikun, D., Sichin, Z., et al., *A Philosophical and Historical Discourse on the True Meaning of the Reptilian Book of Death*:

> The slimly scaled ones, the green masters of disguise, waited quietly in hiding until the time was right. They had perfected the death rattle borne of patience. This allowed them to quickly pounce on their un-suspecting prey once environmental conditions and chaos were afoot on the seven worlds, allowing them to fill universal coffins with spilled blood of trillions of human, Alpha-Centurian, Annunaki, Lyran, Arc-turian, Sirian, and Pleiadian corpses.

> They, the green masters of the Universe, victors of the Orion Wars, had but one challenge that could lead to their demise and downfall. As it was predicted, if one of pure heart and pure mind with selfless motivation and knowledge of the great powers of Spirit were to lead the Rebellion, while another went naked into the bowels of hell to rescue the damned, then humanity and Starseed civilizations would stand a chance.

It wasn't until Prince Ian was born and the awakening of the Star-seed Elders took place that many of the phrases included in the Ak-kadian texts made any sense. It became clear that "setting the land aflame" referred to wildfires in Alaska, California, Oregon, the Brazilian Amazon, and across the globe. "As the storm approaches" referred to impending hurricanes Dorian, Edward, Florence, Ida, and Gilligan, and "later, as the flood comes" referred to the three-foot global sea level rise after the Second Great Climate Change, creating tens of millions of climate refugees as cities across the globe were flooded. These events all heralded impending ecocide, if humanity didn't act in a swift and decisive manner.

Historians were stunned. The rapidly approaching fate of humanity had been predicted centuries ago by the Akkadian epic of Gilgamesh. Under the weight of the present climate crisis born of ignorance, denial, and the Reptilian values of selfishness and greed with disregard for the health and well-being of future generations, humanity was about to enter a final battle for its very existence.

CHAPTER 31:

SYNCHRONOUS SLUMBERING VISIONS

The last individual to wake up that fateful night-morning was Dan Andre of the McMurdo U.S. Antarctic research station.

There were only sixteen people housed at McMurdo Station during the night of August 22, 2042 and the morning of August 23, 2042 because the base was located in one of the most desolate, isolated regions of the globe. The largest Antarctic station, McMurdo, was built on the bare volcanic rock of Hut Point Peninsula on Ross Island, the solid ground farthest south that is accessible by ship.

Established in December 1955, it was the logistics hub of the U.S. Antarctic Program with a harbor, landing strips on sea ice and shelf ice, and a helicopter pad. Its seven dozen buildings ranged in size from a small radio shack to large, three-story structures and boasted facilities, dormitories, a firehouse, power plant, stores, clubs, and the first class Crary Lab. Research included aeronomy and astrophysics, biology and medicine, geology and geophysics, glaciology, glacial geology, and ocean and climate systems. Participants of the Antarctic Artists and Writers Program also worked at sites near McMurdo Station.

Not too bad for someone who just finished his doctorate in philosophy, had a boatload of debt, and couldn't get a job—which Dan's mother had accurately predicted. Science had yet to quantitatively identify the bases for such uncanny abilities in female parents.

A master mathematician and architect, Dan successfully applied to the doctorate program in the mathematical and physical sciences and used his architectural skill set to help solve some of the National Science Foundation's most pressing problems in Antarctica, like how to de-clog a toilet and flush it at fifty degrees below zero centigrade.

Since it was the dead of winter in the Southern Hemisphere, recorded temperatures during that evening had been as low as negative fifty-five degrees centigrade. It was so cold, local politicians had their hands in their *own* pockets. So no one was tempted to go outside, and the buildings were separated by enough distance that, after Dan woke up, there was no one close with whom to talk, and if he dared to tell such as story in the mess hall, the little men in the white coats would surely take him to the mental igloo.

So Dan did what any reasonable person would do—he stayed quiet.

He assumed the general public wouldn't catch wind of his story until he returned home and was settled back in Ann Arbor, Michigan, reunited once again with his wife, teen son, and four-year-old daughter. His departure from Antarctica was only a couple of days away.

• • • •

That first night home, sitting around the kitchen table, he decided to spill the beans.

"Honey, I had the strangest experience down at McMurdo," he'd said. "I woke up from a dream where, exactly as if I were talking to you, an elderly man with a long white beard and wearing a blue and white gown with stars and moons on it appeared to me, along with a young boy. They told me it was time to wake up the seven Starseed Elders of the tribes living on Earth."

His wife nodded but didn't say anything.

Her face was unreadable.

"He proceeded to explain to me about a race of beings called Andromedans and their fight for survival during something called the 'Orion Wars.' Then this man, called Master Dorje, explained that 'my race' of master mathematicians, architects, and computer geniuses had been subjugated and helped this civilization called Draconian Reptilians to build a robot army—spaceships that could move through time and space and 'hybrid power breeds' that dominated civilizations.

"This man, Dorje, said I was the elder of the Andromedan people on Earth, carrying the knowledge of our culture and history...as well as the seeds to help undo the destruction that our race indirectly caused when we were blinded to the misuse of our creations." He paused and tried to gauge his wife's reaction. She just nodded for him to continue. "I'm here to be part of an intergalactic effort to regain our freedom and bring balance back to the five elements. A crazy dream, huh? It didn't stop there, though," he added. "Since then, I've had dreams in which *I'm* the one who's traveling out and finding others—others like me—inviting them to join in. Funny, huh?"

Still no response.

"So, anyhow, how was your day?"

Annie, his wife of twenty-plus years, remained calm. While Dan was away, the media had broken the news of Master Dorje's giant prayer circle. Stuck in the middle of a science experiment in Antarctica, her husband probably hadn't seen any of the coverage.

"Did Master Dor—did the man in the dream tell you *when* and where the meeting of the Starseed Elders would be?"

Dan reached for the plate of soy bacon. "He did, as a matter of fact. Someplace close to New Denver, Colorado called Crestone. Next week. All the Starseed Elders and their spouses and children will be attending for our...*their*...initial orientation."

Annie's face dropped when she heard Dan's words. Her mother had called the day before and let her know her health had taken a turn for the worse and she wanted to see the entire family for one last time before she met her maker. She went to the kitchen counter and picked up a set of airplane tickets. They were for the entire family to fly to New Denver, Colorado on the morning of August 30. It was a strange synchronicity for sure.

• • • •

Dr. Malcolm I. Antware had been the first to take the liberty and embarrassing gamble of searching for the identities, addresses, and phone numbers of all of the Starseed Elders. He'd first reached out to Dr. Sirus, since they shared English as a common language, and found a phone number easily on his Aboriginal Roots website.

"You don't know me, but..." Dr. Malcolm began, and Sam confirmed that he did. He also gave the other five names Dr. Malcolm had written on the notepad. The two then proceeded to call or email each name. Betty came next, then Diana, and one by one, they all connected. But Malcolm and the other Starseed Elders couldn't contact Dan, as he was stuck in transit in Antarctica.

When Annie answered the phone, Malcolm just said he would call back.

• • • •

"We've received several calls this past week from a Dr. Malcolm," she said. "And from—"

"Dr. Sirus," he finished. "And Dr. Sam?"

"Yes," she whispered, eyes going wide.

Dan Andre sighed an enormous sigh of relief. As a kid and teen, he often thought he was the one who didn't belong. He'd thought he was going mad after being stuck in fifty-below for too long without much contact except for his penguin friends. Now all the synchronicities and events leading up to this point in his life finally made sense.

Following the dream, he'd subscribed to the *Synchronous Slumbering Visions and Revelations* podcast, and the most recent installment, in particular, offered important insights:

> The Starseeds described a canoe approaching them as they waited at the banks of a winding river with strong currents. The only way to get to the other side of the river was to accept a ride from the strangers in the canoe. The water was too deep and turbulent to risk going it alone, so they said yes and got in.

> Inside the canoe there was an elderly man and a young boy sitting with a turtle on his lap. They made room for the guests and paddled upstream. Once they arrived at the other side of the river, they moved inland to a large campfire and food. Animals surrounded the site, as if protecting them, including bears, buffalo,

eagles, hawks, racoons, snakes, otters, thunderbirds, foxes, horses, and owls waiting around the perimeter in a circle.

Gingerly moving past the animals, they took their places around the campfire, and the ferryman began to tell them each of their lineage and history. Where they really came from. What they were here to do.

The night seemed to last an eternity and to pass in an instant as the mage Dorje told tales of star systems with destruction and desolation, recounting story after story of desperate people searching for a safe place they could call home.

And then, suddenly, they were all awake, lying in their beds at home in their respective cities on their respective continents.

In the past, when Dan had dreamed of being awake, it usually ended up with yellow pajamas. This was different. Very different. It was clearly a message that the day of reckoning was coming, and work needed to be done. Fast. As Dan prepared to pack for his upcoming trip to meet the Starseed Elders in person, he suddenly remembered the last piece of advice from the mage Dorje given to the dreamers around the campfire:

> "Dorje had said to the gathering, 'Alone we may be weak, but together we stand strong. If our will and resolve are powerful enough, our effort unwavering and our faith uncompromising, we will be victorious in our fight against the Reptiles, victorious in the battle against greed, pride, ignorance and anger, our true common enemies.'"

CHAPTER 32:

INTRODUCTIONS

"One of the greatest discoveries a man makes, one of his great surprises, is to find he can do what he was afraid he couldn't do."

—Andromedan Henry Ford, Sr.

The first Starseed meeting of the elders was held on September 1, 2042 at the secluded Blazing Mountain Retreat Center in Crestone, Colorado. It was chosen despite the facility's address, as the center was located at 2541 West Carefree Way.

Seven hundred fifty-six people from one hundred eight different Starseed families gathered in a shrine hall located at the base of the stunning Sangre de Cristo mountains. Select members of ET Army command and their families, including General Scott, Major Broward, and his wife, Dr. Correro, Dr. Morales and his wife, along with James M. Marks and the secretary of defense were all chosen to be present. Ultimately, they would coordinate military options against the Reptiles, and considering their sincere investment in saving the world, even these non-Starseeds deserved a chance at a deeper understanding of their minds and its power.

The room was chosen for its spaciousness, elliptical wooden ceilings, and practically translucent walls. There were rectangular glass windows around the entire conference hall, which looked out onto the surrounding valley and mountain ranges, all brightly illuminated by the morning sun.

It was time to awaken and stoke the flame of illumination.

"Welcome all," Master Dorje said, speaking even more slowly and deliberately than usual. "Many of you have traveled far from the four corners and eight directions to be with us all today. Our Great Mother and Father and your displaced Starseed civilizations thank you for your leadership and service for the greater good."

Behind him sat the Royal Queen Dawn of Antwar, His Highness King Aston of Antwar, the Royal Mother Helen of Antwar, and me, Prince Ian. They had erected a small throne for me next to Grandmother, from which I could keep her busy. There was special seating for Commander Avorius on one side and Commander Plamorius and his four chattering pugs on the other. Professor Satu and Master Amius flanked the group while Arcturian servants in ceremonial garb lined the shrine hall alongside members of ET Army command and their families.

It was quite a sight.

Amius, who was only rarely seen in public, had been asked to assess the plutonian changes that would occur from 2025 going forward. The experiment of free market capitalism had only survived for a few short centuries before the greed and ignorance of the Reptilian leaders sucked up every resource. The question for the day was whether human beings would be defined by greed, power, and blatant disregard for their own species' survival.

Only a radical shift of values could put the Earth back on track. Amius would explain how the planetary alignments affected our efforts.

Dorje turned and bowed to the seven—the "Dreamers"—and their families who were seated in the first and second rows of the conference hall. Dorje's students from the Copernican-Chiron Magick Academy sat directly behind them, listening attentively.

"Now that you and the lineage holders of your civilizations have recently awoken to the truth," he said to the elders, "it is time to speak of and from your collective memories to unearth the deepest wounds of your civilizations' pasts at the hands of the Draconian Reptiles. You must speak of the atrocities committed to your people so we may understand the depth and power and ultimate corruption of their darkness, and so our newfound knowledge can help us to summon the strength to defeat them by doing exactly the *opposite* of what they've done.

"Today, we will all learn how to access the power and unlimited potential of the light. We are *not* powerless. On the contrary. It is only our imaginations that limit what we can accomplish, and together, we will dive to the depths of our collective unconsciousness and bring light back to the darkness—just as one lit candle in a cave can illuminate that which has been hidden for centuries." Rounds of applause filled the hall. Dorje paused and waited for it to die down. "We are the only ones who can reverse this perilous course that threatens Earth's very existence. We all realize what is at stake. We *must* win back our children's future!"

The young Starseed lineage holders—the fourteen children of the seven Dreamers—jumped to their feet and broke out in wild cheers, howling like a pack of wolves under a full autumn moon. The younger generation was unable to contain their excitement. This was someone giving them hope and providing a plan to regain a future so terrifyingly at risk.

Again, Dorje waited until the reaction died down. He was measured in his rhythm and let the meaning of each of his words settle in.

"Each Starseed," he said, "carries deep within their subconscious a memory of their invasion. The wars that happened on Arcturus, the Pleiades, Andromeda, the Sirius Star System, Lyra, the Alpha Centauri Star System, and amongst the Annunaki people are now playing out on Earth. Many of your Starseed brethren do not remember their history, as the veil came down during their incarnation. We are here today to wake them up fully and then heal their wounds. We will use the respective strengths of *each* star civilization to defeat the Reptilians, as the power of the light we access today illuminates our path."

Dorje took a long breath and continued.

"Our civilizations have been sullied by the Draconian Reptiles, but we do this not to hold onto painful memories or grudges, waiting for revenge. No. We are here today to fully *understand* our pasts and to use that knowledge to liberate ourselves. Help us, Starseed Elders and lineage holders. You are our last bastions of hope!"

Hints from the Star Wars film flickered through my mind, but this was not a movie. If anything, it was more like that academy series on Netflix. And certainly the film rights to our struggle had been sold—for a tidy sum, one which would help monetize us in the coming conflict.

"And be clear, we *will* succeed," Dorje continued. "We *will* change the course of history. So let me introduce to you the seven Starseed Elders, as well as their families and children, the lineage holders."

There was more applause as all seven families stood up in the first two rows of the meditation hall and proceeded to the front of the stage. They all wore traditional outfits of their respective Starseed civilizations provided by the King and Queen of Arcturus for the occasion. Their costumes were colorful and vibrant, reflecting the different races and civilizations, and transcended the race normativity so prevalent in the early parts of the 21st century.

It was passionately argued that the producers of popular science fiction films and programs were inadvertently perpetuating the very racism against which they advocated by operating within the framework of normative whiteness. Deeper examination, however, revealed that the source of this theory was, in fact, a white wealthy Reptilian.

Once everyone was assembled on the stage, Dorje addressed the fourteen children directly.

"Elder offspring, you are the lineage-holders. Each of your families has had one boy and one girl. This was no accident. It was, rather, foreseen in the *Arcturian Book of Everlasting Life*. You and your kin will lead your civilization into the future, melding the best qualities of masculine and feminine wisdom from your native and Starseed cultures." He then addressed the entire group of families. "Please speak to us today. Speak of your pain and sorrow, your hopes, and dreams...*and* your visions for the future."

Dr. Malcolm I. Antware and his wife stood next to their two children, all of them dressed in classical Arcturian fashion with gold and silver tunics sporting turned-up elliptical silver collars. My parents wore smiles on their faces, gazing upon the American family as if reunited again with old friends they hadn't seen in centuries.

"Precious Queen and King," Dr. Antware said, "Royal Mother of Antwar, young Prince Ian, Master Dorje, and the Arcturian court, I salute you. Starseed brethren, I embrace you all." Cheers arose and certain overzealous Arcturians in the audience started shouting.

"Mal-colm, Mal-colm, *Mal-colm.*"

Everyone had to wait for the excitement to die down.

"May I first introduce to you my wife, Yenta," Malcolm continued. "Yen?"

"Good morning, Starseed families," Yenta said. "We'd like to present to you our two precious children, Raziel, which means God's secret, and Eliana, which means God has answered. Indeed, I felt as if God was holding a secret from me when my first-born son—this good-looking boy—refused to become a doctor when he grew up."

The Queen's mother, upon hearing this, wore a large smile on her face. "Now *this* is a yenta I want to get to know," she muttered to me.

"I always prayed my children would turn out to be important when they grew up, but it wasn't until my beautiful little Eliana, sweet child with an IQ of 163 and a mouth to match, decided to become a doctor and bring her mother *nachus.* She wasn't going to be one of those PhD 'philosophers' who never seem to get a job," she said. Dr. Andre squirmed slightly in his seat as Grandmother cackled. "And now, my children…"

Eliana spoke first. "Thank you all for inviting us and waking within us all the pain and suffering of *millions* of Arcturians. Most days, now, we have nothing on our minds but torture, slavery, anguish, and death." Clearly she had the same filter as Grandmother, too.

"It is still a great honor to meet all of you," Prince Raziel said. "You, who have now given us the nearly impossible task of waking up billions of Starseeds and teaching them to give a shit about their miserable existence on this planet whose light grows dimmer every day. Thank you very much for giving my life new meaning, working 'for the man' night and day in what will probably lead to nothing…or certain death for all of us."

Dorje quickly spoke up.

"Well said, Princess Eliana and Prince Raziel! You have a right to your rage, considering how your culture was robbed from you. Whatever future happiness you *thought* you might have here on Earth is fragile. It will be up to you as Arcturian Starseed lineage holders to help bring about the needed changes. To that end, please tell us of your visions for our future. What weakness have you witnessed in the Reptilian overlords while observing the Akashic records of our people? What strengths should we rely upon that may give us some advantage?"

Again, Princess Eliana responded first. "The visions that keep appearing to me," she said, "over and over again during the past weeks always bring me back to when the Reptiles first invaded...breaking down doors and killing innocent children and their parents. Every night now, I hear their screams, witness the rampant panic as people flee for their lives. Nothing the Reptiles took ever seemed to be enough." As I wondered how she could shoulder such a burden, she continued. "Yet as the night goes on, this vision reveals that the antidote to this darkness is generosity. People taking care of one another, feeding one another. This is the quality of the light that I see is required."

"Prince Raziel?"

"I see Arcturian magick," Raziel replied. "In the beginning I also see suffering, yet it quickly changes to a group of master magicians in a prayer circle. And they are performing miracles, opening and closing dimensional doorways, acting as direct channels between the physical plane and someplace else. In that vision, my father stands in the middle of the sacred gathering. These magicians...many of them are here today." He looked at my companions from the Copernican-Chiron Magick Academy. "In the dream, they're chanting as my father reaches down into the ground, as if his arms were made of light, and picks up an old, heavy leather-bound book. The cover says *The Arcturian Book of Everlasting Life*."

A murmur arose in the crowd.

"Wonderful!" Dorje exclaimed. "And how will the two of you help to solve the world's problems, leading the people of Earth out of darkness?"

"As a physician," Princess Eliana said, grinning at her mother, "I will create a new paradigm of healing to help physical bodies weakened by stress, PTSD, infections, and environmental toxins. It will reverse the damage done to brains dumbed down by the constant influx of chemicals and spirochetal infections now present in the majority of the population."

"And despite my mother's disappointment, having just finished *my* PhD in medical technology," Prince Raziel said, smiling at his father, "I will work with my sister to create the biotech required to bring this healing revolution to fruition."

Another round of cheers arose from the crowd. My mother had tears running down her cheeks as Father put his arm around her.

"Thank you both for your service," Dorje exclaimed. "And thank *you*, Malcolm and Yenta, for raising such talented children."

"Our great pleasure," Malcolm replied. Suddenly, he pulled a nail out of his pocket and held it up to the audience, then proceeded to put it through his hand. Gasps gave way to silence as it came out the other side without any blood, bringing *oohs* and *aahs*. "This will be as easy as pulling an Arcturian atmop from a hat!" he exclaimed to a round of laughter. He started to reach for a hat under his chair but was stopped by Yenta.

"And if my husband knows what's good for him, he'll get back to his medical practice and stop pretending to be a magician." She grinned, and Malcolm smiled back.

"Let us now hear from Dr. Betty Centaure and her family from Paris, France," Dorje said. "Doctor?"

Betty, who had conditioned and combed her leg *and* underarm hair for the occasion, sported a ceremonial Alpha-Centurian costume worn by high priestesses during sacred ceremonies. It consisted of a multicolored free-flowing tunic with a tight golden belt and brightly colored parrot feather headdress. She was accompanied on stage by her husband and two teenage children.

"*Bonjour. Ça fait longtemps, dis donc.* I am very pleased to be here today," she said in a lovely Franglais accent as she turned and bowed to the royal family and entourage. "Thank you for giving us the opportunity to work together and save our precious planet and *all* its endangered species."

The Pugs started to whistle and hoot.

"I'll be extinct soon if I don't get a cold beer in this heat," one exclaimed.

"I'm dying alright," a second said, grabbing his throat. "Dying of thirst."

Commander P shot them a nasty glance and held up his two pinkies. The pugs got the message and settled down.

"Starseed brothers and sisters," Betty said, seemingly unperturbed by the outburst. No doubt she was used to temperamental animals. "May I introduce my husband, Archie, and my two children, Veronique and George? *Mes enfants...*"

"Thank you, mother," Prince George said, clearing his mouth. He had been downing a flaky croissant with butter and gruyere cheese, and promptly stowed it into a jacket pocket for later. "I attended Harvard and became an environmental lawyer working for Defenders of Wildlife, and I have had visions of pain and suffering similar to Princess Eliana and Prince Raziel; yet in my dreams, I instead see animals consumed by blazing fires in forests, dying of thirst as rivers run dry, and forced to endure cruel treatment by their Reptilian masters. Then the dreamscape changes, and the darkness is replaced by people caring for all the animals. Respect for life in all of its myriad forms, *la lumiere de respecter la vie.*"

"And how will you use *your* talents to help the Earth during these dark times?" Master Dorje asked.

"I will fight with every fiber of my being to stop and reverse the destruction of species on this planet," the Alpha-Centurian Prince responded. "Setting up animal shelters and climate-protected zoos that care for the weak and sick to ensure that their species survive and flourish once again."

"I recently lost my beloved stallion to the tick-borne infection anaplasmosis," Princess Veronique interjected. "We've already lost one quarter of the diversity of our current plant, animal, and insect species to extinction, and my brother and I will work through the court system to ensure fairness and equality for *all* life on the planet."

"Excellent, Prince and Princess of Alpha-Centuri," Dorje said. "Dr. Samuel Sirus, please introduce yourselves and let us know what weakness you witnessed in the Reptilian overlords during dreams of the Orion Wars, and what strengths of the Sirian people are available for us all?"

"Thank you, Master Dorje," Sirus said. Sam wore typical Sirian ceremonial garb *and* his aboriginal outfit. "It is an honor and privilege for our family—my wife Alinta, my daughter Marlee, and son Cobar—to be here. As many of you know, I have established several environmental organizations in Australia that have since spread throughout the world. Their mission is based on a famous quote: 'Science and reason, the arithmetic of feelings, must prevail, for he that cannot reason is a fool, he that will not is a bigot, and he that dare-not is a slave.' My children will now speak to you of *their* visions and dreams." He first gestured to Marlee.

"In my case, the dream always begins and ends the same way. I am in a large grouping of Sirian scientists and politicians on our home planet, meeting at the Sirian Tower of Knowledge and Technology, debating the future course of our civilization. These powerful men and women sit around a large round table similar to ancient kings, which was natural since he was Sirian. Only our civilization gives every member in society power and leadership roles.

"The scientists and politicians have new information on the Reptilian invasion and the discussion goes back and forth on what to do. Ignorance and denial prevail as the politicians refuse to acknowledge the scientific facts. The vision then shifts to robots, spiders, and Reptilian overlords destroying our city, bringing death and ruin. Yet amazingly, the end of the dream always *resolves* the same. The darkness of ignorance is replaced by wisdom. Scientists and politicians again at the round table, ultimately using science and reason to lead them forward with strong, quick, and decisive action."

I pondered how, for decades, politicians largely ignored the dangers occurring right under their noses, shunning science as coastal cities flooded, forests burned, and hurricanes, earthquakes, hailstorms, and tornadoes decimated entire communities.

"I've had a similar dream," Prince Cobar said. "In the words of Albert Einstein, 'The world is a dangerous place not because of those who do evil, but because of those who look on and do nothing.' *Well, we are going to do something!* Marlee and I both have PhDs in political science from Yale and are members of the Skull and Bones Society. We have become part of the 'power elite' who will work within the walls of our Australian Parliament to effect the necessary changes to save our planet."

This made sense to me. Climbing the political ladder and working from the inside was essential if any outside progress was to be accomplished, and the Yale group definitively wielded power. The Skull and Bones Society had a long, secretive history, said to have a role in the global conspiracy for world control by the Illuminati. Such people would wield enough clout to rapidly shift the balance of power.

CHAPTER 33:

THE CHILDREN SHALL LEAD

Master Dorje continued. "Dr. Gail Lyra from Amdo, Kham, you and your family are next. We warmly welcome you."

Chants arose from the crowd. "Lyra! Lyra!"

"Thank you Master Dorje," Gail said. "It is an honor to be in the presence of such greatness of heart, mind, and spirit." She and her family bowed to the entire royal entourage. "May I introduce my husband, Gesar, and my two children, Agartha and Yeshe, both astrophysicists and lineage holders of the Lyran civilization." The family again took bows to rousing cheers.

"Thank you, darling," Gesar said. He was a handsome Tibetan with a long beard. At four-foot eleven-inches, he stood above Gail's four-foot nine-inch frame. Two-inch differences among Lyrans were considered to be enormous. Gesar and the children were all wearing a mix of traditional, maroon-colored, draped cotton cloth, minus the animal skins in deference to Dr. Centaure, along with expensive Lyran ceremonial green and shimmering gold vests with pointed shiny leather shoes. In all truth, I thought, they looked like space Leprechauns.

"My wife and I have studied physics for several decades," Gesar continued, "as well as traditional Bön magical incantations." This elicited playful hoots of "Bon-bons! Bon-bons!" The Arcturian servants immediately ran out to get candy. Gesar remained calm and continued. "We will bring our skills to bear against the Reptilians, and our children will join us in this endeavor." He gestured to his son.

385

"Greetings to all of my Starseed brothers and sisters, and the royal family," Prince Yeshe said. "Our nightmares begin every night with a similar disturbing theme and tone, except in my case and my sister's, it doesn't commence with war and killing. Our dreamscape always begins with a climate summit, much like the recent Davos conference, where we are on stage and my sister is presenting innovative ways of storing renewable energy. There is a debate with another individual who is a well-known physicist. This individual is unyielding in his attack on our theories, and no matter the quality of science I quote, he is relentless.

"He continuously points to his own scientific achievements in the field and how he is an esteemed and founding member of the International Distinguished Syzygy Society of America. The darkness of pride obstructs his ability to work for the benefit of others, yet as the dream proceeds, the energy shifts, and people begin to work with respect for one another. It is the light of *humility*, the antidote to the darkness of pride, that finally brings everyone together to be part of the global solution." Prince Yeshe turned to his sister and smiled.

"And how, specifically, will the two of you help to solve the climate emergency?" Dorje asked enthusiastically.

"We've established an international physics society called S.O.S—Science Offers Solutions," Princess Agartha said, "where top scientists and researchers come together to discuss current technology and where innovation is needed. Global leaders *not* under Reptilian influence, as well as entrepreneurs and venture capitalists, are part of the process to ensure funding and political will is aligned with our greater purpose." People stood and gave a rousing ovation. The mood in the hall reached a crescendo like sine waves in a physics lab subjected to a strong, magnetic oscillating fields.

"Thank you," Dorje said. "We salute your efforts." He looked at his agenda. "Dr. Dan Andre of Ann Arbor, please introduce yourself and your family of lineage holders."

"May I echo the profound sentiments of my Starseed brethren in thanking *everyone* here for their efforts to make this all possible." Dan bowed to the Royal family and then the other Starseed families. "Please meet my beautiful wife, Annie Andre."

Dan had thoroughly accepted his role, I thought, though there was something about the wife that seemed…pensive. '*It was something about her mother*,' I thought. '*Sickness. Death*?'

"Thank you, Dan," Annie said. "It's a pleasure to be here." She and her children were well over six feet tall with slightly coned-shaped heads and striking features, as if they were literally chiseled out of fine marble by a Renaissance master. Except *she* resembled a tall, stylish, alien Michelle Pfeiffer without hair; *he* resembled an alien Ashton Kutcher on Quaaludes; and the Princess bore a striking resemblance to a vibrant and joyful Anne Hathaway.

The whole family was dressed in Royal Andromedan ceremonial robes with orange and blue tunics, a bright gold belt, and sandals made of leather. They had also shaved their heads in the fashion of their people. Andromedans, by their very nature, were freedom seekers doing whatever was necessary to attain independence.

"May I please introduce to you my precious children," Dan continued, "Prince Andon and Princess Ventra from Andromeda. They will share with you the visions and solutions witnessed in their dreams."

"Thank you, Father," Ventra said, looking much more enthusiastic than her mother. "My brother and I have shared the same vision during the past few weeks, with a political twist to the one described by Princess Agartha and Prince Yeshe. When the dream commences, we're both sitting in a large gallery overlooking a meeting taking place in Congress. The head of the Commerce Department and Secretary of the Interior tout the need to reach energy independence by fracking pristine lands and drilling for oil in conservation sites. Striking anomalies began to emerge as the dream unfolded. The math didn't add up—two plus two was five, and seven plus seven was seventy-seven. The cost of preventing our climate emergency, put at approximately ten trillion dollars, made more sense, yet people weren't paying attention.

"The speakers insisted on following a path of economic destruction. Then the whole dreamscape changed. The Reptilian masters who had infiltrated the highest levels of government began to shapeshift as their faces suddenly became green and scaly. Panic erupted as the Reptilians were finally outed and exposed." She became more excited, and her voice rose. "Those who served on behalf of the people overpowered the Reptilian overlords to regain control of the House and Senate. The darkness of dishonesty was transformed by the light of truth."

"Very exciting," Master Dorje said, caught up in her story. "And how will you and the Prince help to bring about the changes needed?"

Prince Andron responded, "We are creating an organization called the Honest Accounting Federation, which is working with the Global Commission on Adaptation. We must immediately shift our priorities and resources to fund the technology and job creation in renewable energy. The Global Commission on Adaptation has indicated that we must *also* pay to change how we live, concentrated in five categories— weather warning systems, infrastructure, dry-land farming, mangrove protection, and water management. This would yield 18.1 trillion dollars in *benefits*. The new partnership is meant to bring urgency to incorporating climate risk into virtually everything governments and companies do."

"Well done, Prince Andron and Princess Ventra," Dorje said. Then he turned toward the assemblage. "We have two more Starseed families who wish to share the stage together, since their dark challenges and solutions are closely interrelated. Please welcome the elders and lineage holders of the Annunaki tribe, Dr. Diana Anki Alvarez from Peru, her husband Shamash, her young son Prince Enlil, and her daughter Princess Inanna."

Several of the people in the hall suddenly shouted, "Foul!" Far from being insulted, Diana Anki grinned and waved. Having begun to watch basketball myself, I felt a shiver of excitement.

Dorje just ignored the shouts.

"Alongside them are the elders and lineage holders of the Pleiadian civilization, Dr. Mutambe Pleadus from Abidjan, along with his wife Avalon, Indigo son Prince Cleox, and their Indigo daughter Xiyia." He looked up to the towering, seven-and-a-half-foot Annunaki. "Diana, why don't you start?"

"Thank you, Master Dorje," she said. Her whole family appeared as titans on stage, especially next to the Lyrans. Even more striking were their headpieces with seven superimposed pairs of ox-horns. They wore white silk clothing with elaborate decorative gold and silver ornaments and looked like well-dressed Vikings. "I echo the sentiments of my Starseed brethren when I say that we are all honored to be here today." Everyone on stage nodded and bowed to the Arcturian royal family and their entourage.

When they turned to Commander Plamorius, Mutambe jubilantly exclaimed, *"Family love fest!"*

"Pleiadian brother from another mother!" P shouted back. The whole room cheered, and the pugs barreled over to get petted and to see if the Pleadus family had any snacks or cold beer.

"Now that the introductions have been made," Dorje said wryly, "let us hear from Dr. Anki and her family."

"Thank you, Master Dorje, precious King and Queen, Prince Ian, Royal Mother, and all those from the Arcturian court who've made this possible," Diana said. "I have the great honor of introducing to our Annunaki people and all my Starseed brethren my daughter, Princess Inanna, and son, Prince Enlil. They are all a mother could ever hope for. Smart, honest, trustworthy, compassionate, charming, and the biggest badasses you could ever meet."

Far from being embarrassed by the praise, Enlil smiled and stepped forward confidently.

"Thank you, Mother, for that overstated introduction," he replied, facing his audience. "The dream my sister and I have both had in the past several weeks has been shared by our Starseed brethren, the Pleiadian prince and princess. I believe it holds an essential key to our salvation. My dream always begins in a bunker at night, bombs exploding all around me on our home planet of Nibiru. Sleek silver triangular Reptilian star cruisers streak past overhead, shooting laser beams at our resistance fighters on the ground."

His words grew louder, as his voice echoed off of the walls.

"Thousands of mutilated corpses lay strewn across the battlefield. Blood is splashed everywhere. I can hear the lamentations of mothers holding their dead children with fathers alternately fighting for their families and begging for mercy, but none comes. We are outnumbered and outmaneuvered, people cower in fear, and we understand that our culture, world, and life as we know it will soon be no more.

"Just when all seems lost and Annunaki souls have begun their descent into the underworld, a heavy, thick, black-and-red leather book suddenly appears. It is the *Reptilian Book of Death*. Picking it up, I open it to a page where a woman who resembles my mother, with her size and stature, wearing a seven-pointed ox-horned hat and melam, begins her journey into the dark Underworld. As she goes deeper and deeper, she must leave behind her external trappings, and any internal remnants of ego clinging—including fear. She must face her shadow and become pure, without attachment, to liberate the Annunaki caught in the Reptilian soul traps.

"How?" he continued. "By pleading their case before the seven judges of the Underworld—and this warrior queen does just that. She recounts their good deeds and noble qualities, as well as the love they share. This restores the balance and convinces the judges to let our people survive. The darkness and cowardice she and our people faced is transformed by the light of unrelenting courage."

The room was utterly still. Many had experienced the fear Prince Enlil described: cowardice, overwhelming, and helpless, left with an unrelenting nausea, as if they were continuously tortured by a low-pitched hum of a death rattle getting closer and closer to their ears. Yet as everyone in the room visualized the story and Diana's descent, they realized that they, too, would have to face their shadows and find courage. The judges would require nothing less if we were to survive.

"I, too, have had the same dream," Princess Inanna said, "with a difference. My dream continues when Queen Diana emerges from the Underworld. There is suddenly a re-emergence and blossoming of the Nephilim. The sacred half-angel, half-human breeds that walked the Earth centuries ago finally return and help us, as foretold in the Bible and the Book of Enoch. I quote, 'The Nephilim were in the Earth in those days, and also after that, when the sons of God came in unto the daughters of men, and they bore children to them; the same were the giant mighty men that were of old, the men of renown.' And in Numbers 13:32–33, where the twelve spies report seeing giants in Canaan. 'And there we saw the Nephilim, the sons of Anak, who come of the Nephilim; and we were in our own sight as grasshoppers, and so we were in their sight.'

"So the dream, as I interpret it," Princess Inanna continued, "signifies the revival of our connection with angels, as the Nephilim return to walk upon the Earth once again. Men and women alike must confront their mortal darkness and awaken within themselves their fallen angelic souls to bring them back into the light and redemption."

Still the audience remained completely silent.

"My brother and I will help build Arcturian Healing Temples on all seven Earth continents. Using our advanced biotech and frequency technology, we will augment the power of the healing process that needs to be put in place by the Arcturian scientists so Starseeds can wake up more quickly and Earth people can regain their health."

"The Annunaki are a powerful civilization," Dorje said, "with a knowledge of frequency technology that can help our Arcturian scientists create healing chambers." He paused and turned to look at Dr. Pleadus and his family.

"And last but certainly *not* least, I have the pleasure of letting our Pleiadian lineage holders explain how their dreamscape provides the final piece to the Earth's salvation. Dr. Mutambe, would your wife please do the honors of introducing Prince Cleox and Princess Xiyia and have them explain how their visions provide a road map to our future?"

Mutambe smiled and, with an outstretched open palm, invited his wife to speak. She wore traditional red-and-green-striped African ceremonial robes with brown leather sandals and a Pleiadian turban made of silk and gold.

"Sacred brothers and sisters on the journey," Avalon said. "We have all experienced tremendous pain and sorrow as our homes have been destroyed by an imbalance of the five elements. Our lands in Africa, as in other parts of the world, have been flooded, burned, and decimated as forceful winds destroy our homes and crops. It has seemed as if there is no hope of subsisting on this planet, yet my children have experienced a prophecy which corroborates and strengthens the Annunaki vision. Princess Xiyia?"

"Thank you, Mother." Xiyia faced the assemblage. "As you have heard today, six qualities of light must be embraced to overcome six Reptilian qualities of darkness that presently oppress us. Generosity, respect, humility, honesty, courage, and wisdom are needed to restore the balance that has been destroyed by unbridled greed, disdain, pride, dishonesty, cowardice, and ignorance. Yet there is one more: the seventh element that will help bring harmony back to our people and planet.

"In my vision, I am living in the city of Lorea on the island of Lemuria, sister city to Auria from the continent of Atlantis. Our island, which existed more than thirty-five million years ago as a land bridge between Africa and India, provided our people with a paradise where we had all we needed to live a simple, peaceful, and happy existence. We coexisted harmoniously with all life around us, until certain members of our tribe convinced us our simple way of life was insufficient to attain true, lasting happiness.

"Materialist expansion and invading foreign lands, owning more and more—these were propagated as our only way to attain fulfillment. Our people did not critically examine the motives behind the claims, and the consequence led to exactly the opposite result. Therein we sowed the seeds of our own suffering and demise. As we expanded our reach across continents with war and a greater need for resources, our leaders convinced us to mine the land. Debates ensued, but the Reptilian leaders won. Peace and harmony were replaced by fear and instability, as our sins caught up with us.

"Lemuria was situated on a highly unstable tectonic plate, and one day, after assaulting the ground for fuels, an earthquake began, which caused a tsunami, destroying our city. There followed a chain reaction of volcanoes erupting on surrounding islands, which consumed the very earth around us, causing our island to sink.

"Witnessing our fate, many of the inhabitants of Atlantis fled, setting sail on ships before the continent's submergence in 9564 BCE from a violent series of earthquakes. Fear struck the hearts of the people when life as we knew it was gone. Yet miraculously, the dream shifts, and my brother and I find ourselves alive and on the larger continent of Atlantis." Princess Xiyia paused and then continued. "A group of Atlanteans led by King Poseidon sit in a large council chamber on Auria, discussing the future of their civilization. The King had been warned by the local gods his continent would sink if changes were not instituted to reverse the damage that had been done.

"Some Atlanteans were playing God, breeding human-animal chimeras as slaves while genetically modifying clones of their people to produce a superior, 'lighter-skinned' race. Pride, greed, disrespect, and ignorance had gripped their minds and hearts, yet the King was offered a final way to save what was left of their civilization. The six qualities of light had to include the element of *love* to tie them all together. As per the course in miracles: 'Where love is, fear is not.' Love—wanting others to be happy above our own needs—paradoxically brings what we have been searching for all along: peace and joy.

"Master Jeshua explained this centuries ago. Building a house requires a strong foundation, and without the foundation of love as the basis of our civilization, our 'house' will not remain standing. It will succumb to material forces, thus limiting our ability to experience bliss and enter the kingdom of heaven."

The Princess stepped back, and the mood in the room became ee-rily pensive as Starseeds closed their eyes and reflected on what she had said. To sustain the next seven generations on the seven Earth con-tinents, all seven principles of generosity, respect, humility, courage, wisdom, honesty, and love would be needed. It made sense.

The quality of love was always at the heart of the Pleiadian people, but without integrating all of the other qualities, fighting against the powers of darkness would be impossible.

The different Starseed groups in the Burning Mountain Retreat began to open their eyes and come back to the present. Suddenly, there arose a loud cry coming from the Pleiadian prince and princess simul-taneously.

CHAPTER 34:

ANGEL OF LOVE

"*STARSEED LOVE FEST!*"

The room broke out in a scene from Hellzapoppin. People started to dance and hug each other with unbridled affection as they realized for the first time that they had a map to escape the trap that had been set for them. The pugs dashed around and jumped into people's laps. Commander P turned to Master Amius and gave her a giant Pleiadian love squeeze. King Mutambe turned to his wife and children and embraced them for what seemed an eternity. Even the King and Queen of Arcturus joined in, scooping Prince Ian up as they went over to the Royal Mother, embracing her as well.

Just as everyone in the shrine hall was having this profound and moving experience, as if deeply touched by the grace and power of the angel of love, Master Dorje took up the microphone.

"This concludes the morning session," he said, raising his voice over the din. "Before we return this afternoon for our first communal Starseed meditation, Prince Ian—one of the shining lights of our people—has gifted us with a poem and song. Our Arcturian servants learned the song from Prince Ian and will accompany him." The Starseeds in the room began to chuckle. Many had large smiles on their faces.

I pulled out a thick piece of parchment paper and my guitar and read the title. "Angel of Love" and then continued:

> *It was a cold winter night, in December '42*
>
> *We huddled round the table, our fingers turning blue*
>
> *She sat across the table and asked, is it hot in here?*
>
> *There was a fire burning, the man she loves so near.*

Then the chorus of Arcturian servants began to sing:

> *Angel of Love, she came down from above*
>
> *and set my heart on fire.*
>
> *She filled me with desire*
>
> *lifted me up, to places I've dreamed of,*
>
> *filled me with peace and joy that I've longed for.*
>
> *Angel of Love came down from above*
>
> *and taught me to fly.*
>
> *The wings of my heart soared high.*

I continued:

> *It happened in an instant, we met the week before,*
>
> *An ancient recognition, lonely hearts were no more.*
>
> *It happened in an instant, the moment our eyes met,*
>
> *Two hearts became one again, I couldn't understand yet.*

Again, the chorus sang:

> *Angel of Love, she came down from above*
>
> *and set my heart on fire, she filled me with desire.*
>
> *Lifted me up, to places I've only dreamed,*
>
> *filled me with peace and joy for which I've longed.*
>
> *Angel of Love came down from above*
>
> *and taught me to fly.*
>
> *The wings of my heart soared high*

I continued with the break:

> *There are so many times where love can pass you by*
>
> *it would be a crime not to give true love a try.*
>
> *So if you're feeling helpless and if you're feeling blue*
>
> *just call to your Angel and love will come to you.*
>
> *It was a love so true, I'd never felt this way,*
>
> *my heart had been so lonely waiting for this day.*
>
> *I never thought a dream come true could happen to this man,*
>
> *But now that you're in my life, I know that it can.*
>
> *I know that it can*

Again, the chorus sang:

You're my Angel of Love, You're my Angel of Love....

Once I finished, rousing waves of applause arose as the tears flowed. Queen Dawn looked over and smiled lovingly at me, and I smiled back.

The energy in the room settled, and Dorje continued.

"Today is truly a momentous day in the history of the Earth's civilizations. Thanks to the combined efforts of all of the religious leaders on your planet and Arcturian magick, we have managed to finally awaken the seven elders of the Starseed lineages who escaped Reptilian domination. You have all come together on this sacred occasion to hear them share their visions and solutions for this planet, a profound wisdom previously hidden for centuries.

"By incorporating the seven principles of light outlined today, you now have the essential keys to your own salvation. But for these to be effective, for them to help truly transform the world, you must meditate on these qualities every day, incorporating them into your body, speech, mind, and activities.

"This afternoon we will begin sessions to teach you how to do just that. Please return promptly at two o'clock for teachings on the sacred Arcturian meditations that, once properly practiced, will lead you all to awakening and the Fifth Threshold of Knowledge."

Slowly and silently, one by one, everyone got up from their chairs and left the shrine hall, many holding each other's hands. Even Major Broward's wife reluctantly grabbed his hand. Hope was no longer a dream. Having had the profound experience of opening their hearts and minds to divine wisdom and love, they all vowed these seven principles would guide them forward. The full knowledge of the Starseeds had finally been revived.

Planet Earth hoped it would be just enough.

CHAPTER 35:

VISUALIZING WHIRLED PEAS

"All we are saying is give peas a chance."

—Environmental leader, spiritual and social activist Marianne Williamson, discussing the worldwide difficulties of vegetable gardening during her last presidential run in 2040

A s the afternoon meditation session began at the Blazing Mountain Retreat Center, Dorje stood at the microphone, silent and motionless for what seemed like an eternity.

The only sound for almost an hour was the buzz of crickets' melodies filtering through the open windows. It was mesmerizing, as each of the Starseeds—the seven elders, their spouses and children, and all those the elders had found and wakened—quietly focused on the Master, waiting for instructions.

Once Dorje felt he had everyone's undivided attention, he began to motion to the group with several gentle, sweeping gestures of his hands that they should now all breathe in and out, in and out…. He did this silently, illustrating the technique. Everyone followed suit; in the silence, they all took three deep breaths in unison, each inhalation and exhalation becoming stronger and stronger. The first in and out breath was gentle, the second one moderate, and the last one exhaled from the lungs was powerful, fully expelling any remaining stale air.

"Does everyone understand why the meditation teachings you are about to receive are so important?"

Those present in the room reflected on the question, and many of the younger lineage holders immediately pulled out their phones to look up the answer. However, one young person by the name of Paul yelled out.

"Because not all questions can be answered by Google?"

Laughter peppered throughout the prayer hall.

"Correct, young Pleiadian master!" Dorje responded, and the other young people hurriedly tucked away their phones. "Yet it goes beyond that. Anyone else?"

"I know!" It was Kyra, an Annunaki and dental hygienist from Dayton, Ohio. "I do yoga, deep breathing, T'ai Chi, burn candles, light incense and drink camomile tea, yet I still want to smack some people!" Laugher rolled in waves across the room, but it was still clearly mixed with underlying emotions.

"Yes, meditation is for stress reduction, too," Dorje replied, smiling, "but also for much more. We are here this afternoon to learn to access the deep power of our minds. Now that you have awakened to your lineages, you will have access to tools that will help you cope with the difficult situation you find yourselves in *and* help you regain your future. Meditation can provide answers not otherwise easily accessible. Emotions of fear, anger, desire, jealousy, and confusion are like waves on the top of the ocean, battering and afflicting us during difficult times but easily transformed when we dive below.

"There—where our inherent qualities of joy, wisdom, peace, and generosity can manifest—it is always peaceful. It will take energy and patience while we address the immorality and ignorance in this world, but I promise you that if you follow the instructions, you will be successful, and you *will* make a difference."

The assemblage silently reflected on the words of the Master.

"As we perform our meditations," Dorje said, "first embrace the concept of working tirelessly toward the benefit of others, adopting the qualities of loving-kindness and compassion, wanting *all* beings to be happy and free from suffering."

Happy and free from suffering? That was all the pugs needed to hear.

"To be happy, I need to wet my whistle with a little brewski," one said, focusing on an Arcturian servant. "Could you make a cold beer run and relieve our suffering?" The Arcturian was confused. In his experience, beer could not ambulate.

"While you're at it, can you get us some beer pretzels?" the second pug said, rising to the opportunity. "I'm losing tons of sweat over here…panting like a hyena in 120-degree heat."

"Yeah, don't forget the chilled mugs," the third said. "It wouldn't be complete without chilled mugs. Right, boys?"

"Personally, you could all relieve my suffering," the fourth added, "by getting me a six-pack of the brew with those special Colorado herbs."

Dorje found himself questioning his own wisdom in allowing the pugs to participate. *Alas, wisdom must be shared with everyone.* He turned and took some dried cat treats out of his pocket, throwing them over to each of pugs. He then put his finger over his mouth, instructing them to stay quiet. Then he continued.

"This is the fertile ground of our meditation: love and compassion. Working for the benefit of others *limitlessly* through time and space is the soil upon which our seeds today will be planted. Everything that comes from such superior motivation must lead to superior results." He took a long, slow, deep breath. "We all wish to help the world and solve the crisis in which we find ourselves, but if we stay caught only at the level of emotion and superficial thought, worried about the future and-or lamenting the problems of the past, we will lack the ability to tackle the monumental problems before us. Do you understand?" He looked over the sea of eager faces. One head bobbed, then another, then more until everyone in the prayer hall nodded silently.

"After tilling the soil of our sacred intention, the next step is for the farmer to plant his or her seeds. These are our aspiration prayers, which help provide a map. Just as a boat captain must have a chart to properly navigate the waters and reach a distant shore, our consciousness needs to know the direction in which we wish to go and how to get there. Take a moment now to inform the deepest aspect of your mind about what it is that you seek to do here today. Are you looking to access deep, mystical wisdom? Do you wish to understand what *your* special gifts are? What part will *you* play in the awakening and healing of the planet?"

People nodded again, the energy in the room rising in waves of heightened emotion. The words "a man reaps what he sows" resonated through their minds.

"Next, the farmer must care for the seeds that have been planted," Dorje continued. "Just the right amount of light and water and care. To create the right conditions for growth to manifest, we must tame our minds. We will learn to dive down to the bottom of the ocean of consciousness where peace naturally resides. It is, paradoxically, in the silence—the space between thoughts and emotions—that profound wisdom exists.

"To reach this level of wisdom, the instruction is simple: Do not follow thoughts of the past, do not follow thoughts of the future, and do not follow thoughts of the present. Simply turn your attention inward; rest your mind completely and undistractedly. This place of calm abiding is where our seeds take root, and the power of our awakened consciousness can be properly accessed."

Dorje paused and everyone in the room began to meditate.

Miraculously, even the pugs.

• • • •

Only a minute into the meditation, a knocking sound resonated from the walls in the front *and* back of the room. The Starseeds tried to settle their minds, but the incessant knocking sound persisted. Some of the students got up to look out through the windows. Nothing and no one could be seen.

They sat back down and tried to focus—to meditate.

The knocking started again.

"Knock, knock," Dorje said. Everyone was shocked. Scant chuckles trickled throughout the room.

"Knock, knock," Dorje said again.

"Who's there?" the full audience responded in unison.

"Hammering," Dorje said.

"Hammering who?" the group responded.

"Hammering home the point that you're too easily distracted. *Focus!*"

Everyone laughed as they grasped the Master's intention. They began to meditate again, attempting to do so undistractedly despite the noise. Once he felt as if the majority had been successful, Dorje continued.

"Well done," he said. "It is essential to be keenly focused and un-distracted by present-moment awareness. This is a necessary condition for true growth."

One of the tougher Alpha Centurians in the group—known as Babsy or "Bab" for short—raised her hand. He acknowledged her.

"Master Dorje," she said, "you've stressed that we should not be distracted from the present. Well, I stress when *thinking* about stress before stress is even present. Then I stress about *stressing* over stress. Stress that probably shouldn't be stressed about."

The room laughed, for they both appreciated Bab's circular thinking and most unfortunately knew her mental predicament. Dorje smiled.

"Yes, I understand. In order to achieve this state of calm abiding, the instructions are simple. Do not stop thoughts from arising, yet do not *follow* those thoughts into the future—where your fear and stress arise. The key is not to be distracted by whatever is happening in your mind. Pay attention to any thoughts that arise spontaneously, but do not grasp them or follow them. That is the essence of meditation. Please do this now."

The Starseeds began to follow Dorje's instructions. They sat up in their chairs and adopted the specific seven-point posture for med-itation. They made sure their backs were straight as they relaxed their minds, with eyes open, chins tucked in slightly, right hands resting gently on their left hands, with their tongues touching the roof of their mouths. Dorje's earlier students from the Magick Academy had taught them the posture in preparation for this session.

After thirty minutes, Dorje continued.

"Now that we have attained a degree of calm and non-distraction, the next step is 'non-conception.' Whatever arises spontaneously with-in the mind, do not judge it. During the meditation, our thoughts are neither good nor bad. The conceptual mind judges and is limited, but the *absolute mind* we will access is beyond conception. And when even just one percent of a town or city meditates in such a manner at the same time, the level of coherence established within the field of con-sciousness will help physical reality to shift.

"Scientific studies done at Harvard University years ago proved this theorem. This is, in part, is how we will defeat the Draconian Reptiles and save the Earth. Let us all look at the mind non-distractedly and non-conceptually for several minutes, and later, I will illustrate to you the sheer *power* of this approach and its ability to affect the world."

This caused the attendees to pause. *How would the Master prove the power of mind's effect on physical reality?*

Dorje paused, and the group relaxed their minds once again, staying aware of whatever arose spontaneously in their minds in the present moment without judgment. Within moments, the knocking started again.

This time they will not be fooled, Dorje thought.

Indeed, this time the knocking was ignored. But then several young Starseeds jumped up in fright. Amorphous, demonic forms sprung through the floor and walls, romping and gliding around the temple. They had horns, barbed tails, leathery wings, and long, forked tongues.

CHAPTER 36:

FALSE DEMONS

"They're after us, they're after us!" a young Sirian Starseed cried out.

"*What* is after you, young master?" Dorje asked.

When the man looked around again, nothing was there. He appeared perplexed.

"Ah, young Starseed," Dorje said. "The demons of our mind will always tempt and torture us. Be wary of false demons!"

Were those really false demons? I wondered. Certainly, I had seen their like when Michael saved me. *They sure looked real.*

The group again settled back to meditate, ignoring the knocking and occasional demonic forms cavorting around the room. After several minutes, Dorje proceeded to explain the third basic instruction of meditation: the best meditation and that which creates the most fertile soil for our seeds is 'non-meditation,' that which involves no effort. Paradoxically, he said, we do not "try" to meditate. We deeply relax our minds in the present moment by doing…nothing.

Notions of "effort" prevent us from reaching the non-dualistic state of the Fifth Threshold of Knowledge where true wisdom and power resides. The ego filter of the "I" distorts and creates our relative reality, hiding the deeper, more profound truths of ultimate reality. So when thinking "I" want to meditate and be calm and "I" want to help save the world, it is essential for the "I" to be taken out of the equation.

One of the Arcturian Starseeds in the audience, a woman named Avia, raised her hand.

"Master Dorje," she said. "I don't quite understand how to *not* put any effort into meditation. If I don't put in *some* effort, I won't meditate at all…much less even get out of bed some mornings!"

People chuckled and shook their heads, understanding her meaning. It was tough getting out of bed some days when your future had been stolen from you by the Reptiles. Strong coffee, when available, was no longer enough for most.

Avia continued, "If I don't put in some effort to stop my mind from being distracted, it's like a wild elephant roaming through the jungle. Can you explain a bit more about the third instruction of no effort?"

Dorje smiled. "Excellent question, and congratulations on having the courage to raise your hand. I sense many in the room were confused but perhaps were afraid to ask? Let me explain it like this," he said. "You need to use minimal effort to get to the meditation cushion, the most minimal effort to stay focused non-distractedly, and a slight effort is similarly required to be sure you are maintaining the proper seven-point posture. Our meditation is done with the least amount of effort so that we may achieve the ultimate non-dualistic state where true wisdom and power reside."

People in the room nodded their heads, but I was reasonably certain some still didn't entirely grasp the concept. I wasn't sure I had. A young Sirian man by the name of Arthur raised his hand.

"Master Dorje, I find that instead of being mindful, *my mind is full*. I can't shut it off—there are so many thoughts, and it interferes with my meditation. What should I do?"

"The next step we will take is called 'insight,' which provides a solution to this common problem," Dorje replied. "Once we have established the proper motivation and posture, planted our seeds of aspirations, and watered the soil with non-distraction, non-conception, and non-meditation, we will learn how to look at the mind's true nature. To do that, we are not going to focus on the quantity or content of our thoughts that have arisen during 'calm abiding.' Rather, we will look at the *nature* of whatever arises in the mind, addressing it with insight.

"It does not matter how many thoughts we have in this type of meditation, as we are going to use them to deepen the meditation itself. How do we accomplish this? If a thought arises, look to see where it comes from. Look to see where it goes. Look to see if it abides anywhere in space. Look *carefully*. Then observe whether the thought that occurs has a color or form. Does the mind experiencing the thought have a color or form? Again, look carefully." Dorje paused to let his words percolate in everyone's consciousness. "As stated so eloquently by Master Khentyse, 'Mind has no form, no color, and no substance; this is its empty nature. Yet mind can know things and perceive an infinite variety of phenomenon. This is its clear aspect. The inseparability of these two aspects, emptiness and clarity, is the primordial, continuous nature of mind.'

"Yet wonderfully and fortunately for us," Dorje continued, "this emptiness is not a void, a nothingness. Its nature is pregnant with enlightened potential and limitless possibilities. This nature allows *all* things to be possible. That is how and why we will be successful, as long as you all apply yourselves with energy and patience. Whatever seed thoughts are planted in this fertile soil of enlightened, empty, clear, spacious mind must manifest in physical reality. That is the nature of consciousness and how it works. I believe the proper English expression for this phenomenon is 'a man reaps what he sows.'

"Let's meditate again."

We took our meditation positions again and began to look at the mind's clear empty nature, reminding ourselves of the Master's words. The room grew silent as the meditation went deeper than ever before.

The knocking on the doors and windows started again as amorphous demonic shapes emerged from the walls. Now zombies were climbing in through the windows, while elephants trumpeted in the distance. Those of us from the Copernican-Chiron Magick Academy remained focused, as we had been trained, but the rest looked to Dorje to see what was up.

His eyes were closed, his breathing perfect.

Some of the younger Starseeds, gripped with fear, started to get up, but their parents reassured them. None of this was real. They got it. They could remain seated and just meditate. Trusting their parents, they sat back down.

After several minutes, the sounds and visions disappeared. Dorje opened his eyes and gestured to the group for any questions. A young Andromedan by the name of Andrew raised his hand.

"Master Dorje," he asked. "You have told us that, ultimately, life is like a dream happening in the mind of universal consciousness. Yet there *are* days when I feel it's more than real. I am often, in fact, super stressed and can't handle what's happening. The greed and hate. The power struggles by the Reptilians. It's overwhelming and…there *are* days I feel as if I can barely go on. Days I feel like I have lost my mind. What should I do?"

Dorje reflected for a moment. "You feel you have lost your mind, but I have a question for you: Have you ever *found* your mind? There is something deeper to be realized here. Have you ever actually *seen* your mind and/or the thoughts and emotions that are tormenting you?"

"No," Andrew replied. "When I look, I can't find anything. Yet I still experience the feelings and thoughts of being overwhelmed and suffering, similar to what Avia expressed earlier."

"There *is* relative truth, Andrew," Dorje said, "where we feel that we are powerless and suffering at the hands of the Reptilian overlords. Yet there is an absolute, deeper, and more profound truth to help us to shift perception and gain power. It is summed up perfectly by the Indian meditation master, Saraha, who said centuries ago, 'Mind is a wish-fulfilling gem.' Normally we think of mind as being the source of our problem, yet when we use the mind to look at its nature and see its deeper reality, we transcend the mind's limitations and beliefs.

"Let us do this together, resting in this state called *mahamudra* or 'maha-ati.' This is the ultimate state of truth and sanity. Then I will give the final set of instructions for today."

The group began to meditate, and on cue, knocking again came from the walls, while barbed, taloned, fanged, forked demonic shapes zoomed naked and squamous in every direction, zombies clawed at the windows, and elephants called in the distance.

No problem, we thought to ourselves. The Master was testing us. *He's that good. Damn. Focus and meditate.*

We went back to "not" trying, to non-distractedly and non-conceptually look at our minds, and then the strangest thing happened.

All visions and sounds suddenly disappeared, and all that was left was a deep silence. It was like a quiet nothingness, but conscious. A silent awareness. Like a living manifestation of the worst spiritual hotdog joke of all time, "make me one with everything." The group became extremely still as they all bathed in this deep state of abiding. It was so peaceful and wonderful.

Finally. The Master's blessing had kicked in.

Then something frightening happened, and this time it was much worse than the demons and zombies. It was real.

CHAPTER 37:

THE FINAL MEDITATION

Troubled looks appeared on the Starseeds' faces. The Master had led us to a state of consciousness where we had no choice but to come face to face with our worst enemy.

Our own darkness.

I knew intuitively what was happening. Whatever shadow had followed and haunted each Starseed during their lifetime became apparent as vivid images appeared in their minds. Images of anger. Regrets. Worries. Fears. Threesomes with aliens and Major Broward's wife—Broward was a little fixated on that famous day and couldn't let go.

Different images appeared for each Starseed and human as they watched their hidden fears and regrets manifest. Since I could tell what was happening, it was particularly difficult for me. And yet they all stayed in a state of silence, being aware of the thoughts and images but becoming separate from them. They rested, and the room was once more enveloped in a profound silence, except for the occasional rustling of leaves or the sounds of crickets and cicadas, which appeared to be growing louder and louder as time passed and as the group relaxed more and more into their meditation.

"Now that you have all tasted the three stages of meditation—calm abiding, insight, and *mahamudra*, using the techniques of non-distraction, non-conception, and non-meditation while accessing the powerful triad of mindfulness, awareness, and watchfulness—you must learn how to ensure this state is fully empowered so that the seeds we plant in fertile ground finally come to fruition. We will do this with two methods: the power of clear visualization and the power of the sacred word."

Excitement filled the air. Dorje was going to teach everyone how to access the power of enlightened consciousness to truly make a difference in the world. A few cried softly, while others smiled. I could hear many in the group wondering if this was the answer to their prayers. Could this instruction help save the planet and all sacred life living upon it?

"First, we will learn the power of visualization and how visualizing an object clearly and with great detail enables it to manifest. The mind cannot differentiate between a real event and an imagined event and is encoded in memory cells in the hippocampus, the seat of memory, as if it actually took place. This is especially the case when the object is not only visualized clearly and in detail in the mind's eye but also is associated with a strong feeling. This links the seat of memory in the hippocampus with a part of the brain called the amygdala where emotions arise.

"These two steps strengthen the effects." Dorje looked around the room to be sure everyone was following. "The first step is this: begin by visualizing a small, brilliant white sphere the size of a pea in front of your third eye, the anatomical area in the middle of your forehead that is located approximately one inch above and between your eyebrows. Visualize this small, bright, brilliant sphere non-distractedly, as we did in our prior meditation session. Do this with a strong feeling of joy, knowing that in this technique, you are accessing the power of your intuitive wisdom.

"Feel the joy as if it already happened. We are ultimately creators of our own reality and destiny. Healthy seeds planted in this fertile soil grow healthy plants if they are properly cared for, but tainted seeds will have the opposite effect. An expression in your English language that captures that idea is, I believe, 'garbage in, garbage out.'"

Abruptly, a grinding sound could be heard outside, as a garbage truck lifted up a large metal garbage container and dropped the contents. The Starseeds began to laugh. The synchronicities were amazing, and Dorje's intimate knowledge of the culture and language seemed to manifest in reality whenever he chose.

Is that coincidence? I wondered.

"Proper motivation mixed with seeing a vivid picture joyfully while in the non-distracted state will allow us to shift reality—allow our deepest wishes to be accomplished. Therefore, begin by visualizing the sphere. Do not allow your concentration to waver as you clearly see it in your mind's eye."

We all became silent and motionless and raised our eyes in unison, focusing them slightly upward, visualizing non-distractedly the image of a small, luminous pea.

After a few minutes, gasps began to emerge from the group.

Suddenly, the room was filled with hundreds of brilliant spheres radiating light in all directions. It was as if we were personally the creators of all the stars in the universe.

"You may stop now," Master Dorje said. "How was that 'pea break'?" Laughter ensued. Dorje continued. "Centuries ago on Arcturus, our great meditation masters were so adept in this technique, they could create entire cities from the void and had the ability to feed the homeless and poor just by manifesting from their great awakened, compassionate consciousnesses. It is rare to find such masters in this day and age, but some of you here may awaken one day to such power."

Leoto, a Lyran Starseed, raised his hand, and Dorje recognized him.

"Master, these untapped powers are truly amazing, but I am not sure how much I'm adding to the group. My mind keeps getting distracted, as I am often agitated thinking about the state of the world and the worrisome future that lies before us. This isn't the first time I've tried to meditate, but either my mind is so agitated that it's impossible for me to focus, or I find I am so drowsy that I just keep falling asleep. What should I do to remedy this?"

Leoto's wife, Angela, sat beside him and chuckled.

"First," Dorje said, "it is important to get enough sleep so are you not drowsy *during* your meditation." Angela laughed out loud at that. The Arcturian master continued. "It is *also* important, before the meditation, to set the intention that you will try not to follow thoughts during the session. Whatever your concerns are, put them aside for these quick, short sessions. You can even write down any lists, concerns, or things you need to accomplish for the day or the week ahead, but do so before the meditation starts. There is no reason to pay attention to thoughts which arise during meditation."

This made perfect sense to me, and many scribbled notes as the Master spoke. Still, another Starseed by the name of Wanda from Andromeda and Haddonfield, NJ, raised her hand.

"Master, I find it difficult to visualize *clearly* while I'm doing the meditation. My images are vague, and I'm concerned I'm not doing the technique properly."

I grinned. This very complaint came up often during the Magick Academy training. Many humans were so accustomed to swiping at their phones and playing video games that their own visualizations could not compare to the detail and clarity of *Shirtless Spider-Man* or *Super Mario 3D*.

"It is quite simple," he replied. "Visualization is like a muscle that gets stronger and stronger with practice and use. The secret is to relax without effort into this clear, open, spacious state and simply plant your seeds with positive imagery and positive emotion. That is how we co-create with the universe. Is that clear?" He scanned the group, and no one spoke. "Now that you have a sense of how to incorporate this initial visualization practice into your meditation, return to the white, bright, pea-sized sphere."

Everyone went back to the visualization, but Dorje continued to speak.

"Instead of continuing to look at a small, white, vibrant sphere of light, expand the image in your mind's eye, bigger and bigger until the sphere becomes the size of the Earth whirling through space. Focus on that." Dorje waited for the Starseeds to complete the visualization. "Now shift the image of a brilliant white sphere to a visualization of the planet Earth…with vibrant, healthy blue oceans and shimmering green forests covering the planet. Perform this visualization with as much clarity and detail as possible.

"Picture an Earth radiating health, filled with *trillions* of green trees breathing in carbon dioxide and emitting large quantities of life-giving oxygen. Pristine blue oceans teeming with life. Now *feel* the joy associated with the healing and health of the planet and all living beings upon it. When visualizations like this are done clearly and in detail, associated with strong emotions like joy and gratitude, external reality will begin to shift."

The room developed a quiet intensity as hundreds of Starseeds, gathered from different parts of the Earth and different galaxies, meditated in unison. Around the room, people repeated the instructions, reminding themselves of their motivation.

For ten minutes, we proceeded to calm our minds, and then it happened once again. In front of each meditator, instead of the small, luminous, pea-sized spheres, hundreds of rotating healthy planet Earths suddenly filled the temple. First one, then another, and then dozens became hundreds. Gasps arose from the group.

Dorje spoke. "We will now learn to incorporate the sacred word into meditation, further empowering the effects. Examples are abundantly present in your biblical stories, such as those in the book of Genesis. There it discusses the power of the spoken word, yet many among your civilization have overlooked the true underlying significance. It comes down to this: the utterance of sacred words while resting in the open, spacious, non-dualistic state creates a ripple effect in consciousness manifesting the power of the word.

"Your civilization has, for the most part, ignored this because people felt that these stories and the associated power came from a source *outside* themselves. Yet nothing could be further from the truth. The clue to the power of the spoken word was hidden under everyone's noses for centuries. Man is said in Earth's Bible to be created in the image of God. What does this mean?"

For the first time, one of the elders spoke, as Dr. Antware said, "I'm not sure, but…if it was hidden under everyone's noses for centuries, and we *are* created in the image of God, then God's nose must be *huge*—just look at the size of *my* schnoz!"

The room broke out in laughter. Yenta shot him a dirty look.

"Just about anything could have been hidden under *his* nose," she said. "Any bigger and it'd be twelve inches long and become a foot. When the Lord gaveth, he didn't stop."

Unperturbed, Dorje continued.

"Anyone else?" There was silence. No one dared say a word after *that* exchange. "The story of Genesis and creation begins with the words, 'In the beginning God created the heaven and the earth. And the Spirit of God moved upon the face of the waters….and God said, "Let there be light," and there was.' Most have taken this as an allegory, but it points to deeper truths. When God, absolute consciousness, 'moved and spoke the words "let there be light,"' those sacred words and intention, placed into the field of enlightened consciousness, caused a singularity to form where the energy of thought was transformed into matter. This was what you quaintly call the 'big bang.' The expanding universe began at that moment from a dense super-force into an abundance of light elements, where particles and waves were simultaneously created, giving birth to the universe as we know it."

We sat in absolute silence as everyone reflected upon the Master's words. The secret to transforming ourselves and our world had been there all along. It just required some digging.

"The great physician and yogic master Patanjali recognized this centuries ago," Dorje explained, "when he discovered and created the yoga sutras. Please start by placing the seed thought 'cheerfulness' into the field of consciousness, repeating every few seconds, and relaxing."

Everyone in the room followed the Master's instructions. Smiles appeared on faces, and some even began to giggle.

"I said cheerfulness, not *silliness*."

Laughter.

"This can also be completely silent, gently placing the thought into the field of consciousness and then letting go. Place the thought and then let go." After several minutes, he continued. "Now place the seed thought 'kindheartedness' into the mind stream every few seconds and relax." The Master waited. "Now place the seed thought 'friendliness' into the field of awakened consciousness and relax."

The effects of these thoughts started to become evident, and all around me body language shifted and more people relaxed with big smiles on their faces. I knew what was to occur.

"In between resting and doing nothing, after placing these seed thoughts, let go of attachment to outcome, while continuously holding onto your sacred intention to do this meditation for the sake of every living being on the planet and for Mother Earth herself. Place the seed thought into the ocean of enlightened mind and then rest, doing nothing, relaxing non-distractedly in the empty, clear, spacious nature of mind itself."

These were the keys to awaken ourselves and our Starseed brethren who were still asleep.

Perfect awakened clarity and wisdom...

Perfect awakened clarity and wisdom...

The ripple in consciousness, holding this sacred thought and intention like a pebble tossed into a still pond, affected the waters of consciousness throughout all time and space.

"The final meditation," Dorje said, "is a very simple one. We will combine the elements of sacred visualization with sacred word and intention. Please again adopt the limitless motivation of wanting *all* beings throughout the universe to be happy and free from suffering. *No one* can be excluded. Remember, during the Orion Wars, the Reptiles invaded multiple worlds and galaxies, leaving a wake of death and destruction.

"The suffering of your Starseed lineages and the impending destruction of this world are only a small part of this ongoing intergalactic war. If the Reptiles should succeed in their destruction of the Earth, they will become stronger, and neighboring galaxies also will fall. The suffering will be unimaginable. We must win for the sake of all loving and peaceful civilizations."

Hearing these words, the Starseeds could feel the force for good coursing through the subtle energy channels. It was palpable. Dorje's words filled them with a newfound strength they had never before experienced. The power of good. The power of the light. Some of the group let out a howl, and I joined them. The Master waited for the energy in the room to settle down before continuing his instructions.

"How can we ensure victory in battle against such a foe?" Dorje asked. "One who is seemingly invincible? We must connect with the limitless power of spirit—that which is indominable, which is unequalled. That which contains limitless possibilities and which will manifest to support our sacred intention.

"While connecting to your own divine nature, see yourself clearly and in great detail as a liberator. A noble and heroic warrior, relieving suffering and bringing peace and joy wherever you go. Visualize clearly and in detail that you *are* this indominable warrior, that this is your true essence. *Feel it.* Fighting darkness, while intimately connected to the light, wisdom, and power of spirit. See yourself working tirelessly for truth and justice throughout the worlds and winning. For you have mastered the seven principles of light, which is unparalleled in its excellence."

Dorje paused again to let his words sink in.

"In your minds, wear the military uniforms of your respective lineages and see yourself fighting alongside an Intergalactic Starseed Force, beings of light who have come together from across the multiverse to fight the forces of darkness. See yourself on Draconisss, the home planet of the Reptiles, their headquarters, and black heart. The Reptiles have called to the forces of darkness, and vampires and demons fly overhead with them in their cruisers. As you fight alongside your allies, see yourself winning battles against the vampires, demons, spiders, robots, and Reptiles until you surround the citadel of the King and Queen of the Reptiles.

"Laser cannons fire at you from overhead, with robot armies and giant spiders marching through the land trying to destroy every member of your army. Miraculously, effortlessly, you avoid their fire. Once you are at the walls, you storm the citadel, and the barriers crumble under the superior firepower of your intergalactic army, your laser and light cannons breaking through their seemingly impenetrable defenses. Within the citadel, the members of the Reptilian army fall to your superior might. Your battalion slowly climbs the stairs of the Reptilian Tower of Power until you are at the top, where you enter their royal chamber.

"They beg for mercy, trying to deceive you and your troops, claiming that they can be allies and become a force for good, changing their ways—when suddenly, they pull out laser pistols to destroy you. Where others might destroy them, with great compassion, you only subdue both the King and Queen of darkness. *You have captured the Reptilian overlords and won the war!* Their war machines break down and crumble. The demons flee in terror. The giant spiders roll into balls and dissolve into dust.

"Feel the joy. Feel the satisfaction of having won such a long-fought battle. Cries of victory echo throughout the cosmos.

"As you return to planet Earth, you are rewarded for your efforts, and in Washington D.C., you are given what has become the highest medal of honor, the Intergalactic Peace Prize. The crowd around you roars with delight. Bask in the sense of accomplishment, having saved trillions of lives throughout the galaxies and winning the ultimate battle of good against evil."

The air in the room was electric as excitement rippled through me and in every other Starseed.

After a moment, Dorje said, "Say it together," and intuitively, we all knew the words.

We are the great liberators,

effortlessly conquering all evil in our path.

Goodness and light prevail

as we harness the indominable power of spirit.

We are the great liberators,

effortlessly conquering all evil in our path.

Goodness and light prevail

as we harness the indominable power of spirit.

As Dorje and the group finished the sacred incantation, cries of exultation echoed from all four temple walls. Hundreds hugged and cried. Then, after several minutes of celebration, the room grew silent again, as the Starseeds settled down and savored in their good fortune, in the incredible wisdom and power given to them.

"And now you understand," Master Dorje said, "fully and with every fiber of your being. It felt good combining your minds' deepest realities to defeat the great enemy, did it not?"

The whole room acknowledged that it was so.

The recruits still shivered in satisfaction.

"And so that is what you have done," Master Dorje said.

"How so?" the Andromedan named Andrew inquired.

"You have defeated the Reptilian King and Queen," Dorje replied simply. "Through your visualization and the amassed power it yielded, you all invaded their base on Draconisss, imprisoned them, and annihilated their forces."

"In our meditations," Andrew said carefully, looking around as the room grew excited. "Surely only there."

"No," Dorje said. "In reality. Your vision was *actually* harnessing the joint power in the room, making a tangible strike against the Reptilian planet. You may have thought you only *imagined* the fight against the King and Queen of the Reptiles, but it was quite real in the way you use the word. You imagined your best selves in this visualization and have experienced the astonishing power in an even more concrete way than a glowing pea."

The room erupted in cries of confusion, wonder, and liberation.

"Prince Ian gave me the idea," Dorje revealed. "I'd told him at breakfast about my plans for making the peas and then maybe a few trees after lunch—but then he suggested to me that we could do more. Much more. Harness what was to occur as it did so for the very first time, uncorrupted and unfettered."

The whole room turned to me, and I blushed proudly. This was the culmination of my time with the Copernican-Chiron Magick Academy. Cheers erupted throughout the hall, crying my name, and I could only wave back awkwardly. Master Dorje motioned for the group to settle down.

"Let's not give him too big of a head," he said. "There's still plenty of work to do. The Reptilian home world is destroyed, but they are still spread across the cosmos and here on Earth plotting against the work we have begun here today. The work we will do tomorrow."

We all nodded in understanding.

"Before we leave the meditation hall today," Dorje asked, "please return to the visualization we did earlier. A healthy, vibrant, blue-and-green planet Earth spinning in space. Knowing success in defeating the Reptiles, say or think to yourselves 'healthy, happy home…healthy, happy home….' Place this thought into the awakened field of consciousness while deeply feeling joy and gratitude."

Focusing once again, we did as he asked. After several minutes, Dorje rang the meditation bell to wake us from our reveries.

"Please all look outside the windows," he cried as if he had been startled out of a dream. We moved to the large rectangular windows surrounding the meditation hall. A double rainbow—one with brilliant blues and greens and magenta and violet—took shape over the mountain peaks.

The sight inspired awe. The power we were witnessing was magical and showed, in no uncertain terms, that optimism was no longer a pipe dream. Hope had come home and become a reality.

"May I address the Starseeds?" I asked.

Master Dorje bowed deeply and stepped aside.

Stepping forward, I saw the love-filled faces of the Starseeds and those humans who now understood fully. Slowly and deliberately, in a strong, unwavering tone, I chose my words as carefully as my youth would allow:

"See what we can do? Now let us get to work...."

ACKNOWLEDGMENTS

Margaret Doner, author of several books, including *Merlin's War: The Battle Between the Family of the Light and the Family of Dark*, was an inspiration, providing the initial descriptions of Starseeds and the Orion Wars. Lee Horowitz, MA, skillfully provided the astrological insights for this story. Geoffrey Girard, author, helped expertly shape and edit the initial manuscript of *Starseed R/evolution: The Awakening*. Steve Saffel, writer and Senior Acquisitions Editor at Titan Books, skillfully revised the second version of the manuscript. Final edits were done by Rachel Hoge at Permuted Press. The author is enormously grateful to all of the editors and staff at Permuted Press and Post Hill Press for their professional assistance and support in helping *Starseed R/evolution* become a reality.

APPENDICES

1. "A Green New Deal Is Technologically Possible. Its Political Prospects Are Another Question." Lisa Friedman and Trip Gabriel. *New York Times*. Feb. 21, 2019. https://www.nytimes.com/2019/02/21/us/politics/green-new-deal.html.

2. *The Uninhabitable Earth* by David Wallace-Wells. https://nymag.com/intelligencer/2017/07/climate-change-earth-too-hot-for-humans.html.

3. "Impacts of Green New Deal Energy Plans on Grid Stability, Costs, Jobs, Health, and Climate in 143 Countries." Mark Z. Jacobson, et al. *One Earth*. Volume 1, Issue 4, pp 449-463. December 20, 2019. DOI: https://doi.org/10.1016/j.oneear.2019.12.003.

4. "Geoengineer the Planet? More Scientists Now Say It Must Be an Option." Fred Pearce. *Yale Environment 360*. May 29, 2019. https://e360.yale.edu/features/geoengineer-the-planet-more-scientists-now-say-it-must-be-an-option.

5. "Learning Catalysts' Secrets." Caitlin McDermott-Murphy. *The Harvard Gazette.* August 30, 2018. https://news.harvard. edu/gazette/story/2018/08/harvards-cynthia-friend-and-teammates-hope-to-revolutionize-chemical-production/.

6. "Greenland's Ice is Melting Four Times Faster Than Thought— What it Means." Stephen Leahy. *National Geographic.* January 21, 2019. https://www.nationalgeographic.com/environment/ article/greeland-ice-melting-four-times-faster-than-thought-raising-sea-level.

7. "CO2 Emissions Are On Track to Take Us Beyond 1.5 Degrees of Global Warming. Caroline Wilke. ScienceNews. July 1, 2019. https://www.sciencenews.org/article/co2-emissions-global-warming.

8. "Four Decades of Antarctic Ice Sheet Mass Balance from 1979–2017." Eric Rignot, et al. *PNAS.* January 22, 2019. Volume 116, Issue 4, pp 1095-1103. https://www.pnas.org/content/116/4/1095.

9. "Combining Reclaimed PET with Bio-based Monomers Enables Plastics Upcycling." Nicholas A. Rorrer, et al. *Joule.* Published: February 27, 2019. DOI: https://doi.org/10.1016/j.joule.2019.01.018.

10. "Ocean Warming Is Accelerating Faster Than Thought, New Research Finds." Kendra Pierre-Louis. *New York Times.* January 10, 2019. https://www.nytimes.com/2019/01/10/climate/ocean-warming-climate-change.html.

11.   "The World Is Losing Fish to Eat as Oceans Warm, Study Finds." Kendra Pierre-Louis. *New York Times*. February 28, 2019. https://www.nytimes.com/2019/02/28/climate/fish-climate-change.html?rref=collection%2Fsectioncollection%2Fclimate.

12.   "Size Doesn't Matter: How Small Towns and Businesses are Taking Climate Action." Climate Reality Project, Blog. April 27, 2018. https://www.climaterealityproject.org/BLOG/SIZE-DOESNT-MATTER-HOW-SMALL-TOWNS-AND-BUSI-NESSES-ARE-TAKING-CLIMATE-ACTION.

13.   "Impact of Climate and Climate Change on Vector-Borne Diseases." BMC Blog, Florence Fouque. Jun 25, 2019. http://blogs.biomedcentral.com/bugbitten/2019/06/25/impact-of-cli-mate-and-climate-change-on-vector-borne-diseases/.

14.   "More Efficient Solar Cells Imitate Photosynthesis." Lab Manager. University of Erlangen-Nuremberg. January 15, 2019. https://www.labmanager.com/news/2019/01/more-efficient-so-lar-cells-imitate-photosynthesis#.XHV_XsBKjIU.

15.   "Moving Artificial Leaves out of the Lab and Into the Air." Lab Manager. University of Illinois at Chicago. February 12, 2019. https://www.labmanager.com/news/2019/02/moving-ar-tificial-leaves-out-of-the-lab-and-into-the-air#.XHV_tcBKjIU.

16.   "Marine Heatwaves Threaten Global Biodiversity and the Provision of Ecosystem Services." Smale, D.A., Wernberg, T., Ol-iver, E.C.J. et al. Nat. Clim. Chang. 9, 306–312 (2019). https://doi.org/10.1038/s41558-019-0412-1.

17.   "How Fast are the Oceans Warming?" Lijing Cheng, et al. *Science*. January 11, 2019, Volume 363, Issue 6423, pp 128-129. DOI: 10.1126/science.aav7619.

18.   "Pricing Pollution: How We're Pushing for Fair Energy Solutions." Climate Reality Project. May 7, 2018. https://www.climaterealityproject.org/BLOG/PRICING-POLLUTION-HOW-WERE-PUSHING-FAIR-ENERGY-SOLUTIONS.

19.   "The Intergovernmental Panel on Climate Change. AR6 Climate Change 2021: The Physical Science Basis." https://www.ipcc.ch/report/ar6/wg1/.

20.   "The Intergovernmental Panel on Climate Change. Special Report on the Ocean and Cryosphere in a Changing Climate." https://www.ipcc.ch/srocc/.

21.   "Seeking a Breakthrough on Catalysts." Peter Reuell. *The Harvard Gazette*. January 12, 2017. HTTPS://NEWS.HARVARD.EDU/GAZETTE/STORY/2017/01/SEEKING-A-BREAK-THROUGH-ON-CATALYSTS/.

22. "'Sun in a Box' Would Store Renewable Energy for the Grid." Lab Manager. Massachusetts Institute of Technology. December 6, 2018. https://www.labmanager.com/news/2018/12/-sun-in-a-box-would-store-renewable-energy-for-the-grid#.XHV_DcBKjIU.

23.   "Sustainable 'Plastics' Are on the Horizon." Lab Manager. American Friends of Tel Aviv University. December 26, 2018. https://www.labmanager.com/news/2018/12/sustainable-plastics-are-on-the-horizon#.XHWCpcBKjIU.

24.   "Cricket Bread, It Might Just Be Your Jam." Henry Fountain. *New York Times*, Climate Forward. February 27, 2019. https://www.nytimes.com/2019/02/27/climate/marie-kondo-recycling.html.

25.   "Transforming Carbon Dioxide into Industrial Fuels." Lab Manager. Harvard University. November 13, 2018. https://www.labmanager.com/news/2018/11/transforming-carbon-dioxide-into-industrial-fuels#.XHWCGMBKjIU.

26.   "Turning Tide on Greenhouse Gases." Peter Reuell. *The Harvard Gazette*. November 8, 2018. HTTPS://NEWS.HARVARD.EDU/GAZETTE/STORY/2018/11/NEW-SYSTEM-OPENS-THE-DOOR-TO-TRANSFORMING-CO2-INTO-INDUSTRIAL-FUELS/.

27.   "We Could Power The Entire World By Harnessing Solar Energy From 1% Of The Sahara." Quora Contributor. *Forbes*. September 22, 2016. https://www.forbes.com/sites/quora/2016/09/22/we-could-power-the-entire-world-by-harnessing-solar-energy-from-1-of-the-sahara/#27dc1b0fd440.

28.   "What is Holding Back the Growth of Solar Power?" Karl Mathiesen. *The Guardian*. January 31, 2016. https://www.theguardian.com/sustainable-business/2016/jan/31/solar-power-what-is-holding-back-growth-clean-energy.

29.   "Artificial Phototropism for Omnidirectional Tracking and Harvesting of Light." X. Qian, et al. *Nature Nanotechnology*. Published online November 4, 2019. DOI: 10.1038/s41565-019-0562-3.

30. "The Trouble With Chocolate." Steven Mufson. *The Washington Post*. October 29, 2019. https://www.washingtonpost.com/graphics/2019/national/climate-environment/mars-chocolate-deforestation-climate-change-west-africa/?utm_campaign=7d46d53a49-briefing-dy-20191031&utm_medium=email&utm_source=Nature%20Briefing.

31. "Climate Feedback Loops Could Put Human Civilization on the Road to Extinction." Charlie Smith. *The Georgia Straight*. Aug 10, 2019. https://www.straight.com/news/1284161/climate-feedback-loops-could-put-human-civilization-road-extinction#:~:text=Climate%20feedback%20loops%20could%20put%20human%20civilization%20on%20the%20road%20to%20extinction,-by%20Charlie%20Smith&text=A%20summer%20heat%20wave%20over,National%20Snow%20%26%20Ice%20Data%20Center.

32. "Dare to Declare Capitalism Dead – Before it Takes Us All Down With It." George Monbiot. *The Guardian*. April 25, 2019. https://www.theguardian.com/commentisfree/2019/apr/25/capitalism-economic-system-survival-earth.

33. "Hello From the Year 2050. We Avoided the Worst of Climate Change—But Everything Is Different." Bill McKibben. September 12, 2019. One.Five. *TIME*'s Climate Change Newsletter. https://time.com/5669022/climate-change-2050/.

34. "Lifestyle Changes Aren't Enough to Save the Planet. Here's What Could." Michael E. Mann. *TIME*. September 12, 2019. https://time.com/5669071/lifestyle-changes-climate-change/.

35.   "2050: The Fight For Earth." *TIME*. https://time.com/climate-change-solutions/.

36.   "Rethinking Food and Agriculture." RethinX. https://www.rethinkx.com/food-and-agriculture.

37.   "A Green Approach to Making Ammonia Could Help Feed the World." University of Central Florida. *Science Daily*. May 15, 2018. https://www.sciencedaily.com/releases/2018/05/180515131548.htm.

38.   "Pervasive Human-Driven Decline of Life on Earth Points to the Need for Transformative Change." Sandra Díaz, et al. *Science*. December 13, 2019. Volume 366, Issue 6471. DOI: 10.1126/science.aax3100.

39.   "Explainer: Six Ideas to Limit Global Warming with Solar Geoengineering." Daisy Dunne. Carbon Brief. September 5, 2018. https://www.carbonbrief.org/explainer-six-ideas-to-limit-global-warming-with-solar-geoengineering?utm_content=buffer9f299&utm_medium=social&utm_source=twitter.com&utm_campaign=buffer.

40.   "The Beginning of the End of the World." Umair Haque. Eudaimonia & Co. October 12, 2019. https://eand.co/the-beginning-of-the-end-of-the-world-9301a927d383.

41.   "The Short List Of Climate Actions That Will Work." Michael Barnard. Cleantechnica. September 29, 2019. https://cleantechnica.com/2019/09/29/the-short-list-of-climate-actions-that-will-work/.

42. "How Climate Change is Melting, Drying and Flooding Earth—in Pictures." Nisha Gaind and Emma Stoye. *Nature*. September 26, 2019. https://www.nature.com/articles/d41586-019-02793-0?utm_source=Nature+Briefing&utm_campaign=c699f7417d-briefing-dy-20190927&utm_medium=email&utm_term=0_c9dfd39373-c699f7417d-43990557.

43. "World 'Gravely' Unprepared for Effects of Climate Crisis – Report." Damian Carrington. *The Guardian*. September 9, 2019. https://www.theguardian.com/environment/2019/sep/10/climate-crisis-world-readiness-effects-gravely-insufficient-report.

44. "Climate Change: 'We've Created a Civilisation Hell Bent on Destroying Itself – I'm Terrified', Writes Earth Scientist." James Dyke. The Conversation. May 24, 2019. https://theconversation.com/climate-change-weve-created-a-civilisation-hell-bent-on-destroying-itself-im-terrified-writes-earth-scientist-113055.

45. "Majority Rules: American Attitudes on Climate in 7 Stats." Climate Reality Project. May 29, 2018. https://www.climate-realityproject.org/blog/majority-rules-american-attitudes-climate-7-stats.

46. *The Little Prince* by Antoine de Saint-Exupéry. Published by Reynal & Hitchcock (U.S.) and Gallimard (France), April 1943.

47. *The Practice of Tranquillity & Insight: A Guide to Tibetan Buddhist Meditation.* Khenchen Thrangu Rinpoche. Snow Lion Publications, January 1, 1998.

48.   *Essentials of Mahamudra: Looking Directly at the Mind.* Khenchen Thrangu Rinpoche. Wisdom Publications, May 1, 2014.

49.   *Crystal Clear: Practical Advice for Mahamudra Meditators.* Khenchen Thrangu Rinpoche. Rangjung Yeshe Publications, May 18, 2004.

50.   *Vivid Awareness: The Mind Instructions of Khenpo Gangshar.* Khenchen Thrangu Rinpoche. Shambala Publications, January 11, 2011.

51.   *Relative World Ultimate Mind.* Twelfth Tai Situpa, Shambala Publications. January 21, 1992.

52.   *Merlin's Handbook for Seekers and Starseeds: A Guide to Awakening Your Divine Potential.* Margaret Doner. iUniverse, December 19, 2013.

53.   *Merlin's War: The Battle Between the Family of Light and the Family of Dark.* Margaret Doner. iUniverse, April 17, 2012.

54.   *The Path of the Human-Incarnated Angel and Starseed.* Margaret Doner. iUniverse. April 28, 2018.